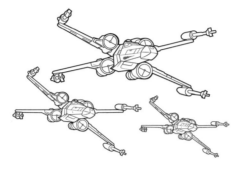

EGMONT

First published in the French language by Hachette Livre in 2017
First published in the English language in Great Britain 2018 by Egmont UK Limited
The Yellow Building, 1 Nicholas Road, London W11 4AN

Direction: Catherine Saunier-Talec
Art Director: Antoine Béon
Project Manager: Anne Vallet

© & ™ 2018 Lucasfilm Ltd.
Original English language translation © Philippe Touboul and Xavier Hanart 2018
Adapted in English by Josh Winning and Natalie Clubb
Cover design by www.blacksheep-uk.com

ISBN 978 1 4052 8479 0
65875/001
Printed in Italy

To find more great *Star Wars* books, visit www.egmont.co.uk/starwars

GEEKTIONARY

1.4 FD P-tower

A combat tower designed for ground confrontations and adapted to the roughest climates, this weapon was intended to defend military positions against light vehicles.

It consisted of a rotating base that allowed the cannon to turn a full 360 degrees on its axis. The cannon was surrounded by an energy dish, which housed the multiple converters and routers that powered the unit.

2-1B Surgical Droid

Produced by Industrial Automaton, the 2-1B droid was designed to help with the treatment of humans, as well as assisting with surgical and cybernetic needs.

The model was assigned to the Alliance's Echo Base on Hoth and treated Luke Skywalker's facial injuries via bacta after he had been attacked by a wampa, as well as overseeing Luke's cybernetic hand transplant after his lightsaber duel with Darth Vader at Bespin.

4-LOM

A glitch in this protocol droid's system enabled 4-LOM to escape his original programming and become a bounty hunter.

Originally manufactured by Industrial Automation, 4-LOM's green sensors and insect-like appearance were clues that he was initially designed to aid communication between insectoid species. However, the logic glitches in his programming, along with the corruption of his personality software, made him a cold and calculating bounty hunter. After the Battle of Hoth, he was hired by Darth Vader, alongside Zuckuss and Boba Fett, to track down the *Millennium Falcon*.

4B-EG-6 Power Droid

This GNK-series power droid was equipped with an internal fusion generator that facilitated its use as a self-powered, mobile energy source.

Responsible for providing continuous energy to the network of runways at the Resistance base on D'Qar, it tried to be constantly available to ensure equipment was always functioning. As was the tradition of the Rebel Alliance, 4B-EG-6 was emancipated and was a devoted member of the Resistance.

4D6-J-A7

An arrogant and mean RA-7 protocol droid, 4D6-J-A7 was stationed at the Imperial Office of Security on Scarif.

Equipped with optical sensors and distinctive glossy black plating, this female-programmed droid was so high ranking that she looked down on her fellow droids, while her access to important Imperial files saw her databanks specially protected against hacking. She was at the Citadel Tower during the Battle of Scarif but, luckily for Jyn Erso and the other rebels, 4D6-J-A7 failed to recognise them as a real threat against the Empire.

74-Z Speeder Bike

A small and ultra-fast reconnaissance vehicle, this speeder bike was manufactured by the Aratech Repulsor Company.

The 74-Z, employed by the Empire, was piloted by scout troopers and was notably used to patrol the forests around the planetary shield generator on Endor, where the troopers worked in squads of two or four and coordinated their actions to optimise their surveillance of the strategic site. At 3.2 metres long and equipped with a forward Ax-20 blaster cannon, these speeders could theoretically reach speeds of up to 500 kph.

8D8

This towering 8D-series droid struck fear in the power cores of even the bravest droids.

Working at Jabba the Hutt's Palace, this male-programmed droid took great pleasure in his role as a terroriser of misbehaving droids. With his ghostly white appearance, 8D8 was originally programmed by Roche Hive to work in ore-extraction facilities. He was reprogrammed for torture when he was purchased by Jabba, and 8D8 enjoyed bullying and tormenting other droids – on one occasion, he sadistically branded a 'gonk' power droid's feet.

975th Stormtrooper Garrison

Imperial troops stationed on the planet Eadu, the 975th garrison were employed to protect the biggest secrets of Emperor Palpatine's evil regime.

Their mission was to stop spies from infiltrating the Tarkin Initiative facilities, and to prevent any staff members from escaping or leaking confidential information to the enemy. The 975th garrison failed to prevent the data theft orchestrated by Galen Erso and Bodhi Rook, and paid a heavy price during the rebel attack on their base.

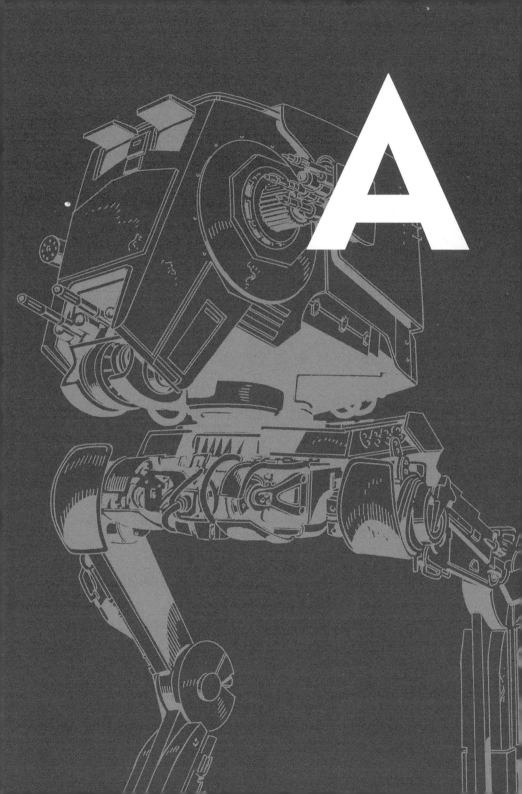

A/SF-01 B-wing Starfighter

Produced in secret by Slayn & Korpil for the Rebel Alliance, the A/SF-01 B-wing starfighter was easily identifiable by its cross-shaped silhouette.

Not conceived as a craft that would take part in space dogfights, B-wings were instead used to strike at the biggest Imperial warships, such as Star Destroyers. To ensure they had the necessary heft, they were kitted out with heavy weapons, such as an ion cannon and proton torpedoes, which were installed opposite the cockpit at the end of the main 17-metre-long wing. The twin laser cannons were positioned on the two extremities of the smaller wings, and they boasted firepower that was without equal among the rebel fighters. In order to guarantee the pilot's stability no matter how the craft was oriented, the cockpit was built on a gyroscope capable of turning through 360 degrees. The hyperdrive and four efficient engines helped to make this assault ship an invaluable asset at the time of the Battle of Endor.

A-wing Starfighter

See RZ-1 A-wing Starfighter

A99 Aquata Breather

This miniaturised breathing apparatus was used by the Jedi Knights in thin air, toxic atmospheres and under water.

Qui-Gon Jinn and Obi-Wan Kenobi used these respirators while on the planet of Naboo, donning them on the banks of Lake Paonga in order to reach the undersea city of Otoh Gunga.

Aayla Secura

A brave Jedi Knight who hailed from the planet Ryloth, Aayla Secura was loyal to the Jedi Order and the Republic.

A gifted fighter, she possessed all of the admirable qualities of the Jedi Knights, and was a formidable opponent during some of the fiercest battles between the forces of good and evil. During the Battle of Geonosis, Aayla was part of the Jedi battalion sent to save Anakin Skywalker, Obi-Wan Kenobi and Padmé Amidala in the Petranaki Arena.

During the Clone Wars, she led a Republic fleet, and fought the Separatist general Lok Durd. After losing her ship in battle, Aayla Secura found herself on the planet of Maridun, accompanied by Anakin Skywalker and Ahsoka Tano. There, she showed her diplomatic skills with the Lurmen people, and eventually defeated Lok Durd, gaining a senior position on Coruscant alongside the great Jedi Masters Yoda and Mace Windu. At the end of the Clone Wars, Aayla Secura became a Jedi Master and assumed command of the 327th Star Corps, fighting the last Separatist forces on the Outer Rim. While conducting an operation in the jungles of the planet Felucia, she was shot in the back by Commander Bly and her clone troopers, who blindly obeyed Order 66 as commanded by Darth Sidious from Coruscant.

Acclamator-class Assault Ship

The first Republic warship to be used during the Clone Wars was produced by Rothana Heavy Engineering.

Measuring over 700 metres in length, the *Acclamator* served as the main troop and equipment freighter throughout the whole conflict. Heavily armed with laser cannons, turbolaser turrets and torpedoes, it was able to land on the ground and played a decisive role in the conflict, notably against the Separatist navy. Its bevelled design foreshadowed the look of the infamous Imperial Star Destroyer.

Acklay

An amphibious creature native to the planet Vendaxa, acklays were extremely aggressive carnivores, which made them perfect executioners on the planet Geonosis, where they were frequently unleashed on unsuspecting prey in the Petranaki Arena.

With their hard, shell-like bodies mounted on six, claw-like legs, acklays resembled mobile crustaceans. At 3 metres tall, they towered over their prey, and their fanged jaws could easily crush weapons. These wild creatures were also canny hunters. They possessed an organ under their lower mandible that helped them detect the electricity produced by a living organism, making them expert trackers. Obi-Wan Kenobi fought an acklay in the Petranaki Arena on Geonosis, cleverly using the beast's claws to break his chains. He failed to wound the creature with the picadors' spears, but recovered his lightsaber in time to defeat the beast.

Adi Gallia

A Jedi Master and Tholothian who sat on the Jedi High Council, Adi Gallia was present when Qui-Gon Jinn appeared before the Council to warn them that the Sith had returned.

Despite this extraordinary announcement – which Qui-Gon Jinn combined with introducing a young Anakin Skywalker, whom he told the Council was the Chosen One – Adi Gallia failed to speak up. An experienced pilot and formidable when fighting with a sword, she became a general in the Grand Army of the Republic. During the Clone Wars, while on a mission with Obi-Wan Kenobi, Adi Gallia was gravely injured by the Sith Apprentice, Savage Opress.

Admiral Ackbar

See Gial Ackbar

Airen Cracken

Despite his high rank as a general in charge of Rebel Alliance intelligence, Airen Cracken was often found on the battle front lines.

During the Battle of Scarif, Cracken was busy building a network of spies on the Outer Rim, leaving General Draven to represent him at the rebel council on Yavin 4. Cracken was aboard the *Millennium Falcon* with Lando Calrissian, Nien Nunb and Lieutenant Blount during the Battle of Endor. Acting as gunner in the legendary Corellian freighter, he contributed to the destruction of the second Death Star and lived to tell the tale.

Ak-rev

As well as playing as the percussionist in the Max Rebo Band, Ak-rev was also Jabba the Hutt's personal bodyguard.

While beating his enormous drum in duet with the Klatooinian Umpass-stay, this Weequay was interrupted by a commotion created by the Twi'lek slave Oola, whose disobedience led to her being fed to Jabba's rancor. Despite his role as bodyguard, Ak-rev was not taken aboard Jabba's sail barge to attend the execution of Han Solo, Luke Skywalker and Chewbacca, and his fate remains unknown.

Aks Moe

A perfect example of the sorry state of the Galactic Senate during the time of the Separatist Crisis, Aks Moe was the Gran senator and represented the Malastare Congress at the Senate.

When Queen Amidala begged for help against the droid armies invading Naboo, Aks Moe supported the Trade Federation's delaying tactics. Despite the three eyes particular to his species, Moe appeared blind to the unfolding tragedy ... or perhaps his support of the Trade Federation was motivated by a more shameful, and greedier, reason.

Aldar Beedo

This long-snouted Glymphid from Ploo II was the podracer pilot who was positioned on the front line of the starting grid for the famous Boonta Eve Classic Podrace on Tatooine.

Despite his better efforts, he ended up finishing third behind Gasgano and the young Anakin Skywalker.

Alderaan

Famous for its beautiful landscapes and the peaceful nature of its inhabitants, this rocky planet was located in the Alderaan system of the Core Worlds.

It also boasted centres of culture and education, two values dear to the Alderaanians' hearts. During the time of the Galactic Republic, Alderaan was an important world. Its senator, Bail Antilles, was in line to succeed Chancellor Valorum when he was removed from his position.

During the Clone Wars, Alderaan refused to arm itself and remained peaceful. When Chancellor Palpatine activated Order 66, Bail Organa, Antilles' successor as senator, helped the Jedi to flee. He adopted Leia – Padmé Amidala and Anakin Skywalker's daughter – and raised her as the princess of Alderaan.

Years later, when Bail Organa was one of the leaders of the Rebellion, Leia was arrested and imprisoned on the Death Star. To convince her to reveal the location of the rebel base, Grand Moff Tarkin threatened to test the Death Star's awesome firepower on Alderaan. Leia finally revealed the name of an abandoned rebel base on Dantooine, hoping to save her homeworld. However, Tarkin fired anyway, destroying Alderaan, leaving only an asteroid field where the planet once was and creating a huge disturbance in the Force.

All Terrain Armoured Cargo Transport

A larger version of the All Terrain Armoured Transport (or AT-AT), the AT-ACT was designed by the Kuat Drive Yards with a hold purpose-built to transport ammunition or construction materials.

These four-legged units were usually used by the Empire during the construction of large-scale projects, such as shipyards or research centres. The AT-ACT's large hangars could carry an impressively heavy load – usually several thousand tonnes inside the 550-cubic-metre module. Even with this heavy load, the AT-ACT made steady progress using powerful motors and an electromagnetic field tensor that kept its legs in the necessary alignment. Despite its great height of 31.85 metres, this steel monster didn't require a pilot in the same way as the AT-AT. The AT-ACT wasn't designed for the battlefield, with the Imperial army preferring to use tanks, AT-ATs and other ground vehicles during combat.

Despite the fact that it wasn't considered a combat unit, the AT-ACT came equipped with armour and two heavy laser cannons that could be used in the event of an external attack. During the Battle of Scarif, Baze Malbus, Chirrut Îmwe and the other rebel soldiers from the Rogue One team quickly discovered that the AT-ACT could be a formidable foe on the battlefield. While Rogue One successfully infiltrated the Citadel Tower and had no trouble tackling the Empire's ground troops, the arrival of four AT-ACTs posed a very real threat to the outcome of the rebels' mission. The units forced the rebels out of the jungle and pushed them onto the open beaches, resulting in the first big losses for the Rebel Alliance. Baze Malbus attempted to take down one of the AT-ACTs using his HH-12 rocket launcher, but it barely dented the enormous vehicle. Only the firepower of the X-wings and the U-wings of Blue Squadron proved effective in destroying the AT-ACTs, which were eventually blasted into oblivion when the Death Star targeted Scarif.

All Terrain Armoured Transport

The most heavily armoured ground vehicle in the Imperial army, this four-legged combat walker came to be synonymous with the might of the Empire during the war years.

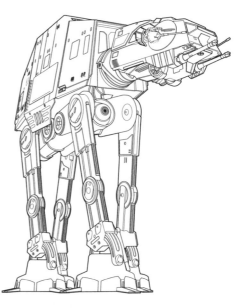

Manufactured by Kuat Drive Yards, the All Terrain Armoured Transport was a powerful display of 'walker' technology and cut an imposing figure on the battlefield where, at least until the Battle of Hoth, they were widely considered to be invincible owing to their immense size and armour which could withstand blaster fire. A mechanised infantry capable of moving under its own steam, the AT-AT (also known as an Imperial Walker) was also used to transport troops.

The massive machines were operated by a pilot located in the cockpit, but owing to their huge size and powerful walking controls, only pilots with the greatest physical strength were able to drive them.

All Terrain Recon Transport

An off-road reconnaissance transport developed by the shipyards of Kuat for the Grand Army of the Republic.

This single-seater, two-legged walker was used by clone troopers to easily manoeuvre a wide variety of terrains. Despite some structural weaknesses and an open cockpit that left the pilot somewhat exposed, the vehicles were stable and extremely nimble owing to their state-of-the-art gyroscopic system. Ergonomically designed, the All Terrain Recon Transport was piloted like a jet ski and featured a front-mounted repeating blaster, as well as a highly developed communication array, which sent up-to-date situation reports to command bases. A popular mechanised unit, its design inspired the Empire to later develop larger 'walker' vehicles, such as the AT-ST.

All Terrain Scout Transport

A two-legged walker, the AT-ST or 'Scout Walker' was primarily used for reconnaissance and anti-personnel hunting.

At just over 9 metres in height, the AT-ST was smaller than the full-size Imperial AT-ATs and was fitted with a gyroscopic stabiliser, which made it more suited to navigating dense and uneven terrain, such as forests and rugged inclines.

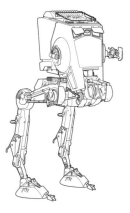

Operated by a crew of two (a pilot and a gunner), AT-ST pilots needed to possess a good sense of balance, dexterity and agility to efficiently drive the vehicle. With the capability to reach speeds of up to 90 kph, the Scout Walker played an important role in the Empire's mechanised infantry, but it was not without its weaknesses. Despite being equipped with twin blaster cannons and a concussion grenade launcher, its firepower was only effective on close-range, lightly armoured targets, and defensively, as the AT-ST itself was only lightly armoured (in order to retain its speed and agility), it was vulnerable to attack. In addition, its small size rendered it unable to carry a full-size power generator and fuel, which restricted its range.

All Terrain Tactical Enforcer

An assault vehicle and a transport module, this Clone War-era, mass-produced tank was essential to the ground operations of the Republic.

Its arachnoid form, which boasted six mechanical legs, was characteristic of the 'walker' technology developed by Rothana Heavy Engineering. Equipped with magnetic feet, its great stability enabled it to adapt to any terrain, and to easily climb metallic walls.

Requiring a crew of seven (one pilot, one lookout and five gunners, one of them exclusively dedicated to the operation of the main cannon), the AT-TE could safely transport up to twenty clone troopers, and efficiently cover a vast area. The rather slow firing rate of the AT-TE was compensated by its durable armour and its support laser cannons, which were directly placed on its hull and could counter the assaults of enemy troops and combat droids.

Alliance Cabinet

A branch of the Alliance to Restore the Republic's Civil Government, the Alliance Cabinet had Mon Mothma at its head.

It was composed of six ministers, among whom were Bail Organa, Nower Jebel, Tynnra Pamlo and Vasp Vaspar. Each minister had specific responsibilities, such as education, industry and finance. The existence of this governmental system within the Rebellion was dedicated to its ultimate goal: to re-establish equality and democracy within the Senate and the Republic regime.

Alliance Council

A political organism that sat alongside the Alliance Military in the Rebellion.

Also named the rebel command, the Rebel Alliance High Command, and the Civil Government of the Alliance, it was led by the rebel and former senator Mon Mothma. Its purely governmental branch, the Alliance Cabinet and its ministries, formed a large part of the Council. On the eve of the Battle of Scarif, a passionate meeting of the Alliance Council was held to debate the existence of a gigantic Imperial vessel known as the 'planet killer': the Death Star.

Amanaman

A gangly bounty hunter with cruel red eyes and enormous hands, Amanaman was a member of Jabba the Hutt's crime syndicate.

This Amani, a species from the planet Maridun, had a reptilian appearance, with a yellow body and green streaks on his back. He was a headhunter who never showed mercy, and was skilled with a variety of traditional weapons.

Amee

A human girl who lived on Tatooine, Amee was one of the girls who knew Anakin Skywalker as a youngster.

She was the only one in her group of friends who had braces. While Skywalker worked on his podracer, she doubtfully pointed out that he had been tinkering with it for years, and claimed it would never fly. Happily, Skywalker proved her wrong.

Ames Uravan

A pioneer in delicate operations involving kyber crystals, Ames Uravan was a specialist on the scientific team of the Tarkin Initiative.

At the Imperial refinery on Eadu, he received the shards stolen from Jedha by the Empire, and merged them to create even bigger crystals. With this unmatched skill in engineering, he was able to perfectly preserve the crystals' properties. However, this native from Christophsis would never see his homeworld again as, alongside his colleagues, he was randomly killed by Orson Krennic's death troopers. Despite his contributions to its cause, in the eyes of the Empire, he was obviously viewed as dispensable.

Anakin Skywalker

Easily the most controversial person in the history of the galaxy, Anakin Skywalker was defined by the fact that he was dramatically torn between Jedi philosophy and Sith corruption.

Considered by some as the Chosen One from a prophecy about a great Jedi that would restore balance to the Force, Skywalker's inevitable slide into the dark side had terrifying consequences for the entire galaxy. However, despite decades as a Sith Lord, Anakin Skywalker eventually redeemed himself, and with the help of his son, Luke Skywalker, he fulfilled the prophecy.

Born into slavery on Tatooine, Skywalker always felt that his life was not his own. Stripped of any kind of freedom, he knew that if he attempted to escape his miserable life, he would be killed by the detonation of an explosive implant in his body. Even though his owner, Watto, was not the worst of the slavers on Tatooine, Skywalker learned to live in fear, and worried for his mother Shmi Skywalker, who was also enslaved to Watto.

Skywalker's daily life involved working at Watto's shop and, in his spare time, socialising with his close friends Amee, Wald and Kitster Banai. He also developed his talent with technology by reconstructing a protocol droid, C-3PO, and dreamed of one day becoming a podracer.

When Skywalker was nine years old, the arrival of a Jedi, a young woman, an astromech droid and a Gungan forever changed the course of his life. Among this group, Skywalker was most interested in Padmé Amidala, who made an enduring impression on him. Attempting to help Amidala and her friends find a hyperdrive that would get their ship operational once more, Skywalker showed considerable kindness and selflessness by putting his life in danger during the Boonta Eve Classic, an incredibly dangerous podrace. He won the race and earned his freedom thanks to a bet Qui-Gon Jinn made against Watto.

Sadly, winning the bet only earned Anakin Skywalker his freedom, leaving his mother Shmi behind. After an emotional goodbye, Skywalker departed with Qui-Gon Jinn, who had made a surprising discovery – Skywalker had a phenomenally high rate of midi-chlorians in his blood. This was so exceptional that the Jedi Master took Skywalker to Coruscant to present him to the Jedi High Council. Although Jinn claimed that Skywalker was the Chosen One of the Jedi Prophecy, the Council rejected him and advised Jinn against training him. This marked the beginning of a complicated relationship between the young Skywalker and the Jedi Masters.

During the retaking of the capital, Theed, in which Jinn and Obi-Wan Kenobi fought Darth Maul, Skywalker took shelter in the cockpit of a Naboo Royal N-1 starfighter. He accidentally engaged the automatic pilot and his ship was thrown into the space battle around the Trade Federation's capital ship. Thanks to the combination of his natural talents as a pilot and the help of R2-D2, the reluctant hero survived, and ended up landing in the hostile vessel's hangar. Firing on the main reactor, Skywalker created a chain reaction that resulted in the vessel's reactor exploding, provoking the deactivation of the entire invading droid army on the surface of Naboo.

But the victory was tarnished by the fact that Qui-Gon Jinn lost his life while duelling Darth Maul. In the wake of Jinn's death, Obi-Wan Kenobi announced to the Jedi Council that he would train Skywalker to become a Jedi, just as Jinn had wanted. Reticently, Yoda agreed.

Kenobi attempted to teach Skywalker patience, selflessness and obedience. Ten years after the Battle of Naboo, Skywalker was hired to protect Padmé Amidala. Now a senator, Amidala was being targeted by an unknown assailant, and with Kenobi away on his own mission, Skywalker stayed to protect her. Despite the reserve imposed on the Jedi, he confessed his love to Amidala. She rejected his advances, despite her feelings for him. She had become a queen at age fourteen and was elected to the Galactic Senate when she was twenty-four, and she understood that both she and Skywalker had important responsibilities that they couldn't put aside for their relationship.

Later, Skywalker suffered a terrible vision of his mother suffering. He immediately left with Amidala for Tatooine where he discovered that Watto had sold Shmi to a farmer. Cliegg Lars, Shmi's new owner had freed and married her, but she had been kidnapped by Tusken Raiders, nomads who were known for their brutality. Skywalker located the Tusken Raiders' camp and found his mother, but she was badly injured and died in his arms. The pain of the loss became unbearable for Skywalker, and was made worse by his own feelings of guilt at having left his mother on Tatooine. In a blaze of anger, Skywalker slaughtered every Tusken Raider he could find: men, women and children. It was his first step towards the dark side.

In the wake of his mother's death, Skywalker became determined to protect those he loved by becoming the most powerful Jedi of all. However, his plan suffered a setback when, after a failed rescue attempt on Geonosis, he was sentenced to death alongside Amidala and Obi-Wan Kenobi. With their lives on the line, Amidala finally confessed her love for Skywalker. The group was finally saved by Yoda and the Jedi, but not before Skywalker was injured in a duel against the leader of the Separatists, Count Dooku. Even though it contradicted the Jedi Code, Skywalker married Amidala in a secret ceremony.

After being promoted to Jedi Knight, Skywalker was named General in the Grand Army of the Republic, where he participated in numerous missions with the 501st Legion. The conflict was arduous and exhausting, and Skywalker knew that the Jedi and the Republic regime were losing their ground. He and Obi-Wan Kenobi infiltrated General Grievous' vessel, the *Invisible Hand*, and discovered an imprisoned Palpatine. When Count Dooku appeared, he duelled with the Jedi and, with Kenobi out of the fight, Skywalker unleashed his full fury against Dooku, severing both of his hands. Then, on Palpatine's order, the young Jedi killed him. Later,

Skywalker expressed regret at not having acted according to the Jedi's principles.

After the crash-landing of the hostile vessel, Skywalker joined his wife, who revealed that she was pregnant. He was overjoyed, but that night he suffered a terrifying vision of Amidala dying during childbirth. He immediately began searching for a way to ensure that the nightmare never became reality. As a Jedi Knight, Skywalker implored the Order for help, but Yoda ignored his call and told Skywalker that he must understand that death is a natural part of life.

Disturbed and obsessed with saving Amidala, Skywalker became easy prey for Palpatine and his evil agenda. Palpatine summoned Skywalker, which displeased Obi-Wan Kenobi who told Anakin to be careful. Palpatine explained to Skywalker his concerns about the Jedi Council and, as proof of friendship and goodwill, the Chancellor designated Skywalker as his personal representative. Having been denied the title of Jedi Master by the Council, Skywalker quickly accepted Palpatine's offer.

Confident that he had Skywalker's trust, Palpatine pressed on with his designs to lure him to the dark side. He took Skywalker to the Opera of the Galaxies, where they watched the Mon Calamari Ballet in a private stall. As the opera cast them in an ethereal and hypnotic aura that resembled a bad dream, Palpatine told Skywalker the story of Darth Plagueis the Wise. While the tale's reference to the Sith alarmed Skywalker, it involved some tempting information – there was a way to stop death.

While Obi-Wan Kenobi's troops advanced against General Grievous, the Chancellor finally revealed his connection with the dark side to Skywalker. Skywalker realised that Palpatine was the Sith Lord his Order was hunting, but he knew revealing Palpatine's true identity to the Jedi would destroy any chance he had of saving Amidala's life.

Torn between the Jedi and the Sith, Skywalker struggled with his loyalty to the Jedi, and warned Mace Windu about Palpatine. With three Jedi as back-up, Windu went to confront Palpatine, but Windu's accomplices were killed before Windu had a chance to disarm the Chancellor. At that moment, Skywalker arrived on the scene horrified to discover that Mace Windu wanted to kill the Chancellor, regardless of the fact that it went against the Jedi Code. Skywalker surrendered to the dark side, knowing that if he allowed Windu to kill Palpatine, he would also condemn Amidala to death. As Mace Windu prepared to drop the final blow against Palpatine, Skywalker shouted out and cut off Windu's arms. Triumphant, Palpatine shot Force-lightning at his adversary, propelling him through a broken window to his death.

Stunned by his actions, Skywalker knew there was no going back. He pledged allegiance to his new master, Darth Sidious, who renamed him Darth Vader. He was commanded to execute all Jedi in the Temple. Order 66 converted the control of all of the 501st legion clone troopers to Palpatine, who had declared himself the Emperor, and they killed almost all the Jedi around the galaxy.

In the wake of the slaughter, Skywalker returned to Amidala to tell her that the Jedi were plotting against the Republic. Sceptical of his story, Amidala nevertheless heard him out before he departed for Mustafar to eliminate the Separatist leaders. After succeeding, Skywalker fulfilled another of Darth Sidious' orders by transmitting a deactivation signal to the droid army of the Confederacy of Independent Systems.

Amidala arrived on Mustafar to confront Skywalker over his actions. He flew into a rage, accusing her of being ungrateful. Everything he did was for her. He suggested they could overthrow the Emperor and rule the galaxy together, but Amidala rejected his proposition. Obi-Wan Kenobi had already warned her of her husband's fall to the dark side. She didn't want to believe it and tried to convince Skywalker to leave with her and raise their child in peace.

At the worst possible moment, Obi-Wan Kenobi emerged from Amidala's vessel, and Skywalker became convinced that the pair had plotted to kill him. Convinced of his wife's betrayal, Skywalker used his Force powers to choke her and left her unconscious. He then turned on Kenobi, who tried to argue with Skywalker to help him see sense, but the inevitable came to pass – an epic confrontation between master and apprentice.

The duo fought without mercy. Skywalker's anger came to the fore as he faced off against his former master, while Kenobi succumbed to increasing despair. The pair battled across Mustafar dodging flowing streams of lava, before the duel reached its climax when the Jedi Master leapt to safety on the rocky shore beside the flowing lava. Tactically better placed than his Sith adversary, Kenobi warned Skywalker not to attack, but Skywalker viewed the gesture as condescending. Skywalker launched himself at Kenobi. The Jedi Master was forced to protect himself, and used his lightsaber to sever Skywalker's legs and left arm. Suffering excruciating pain, Skywalker slipped closer to the lava and became horribly burnt.

Transported back from Mustafar by the Emperor, Skywalker was worked on by a team of physicians and scientific droids. They encased him in protective black armour equipped with life-support systems and a respiratory aid. When Skywalker asked what had become of his wife, the Emperor answered that Skywalker had killed her in his rage. Sealed in his mobile tomb, Anakin Skywalker was no more and only the Sith Lord remained.

As the Emperor's right-hand man, Vader's previous identity was known to only a few people. Vader was mistrusted by some of the senior officers, who ignored the fundamental importance of the Sith Order in the creation of the Empire. Vader became the leader of the 501st legion who became known across the galaxy as 'Vader's Fist'. Tracking down the surviving Jedi and Republic sympathisers remained a top priority for Vader.

Nineteen years later, Vader remained close to the head of the Galactic Empire, and knew about one of its biggest military secrets – the Death Star. After the development of the project and a successful test-run by Director Krennic, Wilhuff Tarkin gained control over the Death Star, with Vader by his side, until its completion. Vader was sent on a mission to recover the Death Star plans that had been stolen by an active group of dissidents named the Rebel Alliance. He intercepted a vessel in which Senator Leia Organa, Princess of Alderaan, was in possession of the electronic documents. To keep the plans out of Vader's hands, Leia hid them in the astromech droid R2-D2 with a message for Obi-Wan Kenobi and sent the droid to Tatooine. After interrogating and then executing Captain Raymus Antilles for not cooperating, Vader arrested Leia, unaware that she was his daughter. Despite her diplomatic immunity, he charged her with treason and for aiding the Rebel Alliance.

After a meeting with the Imperial military council, Vader resolved to torture Leia to discover the location of the rebels' base. When she refused to answer, Vader and Grand Moff Tarkin chose to blackmail her. They transported the Death Star close to Alderaan and threatened to annihilate the princess' homeworld if she refused to provide them with the information they wanted. But even after she revealed Dantooine as the base of the Alliance, the Grand Moff used the Death Star to destroy Alderaan right in front of her eyes. After a scout operation to Dantooine proved to be fruitless, Tarkin ordered Vader to execute Princess Leia.

However, the order was delayed by the arrival of the *Millennium Falcon*. Vader sensed the presence of his old master, Obi-Wan Kenobi, who had come to rescue the princess. Vader confronted Kenobi, who had become weakened with age. The two engaged in a duel, lightsaber against lightsaber, while Kenobi's accomplices helped the princess escape.

Serenely, Kenobi declared that Vader could not win because, even dead, Kenobi would become more powerful than Vader could imagine. The Jedi smiled as he surrendered as Vader's lightsaber plunged at him, but the weapon was met with emptiness – the body of the old master had vanished.

The princess was free and the Death Star plans were safe in the hands of the Rebel Alliance. They plotted an attack on the Death Star and engaged in the Battle of Yavin. While the Grand Moff was convinced his station was indestructible, Vader personally set off to fight the rebel fleet. Aboard his TIE Advanced x1 and with two TIE fighters at his side, Vader mercilessly destroyed the rebels' Gold Squadron, and then began to do the same to Red Squadron. He brought down its leader, Garven Dreis, then put Wedge Antilles out of the fight before killing Biggs Darklighter. He then began to pursue the last X-wing. Feeling that the Force was strong with the mysterious and dangerous rebel pilot, Luke Skywalker, Vader successfully targeted him and lined up his shot. Suddenly, the *Millennium Falcon* came out of nowhere and destroyed Vader's escorting TIE fighters, an action that destabilised Vader's vessel, sending him spinning off into space. Luke Skywalker fired his missile and the Death Star exploded, along with Tarkin. The Alliance had succeeded in delivering a heavy military and psychological defeat on the Empire.

Three years after the Imperial failure, Darth Vader was on the hunt. He was determined to track down the rebels responsible for the destruction of the Death Star, and in particular Luke Skywalker. From his flagship, the *Executor*, he released thousands of probe droids into the galaxy, searching for the rebels. One of them reported back from the Hoth system, and its sketchy information was sufficient enough for Vader to believe the rebel base was located there. After executing Admiral Ozzel for failing to conduct an orbital attack on Hoth, Vader immediately promoted Captain Piett in his place. General Veers entered into a victorious ground fight with his AT-AT walkers, which destroyed Echo Base's shield generator. Vader was able to land in order to attack with his troops, but he discovered Echo Base empty.

With his military victory having pushed the Alliance into retreat, the Sith Lord concentrated his fleet on the pursuit of the *Millennium Falcon*. Not only was it partly responsible for the destruction of the Death Star, but its occupants seemed to be linked to Luke Skywalker. While pursuing the *Falcon* into an asteroid field, Vader momentarily removed himself from the hunt to contact the Emperor. His master told him that he felt a new threat in the Force – the famous Luke Skywalker. He hoped that Vader could draw Skywalker to the dark side, and Vader stated that the newcomer would join them or die.

In order to find Skywalker, Vader convened a group of bounty hunters, among them Boba Fett, to hunt the young Jedi down. Informed of the destination of the *Millennium Falcon* by Boba Fett, who anticipated Han Solo's cunning escape, Vader journeyed to Cloud City at Bespin. Pledging that the Empire would leave Cloud City alone, Vader convinced the Baron Administrator Lando Calrissian to set a trap for his old friend the *Falcon's* pilot Han Solo, and the rebels. Vader used Solo to test a carbonite freezing system, which he planned to later use on Skywalker. Although too late to save Han from being interned in a solid block, Luke Skywalker arrived to rescue his friends and confront Vader.

The two engaged in a duel where the Sith Lord decided to demonstrate the full extent of his Force abilities. He pushed Skywalker back onto a footbridge and sliced off Skywalker's hand, sending it and his lightsaber tumbling into the depths of an immense duct. Facing Skywalker, who was in a state of shock, Vader revealed the truth to him. He was his father. Vader told Skywalker that, together, they could destroy the Emperor and bring order back to the galaxy.

But like Vader's wife, Amidala, his son also rejected this idea, and chose to die by launching himself into the void. Vader returned aboard the *Executor* to discover that Skywalker was still alive, having been recovered by his friends and was safe aboard the *Millennium Falcon*. Through the Force, Vader contacted Skywalker to tell him that his destiny was to join him, even calling him 'son', but the rebels soon disappeared into hyperspace.

The next time the Sith Lord felt Skywalker's presence was on an Imperial shuttle that had requested permission to land on the forest moon of Endor. Despite the fact that this sector was highly restricted because the second Death Star was being constructed there, Vader let the shuttle pass and informed the Emperor of the situation. The Emperor ordered Vader to go to the Endor moon shield, where he predicted Luke Skywalker would be found.

The young Jedi tried to convince Vader to turn against the Emperor but Vader believed himself to be past redemption, and had been for a long time. He escorted his son to the Imperial throne room aboard the second Death Star. Very quickly, the Emperor attempted to break Skywalker and threatened him, telling him that if he didn't succumb to the dark side, he would die. Father and son faced each other again. Enraged, Skywalker unleashed a violent attack and severed Vader's hand – the same hand that had been sliced off by Dooku years earlier.

Vader listened as Darth Sidious urged Skywalker to finish him off and take Vader's place. Weakened, Vader was easy prey, but his son refused the offer and threw away his weapon, declaring he was a Jedi, like his father was before him. Frustrated, the Emperor threw a torrent of Force lightning at Skywalker. Seeing his son on the verge of death, Anakin Skywalker, the Jedi Knight, stirred inside Vader.

Seizing hold of the Emperor despite his injuries, Vader raised him above the vent of a reactor. In spite of his previous loyalty to the Empire, Vader chose to save his son, living proof of the love that had once existed between him and Padmé Amidala. Vader's betrayal incensed the Emperor, who diverted all his destructive energy into his former apprentice. At the cost of crippling pain and the failure of his life-support system, Vader threw the Emperor into the reactor. Carried by Skywalker back to his shuttle, Vader asked his son to remove his helmet, revealing his face before he died.

Unable to leave the remains of the father he had just rediscovered, Luke Skywalker took him aboard the shuttle just before the destruction of the second Death Star. In the forest of Endor, he laid his father to rest with a Jedi funeral. By killing the Emperor, Anakin Skywalker, the

Chosen One, had finally fulfilled his destiny and restored balance to the Force. Alongside the rebels' victory celebrations, Anakin appeared as a spirit beside Yoda and Obi-Wan Kenobi for a silent communion among the Jedi, living and eternal in the Force.

Thirty years later, Anakin Skywalker's controversial legacy survived through two artefacts that once belonged to him. The first was his deformed Vader helmet, salvaged from the funeral pyre. The Sith relic was used as a source of inspiration for his grandson, Ben Solo, who became Kylo Ren and joined the First Order. The second was his Jedi lightsaber lost by Luke at the time of the duel on Bespin, which resurfaced at Maz Kanata's Castle. There it was found by Rey who used it to fight Kylo Ren on the First Order's Starkiller Base.

Anakin Skywalker's Mechno-arm

This cybernetic prosthesis was given to Anakin Skywalker after he lost his arm while fighting Count Dooku during the Battle of Geonosis.

Tailor-made for the young Jedi, Skywalker recovered all of his abilities thanks to this droid arm. Although the mechanics and articulation of the arm were fully visible and exposed, it enabled the Jedi Knight to have a stronger grip than ever before.

Anchorhead

Despite its modest size, this town on Tatooine played an important role in the development of the desert planet, as it connected all of the planet's main cities, including Mos Eisley.

Before his aunt and uncle were brutally killed, Luke Skywalker offered to accompany Obi-Wan Kenobi to Anchorhead. There, they hoped to find a way to reach the Mos Eisley spaceport and find a pilot who could take them to Alderaan.

Angber Trel

A member of the Disciples of the Whills, Angber Trel was in Jedha City at the moment of its destruction by the Death Star.

Dressed in the traditional red robes of his religion, this old pilgrim had a distinctive white beard and used a walking stick made from salvaged power cells, making him easy to spot in a crowd.

Ann and Tann Gella

See Twi'lek Twins

Anoat System

The Anoat system was an area located in the Outer Rim Territories of the galaxy.

Shortly after the Battle of Hoth, Han Solo and his crew experienced difficulties while in the sector when the *Millennium Falcon*'s hyperdrive broke down. Solo made the decision to visit Lando Calrissian in Bespin in order to carry out repairs on the ship.

Ansin Thobel

An infantry corporal, Ansin Thobel was a member of the Imperial fleet posted on the first Death Star.

His primary role was securing the combat station of the Empire using sentries and patrols. In order to protect the headquarters and important individuals, such as Director Krennic and Grand Moff Tarkin, he was sometimes posted on sentry duty on the command bridge. He was present during the Death Star attacks on Jedha City and Scarif, but it was unclear if he also witnessed the destruction of Alderaan, or what happened to him during the Battle of Yavin.

Ansion

A planet allied with the Galactic Republic.

Obi-Wan Kenobi and Anakin Skywalker settled a border dispute on Ansion just prior to the outbreak of the Clone Wars.

Antiquated Data Storage Unit

This portable storage unit was the most precious item belonging to Lor San Tekka, an elderly man who resided in the village of Tuanul on Jakku.

Stored for safety in a leather purse, the unit held essential information on the most remote regions of the galaxy. As an explorer, San Tekka had gathered the data during his many travels, including information pertaining to the whereabouts of the legendary Jedi Luke Skywalker, who had exiled himself in a secret location. The unit was made up of different-sized white hexahedra, and being no bigger than a finger, Resistance pilot Poe Dameron was able to hide it in the tool compartment of his astromech droid, BB-8, when the First Order troops began their assault on Tuanul.

Antoc Merrick

This leader of Blue Squadron was also a general in the Rebel Alliance.

Along with his fellow pilots, he participated in the aerial assault at the Battle of Scarif in order to support the operation conducted by Rogue One to retrieve the Death Star plans. A forty-six-year-old man of action, Antoc Merrick was born on Virujansi, where he was the leader of a squadron of the Rarified Air Cavalry. With the advent of the Empire, Palpatine placed

Merrick's homeworld under a governor's authority. With its reigning council replaced, the planet's global defence forces were dissolved and Merrick was invited to join the Imperial fleet, where he would likely have piloted a TIE fighter. Rejecting the invitation, Merrick left to join the Rebellion with fellow pilot, Garven Dreis.

As a military man, Merrick was a natural leader and naturally commanded authority within the Alliance. He was one of the most important rebels on the eve of the Battle of Scarif. Besides his general rank, he was the commander of all the starfighters at the site of Massassi on Yavin 4. He also attended high-ranking briefings, such as Jyn Erso's cross-debriefing after her release. Merrick was also a member of the Rebel Council. By attending this cabinet of the Civil Government of the Alliance, he learned about the operational function of the Death Star, and the offensive position of Jyn Erso. He noted, 'It is simple; the Empire has the means of mass destruction. The Rebellion does not.'

Aware of the danger that the enemy represented, he threw himself into battle with all the determination of a true general. Working with Admiral Raddus, he fought to ensure that the small hope ignited by the successful infiltration of Rogue One would not be extinguished. In a brave gesture typical of him, Merrick was among the first of Blue Squadron to pilot his X-wing, Blue One, through the shield gate around Scarif. Only five X-wings and one U-wing managed to follow him before the access closed, but this daring breakthrough proved invaluable in establishing a rebel assault on the ground.

Merrick's squadron annihilated three AT-ACTs before it was weakened by the walkers. The squadron then unloaded reinforcements that delivered a second wind to the combat around the Citadel Tower; finally, it gave the rebels an aerial cover as they faced the dangerous TIE strikers. It was a TIE striker that shot Merrick down. His X-wing spiralled as it plunged to the ground, and Merrick died when his starfighter crashed close to the Citadel Tower.

ARC-170 Starfighter

The Aggressive Reconnaissance-170 starfighter was used during hostile scouting missions and built by the Incom Corporation.

This multitasking ship combined the qualities of a starfighter and a bomber, which meant it was able to handle a number of different scenarios. Requiring a pilot and a gunner, it was equipped with powerful laser cannons that were placed at the front and back of the ship, as well as deadly proton torpedoes. Its firepower was a serious threat for enemy cruisers and, like the ETA-2 Jedi starfighter, many of its design elements, such as its flower-shaped wings, were retained for later models, such as the X-wing starfighter of the Rebel Alliance.

Ark 'Bumpy' Roose

A podracer pilot, Ark Roose's nickname, 'Bumpy', hints at his reputation for becoming a little aggressive during races.

His starting place during the Boonta Eve Classic was at the outside of the fourth row, but that didn't deter him. The Nuknog was introduced to the crowd by announcer Fodesinbeed Annodue, and when a band played a piece in his honour, Bumpy saluted the musicians before strapping into his podracer. Well-placed in the lead group, Bumpy skilfully evaded shots fired by Tusken Raiders, but the pilot was forced to stop at the beginning of the second lap so that maintenance droids could conduct repairs. Getting back on the track at full speed, he was overtaken at the end of the lap by Anakin Skywalker. While Bumpy dangerously gained on Skywalker during the last lap, another competitor, Dud Bolt, crashed into him and sent Bumpy into a tailspin, which meant he ended up biting the dust. Or rather, the golden sands of Tatooine.

Armitage Hux

The undisputed leader of the First Order's armies, Armitage Hux was also the commander of Starkiller Base.

His father was the head of the old Imperial Academy, and Hux personified the new generation of the First Order's commanders. Still a child during the fall of the Empire, he grew up on Arkanis alongside his father, and became part of the Imperial exodus to the Unknown Regions. Lulled by epic tales of the Clone Wars, and nostalgic stories about the peace imposed by the Empire, which valiantly fought back against Republic uprisings, Hux was convinced that the galaxy needed to be saved from itself and its leaders' weaknesses. A disciplined and driven officer, Hux rapidly climbed the Imperial ladder to gain Supreme Leader Snoke's trust.

As a skilled military operator, Hux designed the training simulations used for the First Order's various specialised troops. He had total faith in the programme's efficiency and was sure that it inspired absolute loyalty in his soldiers. However, Hux's blind faith in his stormtroopers and their devotion to the First Order – something that Captain Phasma often warned him about – was weakened by the shocking defection of FN-2187, who helped prisoner and Resistance pilot Poe Dameron to escape. Hux's rivalry with Kylo Ren stemmed from his belief that technology and science were the most important elements for increasing Imperial power. In contrast, he viewed Ren's faith in outdated Force mysticism with scepticism. A confident leader whose passion for the First Order ran through to his core, Hux never hesitated to put himself front and centre, famously bragging about the power of his army and Starkiller Base while addressing his troops.

Armoured Assault Tank

This heavily armed vehicle, manufactured by the Baktoid Armor Workshop, was deployed on battlefields but also used on patrol by the armies of the Trade Federation, then by the Confederacy of Independent Systems.

Crewed by four combat droids – a commander at the turret, an interior driver listening to orders and two gunners) – its artillery consisted of a heavy laser cannon, two lateral lasers and six energy-shell projectile launchers. On Naboo, the droid commander OOM-9 conducted his attack against the Gungan forces from aboard his AAT.

Arro Basteren

A first-class rebel soldier, Arro Basteren took part in the Rogue One mission to steal the Death Star plans from Scarif.

Born on the agricultural world of Ertegas, Basteren grew up protecting the harvests from a number of dangerous creatures, a job that helped him develop a skill for seeking out and destroying the enemy. After joining the Alliance, he found a natural place as a scout who would use his Fabritech Q4-E quadnoculars to uncover targets. That information would then be passed on to marksman Corporal Rostok. On Scarif, Basteren successfully infiltrated Scarif beach and diverted attention away from Jyn Erso and her assault, but the battle went south with the arrival of the AT-ACT walkers. Basteren grew worried when Baze Malbus was unable to destroy one of the behemoths with his rocket launcher. While Blue Squadron, led by General Merrick, solved the problem a few seconds later, Basteren lost his life in the face of the enemy's superior forces.

Arvel Crynyd

Leading Green Squadron during the Battle of Endor, Arvel Crynyd seized a golden opportunity when the Super Star Destroyer _Executor_ lost its shields.

Choosing valour over caution, Crynyd piloted his A-wing at high speed straight into the enormous Imperial flagship. Crynyd died instantly in the ensuing fireball, but his efforts were not in vain as he also took down the _Executor_'s bridge crew, including Admiral Piett. The _Executor_ crashed against the surface of the second Death Star, piercing it like the tip of an arrow, and causing an enormous explosion.

ASP-7

A labour droid produced for the Empire by Industrial Automaton, the ASP-7 model was slightly smaller than the average human.

A multitasking droid, its shape was based on the anatomy of a biped, which gave it great flexibility, including the ability to hold and use a variety of tools. However, its ability to communicate was rather limited. The ASP-7 used a very rudimentary speech module, which nevertheless enabled it to express its moods through a series of organised sounds.

Astromech Droid

These mechanical droids could be found installed either in a compartment on a large ship, or in a specific socket on the outside of a starfighter, where they would be exposed to deep space and enemy fire.

The droids had multiple functions including piloting, hyperdrive calculation and repair, and were able to communicate through the on-board computer, or sonically using a binary language made of beeps, clicks and electronic signals. The most popular brand of astromech droid was the R-series, of which R2-D2 was a model. Following the destruction of the second Death Star, a new class of astromech droid, known as the BB-series, was manufactured. This design featured the domed head of the R-series, but it was paired with a spherical body. BB-8 was a droid from this astromech generation.

AT-ACT

See All Terrain Armoured Cargo Transport

AT-AT

See All Terrain Armoured Transport

AT-AT Pilot

These pilots were responsible for controlling the weapons and manoeuvres of the walking ground vehicles known as All Terrain Armoured Transports.

They were also trained and equipped to take part in ground assaults, if required.

AT-RT

See All Terrain Recon Transport

AT-ST

See All Terrain Scout Transport

AT-TE

See All Terrain Tactical Enforcer

AT-TE Transport

Built by Rothana Heavy Engineering, this large, conveyor-type transport was a freighter used mainly to transport All Terrain Tactical Enforcers to the battlefield.

Fitted with a strong magnetic grip to keep the cargo secure during flight and powerful laser cannons, activated from the cockpit, to assist with landing, the transport could reach speeds of up to 620 kph. Requiring only one pilot, the transporters were first put to use during the Battle of Geonosis, but went on to take part in many more conflicts.

Attark

This black-eyed, weak-bodied creature was surprisingly intelligent and a talented weapons repair worker.

This male Hoover lived in Jabba the Hutt's Palace, where he worked in repairs. At night, Attark had the habit of using his trunk to suck people's blood. It was a dangerous habit to have, given that Jabba's Palace was mainly populated with criminals, who didn't take kindly to being attacked in the dark.

Attico Wred

A rebel pilot who used the call sign Green Four during the Battle of Scarif, Attico Wred originally had a career in the Imperial fleet.

However, the TIE fighter pilot's life took a turn for the unexpected when he refused to shoot a disarmed civil vessel. Wred's crisis of conscience was viewed as treason by the Emperor, and Wred immediately defected, joining the Rebel Alliance. On Yavin 4, he met another Corellian, Nozzo Naytaan, with whom he enjoyed an easy-going rivalry. Together, Wred and Naytaan destroyed the outpost of Massassi to support the Rogue One operation.

Aurra Sing

A fearsome bounty hunter, sharpshooter and assassin.

Aurra Sing had chalk-white skin and an antenna in her skull. She watched the Boonta Eve Classic Podrace on Tatooine, which was won by Anakin Skywalker, from a balcony above Beggar's Canyon. She was armed with an Adventurer Slugthrower rifle that enabled her to take out a target at an impressive 450 metres. She was a veteran of the underground world, and during the Clone Wars she was hired by Ziro the Hutt to kill Padmé Amidala.

Avenger, the

A famous *Imperial*-class Star Destroyer of the Imperial fleet that was in service during the Galactic Civil War.

The Star Destroyer *Avenger* acquired its terrifying reputation under the command of Captain Lorth Needa, and formed the armed wing of the Imperial takeover in many systems. The ship took part in hundreds of missions of order enforcement, meaning it was involved in the violent intimidation of many worlds across the galaxy.

After the Battle of Yavin, Needa and the *Avenger* were assigned to the prestigious Death Squadron, and ordered to search for the new rebel base. Having located it on Hoth and revelled in the biggest military victory of the Empire against the Rebel Alliance, Needa failed to keep track of the *Millennium Falcon,* which pulled off a series of incredible manoeuvres, blasting through an asteroid field and even hiding against the hull of the cruiser, causing it to disappear from the Star Destroyer's sensors. Needa was executed by Darth Vader for his mistake, but the *Avenger* retained its excellent combat reputation, which endured even after the Battle of Endor.

B-U4D 'Buford' Droid

This bulky droid, often found on Resistance airstrips, managed the loading of heavy equipment.

Featuring hydraulic compressor grippers and a large, stable base to aid with safely transporting heavy equipment, its brightly coloured, ceramic armour also helped warn Resistance technicians of hazardous loading zones. Buford was part of the droid team that worked continuously to help the Resistance by maintaining equipment and preparing operations. As was the principle of the Resistance command, Buford and all the other droids were granted independence.

B-wing Starfighter

See A/SF-01 B-wing Starfighter

B'omarr Order

This community of monks, who built their monasteries throughout the galaxy, followed a curious practice in which they would surgically transplant their brain into a jar containing nourishing fluid.

If they then wanted to move, they would use spider-like droid walkers to carry the jar. Jabba the Hutt's Palace on Tatooine was once a B'omarr monastery, before it was refurbished by the crime lord. This explained the presence of at least one of the monks in the palace, who could be seen wandering the building when R2-D2 and C-3PO arrived there.

B1 Battle Droid

Produced by Baktoid Combat Automata on Geonosis, this combat model symbolised the transformation of the Trade Federation from a business organisation into an armed force.

Seeking out a complete military solution that would offer defence against minor threats without the need to develop complex military strategies, the Neimoidians opted for a fully mechanised and automated army, with an electronically centralised command centre – all of which could be provided by the B1 battle droid. Armed with an E-5 blaster rifle, or thermal charges, this soldier would fearlessly enter into combat, without being tempted to desert or question orders. With the ability to pilot STAPs and AATs, its only weakness was its vulnerability to electromagnetic weapons.

Bacta Tank

A piece of medical equipment used to accelerate the healing process.

The substance used in the tank, bacta, was a thick gelatinous matter that encouraged the regeneration of organic tissues, such as skin and muscle. Bacta was, for some species, a substance that appeared to have magical properties, but it wasn't able to heal an otherwise incurable injury. Bacta merely accelerated the body's own organic and natural reconstructive processes. Echo Base, the rebel base on Hoth, was fitted with a bacta tank in its medical quarters. After Luke Skywalker's encounter with a wampa left him with numerous injuries, he was placed in a bacta tank to heal, accelerating his return to fight against the Empire.

Bail Organa

A Galactic senator representing the planet Alderaan, Bail Organa was the viceroy of House Organa on Alderaan, and one of the fervent defenders of peace and the Jedi Order.

Close to such politicians as Mon Mothma from Chandrila and Padmé Amidala from Naboo, he took an active role in the handling of the Separatist Crisis, and became one of Chancellor Palpatine's most trusted counsellors, serving on the loyalist committee. Concerned by the chaos and political tension generated by the Clone Wars, Organa didn't hesitate in leading rescue missions on Christophsis.

His honesty made him one of the first people to witness Palpatine's power going astray, and the progressive transformation of Palpatine's mandate into a military dictatorship. At first, he attempted to oppose the financing of supplementary troops, but the suspicious deaths of some of his colleagues, such as Onaconda Farr from Rodia, confirmed Organa's suspicions. After witnessing the massacre of the Jedi by Republic troops at the Jedi Temple, he quickly helped Obi-Wan Kenobi and Master Yoda escape into hiding. With his wife Breha, he took in the newborn Leia after the death of her mother Padmé Amidala.

Always concerned with preserving hope for the future generations, and fighting against the oppression of the emergent Empire, Senator Bail Organa and his friend Mon Mothma secretly created what would become the Rebel Alliance. He died on Alderaan when it was destroyed by the Death Star.

Bala-Tik

The leader of the Guavian Death Gang, an Outer Rim criminal organisation formerly based in the Core Worlds.

Anxious to preserve his organisation's reputation, Bala-Tik specialised in debt recovery. He never hesitated to confront an individual who appeared to be trying to rip off his gang, threatening debtors with his harsh Core Worlds accent. He could frequently balance the books using concussive cannon shots. A cautious leader, familiar with underworld scams, he was usually accompanied by cybernetically improved Guavian guards. They proved to be valuable assets when it came to intimidation. As with any good businessman, Bala-Tik knew when to use skilled smugglers and bandits to develop profitable plans, even if those associates weren't entirely reliable, such as Han Solo.

Bantha

Four-legged, herbivorous creatures that lived on the planet Tatooine. Banthas were easily domesticated, and formed an integral part of the Tusken Raider culture and folklore.

Used as a mount by the Tusken Raiders, also known as the Sand People, banthas shared a unique bond with their masters. Although peaceful by nature, the males of the species had two huge tusks at the top of their skulls that they used to protect themselves against other creatures, or to participate in blood duels. Banthas were also at the centre of a whole food-processing industry, with banthas prized for their milk and meat. Even their skin was used to make popular clothes and accessories. The banthas from Tatooine were the most famous, but the species was common throughout the galaxy. Their benevolent nature inspired the creation of merchandise on many worlds, such as the toy banthas that Wookiee youngsters played with on Kashyyyk.

Bantha-II Cargo Skiff

A repulsor-equipped vehicle manufactured by Ubrikkian Industries.

Although mainly used to escort goods, this type of skiff could also be used to transport passengers, as Jabba the Hutt demonstrated on Tatooine, where he used them as execution vehicles to carry his prisoners to the Great Pit of Carkoon. However, when it came for their transportation to the pit, Luke Skywalker and his friends had different ideas. They destroyed Jabba's sail barge and made their escape on a sand skiff.

Barada

Jabba the Hutt's henchman, a Klatooinian who wore a white shirt, blue trousers and orange scarf.

Barada was aboard the second skiff that accompanied Jabba and the prisoners, Luke Skywalker, Han Solo and Chewbacca, to their execution at the Great Pit of Carkoon. However, Barada met his demise when Skywalker freed himself with his lightsaber. Skywalker then jumped onto the vehicle where the Klatooinian stood, and easily dodged Barada's blows before killing him.

Barion Raner

A Rebel Alliance pilot who used the call sign Blue Four during the Battle of Scarif, Barion Raner was born on Ord Mantell.

A T-65 X-wing starfighter specialist, he wrote the X-wing flight manual, a document that proved vital to many Rebellion pilots. Raner also served for three years under General Antoc Merrick's command. At the beginning of the operation to support the Rogue One mission, Raner failed to follow his squadron leader, as Merrick took advantage of the opening in the orbital shield gate and flew towards the beaches around the Citadel Tower. As the gate closed, Raner only just managed to avoid crashing into it and flew on to fight another day.

Barquin D'an

A professional musician who played the wind instrument kloo in the Max Rebo Band at the Court of Jabba the Hutt.

Like all of his fellow players, he witnessed the fate of dancer Oola, who was devoured alive by Jabba's rancor. He was also present when the bounty hunter named Boushh arrived at Jabba's Palace with a new prisoner, Chewbacca.

Baskol Yeesrim

The Gran senator from Malastare, Baskol Yeesrim represented the Gran Protectorate.

During the presentation of the Naboo crisis by Queen Amidala, Yeesrim was among those who pointedly agreed with Senator Lott Dod's proposition to create a committee to decide if Amidala was telling the truth.

Battle of Coruscant

A decisive space battle during the Clone Wars, the Battle of Coruscant set the Separatist fleet, led by the cyborg General Grievous, against the forces of the Republic.

Many starships, including the notorious Separatist starship *Invisible Hand* and the droid control starship of the Trade Federation, were involved in the battle, which marked a true turning point of the Clone Wars.

The battle was initiated by General Grievous who, in a bold move, kidnapped Chancellor Palpatine. The battle launched the siege of the planet Coruscant. During a particularly risky rescue mission, Obi-Wan Kenobi and Anakin Skywalker slipped inside the *Invisible Hand* to beat Count Dooku and free the Chancellor. Unfortunately, General Grievous was able to flee in an escape pod, abandoning his troops, and losing the battle. The *Invisible Hand*, much damaged, finished its course on Coruscant after Anakin Skywalker executed an impressive crash-landing.

The battle of Coruscant marked the beginning of the end for the Separatists. After their failed landing on Kashyyyk and the death of their leaders on Mustafar, the Republic troops soon took control across the galaxy.

Battle of Endor

A crucial conflict in the system of Endor during the Civil War between the Rebel Alliance and the Galactic Empire.

This battle of wills led to a difficult victory for the rebels, who drew the Empire into an elaborate ambush. For the Empire, the battle concluded with a double defeat, both military and religious, with the destruction of the second Death Star, a large part of its fleet, and the deaths of the Emperor and Darth Vader.

Palpatine set in motion one of the Empire's greatest operations by leaking misinformation about the second Death Star, leading the rebels to believe that the Empire's new secret space combat station wasn't fully operational. With its existence and location revealed, the rebels also learned the Emperor would be attending the second Death Star in order to oversee the final phase of its construction.

Seizing an unexpected opportunity, two rebel forces were sent to tackle the Empire one last time. A fleet was sent into orbit, while an infiltration team landed on the forest moon of Endor to deactivate the shield generator protecting the second Death Star. The sabotage mission was thrown into disarray when the rebel fleet, commanded by Admiral Ackbar, arrived at the second Death Star and discovered that it was still protected by its energy field. Meanwhile, the Imperial fleet ambushed them and the second Death Star's massive weapon proved to be fully functional. War broke out between the rebel and Imperial fleets. Luke Skywalker could do nothing but watch, imprisoned in the Imperial throne room with the Emperor and Darth Vader, as the battle turned to a slaughter for the rebels.

Everything changed thanks to Chewbacca and the Ewoks, who helped Han Solo and Princess Leia to destroy the energy field generator. After receiving the attack signal, General Lando Calrissian and the survivors of Gold and Red Squadrons bombarded the main reactor of the second Death Star. With rebel pilot Wedge Antilles in support, Calrissian reached the heart of the station, causing a critical chain reaction. Saved by his father, Darth Vader, Luke Skywalker escaped the Emperor's clutches and barely had enough time to return to his shuttle to blast a safe distance away from the second Death Star. Skywalker, Calrissian and Wedge managed to escape a short moment before the Imperial space station detonated in the skies above Endor.

As news of the defeat spread through the galaxy, celebrations were held on numerous worlds, from Tatooine and Bespin to Naboo and Coruscant, where the Emperor's giant statue was pulled down. Although the Empire managed to salvage part of its fleet by jumping into hyperspace, with a broken chain of command and constant infighting, it was unable to avoid its ultimate defeat one year later during the Battle of Jakku. After this final defeat, the Galactic Accord was signed, marking the official end of the terrible Galactic Civil War.

Battle of Hoth

This historic conflict of the Civil War saw the Rebel Alliance going up against the Galactic Empire on the frozen planet of Hoth.

The confrontation turned into a major failure for the rebel forces. Despite the destruction of the Death Star, the Empire maintained a dangerous fleet whose main objective was to track down the rebels and to recover Luke Skywalker, the pilot who destroyed the Death Star. Skywalker's victory caught the interest of the Emperor, who ordered Darth Vader to bring the young pilot to him. The Sith Lord took command of the squadron that met on the outskirts of the planet Hoth after a probe droid detected a presence on its surface.

The Battle of Hoth was initially intended to take place in space. With the help of an attack by the fleet in orbit around Hoth, the Empire intended to destroy the rebels from the air as quickly as the rebels had destroyed the Death Star. But a poor strategic choice made by Admiral Ozzel revealed the Empire's plans to the rebels, and gave them time to activate their deflector shield, ensuring they were safe from any distant bombardment. In response, the Empire deployed its troops to the ground through the use of armoured, four-legged units called AT-ATs. Their mission was to destroy the shield generator in order to weaken Echo Base's defences. On their side, the rebels put in place a strategy that seemed contradictory – they intended to defend the base while secretly evacuating it.

The ground troops faced the Imperial might as snowspeeders offered aerial support, destroying some of the advancing AT-ATs. In order to buy enough time for the rebel base to be evacuated, a number of shots were released by an ion cannon, clearing the path for the fleeing transports.

Echo Base's shield generator was destroyed by the Imperial advance, allowing Vader's troops to infiltrate the base. The Sith Lord went in search of Luke Skywalker, who was part of Rogue Squadron. After his snowspeeder crashed, the young pilot destroyed an AT-AT and eventually fled the Hoth system aboard his X-wing. Despite the unquestionable victory of the Imperial forces, Vader arrived too late and could only watch as the last rebel vessel, the *Millennium Falcon*, blasted off with Han Solo, Princess Leia, Chewbacca and C-3PO aboard.

Battle of Naboo

The third and final phase of the crisis known as the 'Invasion of Naboo' saw the Trade Federation's occupation of the planet come to an explosive end.

After her unsuccessful plea in front of the Galactic Senate, Queen Padmé Amidala came up with a battle plan that required one essential element – the Gungans' full commitment to the war effort. Returning to Naboo, Amidala first resolved to convince the Boss of the Gungan people, Rugor Nass, to become an ally, despite the historical conflict between the Gungans and the Naboo. After his agreement, the battle began outside the capital Theed, with a massive confrontation between the Great Gungan Army and the droid army of the Trade Federation. Meanwhile, a second, aerial front line was created as the Naboo forces liberated starships in the hangar and dispatched a squad into orbit to attack the Neimoidian command vessel. Finally, a third front line saw Amidala's troops infiltrating the Royal Palace in order to capture the head of the Trade Federation.

At the end of the battle, the droid capital ship was destroyed by a young Anakin Skywalker, which aided the courageous Gungan army by deactivating its adversaries. Meanwhile, Amidala arrested Viceroy Nute Gunray and his adviser Rune Haako, stifling their work as warmongers. In fact, the Crisis of Naboo was secretly orchestrated by the senator of Naboo, Sheev Palpatine – who was also Darth Sidious, a Sith Lord – and despite the apparent failure of the Trade Federation, their loss was actually Palpatine's success as he was elected the new Supreme Chancellor of the Galactic Republic.

Battle of Scarif

The first confrontation between the Rebel Alliance and the Galactic Empire took place in space while a convoy of rebels below on Scarif, attempted to steal the secret plans of the Death Star.

Although the battle was eclipsed later by the more famous Battle of Yavin, it has retained its historic value as the official start of the Galactic Civil War. The Battle of Scarif was notable for its largely improvised nature. After the Alliance Cabinet rejected the notion of direct and immediate military action against Scarif, a group of rebels led by Jyn Erso decided to embark on an unauthorised operation that hadn't received the approval of the Rebellion. This group of rebels included two Guardians of the Whills, a droid, an intel officer, a pyrotechnician, a sniper, an ex-delinquent and a former Imperial pilot, who chose the team name of 'Rogue One'. They succeeded in landing near the doors of the Imperial Centre of Military Research using a stolen shuttle, which had been approved for landing by air control. While Erso headed up the infiltration into the base, the rest of the rebels planted charges on several sites around Scarif as an explosive distraction.

Rogue One's declaration of war stunned the Citadel Tower's command room, with the exception of Director Orson Krennic, who ordered troops to spread out across Scarif and confront what appeared to be a huge ground attack. News of this strike quickly reached Yavin 4, where Mon Mothma dispatched official militarily support to aid the clandestine mission – a good thing, as Admiral Raddus' fleet was already on their way to Scarif.

As soon as the rebel fleet arrived, the Mon Calamari dispatched Red and Gold Squadrons to protect the Alliance ships, while Blue Squadron was ordered to provide cover for the soldiers fighting on the ground. Only one U-wing and twelve X-wings, among them Blue Leader Antoc Merrick, passed through the shield surrounding Scarif. Red Squadron attempted a diversion with ten of its X-wings, allowing ten Y-wings from Gold Squadron to bomb the shield. Three Y-wings were shot down as a swarm of TIE fighters was launched, so the rebel fleet turned its attention on the Star Destroyers, the *Intimidator* and the *Persecutor*.

On the ground, Rogue One's troops were struggling. The initial ruse confused the enemy and allowed the rebels to concentrate their firepower on Imperial troopers, forcing them to emerge from their bunker into the open. But the arrival of the AT-ACTs changed it all. The rebel soldiers were pushed back onto the beach and were about to be wiped out when Blue Squadron arrived.

New troops were unloaded from the U-wing on the order of Blue Leader, a move that provided the rebels with a second wind after they had suffered serious losses. Supported by aerial cover, with the X-wings fighting the TIE strikers, the soldiers on the beaches continued to lure the garrison out of its base, buying time for Jyn Erso, Cassian Andor and K-2SO to conduct their break-in. The aerial dogfights around the Citadel Tower cost the lives of pilots in both camps, including General Merrick, while the deployment of an elite unit of death troopers brought a death blow to the rebel soldiers. Considerably weakened, the rebel forces were so depleted that there were soon only Baze Malbus and Chirrut Îmwe left to activate a button that would make it possible for Erso to transmit the stolen plans to an Alliance ship in Scarif's orbit. Malbus and Îmwe succeeded, but at the cost of their lives.

In orbit, the rebel fleet fared no better as they were faced with an onslaught of TIE fighters. The shields of the *Profundity* were reduced to fifty per cent and, among the Imperial fighters' victims, were a GR-75 transport and a Nebulon-B frigate. Pushing its advantage, the Imperial fleet failed to notice that it had left an opening for Admiral Raddus to exploit. Then five starfighters of Gold Squadron launched their ion torpedoes on one of the Star Destroyers, immediately cutting the power on the *Persecutor*. Aware that the Scarif shields still needed to be deactivated, the Mon Calamari admiral had a sudden flash of genius that changed the outcome of the battle and the fate of those involved. He ordered the *Hammerhead*-class corvette *Lightmaker* to ram into the Imperial starship from an angle that would push it off course, forcing a collision with another Star Destroyer. Admiral Gorin attempted to manoeuvre the Imperial ship to avoid the collision, but was too late and the bridge of his *Intimidator* was destroyed. The two enormous ships plunged into Scarif's atmosphere and destroyed the shield gate, making it possible for Erso to transmit the precious files to the *Profundity*.

Arriving just in time to witness the confrontation from the Death Star, Grand Moff Tarkin attempted to prevent the Death Star plans from being transmitted, but was too late. The Death Star's superlaser then vaporised the summit of the Citadel Tower. Having received the transmission of the station plans, Admiral Raddus realised that the Rogue One team had succeeded, but Jyn Erso and Cassian Andor were both destroyed along with the Imperial complex in an apocalyptic fireball. Without wasting a moment, the rebel leader of the fleet commanded all ships to jump into hyperspace, but the sudden arrival of the *Devastator*, Darth Vader's capital ship, prevented them. Two Y-wings, an X-wing and a Dornean gunship made evasive manoeuvres but only a GR-75 transport was able to avoid crashing against the *Devastator's* hull. Instantly, the Sith Lord's cruiser launched a violent barrage of fire on the *Profundity*, breaking a Nebulon-B frigate in two and disabling the Mon Calamari ship.

Vader boarded the *Profundity*, but the stolen plans escaped the Sith Lord's grasp as they were given to the crew of a corvette that was under the command of Captain Raymus Antilles and escorting Princess Leia Organa. The hyperspace departure of this starship marked the end of this short, improvised and intense battle in which the Rebellion were revealed to possess considerable strategic skill, despite the great losses on their side.

Battle of Taanab

An encounter between Lando Calrissian and a fleet of pirate vessels in the orbit of the planet Taanab during the Galactic Civil War.

Little detail exists about this famous battle, during which the former administrator of Bespin won the fight by a daring and successful manoeuvre. Calrissian mentioned it just before the Battle of Endor, deciding that his promotion to General in the rebel fleet was thanks to his successes during the Battle of Taanab.

Battle of Yavin

A major confrontation between the forces of the Rebel Alliance and the Galactic Empire, which led to the destruction of the first Death Star.

The impact of this rebel victory was so significant that the clash became known as the 'Year Zero' of all the events that happened before and after it in the galaxy. The Battle of Yavin took place nineteen years after the creation of the Empire. For the small fleet of rebel starfighters, it took the form of a huge race against time. Their mission was to annihilate the lethal space station, the Death Star, before it could reach the moon Yavin 4, where the headquarters of the Rebel Alliance were located. Rebel Generals Dodonna and Willard developed, coordinated and supervised the battle. According to analysis of the data the rebels had in their possession, the Death Star was mere seconds away from blowing up Yavin 4 when it was destroyed.

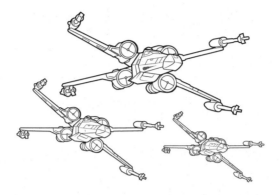

This victory wouldn't have been possible if it hadn't been for the Rogue One mission that obtained the complete technical read-outs of the Death Star, which Princess Leia had stored in the memory banks of R2-D2. By analysing the plans, the rebels were able to pinpoint a flaw in its design – a small thermal exhaust port leading directly to the core. A direct hit by a proton torpedo would start a chain reaction, thereby destroying the space station. But the mission was nevertheless risky with a very small chance of success. The rebel forces were sparse, and from the outset, it looked like a futile mission. The rebel fleet comprised of thirty starfighters – twenty-two X-wings from Red Squadron, and eight Y-wings from Gold Squadron. After most of the rebel fleet was destroyed, Luke Skywalker, with a timely intervention by Han Solo in the *Millennium Falcon*, used the Force to land a one-in-a-million shot that resulted in the Death Star's destruction.

However, casualties were high, and only Skywalker, Solo and two other pilots survived the assault. While the Rebel Alliance was able to deal a catastrophic blow to the Empire, their victory was short-lived as the rebels were forced to abandon Yavin 4 in search of another hidden base, eventually settling on Hoth.

Baze Malbus

A former Guardian of the Whills, Baze Malbus fought as a vital part of Rogue One, the group of rebels who succeeded in stealing the Death Star plans from Scarif.

Despite losing his faith in the Force, he willingly followed his friend Chirrut Îmwe into battle. Born on the desert moon of Jedha, a world that existed at the intersection of many of the galaxy's religions, Malbus' destiny seemed to be to live a restful life dedicated to spirituality. He enlisted in the ranks of one of the most respected holy orders, the Guardians of the Whills, with his friend Chirrut Îmwe, who shared his beliefs. During the era of the Republic, Malbus' life revolved around the study of the Force, and he devoted himself to practising kindness. He ultimately became a guard in Holy City, also known as Jedha City, and was stationed as a protector of the Temple of the Kyber.

The advent of a new type of galactic regime, overseen by Sheev Palpatine, marked a profound change in Malbus' environment. Jedi were hunted and killed, giant holy statues were brought down and the situation gradually deteriorated for the guards, too. Jedha fell under Imperial occupation when the Empire got involved in the exploitation of kyber crystals, not only taking over the mining of the precious minerals, but also the seizure of existing stocks. The Temple of the Kyber, which Malbus guarded, became a restricted area and Malbus and his fellow guards were cast out.

Disillusioned, Malbus and Îmwe made a life on the Jedha streets. While his friend Îmwe saw their dire situation as a test, Malbus became cynical and lost his faith in the Jedi, transforming himself into a soldier who fought the Imperial forces. It was at this time that the duo were contacted by Saw Gerrera, who wished to invite them to fight at his side. While Malbus was immediately tempted, Îmwe was more reticent, but they both eventually accepted Gerrera's offer and enlisted with his rebel group. During a mission, Malbus acquired a new weapon, stolen from an Imperial warehouse – a dangerous MWC-35c 'Staccato Lightning' repeating cannon, which was built to be mounted on a vehicle, but which Malbus operated by hand.

Wrapped in combat armour and wielding the MWC-35c, Malbus rescued a group of rebels, including Jyn Erso and Cassian Andor, from stormtroopers on Jedha, while blind Îmwe impressed the rebels by taking out a squadron of stormtroopers using only his staff. All four were then captured by Saw's gang and taken outside of the city to their hideout located in the Catacombs of Cadera. There, jailed in a summary cell, Malbus wanted to kill another captive, the ex-Imperial pilot Bodhi Rook. But when Grand Moff Tarkin targeted Jedha with the Death Star, Malbus was forced to flee taking Rook with him. After Tarkin's lethal attack, the Holy City – or NiJedha as Malbus liked to call it – no longer existed. It was destroyed by the Empire's new superweapon, along with its thousands of inhabitants and treasures.

With nothing to live for except his friend Îmwe, Malbus joined the Rogue One team bound for Eadu. He went along with a mission against his hated enemy, and during the Rogue One operation on Scarif, his talents came to the fore. While Erso and Andor infiltrated the Citadel Tower, Malbus and Îmwe tackled the Empire's forces on the ground, and ended up the only two survivors after a violent confrontation in the jungle and on the beaches.

Fighting back against the AT-ACTs and the TIE strikers, they resisted, but were driven back to a bunker by death troopers. The success of their mission depended exclusively on the activation of a button located out in the open, which would allow Erso to transmit the stolen Death Star plans to the Alliance ships in Scarif's orbit. In a show of real bravery, Îmwe strolled out into the battlefield to press the button, but at the cost of his life. Malbus reached his dying friend and comforted him in his very last moments.

Certain that he would never leave Scarif alive, Malbus repeated the mantra of his deceased friend, 'I am one with the Force, the Force is with me'. He succeeded in bringing down many elite Imperial soldiers before being blown up by a C-25 grenade.

Bazine Netal

This undercover spy working for the First Order was a patron at the court of Maz Kanata's Castle on Takodana, and would often cast her eye over the groups of pirates and travellers in search of vital intel.

Bazine Netal maintained her cover as the love interest of the mercenary Grummgar and, seated on his knees, enjoyed a unique view over the castle's main hall. For her own protection, she owned a dagger soaked with venom, while the complex pattern of her outfit was designed to cause interference to sensors so she could evade detection while she discretely transmitted information to the First Order.

BB-8

A new generation astromech droid with a spherical body who was in service to Resistance pilot Poe Dameron.

BB-8 assisted in the on-board energy allocation and navigation of Dameron's X-wing. He expressed himself using 27th generation droid code-language, and his six interchangeable tooling discs gave him great adaptability whenever damage or a technical problem occurred. BB-8's motor allowed him to make his spherical body roll in any direction, while keeping his head vertical using magnets. To move on uneven ground, BB-8 used a wire system that allowed him to reach even the most seemingly inaccessible locations, while BB-8's armour protected his servomotors from impurities, such as dust and sand.

He was the ideal faithful companion to Poe Dameron, who took care of him and often praised the droid as 'one of a kind'. BB-8 accompanied Dameron in all his operations and, like his famous elder R2-D2, showed a great sense of duty whenever he was undertaking an important mission. BB-8 was in possession of a map fragment that would allow the Resistance to track down Luke Skywalker. The fragment was retrieved on Jakku from explorer Lor San Tekka, who had given it to Dameron before Kylo Ren and his stormtroopers arrived and killed him.

Beedo

One of the two Rodians who were present at the Court of Jabba the Hutt.

According to rumour, Beedo was used by the crime lord Jabba the Hutt as a bounty hunter, much like his cousin Greedo, who was famously killed by Han Solo at the Mos Eisley Cantina.

Beezer Fortuna

Bib Fortuna's cousin was the strategic councillor of Saw Gerrera's partisans at the time of Jedha City's destruction.

A descendant of an influential family, this Twi'lek was more of a political idealist than the rest of his clan, which was compromised by its connections with the underworld. Frustrated with his familial association with gangsters, Fortuna watched with interest as the Confederacy of Independent Systems occupied his native world, Ryloth, during the Clone Wars. After its liberation by the Republic and leader Cham Syndulla's freedom fighters, Fortuna became a rebel at the capital, Lessu.

He participated in the fight against the army of the new Galactic Empire and when he was captured, he was freed during an unexpected raid by Saw Gerrera. Faithful to his saviour, Fortuna joined Gerrera's rebel militia, and his bravery often saw him operating out in the field, along with his trusty electrified staff. During one such mission, he intercepted the Imperial deserter Bodhi Rook, and he was present at the partisan base in the Catacombs of Cadera, when Jyn Erso was brought in after the incident at Tythoni Square in Jedha City. Shortly after that event, Gerrera's den erupted in a terrifying deluge of rock, rubble and sand as the Death Star destroyed the Holy City.

Beggar's Canyon

Situated on the desert planet of Tatooine, Beggar's Canyon was a dry riverbed that sliced through the mountains of Ben's Mesa.

As with all the canyons on Tatooine, it served as a den for the planet's fearsome krayt dragons and the somewhat less fearsome womp rats. Beggar's Canyon was famous among the thrill-seeking youths of Tatooine – it was where they practised the extreme sport of podracing. Luke Skywalker and Biggs Darklighter made their mark on this place by repeatedly gunning their T-16 skyhoppers through the treacherous ravine, which was so vast it permitted them to push their hoppers to the limit.

Ben Kenobi

See Obi-Wan Kenobi

Ben Quadinaros

An innovative podracer pilot who took part in the Boonta Eve Classic Podrace, this Toong from the Tund system drove a four-engine podracer, when his opponents usually only had two.

That additional power didn't prove much of an advantage, as Ben Quadinaros' vehicle refused to start at the beginning of the race. Despite the intervention of his pit droids, the worst happened – total breakdown. This led to the deactivation of the power couplings between the engines, which sent the podracer into a chaotic tailspin around the arena.

Ben Solo

See Kylo Ren

Benthic

A Tognath mercenary and marksman, Benthic was a key member of Saw Gerrera's rebel militia.

Along with his eggmate 'brother' Edrio, Benthic escaped Yar Togna, a world occupied by the Empire, and became a political refugee. The duo shared the nickname 'Two Tubes' because of the respiratory gear that allowed them to survive in an oxygen atmosphere. Although the partisans weren't assigned formal ranks, Benthic was considered one of Gerrera's lieutenants. He was in charge of the teams which transported important prisoners, such as the Imperial deserter Bodhi Rook. He also personally delivered Jyn Erso to his chief. During the destruction of Jedha City and Gerrera's den, he barely managed to escape in a ship.

Beru Lars

Born on the desert planet of Tatooine, Beru Lars, whose maiden name was Whitesun, was Owen Lars' spouse.

After the fall of the Republic, she and her husband Owen Lars raised Luke Skywalker on the family farm, which Owen had inherited from his father after he and his stepmother, Shmi Skywalker, died. A few years after that, Beru and Owen received a surprise visit from Obi-Wan Kenobi, who gave them Luke, the newborn son of Anakin Skywalker (who they believed to be dead) and Padmé Amidala, who had indeed died during childbirth.

Beru raised Luke as her own son. As he grew up, Luke occasionally clashed with Owen over his future. While Owen wanted Luke to become a peaceful farmer on Tatooine, his nephew was determined to enrol in the Academy and train as a pilot. Each harvest period involved arguments orchestrated to postpone Luke's departure. However, Beru was more attentive to what Luke wanted, and she managed to convince Owen to let Luke leave when he turned nineteen, at the end of the harvest period. However, their fate was sealed when Owen bought two droids, one (R2-D2) having in its possession the secret plans of the Death Star. The droids were being hunted by the Empire's troops, who tracked them to the Lars farm, and Beru and her husband were killed.

Bespin

Located in the Outer Rim, this gas planet was part of the Anoat system.

Its mainly human population co-habited with the Ugnaughts, whose numerous clans helped to build the floating mining outpost of Cloud City. Bespin owed its economic success to the presence of tibanna gas in several layers of its atmosphere. After being refined in large mining complexes, such as the one at Cloud City, the tibanna gas could be used in the manufacture of weapons and hyperdrive engines, which made it an extremely valuable commodity.

Bespin Guard

A member of the security force at the gas-mining outpost of Cloud City at Bespin.

Between the production of the rare and precious tibanna gas and its gambling industry, the commercial activities of Cloud City often attracted entrepreneurs of a questionable honesty. The prospect of making a quick buck in an environment relatively independent from the Empire had a tendency to lead to envy, corruption and embezzlement, which subsequently resulted in the need for a permanent civil police force.

Bib Fortuna

A native of Ryloth, this Twi'lek worked as a servant to the crime lord Jabba the Hutt.

He was by his master's side at his private stall when Jabba attended the podrace won by a young slave named Anakin Skywalker. Three decades later, Fortuna welcomed two droids named C-3PO and R2-D2 to Jabba's Palace, unaware that they were on a mission with Luke Skywalker to rescue Han Solo. It was also Bib Fortuna who permitted the Jedi Knight entrance to the palace, failing the one order that the Tatooine crime lord had asked of his servant – do not let Skywalker in before the end of his nap. However, Fortuna succumbed to Skywalker's Jedi mind trick, and led the Jedi Knight quickly to his master's throne room. Despite acting against his will, Fortuna was dismissed from the throne room by an angry Jabba. The Twi'lek was also present during the preparations for the execution of Skywalker, Solo and Chewbacca, which proved unlucky for Fortuna when the rebel heroes escaped and blew up Jabba's sail barge with Fortuna aboard.

Biggs Darklighter

A rebel pilot hailing from Tatooine, Biggs Darklighter grew up with Luke Skywalker and became one of the future Jedi's close friends.

The boys shared the same dream of leaving behind their homeworld in order to enrol at the Imperial Academy. They met often to test their piloting skills at the helm of their T-16 skyhoppers in the winding ravines of Beggar's Canyon.

Darklighter went to the Academy, while Skywalker remained stuck on Tatooine. At the end of his training, Darklighter returned to Tatooine to tell his family and friends that he was joining the emerging Rebel Alliance. He was soon assigned to the rebel base on Yavin 4, and was selected to become part of Red Squadron during the assault on the Death Star. It was under the call sign Red Three that he took part in the Battle of Yavin. During the attack, Darklighter showed great courage and exceptional skill, but he was shot down and killed by Darth Vader in the Death Star's trench while serving as Skywalker's wingman.

Biker Scout

See Scout Trooper

Bistan

A hot-headed corporal gunner who took part in the Battle of Scarif, Bistan joined the Rebellion after giving it a helping hand on his homeworld, Iakar, and engaged in the SpecForces for six months.

His homeworld was torn apart by the pharmaceutical lobby then occupied by the Empire. Although he was motivated by Jyn Erso's speech in front of the Rebel Alliance on Yavin 4, he didn't join her because he had too many insubordinations in his file. Only after receiving official orders did he arrive as part of reinforcements above the beaches of the Citadel Tower. Wearing his khaki spacesuit, he stationed himself at the door of a U-wing, where he could make the most damage using his 'Roba' M-45 repeating ion blaster. Upon arrival, the Iakaru gunner pierced the front right leg of an AT-ACT, making it collapse to the ground. Unfortunately, a little later in the battle, a laser blast struck one of the U-wing's engines, causing it to crash on the ground. The ferocious Bistan, who was popular among his equals, was killed in the crash.

Black-Saber

The codename of an Imperial secret stored in the Citadel Tower vaults on Scarif.

It was just one among the thousands of files in the Imperial databank that Jyn Erso and Cassian Andor – the two rebel agents looking for the Death Star plans – skimmed through during their search. Other files included 'Cluster Prism', 'War Mantle', 'Mark Omega', 'Pax Aurora', 'Celestial Power' and 'Stratosphere'. Even though it was classified in the structural engineering division, 'Black-Saber' remained a secret.

Blanaid

An AT-ST and transport pilot in the Imperial army, Blanaid was stationed at the forest moon of Endor.

During the Battle of Endor, he was alerted to the presence of Ewoks on the roof of his walker's cabin. Following the orders of Major Newland, he opened the hatch to get rid of the Ewok, but was dragged out of the walker by Chewbacca, and thrown more than 9 metres to the forest floor below, landing at the feet of the mechanic biped.

Blockade of Naboo

The first phase of the invasion of Naboo by the Trade Federation, the blockade involved immense military ships remaining in orbit around the peaceful planet, and forbidding the entry and exit of any starship.

The blockade was made possible by the laws of the Republic that governed the commercial legislature between merchants and Naboo, although it was contested whether these laws were in fact flouted by the blockade. With the blockade in place, the Trade Federation organised a military invasion, understanding that they should attempt to conceal their illegal actions. Trusting their adviser, Darth Sidious, the Trade Federation failed to comprehend that it was being used as a pawn in the Sith Lord's power games.

Bloodfin

See Sith Speeder

Blue Eight

See Heff Tobber

Blue Eleven

See Laren Joma

Blue Five

See Farns Monsbee

Blue Four

See Barion Raner

Blue Leader

See Antoc Merrick

Blue milk

Produced by the female bantha, this milk was sold all across the galaxy.

It possessed huge nutritional qualities and could be consumed in its natural state as a drink, or made into dairy products.

Blue Nine

See Calum Gram

Blue Squadron

A group of starfighters of the Rebel Alliance that were heavily involved in the Battle of Scarif, but took heavy losses as a result.

Under the command of General Antoc Merrick, the squadron plunged through the open gate of the global shield in order to support the ground troops during operation Rogue One. Only twelve X-wings and one U-wing made it through before the entrance closed, destroying two other X-wings in the process. The remaining surviving units defended the rebel fleet in orbit. Those that fought in the Scarif atmosphere engaged the four-legged AT-ACTs and faced the dangerous TIE strikers, of which Merrick became a casualty when he was shot down. Ultimately all ships were lost when Scarif was decimated by the Death Star.

Considering these major losses, including that of their leader, it was no surprise that Blue Squadron didn't take part in the assault on the Death Star. Instead, only Red and Gold Squadron fought in the famous Battle of Yavin. It wasn't until the Battle of Hoth that Blue Squadron had been rebuilt enough to take its revenge on the Empire, when it had the responsibility of defending Echo Base during its evacuation. Several AT-ATs were destroyed during the confrontation, which allowed rebel transports to get through the Imperial blockade. During the Battle of Endor, Blue Squadron participated once more in the successful battle above the forest moon.

Blue Three

See **Jaldine Gerams**

Blue Twelve

See **Paril Ritta**

Boba Fett

A bounty hunter from the planet Kamino, Boba Fett was the sole unmodified clone of his 'father', Jango Fett.

When Jango Fett was chosen by the Republic as the model from which the clones of their army would be created, he kept a clone for himself to raise as his son. Boba Fett received a normal father–son education with Jango, and became well versed in the techniques and expertise vital to the practice of his future profession as a bounty hunter. Despite his artificial conception, Fett's physical development was similar to any human child because he didn't undergo the genetic modifications of the other clones, notably accelerated growth and compartmental conditioning. That more 'regular' upbringing gave the young boy the ability to empathise, and he was able to feel emotion in a way that the clone soldiers of the Republic couldn't.

Boba Fett's fate was sealed the day his father died in the Battle of Geonosis. His destiny as a dangerous and merciless bounty hunter was born the instant he witnessed Jedi Master Mace Windu cut off his father's head. Fett vowed to get revenge, and created a union of bounty hunters on Tatooine. Fett gradually transformed into a formidable bounty hunter, wearing Mandalorian armour in memory of his father, and equipping it with a number of deadly gadgets and weapons. The armour also included a series of braids, similar to those of the Padawans, which he took from his victims. His ship, *Slave I*, was previously owned by his father, and was composed of various spare parts, including a multicoloured hull.

During the Civil War, Fett accepted a job from Jabba the Hutt. When the previous bounty hunter, Greedo, failed to recover a debt Han Solo owed to Jabba, Fett embarked on a quest to find the smuggler. Han Solo had attracted the interest of the Empire, which put its own bounty on his head. Darth Vader offered a contract to several mercenaries to bring back Han Solo alive, while Solo would also act as bait to lure Luke Skywalker. It was on Cloud City that Solo was finally captured, and frozen in carbonite to be delivered by Boba Fett to Jabba's Palace on Tatooine.

Remaining at the palace, Fett witnessed the capture of Solo's friends after their failed attempt to free the smuggler from Jabba's prison. Taken to the heart of the desert, Solo and his friends were to be executed by being fed to the Sarlacc at the Great Pit of Carkoon. Aided by R2-D2, Luke Skywalker succeeded in counter-attacking. During the confrontation, Fett fell from Jabba's sail barge and was unable to prevent himself tumbling into the gaping mouth of the sarlacc where, according to popular legends about the creature, it began its slow, thousand-year digestion of the unfortunate bounty hunter.

Bobbajo

Bobbajo is a Nu-Cosian arthritic salesman living on Jakku.

This old salesman had a calm nature and travelled slowly because of his ailments. He owned a domestic worrt and sold animals at market, mostly sneeps, keeping them in cages that were integrated into the towering backpack he always carried. Sometimes, he visited the Niima outpost to offer his merchandise to Unkar Plutt.

Bodhi Rook

Formerly a pilot for the Imperial Empire, Bodhi Rook deserted to join the Rebellion, and became an important part of history when he joined the Rogue One mission.

Rook's youth was rather tumultuous. Born and raised on Jedha, he got into trouble with the law on two occasions: first for illegal betting on sporting events, and then for dangerous conduct on a speeder. These indiscretions weren't serious, but showed how Rook tended to end up on the wrong side of the law. In an attempt to get back on track, he decided to pursue a career as an Imperial fighter pilot. Despite two years of practice at the academy of Terrabe, he lost out on a place in the fleet. He persevered, and a couple of years later he earned the rank of lieutenant, and was authorised to transport Imperial freight. The position led him into more and more confidential missions, including transporting kyber crystals from his homeworld of Jedha to a secret refinery on Eadu. There, he made the acquaintance of a remarkable man whose life had been destroyed by the Empire, Galen Erso. Rook, was touched by the captive scientist's story and was haunted by the revelation that his cargo was being used to build a monstrous superweapon.

With this information, the pilot decided to defect from the Empire and help the scientist, and agreed to transport a holographic message from Galen Erso to Saw Gerrera, the leader of a rebel militia. The rebels were difficult to find, and when he finally found them they treated him as an enemy. Suspicious of Rook, Gerrera subjected him to a torturous and painful mental cross-examination by a bor gullet. The interrogation caused Rook to temporarily lose his mind, until Cassian Andor was locked up in the neighbouring cell. Regaining awareness, Rook managed to flee Gerrera's den, along with Andor, Jyn Erso, K-2SO and two Guardians of the Whills, just as Jedha City was destroyed by the power of the Death Star.

Rook returned to Eadu to guide the rebels to the location of Galen Erso, where they made a crash-landing aboard their U-wing. While Jyn Erso and Andor attempted to reach Galen, the base was attacked by Alliance starfighters. Rook stole a cargo shuttle and used it to shoot down the stormtroopers pursuing Jyn Erso and Andor. This act of heroism finally convinced the group that Rook was one of them.

Truly committed to the rebel cause, Rook decided to take part in Jyn Erso's clandestine mission to steal the Death Star plans from Scarif. His knowledge of Imperial procedures would prove invaluable during the mission, particularly in gaining access to Scarif through the planet's protective shield gate. Although the rebels' shuttle wasn't on the list of arrivals at Scarif, he explained to control that he had been re-routed from Eadu, and transmitted the access code through the intermediary of his co-pilot, K-2SO. After the code was accepted, Rogue One was permitted to land on Platform 9 of the Imperial Centre of Military Research.

While Jyn Erso, Andor and K-2SO infiltrated the base, the Guardians of the Whills masterminded a sizeable diversion, and Rook remained aboard Rogue One with a handful of men. Rook's job was to ready the ship for departure once Erso had secured the Death Star plans. As explosives planted by Malbus and Îmwe detonated around the beaches of Scarif, Rook established a connection to transmit the plans of the Death Star. After successfully opening up a line of communication, Rook returned to the safety of the Rogue One hangar, but was killed by a grenade.

Despite his brutal end, Rook was an essential part of the operation, and had helped Jyn Erso succeed in her mission to steal the plans of the Empire's terrifying space station. After that, Princess Leia recovered the files, which led to the rebel victory at the Battle of Yavin.

Bogwing

This flying reptilian creature could be found in the swamps of Dagobah and was known to be highly territorial.

It would hunt by diving and catching prey in its powerful talons, and could carry weight far heavier than itself. Once caught by a bogwing, it was almost impossible for any prey to free itself.

Boles Roor

One of the best podracer pilots in the Boonta Eve Classic Podrace, Boles Roor enjoyed two victories on the circuit, which the Mos Espa crowd were reminded of at the start of the event by the two-headed Troig broadcaster.

Placed on the starting grid just behind the young Anakin Skywalker and Clegg Holdfast, and between Gasgano and Teemto Pagalies, the Sneevel failed to make much of a mark during the race. He was overtaken by Anakin Skywalker in the Laguna Caves during the first lap, and ended up finishing sixth, a disappointing position for this two-time winner.

Bongo

An underwater Gungan vehicle, used by Qui-Gon Jinn, Obi-Wan Kenobi and Jar Jar Binks to reach the city of Theed while going through the oceanic heart of Naboo.

Variations of this submarine model existed: monobubble, tribubble, military and luxury. The famous bubble element of the vehicle was actually a hydrostatic shield, which was incorporated into an organic hull. Quite how the vehicle functioned was a secret the Gungans guarded very closely.

Booma

See Energy Ball

Boonta Eve

An annual celebration held on the desert planet of Tatooine in the Outer Rim Territories.

During the festive celebrations the ruling Hutts hosted the much-watched Boonta Eve Classic Podrace in the Mos Espa Grand Arena.

Bor Gullet

A multipod creature with white, veiled eyes that had the ability to read minds.

The creature's soft and vast body moved on its tentacles, which it used to seize its victims. It then stuck a tentacle to each of its victim's temples to read their mind. In his hideout in the Catacombs of Cadera on Jedha, Saw Gerrera used a bor gullet to torture and gain information from Bodhi Rook. The deserting Imperial pilot nearly succumbed to the secondary effect of the bor gullet's formidable power – losing his mind.

BoShek

A human born on the planet Corellia, BoShek was a smuggler and a pilot during the time of the Galactic Empire.

This Force-sensitive ace pilot crossed paths with Obi-Wan Kenobi in the Mos Eisley Cantina, where he introduced the old Jedi to Chewbacca.

Boss Nass

See Rugor Nass

Bossk

A bounty hunter from the planet Trandosha, Bossk's dedication to business allowed him to work with many customers who often had opposing interests.

Although fiercely independent, Bossk took the young Boba Fett under his wing during the Clone Wars. He even accompanied Fett on his quest to find and kill Mace Windu, the Jedi Master responsible for Fett's father's death.

A few years before the Battle of Yavin, Bossk met Ezra Bridger on Lothal, where they joined forces to fight a corrupt Imperial agent. After the destruction of the Death Star by the Rebel Alliance, the Empire called on the services of this bounty hunter to help them locate the rebels. Bossk was hired by Darth Vader to find the

Millennium Falcon and its crew, but it was Boba Fett who eventually won the bounty after following Solo to Cloud City. Bossk was also a guest aboard Jabba the Hutt's sail barge, the *Khetanna*, when the crime lord intended to feed Luke Skywalker and his friends to the Sarlacc at the Great Pit of Carkoon.

Bothan

Mentioned by Mon Mothma, a team of Bothan spies succeeded in discovering where the second Death Star was being constructed, as well as information about when the Emperor would be on board.

The Bothans recovered this information at the cost of numerous lives, and transmitted it to the Rebel Alliance to aid the military operation against the Imperial superweapon. The Bothans went one step further and also collected other vital information, such as the door code for the bunker on Endor, which allowed the rebels to deactivate the SLD-26 global shield generator protecting the second Death Star.

Boushh

A bounty hunter from Uba IV, Boushh was believed to have been killed by a revengeful crime syndicate.

Taking advantage of his disappearance, Princess Leia Organa used his identity and appearance as a disguise to infiltrate Jabba the Hutt's Palace and free Han Solo. To gain entry to the palace, she presented Chewbacca to Jabba as her prisoner. She also spoke in Ubese, the language of the bounty hunter she was impersonating. However, the next night, while attempting to free Solo, Leia was unmasked and captured by the crime lord and enslaved in chains.

Bowcaster

The Wookiees' weapon of choice, the bowcaster came in two forms.

The first shot a metallic cartridge surrounded and guided by a plasma bullet. The second was a weapon customised to only shoot an energised bullet. The bowcaster's incredible power was down to the fact that, originally, the Wookiees were forced to develop means to defend themselves against the dangerous predators that inhabited their homeworld of Kashyyyk. Owing to the tremendous strength required to withstand the bowcaster's recoil, few other species used the weapon, although Han Solo really enjoyed using Chewbacca's bowcaster.

Bozeden Jeems

Based on Scarif, Bozeden Jeems was the general inspector of the Imperial Security Office.

With his black cap and pure white uniform, he looked every bit the soldier who had been promoted a great career during the era of Emperor Palpatine. Working for an intel agency, a sub-division of the Commission for the Preservation of the New Order, he knew many of the regime's closely guarded secrets. However, his dream of one day being promoted to Deputy Director were ruined by the arrival of the Rogue One team on Scarif. While Jeems fiercely deployed his troops in an attempt to salvage the future he dreamt of, it was unclear if he survived the Battle of Scarif.

Brasmon Kee

A representative from the planet Abednedo at the Galactic Senate of the New Republic, Brasmon Kee was usually attired in a senator robe and a regent turban.

In later life, he was a resident of Hosnian Prime, where he died when the planet was targeted by the First Order's terrifying superweapon, Starkiller Base.

Bren Derlin

A Rebel Alliance officer originally from Tiisheraan, Bren Derlin notably took part in the Battle of Hoth.

He was promoted quickly after the Battle of Yavin, and placed under the command of General Rieekan, taking responsibility for the security of Echo Base on Hoth. Derlin was the officer who decided to secure the base by closing the access doors overnight when Han Solo and Luke Skywalker failed to return from a routine patrol.

Bright Tree Village

This small forest settlement of the Ewok tribe rallied to support the rebels during the Battle of Endor.

A group of dwellings suspended 15 metres above the ground, it was nestled amid the foliage of immense conifer trees and was home to roughly 200 Ewoks. In the centre of the village was the home of Chief Chirpa, as well as meeting places used by the Council of the Ancients. The large huts that were constructed for the many families were located at the periphery of the settlement, while the bachelors were lodged in small huts below the main village.

It was their job to keep watch for any dangers coming from the ground, and defend the village in the event of an attack. All of the huts were linked by a special network of ropes, bridges and platforms.

Just below the canopy of Bright Tree Village stood the launching pad for the Ewoks' gliders, which allowed them to detect aerial threats, such as the condor dragons, and to patrol the surroundings for large predators, such as the gorax. At night, torches and fires illuminated the village. The inside of each hut was simple, warm and comfortable, with braided, fur-covered mattresses. In the middle of the village rested a hearth for cooking meats and soup, while the roofs held wood reserves.

The towering conifers around which the village was built had fireproof bark, which also served as an insect repellent. The trees also aided the Ewoks in their hunting while providing branches and trunks for strong bows, spears and catapult arms should they need to fight to defend their home. Bright Tree Village was used as a war base when C-3PO, with the help of Luke Skywalker, convinced the Ewoks to fight the Empire. After the victory at the Battle of Endor, it was in Bright Tree Village that the heroes of the Rebellion celebrated the death of the Emperor and the Imperial defeat.

Broan Danurs

A versatile rebel pilot who served during the Battle of Scarif.

On Dantooine, he flew an A-wing starfighter in Gold Squadron, but he was brought in to replace one of his wingmen in Green Squadron, and became a pilot of an X-wing starfighter. Promoted to captain, Danurs discovered that one of his best friends and mentors, Davish Krail, was in the squadron with him. Danurs' ability to master his new craft was remarkable, and under the call sign Green Ten he participated in the orbital fight above Scarif as Rogue One embarked on its dangerous mission to steal the Death Star plans.

Buboicullaar a.k.a. Bubo

A male frog-dog who lived at the Court of Jabba the Hutt, Bubo had sharp teeth that protruded from his wide mouth, and his appearance was often considered both ferocious and ridiculous.

His grotesque appearance meant that many inhabitants of the crime lord's den assumed Bubo wasn't an intelligent being, but that couldn't be further from the truth, in fact, he was considerably smarter than a lot of Jabba's thugs.

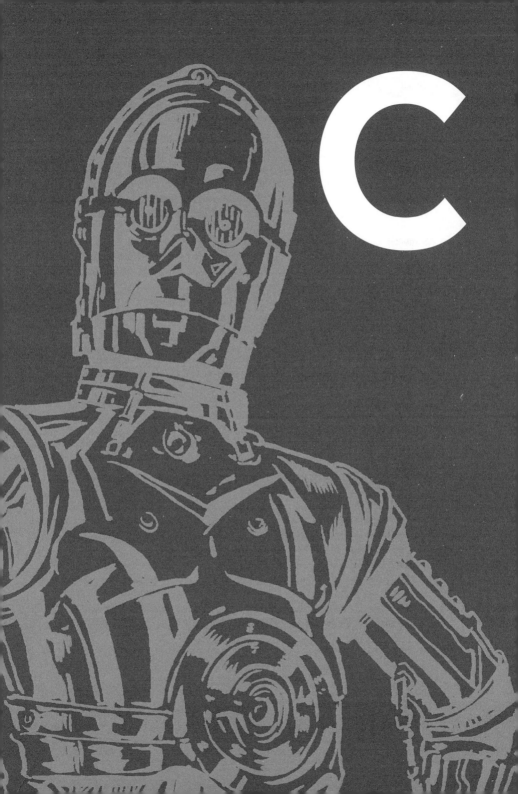

C-3PO 'Threepio'

A humanoid droid specialising in human-cyborg relations, whose destiny was to embark on many epic adventures with fellow droid R2-D2.

Together with the Skywalker family, C-3PO and R2-D2 were present for many of the key moments in galactic history. C-3PO was manufactured by the firm Cybot Galactica for etiquette and protocol. He played an important role as an aide to the chief negotiator of the Manakron system and, according to C-3PO, he was also once tasked with programming loadlifters in a binary language very similar to that used by hydroponic farm vaporators.

Somehow, C-3PO ended up as spare parts in a scrapyard on Tatooine. He was rescued by the talented young slave Anakin Skywalker, who repaired and turned C-3PO into a domestic helper for his mother, Shmi. Although the young boy was unable to cover up C-3PO's wirings and joints, he was able to protect the droid against the harsh conditions of Tatooine, namely the heat and the sand. Skywalker and C-3PO's lives took an unexpected turn when four strangers – Qui-Gon Jinn, Padmé Amidala, Jar Jar Binks and R2-D2 – turned up at the shop of Skywalker's owner, Watto.

The prim C-3PO established a quick rapport with the mischievous astromech droid R2-D2, even though R2-D2 commented that C-3PO was in fact 'naked' without his outer plating. The two soon worked together on the technical team in charge of Skywalker's podracer, which took part in the Boonta Eve Classic, where C-3PO proudly carried the flag of his young master during the parade preceding the race. When Anakin left Tatooine with Qui-Gon Jinn, C-3PO was left with Skywalker's mother.

Shmi was sold to a farmer, Cliegg Lars, who integrated C-3PO into his farm and gave him new silver armour. C-3PO worked there until Shmi was abducted by Tusken Raiders. This dramatic development resulted in the return of Anakin Skywalker, who was by then a Jedi Padawan. It had been many years since C-3PO had seen Skywalker, and he had changed so much that, at first, C-3PO didn't recognise his former master. When Skywalker departed, the protocol droid followed him and was reunited with R2-D2.

From that point on, C-3PO became involved in a series of unfortunate events. On a mission to Geonosis before the Clone Wars began, C-3PO's head became separated from his body and was transplanted onto parts of two B1 battle droids. When he was returned to his natural state by R2-D2, C-3PO attended the secret marriage of Anakin Skywalker and Padmé Amidala, and was gifted to Amidala as a wedding present.

After the Clone Wars, the new, golden C-3PO accompanied the pregnant senator to Mustafar, where she joined her husband, who had turned to the dark side. Following a dispute with Kenobi, Skywalker, now known as Darth Vader, attacked Amidala leaving her unconscious. After the duel between Kenobi and his former apprentice, C-3PO, R2-D2 and Kenobi returned with Amidala just in time for her to give birth to twins, Luke and Leia. Amidala died from her injuries and Kenobi now had the task of rehoming the twins, but also of keeping their births secret from Vader. Leia was adopted by Amidala's friend, Senator Bail Organa, who also took possession of C-3PO and R2-D2. He ensured that C-3PO would keep Amidala's children secret by erasing the droid's memory.

Nineteen years later, C-3PO was aboard the vessel, *Tantive IV*, when it was attacked by Darth Vader. Having had his memory banks wiped, C-3PO didn't recognise the Sith Lord as his former master. Vader captured the small ship to retrieve the stolen Death Star plans, but Princess Leia was able to record a message and store the plans in R2-D2. She instructed the droid to travel to Tatooine and deliver his cargo to Obi-Wan Kenobi. C-3PO escaped from the ship along with R2-D2, landing on Tatooine only to be captured by Jawas. These scavengers sold both droids to a farmer named Owen Lars. The droids were then fixed up by Lars' nephew, Luke Skywalker. While following his new owner's nephew, who was searching for the disobedient R2-D2, C-3PO lost his arm while attempting to escape from a Tusken Raider.

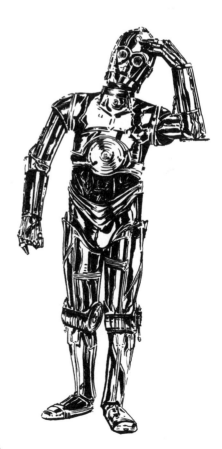

C-3PO, R2-D2 and Luke Skywalker fled Tatooine aboard Han Solo and Chewbacca's ship, the *Millennium Falcon*. When they exited hyperspace in the Alderaan system C-3PO discovered that Alderaan had been vaporised by an enormous space station. When the *Millennium Falcon* was drawn into the Death Star by a tractor beam, C-3PO and the rest of the crew were forced to hide in secret compartments on the smuggler's ship. Later, C-3PO's companions were stuck in a functioning trash compactor and they faced certain death. Luckily, R2-D2 intervened, but C-3PO mistook the rebels' screams of joy for those of agony.

Fleeing the Death Star aboard the *Millennium Falcon*, and under the heavy fire of a squadron of TIE fighters, C-3PO was thrown around so much that he ended up in a heap of electrical wires. The misfortune continued during the Battle of Yavin, which C-3PO survived, but his best friend, R2-D2, ended up severely 'wounded'. After those battles, in which C-3PO had expected to be annihilated, he proved his deep affection for R2 by stating that he'd donate some of his own circuits to help repair the R2 unit. Fortunately, such extreme lengths weren't necessary, as the rebel technicians worked marvels and the two droids were reunited and received medals for their bravery during the battle.

Now allied to the rebels, C-3PO was forced to adopt a life as a fugitive. He was present during the defeat on Hoth, and fled aboard the last vessel remaining on the icy planet, the *Millennium Falcon*, only just evading Darth Vader and his snowtroopers. A new interstellar journey began with Han Solo, but it wouldn't be a relaxing one, particularly when the *Millennium Falcon*'s hyperdrive stopped working. C-3PO failed to help lighten the mood when he revealed the low survival odds of navigating an asteroid field, and he further irritated Solo when he interrupted a kiss between the Corellian smuggler and Princess Leia. Later, C-3PO became so upset about a supposedly deadly plan to confront a Star Destroyer that Leia was forced to temporarily deactivate him.

The group travelled to Cloud City where C-3PO faced yet another sticky situation. He left his friends to investigate what he thought was another droid, but was met by a troop of hidden stormtroopers, who were there as part of a trap set by Darth Vader to capture the rebels. Shot at point-blank range, C-3PO was blown into a number of pieces. The Imperials then gave the pieces to Ugnaught scavengers who would have disintegrated them if Chewbacca hadn't intervened.

Soon after that, the Wookiee and his companions were arrested by the troops of the Sith Lord. Solo's co-pilot took advantage of his confinement by attempting to reassemble C-3PO, but he had a few problems with the droid's head, which he attached backwards. When C-3PO complained, Chewbacca turned him off. Before Chewbacca could reconnect C-3PO's legs, he and the golden droid were transported to witness Han Solo being frozen in carbonite. C-3PO and his friends were to be imprisoned aboard Vader's starship but Lando freed them and they headed to the *Millennium Falcon*. When R2-D2 returned with Luke Skywalker, the little robot finally helped put the protocol droid back together. He also managed to repair the *Millennium Falcon*'s hyperdrive, which allowed them to escape the Empire's clutches once more.

Six months later, C-3PO unwittingly became part of an attempt to rescue Han Solo from Jabba the Hutt's Palace on Tatooine. Afraid that C-3PO might blow their cover, Luke Skywalker neglected to tell C-3PO of his plan and the droid became particularly upset when, along with R2-D2, he was offered as a gift to Jabba by Skywalker. After they had gained access to the fortified palace, C-3PO discovered that Solo was being used as decoration in Jabba's throne room, where droids tortured other droids, a dancer was devoured alive by a rancor and negotiations involved the threat of thermal detonators. The rescue didn't quite go to plan, as Chewbacca was jailed, Leia unmasked and Skywalker was condemned to death.

Serving as Jabba's personal translator, C-3PO travelled with his new master on his sail barge to the Great Pit of Carkoon. Jabba's Kowakian monkey-lizard, Salacious Crumb, tormented C-3PO by damaging one of his photoreceptors. R2-D2 helped Luke escape his fate and the group were rescued, but not before C-3PO was pushed off the exploding sail barge and fell head first into the sands of Tatooine.

During the rebel assault on the forest moon of Endor, C-3PO came across a group of Ewoks. The Endor natives thought he was a god, and saved him and his friends from being sacrificed. C-3PO's mastery of six million types of communication proved particularly useful as he was able to communicate with the natives. By telling the story of the rebels' adventures against the Empire, he convinced the Ewoks to join the Alliance, earning the rebels a vital ally in their quest to destroy the second Death Star. The Ewoks' contribution proved hugely important during the Battle of Endor, especially as they were able to help bring down the second Death Star's shield generator, which allowed Lando Calrissian and the other rebels to destroy the space station. As an architect of this victory, C-3PO participated in the rebels' celebration at the Ewoks' Bright Tree Village.

C-3PO returned to work for the Resistance, under the rule of General Leia Organa, to fight the First Order. C-3PO was on Taul when news arrived that Admiral Ackbar had been captured. C-3PO was attacked by a tentacled creature, which pulled his left arm clean off. Saved by Poe Dameron, his arm was replaced by a red one, which C-3PO considered ugly. As a leader of the network of droid spies of the Resistance on D'Qar, he used his talent to decipher important data that led them to BB-8, who had been lost by Poe on Jakku. C-3PO was part of the team dispatched to Takodana to recover the droid. Shortly after the assault on Starkiller Base, C-3PO's old friend R2-D2 – who had been in stand-by mode ever since Luke Skywalker's disappearance – woke up, to C-3PO's excitement. Before Rey left to meet the Jedi Master, C-3PO replaced his red arm, returning to his original, golden-armoured appearance just in time for further adventures.

C-9979 Landing Craft

A Trade Federation craft used by the Confederacy of Independent Systems, and conceived for heavy transportation.

At the time of the Invasion of Naboo, these craft delivered the droid army, along with vehicles, tanks and troops to the battlefield. They also provided a means of escape for Qui-Gon Jinn and Obi-Wan Kenobi, who used the landing craft to flee from the Trade Federation flagship *Saak'ak* to the surface of Naboo. With a span of 370 metres, each craft had the capacity – thanks to the optimisation of its interior space by its manufacturer Haor Chall Engineering – to carry 11 troop transporters, 28 combat droid transporters and 114 Armoured Assault Tanks.

C1-10P 'Chopper'

Nicknamed 'Chopper', this astromech droid with masculine programming was active during the time of the Clone Wars and Imperial rule.

A member of the Spectres, also known as *Ghost* team, which was led by Captain Hera Syndulla and the Jedi Kanan Jarrus, C1-10P helped the Rebellion fight the Empire. He was in charge of the maintenance of the team's vessel, the *Ghost*. This small droid was present at the Massassi outpost on Yavin 4, and was near generals Merrick, Dravens and Mon Mothma, when they were informed of the clandestine operation 'Rogue One' on Scarif.

C2-B5

A black-plated astromech droid based at the Citadel Tower on Scarif.

C2-B5 roamed around the Imperial complex tasked with solving maintenance problems in the computer network. Unlike other astromech models, it didn't possess a personality as its memory was regularly erased.

Cal Alder

A rebel lieutenant from the planet Kal'Shebbol, and a member of the High Command of the Alliance during the Battle of Hoth.

His brilliant service record convinced Major Bren Derlin to give him the responsibility of undertaking various patrols around Echo Base to ensure its security. Alder was a ground-mission specialist, and for that reason he participated in talks regarding which planet to select for the new rebel base.

In particular, he took responsibility for ordering Derlin to close the doors of the base when Luke Skywalker and Han Solo were reported missing. He reasoned that the intense cold of the night, plus the possibility of wampa attacks, posed a security risk for the entire base, and he wasn't willing to risk its safety, despite the high ranking of the two missing rebels.

Alder also took part in the Battle of Hoth, coordinating the defence perimeter of Echo Base, which had air cover by a fleet of snowspeeders. Alder survived the confrontation, which remained the biggest military defeat in the history of the Alliance.

Caluan Ematt

A Resistance High Command officer who worked with General Leia Organa, Caluan Ematt was an experienced soldier and a veteran of the Rebel Alliance.

After fighting in the Battle of Yavin, the enemy's strategies, whether masterminded by the Empire or the First Order, always seemed familiar to him. It was quite natural for him to join forces with General Organa and the Resistance on D'Qar, where he ensured that the new generation benefited from his considerable experience. He knew all about the Death Star and the havoc it wreaked, which meant that he remained cautious when he first encountered the enormous Starkiller Base.

Calum Gram

A Blue Squadron pilot who fought under the call sign Blue Nine in the Battle of Scarif.

Before becoming a key player in the Galactic Civil War, Calum Gram was a first-aid pilot who worked for the Wilderness Preserve service on Atrisia. It was in that environment that the future Blue Nine learned to master precision landing in the middle of dense vegetation, a skill that proved invaluable on Scarif.

Cam Droid

Also known as a hovercam, this was an intelligent, repulsorlift camera that could record images and sounds in places not accessible to other devices.

Both the Boonta Eve Classic Podrace track and the Galactic Senate Chamber used cam droids to record events.

Camp 4

A camp for prisoners of war created by the Trade Federation specifically to hold the political prisoners from Naboo.

If she had not escaped with Qui-Gon Jinn and Obi-Wan Kenobi, it was at Camp 4 that Queen Amidala would have been held.

Cane Adiss

A member of Jabba the Hutt's criminal clan, this two-headed Yuvernian, who boasted two long necks and spotted heads, was present when the heroes of the Rebellion arrived at Jabba's Palace on Tatooine.

He was there to witness Princess Leia Organa's attempt to rescue Han Solo. Disguised as Boushh, Leia threatened to use a thermal detonator that would destroy the palace. Cane Adiss was also aboard Jabba's sail barge *Khetanna* when it was destroyed, and it's uncertain if he survived the explosion.

Carbon-freezing Chamber

A technological device designed to protect fragile cargo during long-term transportation.

The chamber mixed tibanna gas and liquid carbon, a combination that instantly encased the cargo in an extremely strong and long-lasting alloy. The technique could be used for the transportation of living beings, but freezing a living creature came with a high risk of death. At the point of freezing, the item, or the person, entered into a state of hibernation, from which they would emerge only when they were defrosted. The side effects of freezing a person included a temporary loss of their senses, something that often wore off after a period of time.

Han Solo served as a carbon-freezing test subject to Darth Vader. The Sith Lord wanted to use the chamber to capture and confine his son, Luke Skywalker, and take him to the Emperor, but

Skywalker escaped before he could be frozen. Despite the odds, Solo survived the freezing process and was delivered to Jabba the Hutt, who kept him like a hunting trophy until Solo's friends came to his rescue.

Carlist Rieekan

A general of the Rebel Alliance who was originally from the planet Alderaan.

Carlist Rieekan was one of the lucky and rare individuals who survived the destruction of Alderaan. He became one of the founding members of the Alliance at a time when his own organisation was formed of a group of disorganised cells who were only united by their struggle against Imperial control. At the end of the Battle of Yavin, Rieekan participated in the search for the ideal place to build a new base, and after settling on Hoth, he was promoted to general and military chief of Echo Base. A tall and pragmatic man, he made the difficult decision to evacuate the base just one month after its creation, suspecting that the Empire had discovered them.

Cassian Andor

An intel officer for the Rebel Alliance, Cassian Andor served in the Alliance to Restore the Republic during Operation Fracture and the Galactic Civil War.

He was also an integral part of the clandestine mission codenamed 'Rogue One'. Like Jyn Erso, his childhood was sacrificed to war. Born on the planet Fest, he was already showing anti-Imperial behaviour as early as six years old when he threw stones at Imperial soldiers and the four-legged transports of the Great Army of the Republic. Indeed, although he wasn't a separatist, he joined an insurgent cell supported by the Confederacy of Independent Systems. His father had been killed at the military academy of Carida during a protest demonstration against the growing Republic militarism. With the advent of the Empire, Andor began to attend the anarchist movements, which led to him joining the Alliance to Restore the Republic.

Recruited by General Davits Draven, Andor became a veteran spy. That fact was pretty remarkable, considering the rebels predicted that Andor had only a twenty-three per cent chance of surviving his first twenty missions. Promoted to the rank of captain, Andor built a network of contacts throughout the galaxy, all of which kept him informed about hostile secret activities. On some missions, he was accompanied by K-2SO, an Imperial security droid that he had reprogrammed to serve the Rebellion.

Shortly before the Battle of Yavin, Andor arrived on the Ring of Kafrene, after a frustrating quest that led him from Coruscant to Corulag. Without any substantial information, despite running up a huge debt, Cassian refused to return to Yavin 4 empty handed. Tivik, his informant among the men of Saw Gerrera, told him that, according to an Imperial deserter in contact with Galen Erso, the Empire had built a superweapon described as a 'planet killer'. Interrupted by a patrol of stormtroopers, Andor was forced to eliminate them, alongside Tivik, who he shot in the back without hesitation.

Back in the Massassi great temple, Andor attended the briefing of the mission assigned by Mon Mothma to Jyn Erso. He had been given his own secret objective, to assassinate Galen Erso in order to stop all development on the dangerous new weapon. Bound for Jedha, he showed Jyn Erso that he trusted her by allowing her to use a blaster, much to the annoyance of K-2SO. While searching for Saw Gerrera in the Holy City, the duo were caught in a full confrontation between Gerrera's militia and Imperial forces. To protect Erso, Andor was forced to shoot down one of the partisans, before they were stopped by the stormtroopers.

Liberated by Chirrut Îmwe and Baze Malbus, the four new companions were immediately captured by Gerrera's rebels for the death of one of their own. Taken into Gerrera's den, Andor was confined to a cell with the Guardians of the Whills. And in the cell beside them was the notorious Imperial deserter, Bodhi Rook. Andor helped revive Rook, who had slipped into temporary madness after being mentally tortured by Gerrera's bor gullet. Andor then learned the location of the Imperial scientist he was supposed to eliminate. Outside, the consecrated city of Jedha was destroyed by a test shot unleashed by the Death Star's superlaser. With the foundations of their jail buckling, Andor used his talents as a spy to get everyone out, including Jyn Erso. Using their U-wing, Andor, K-2SO, Erso, Îmwe, Malbus and Rook fled the cataclysmic nightmare and headed for the planet Eadu.

Upon arrival at Eadu, Andor succeeded in tracking down Galen Erso and lined up the perfect aim to take down his target. But after Jyn had told him that her father had allied himself with the Alliance, and he witnessed what appeared to be a confrontation between Galen Erso and his director, Andor made the difficult decision to disobey his orders to assassinate Galen. But, just then, a squadron of rebel starfighters attacked and killed the scientist. The rebel team escaped aboard a stolen cargo shuttle, blasting off for Yavin 4. During the journey, Erso confronted Andor, having guessed his real objectives on Eadu. Despite revealing that he had disobeyed his orders, Andor failed to convince Erso that he was on her side, and they ended up separating upon arrival on Yavin 4.

After Mon Mothma rejected Jyn Erso's planned assault on Scarif, Andor secretly gathered a convoy of ground soldiers who were convinced that Erso's plan was the only way forward. Andor's strong and unexpected support marked the beginning of a new friendship between him and Erso. Perhaps understanding that this was a mission they probably wouldn't emerge from alive, the two rebels finally understood and respected one another.

Together, they took off for the Imperial Centre of Military Research, despite the fact that they hadn't received authorisation to do so. The 'Rogue One' mission was underway! After successfully landing on Scarif, Andor and Erso dressed in stolen uniforms and gained access to the base, along with K-2SO, while the other members of the mission created a diversion outside to distract the Empire's garrison. Familiar with infiltration, Andor and his fellow rebels reached the inside of the Citadel Tower's secure vault. While K-2SO guided them towards the Death Star plans from a remote console, stormtroopers attacked the droid. K-2SO locked Andor and Erso safely inside the vault, then sacrificed himself to ensure their survival.

With no time to grieve the loss of their droid friend, Andor and Erso were pursued by Director Orson Krennic and two of his death troopers. During the shoot-out, Andor was wounded and fell from a column in the vault, landing unconscious on a platform. When he awoke, he summoned all of his strength to track Erso down. Discovering her at the summit of the tower, he shot Director Krennic from behind before the Imperial officer could kill Erso. Together, Andor and Erso succeeded in transmitting the plans of the Death Star before making their way back to the beach. In the descending elevator, they shared a small moment of tenderness, relieved that they had succeeded in their mission.

The Death Star arrived from hyperspace and shot its superlaser at the Citadel Tower. The shot struck the planet surface several kilometres away across the ocean. As on Jedha, it triggered a tsunami of energy that the two rebels were unable to escape. Without a word, kneeling face-to-face on the beach, Andor and Erso embraced each other, awaiting the end.

Cassio Tagge

Born on the planet Tepasi, Cassio Tagge was the Chief of the Imperial Army, and part of the executive advice council supporting Grand Moff Tarkin during his time as governor of the Death Star.

Tagge was one of the few Imperial commanders who took the rebel threat seriously. From a political standpoint, he suspected that the Alliance would benefit from support within the Imperial Senate, which would help to increase its number of rebels. On a military level, he also expressed his concern about how the rebels could exploit the Death Star's weaknesses when they managed to get their hands on the superweapon's technical plans.

On this point, he strongly opposed Admiral Motti, who couldn't imagine for one second that the rebels would ever become a threat, with or without the information in their possession. However, Tagge was quickly proved right, and unlike many of his Imperial colleagues, he survived the destruction of the space station. During the Battle of Yavin, he was present on Dantooine, after Tarkin succeeded in extracting information from Princess Leia. Tagge found evidence of a former rebel base, which had clearly been abandoned for a long time. He remained on Dantooine to investigate, both delaying his return to the Death Star and saving his own life. The Emperor rewarded him for his accuracy concerning the rebel threat by naming him Grand General.

Catacombs of Cadera

A series of ancient ruins located near Holy City on the moon of Jedha, which were used as a hideout by Saw Gerrera's rebel militia.

Once a monastery, the catacombs were originally dug out of the planet's rock, and then used to lay to rest the dead of a society whose name and history was long forgotten. The fact that the catacombs were once used as a burial ground led to stories that they were haunted by spirits, which discouraged the locals from visiting them. Later, the Church of the Contained Crescent used this rocky place for several years, and they left behind evidence of their time there in the symbols carved into the catacombs' lattice windows.

The last occupant of the catacombs was none other than the famous Onderonian leader, Saw Gerrera. With his militia, Gerrera transformed the catacombs into headquarters from where he planned and launched raids against the Empire. The operational base was equipped with weaponry, a prison that was nicknamed 'The Gut', and several ships that were parked in nearby caves. When the Death Star destroyed Jedha City, the catacombs trembled and the gigantic statues collapsed from walls before the ruins were swallowed by the moon.

Cave of Evil

This natural excavation, located below the base of a gnarltree on Dagobah, was inhabited by the dark side of the Force.

It possessed the ability to produce a powerful manifestation of the Force which would feed on the torment and fears of anyone who entered it. Going into the cave was the climax of Luke Skywalker's Jedi training and the trial presented him with visions of the consequences that could lay ahead should he be tempted by the dark side. For every person who entered the cave, the visions would be different, as the malevolent Force fed on the thoughts, fears and weaknesses of each specific individual.

Skywalker's biggest weaknesses were anger and fear, and it was while experiencing these emotions that he would be most susceptible to the temptation of the dark side. Inside the cave, this presented itself in the form of a premonition in which he confronted Darth Vader in a lightsaber duel. Eventually, Skywalker cut off the Sith Lord's head, but when the helmet fell to the ground it opened to reveal the young Jedi's face inside. Skywalker and Vader shared a tie which suggested their common weaknesses were anger and fear, but it also hinted at another connection, which was yet to be discovered.

Caysin Bog

A cybernetic humanoid in Jedha City who had been Decraniated.

After being seriously crippled by an explosion during an operation led by Saw Gerrera's militia, he owed his survival to the skills of Dr. Cornelius Evazan. The sinister surgeon, who worked in the Holy City under the pseudonym 'Roofoo', took the remainder of Caysin Bog's body and rebuilt it. But was the new cyborg still Caysin Bog? Despite having the same chunky frame, the rest of Bog had been drastically modified. The surgical techniques used to save him were very similar to those used by Evazan to create the frightening class of Decraniateds. Surviving without a head, Bog also had a cybernetic abdomen. It was when he had taken on this new appearance that his path crossed with Jyn Erso and Cassian Andor – he was in the front line during the duo's ambush of Tythoni Square. Shortly after, Holy City was levelled by the Death Star.

Central Isopter

An intriguing cult who were fascinated by and worshipped death itself.

This morbid religion led its followers to the most dangerous places in the galaxy in order to study phenomena bound to violence, disease and death, after which they would meditate on questions of morality. Nesta Term, self-proclaimed Lens of the Central Isopter, and two other cult members were based in the Holy City of Jedha, dressed in big, thick shawls and masks. The trio studied the harmonies of disturbance in the Consecrated City, each second coming closer to one of the things they worshipped – chaos.

Chewbacca

A male Wookiee and co-pilot of the *Millennium Falcon*, Chewbacca was a native of the planet Kashyyyk.

Nicknamed 'Chewie', he played a major role in the conflicts of the galaxy. Over a period of fifty years, he took part in the Clone Wars, fighting alongside the Republic, and then in the Civil War, fighting with the Rebel Alliance against the Empire. Much later, he fought to oppose the First Order as part of the Resistance. In addition to those vital military operations, Chewbacca was also known as the co-pilot and faithful friend of Han Solo, the famous smuggler and general of the Alliance.

During the Clone Wars, Chewbacca became a slave and freed himself from captivity with the help of Ahsoka Tano, a Jedi Padawan. He made the best use of his technological expertise by constructing an emitter through which he could send messages to his friends. Along with General Tarfful, he took command of the Wookiee army during the Battle of Kashyyyk, helping the Republic and their army of clones tackle the Separatist droid army. This confrontation was supervised in person by Jedi Master Yoda, who was at that time a general of the Republic. Chewbacca and Tarfful were at Yoda's side when Order 66 was given, and they witnessed the attempt on Yoda's life by the clone Commander Rigs. Chewbacca helped Yoda flee the planet, and the Jedi Master went into self-imposed exile on Dagobah.

When the Galactic Empire replaced the Republic, the Wookiees were enslaved and most were sent to work in mines. Chewbacca was freed from captivity by Han Solo, a Corellian smuggler. Chewie joined Solo in the smuggling trade, and they often worked for the Hutt clan on Tatooine. During one job they had to dump their cargo to avoid Imperial sanctions. This angered the Hutt crime lord Jabba, and a bounty was placed on their heads. While relaxing in the Mos Eisley Cantina, Solo and Chewbacca met with Obi-Wan Kenobi and Luke Skywalker, and considered their offer of work a fantastic stroke of luck. The amount Kenobi promised the smugglers for safe passage to Alderaan would cover their debt. But Chewbacca and Solo quickly discovered that their passengers weren't plain tourists, as they were targeted by an Imperial fleet, including two enormous Star Destroyers.

Once they had safely arrived at Alderaan's coordinates, the crew discovered that the planet had been destroyed by the Death Star. The space station's tractor beam then captured and drew in the *Millennium Falcon*. Chewbacca succeeded in escaping alongside Skywalker and Solo, and they freed Princess Leia Organa, who had been a prisoner aboard the station, before making it back to the *Millennium Falcon*. Only Obi-Wan Kenobi failed to escape, having sacrificed himself during his duel with Darth Vader.

Chirpa

An Ewok with grey and white fur, he was chief of the Bright Tree Village tribe.

During his reign as chief of Bright Tree Village in the forest of Endor, Chirpa's tribe underwent a terrible test. For him, it began with the invasion of a strange human army and the arrival of a huge domed structure in the sky that resembled a gigantic star. When Chirpa's tribe then encountered a golden steel god by the name of C-3PO, the god revealed that the human army was in desperate need of the Ewoks' help. Respectful of the deity, who appeared to magically float in the air, Chief Chirpa allied himself with the rebels and threw his tribe into battle. While the Ewoks suffered great losses during the fight, they contributed greatly to the victory over the Empire. However, this humble chieftain couldn't possibly imagine the intergalactic repercussions of his tribe's modest but determined contribution to the war.

Chirrut Îmwe

A blind Guardian of the Whills, Chirrut Îmwe lived a spiritual life on Jedha, before travelling to the tropical beaches of Scarif along with the rebel group known as 'Rogue One'.

Being born on the desert moon of Jedha inspired many people to choose a life of spirituality, Îmwe, an avid follower of the Force, ended up in charge of protecting the Temple of the Kyber. Following the rise of the Empire, Jedha was occupied by Imperials who took over the mining of kyber crystals, while also attacking the temple that Îmwe, alongside his friend Baze Malbus, was in charge of protecting. When the Imperials restricted access to the temple, both Îmwe and Malbus were ejected from their home.

Lost and struggling after the severing of his connection with his home, Îmwe and Malbus struggled to make lives for themselves. While Malbus sank into self-doubt and lost his faith in the Force, Îmwe attempted to persevere with his spirituality. Meanwhile, his lack of sight didn't prevent him from being a warrior equal to Malbus. Having practised the martial art of Jedha, the zama-shiwo, he mastered Jedi techniques that the non-Jedi population considered supernatural. Equipped with his staff and lightbow, Îmwe's survival was assured even in the hostile environment of a city under immense pressure.

Îmwe rescued Erso and Andor from a squad of stormtroopers, but was unable to prevent Saw Gerrera's militia from kidnapping them along with Malbus and locking them up in his den in the Catacombs of Cadera. Six months previously, Malbus and Îmwe had come to blows with the leader of the partisans. Gerrera was anxious for them to join his militia, but Îmwe was resistant to Gerrera's extremism, and only cooperated with him on a mission to help some Jedha orphans.

While the pair were jailed in one of Gerrera's cells, the future seemed bleak for the monk-warrior and his companion. Chanting a mantra, Îmwe was able to sense another prisoner being brought to the jail, Bodhi Rook, a deserter from the Empire. When Îmwe's home, Jedha City, was destroyed by the Death Star, he managed to escape with the others aboard a U-wing. Blind, but also unable to cope with such a horrible reality, he asked Malbus to confirm that his Holy City had indeed been destroyed, and was horrified to discover it had.

He emerged from his stupor as they arrived on Eadu, the workplace of Jyn Erso's father, whom Andor had the secret order to eliminate. Îmwe explained to Erso that the Force was darker around a creature who was preparing to kill, letting her know Andor's true mission. During a moment of quiet, when Îmwe was alone with Malbus, he justified their allegiance to Erso by explaining that her destiny was important to the balance of the Force, something that the devout Îmwe couldn't ignore. In the air combat that followed between rebel and Imperial fighters, the blind monk brought down a TIE fighter using his simple yet powerful lightbow.

On Yavin 4, Erso's call to arms against Scarif was rejected before the Council of the Alliance, but that didn't make any difference to this Guardian of the Whills, who already knew that he would fight for and with her to the end. When he and the rest of the group codenamed 'Rogue One' landed at the Imperial Centre of Military Research on Scarif, he and Malbus led an assault that would act as a diversion for Erso, Andor and K-2SO to infiltrate the Citadel Tower. During the mission, Îmwe proved deadly with his staff, which he used to silently take down sentries around the beaches of Scarif.

At the start of the rebels' attack on the Imperial garrison, Îmwe's precision with his lightbow helped to contain an enemy that was vastly superior in number. Facing the AT-ACTs, the rebel losses increased and, when death troopers arrived, Îmwe and Malbus were left as the only survivors on the beach, driven back into the corners of a bunker's entryway. The last thing required of them to complete their mission was to activate a button located out in the open, which would permit the stolen Death Star plans to be transmitted to the rebels in Scarif's orbit. It was a seemingly impossible feat that had already claimed the lives of several rebels.

Trusting in the Force, Îmwe walked out onto the battlefield to complete his part of the mission. He repeated to himself, 'I am one with the Force, the Force is with me.' Using the art of zama-shiwo, he felt invisible to the world, protected by the invisible energy field that was the Force, until he reached the console and activated the button. But as he attempted to return to his friend Malbus, Îmwe was hit by the explosion of a container shot by a death trooper. Fatally wounded, the blue-eyed blind monk was cradled by Malbus, who had hurried out onto the battlefield to help his injured friend. With his dying breath, Îmwe reassured his friend that if he looked for the Force, he would surely find it.

Chirrut Îmwe's Lightbow

Built and wielded to devastating effect by Chirrut Îmwe, this traditional weapon was created by the blind monk as part of his training to become a Guardian of the Whills.

Îmwe forged his lightbow as part of the seventh duan, when his abilities approached perfection, and his lightbow was considered to be a powerful example of his faith in the Force. A modified E-11 blaster, the lightbow weighed 8 kilograms and required all the mastery of its creator to be wielded in combat. Its polarising blasts were even more powerful than a traditional blaster – Îmwe once used it to shoot down a TIE fighter on Eadu. The lightbow deployed its lethal blasts by extracting a charged particle from the powering barrel. It also came equipped with a telescopic viewer, which Îmwe didn't actually need, and even though he was blind, he was an ace shot.

Chirrut Îmwe's Staff

Both a tool that helped the blind monk Chirrut Îmwe to walk, and a dangerous weapon in close combat, this stick was made of fire-hardened uneti-wood.

Although polished, it nevertheless retained an irregular and gnarled appearance. The strapping at the centre of the handle was intended to give a better grip, while the staff's metallic lamp contained a silver kyber crystal, a symbolic source of light. The kyber crystal's vibrations allowed the blind Guardian of the Whills to discern his surroundings. During his second meeting with Jyn Erso in Jedha City, Îmwe managed to take out a whole squad of stormtroopers with his staff, which, at first sight, appeared harmless in the blind man's hands. On Scarif, during the infiltration phase of the Rogue One mission, the staff showed itself as the perfect silent weapon as Îmwe used it to eliminate stormtroopers outside the Imperial complex.

Chopper

See C1-10P 'Chopper'

Citadel Tower of Scarif

See Imperial Security Complex

Clan of the Toribota

Originally a nomadic tribe, the clan eventually settled on the desert moon of Jedha.

The tribe's ancestors once lived in an enclave on the planet Isde Naha, where its religion, 'The First Gleam', was named after the first star they observed in the sky during primitive times. During their history, the travelling Clan of the Toribota was convinced they had to find somewhere to settle, and after making a number of astronomical calculations, they decided that the location of the 'The First Gleam' was in fact Jedha. Having made their home there, the members of the clan always wore large, semi-spherical helmets, which served as receivers of their first encounter with 'The First Gleam'.

Class-A Thermal Detonator

A small, handheld explosive which made use of volatile baradium encased in thermite, which was powerful enough to cause damage up to a 20-metre radius.

This detonator, manufactured by Merr-Sonn Munitions, was used extremely effectively by Princess Leia while she was disguised as the bounty hunter Boushh during a rescue attempt at Jabba's Palace.

Clegg Holdfast

A podracer pilot placed on the front row during the Boonta Eve Classic Podrace, Clegg Holdfast rode a Voltec KT9 *Wasp* podracer.

When he was introduced to the crowds before the race, the collection of medals adorned on his chest along with the rather distinguished gesture he made to the spectators, revealed his aristocratic roots. This Nosaurian from New Plympto saw his hopes of victory crushed during the second lap, when his podracer was destroyed by his rival, the fearsome Sebulba.

Cliegg Lars

A moisture farmer from Tatooine, Cliegg Lars was the husband of Shmi Skywalker.

Like the dry desert plains of the sand planet that he called home, Cliegg was a tough and sturdy man. He worked on his moisture farm with his son and his daughter-in-law. After falling in love with Shmi Skywalker, he bought her freedom from Watto, her owner, before marrying her. When his wife was kidnapped by Tusken Raiders, Lars didn't hesitate in leading a rescue party. Sadly, this endeavour failed miserably, and Lars lost his leg in a Tusken Raider trap. As Anakin Skywalker's stepfather, he had the hard task of telling him the terrible news about his mother.

Clone Trooper

The main force of the Republic army, the clones were at the centre of the historic turning point in which the Galactic Empire rose to prominence.

Created by the Kaminoan clone masters for the Jedi Master Sifo-Dyas, who was under the influence of Count Dooku, the clone army was destined to become the Republic's main force in fighting the Separatists. It represented an important step in the plot that would eventually bring absolute power to Supreme Chancellor Palpatine.

Each clone was a modified version of the bounty hunter Jango Fett, and was artificially grown, then programmed to fight. Some were elected to elite posts, like the commandos, while others were taught military tactics in order to become officers. Whatever their role, they were created with a fundamental inability to disobey an order. Their physical characteristics enabled them to use standard and advanced equipment. They were equipped with tailor-made armour composed of twenty plastoid alloy plates, sealed to protect them from temperature fluctuations in the field, which were modulated using magnatomic grip pads. The structure and design of the armour was based on one worn by Jango Fett.

The clone troopers gave their collective name to the conflict between the Separatists and the Republic – the Clone Wars. During this troubled time, they were deployed across the galaxy from Christophsis to the Kaliida Nebula, and from Maridun to Ryloth. Led by Jedi generals, their loyalty and efficiency in the use of heavy equipment, such as the AT-TE, ensured them many victories. The first generation of clone troopers distinguished itself during the Battle of Geonosis. Under Master Yoda's command, they defeated the Separatist droid army, and saved the Jedi Knights, who then led the charge to save Obi-Wan Kenobi, Anakin Skywalker and Padmé Amidala.

Despite the fact that all clone troopers were created alike, some battles, such as the taking of the capital of Umbara, saw certain personalities emerge, such as Captain Rex and Commander Cody, who were remarkably loyal and heroic. The clone troopers were also the secret weapon used by Chancellor Palpatine, who used Order 66 – a secret directive the clones were forced to obey because of an inhibiting chip installed by the Kaminoans – to kill all the Jedi. It was executed by the clone troopers without hesitation at the end of the Clone Wars.

Clone Wars

This major intergalactic conflict opposed the Separatist movement of the Confederacy of Independent Systems and the Galactic Republic.

Its name was taken from the soldiers of the Republic, the clone troopers, who hailed from Kamino. The Clone Wars began at the Battle of Geonosis and ended after the death of all the Separatist leaders on the volcanic planet of Mustafar. Paradoxically, it saw the fall of the Republic which was replaced by the Galactic Empire under the authority of Darth Sidious.

The Sith Lord had secretly devised an evil plan to help him climb the steps of power, gain total control of the Senate and eventually destroy the Jedi Order. Firstly, he helped discredit the Republic using the crisis on Naboo, which allowed his alter ego, Sheev Palpatine, to take the helm of the Senate as Chancellor. He then used a Jedi Master, manipulated by his apprentice Count Dooku, to secretly order an army of clones from the master geneticists of Kamino. At the same time, he stirred up hatred against the Republic and boosted the development of a Separatist movement that threatened the Republic. It was an exceptional situation, combining an enemy that threatened democratic values, an army that was ready to serve, and a Jedi Council, which had been blind to the actions of the Sith, taking control of the Republic troops.

During the conflict, the main source of troops for the two factions – Geonosis for the Separatists and Kamino for the Republic – represented major strategic stakes. The Jedi actively participated in the most dangerous operations, but the war, and the Sith's scheme, ended with the help of the clone troopers themselves. With no choice but to obey Order 66, triggered by Chancellor Palpatine, they shot down every Jedi across the galaxy.

Cloud Car Pilot

This member of Bespin's Cloud City police was assigned to aerial security patrols.

The Cloud Car pilot was always accompanied by a gunner in the second pod of the security vehicle.

Cloud City

A city located in the upper atmospheric layers of the planet Bespin, Cloud City was dedicated to luxury tourism and the mining of tibanna gas.

It was comprised of an immense disc that was over 15 kilometres in diameter. With close to 400 levels and a central well, it was kept airborne by 36,000 propulsors. It was constructed to hover in the air so that it could offer tourists panoramic views of the gas giant's 'life zone', which also meant that the lower atmosphere of the planet was free for the mining of tibanna gas. This precious gas was used to build weapons and hyperpropulsors.

Cloud City was managed for a long period of time by Lando Calrissian, before he joined the Rebel Alliance, with the discreet and efficient aid of Lobot, a man whose faculties were improved by cybernetics. Cloud City became a battlefield on numerous occasions during the Civil War. The rebel hero Luke Skywalker came to rescue his friends who had been trapped in an ambush orchestrated by the Empire. Han Solo was captured by Boba Fett, who took him to Jabba the Hutt after the Corellian smuggler had been frozen in carbonite. Darth Vader had wanted to test the carbon-freezing chamber on a human before using it on his son, Luke Skywalker. But the young Jedi managed to escape at the end of a lightsaber duel in the city's mining facilities, as Calrissian helped the other rebels to escape.

Cluster Prism

An Imperial secret project hidden on Scarif in the secure vault of the Citadel Tower, this name could have perfectly designated the Death Star, had it not been for the fact that the project names were required to be encoded.

However, while searching through the structural engineering files, Jyn Erso was certain that the file titled 'Stardust' was the one she was looking for, knowing that in the event of anything happening to him, her father would have given the file a codename that only his own daughter would recognise.

Colo Claw Fish

This giant aquatic creature, measuring over 40 metres long, lived in the watery abyss on the planet of Naboo.

An enormous underwater, snake-like creature, the colo claw fish had a bioluminescent tail and was capable of staying still for hours, lying in wait for an unsuspecting prey to pass within its reach. It would seize its prey using its two long, pectoral mandibles and then devour it using its snout-like, razor-toothed jaws. When passing through the core of Naboo in a bongo, Qui-Gon Jinn, Obi-Wan Kenobi and Jar Jar Binks were pursued by a colo claw fish. However, the animal failed to catch them, instead falling prey itself to the enormous sando aqua monster.

Comlink

A small, portable communication device.

There were numerous varieties of comlinks throughout the galaxy, but one of the most popular was the C1, the standard model used by the Empire and produced by the SoroSuub Corporation. The technology was roughly the same as the type used for the internal transmitters placed in the helmets of Imperial soldiers.

Command Shuttle

An *Upsilon*-class command shuttle designed by Sienar-Jaemus Fleet Systems, this vehicle, with its disturbing appearance reminiscent of a bird of prey, was one of the crowning jewels in the First Order's technology.

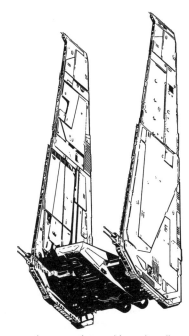

Developed in the greatest secrecy, it was given to the First Order's officers and dignitaries and provided them with the perfect means of transportation. A collaboration between the First Order's secret shipyards and laboratories, the shuttle's main strength was its defensive capabilities. It benefited from reinforced armour and its disproportionate, retractable wings, which measured 30 metres in length, were able to generate powerful shields which protected the cockpit and passenger compartment during take-off and landing – times when the ship was at its most vulnerable.

The wings were also equipped with advanced jammers and sensors that could monitor all surrounding real-time communications at an outstanding distance, therefore identifying potential threats long before the shuttle entered the firing range of any enemy craft.

Kylo Ren used one of these command shuttles to travel to the Kelvin Ravine on Jakku, where he then found and killed the honourable explorer Lor San Tekka.

Commander Cody

The emblematic leader of the Republic's Ghost Company of the 7th Sky Corps and the 212th Attack Battalion.

His armour sported the colours of his battalion: white and orange. As a clone, he was designated the number CC-2224, but in the field he took the name 'Cody'. He was the comrade in arms of Captain Rex and fought alongside General Obi-Wan Kenobi on Christophsis, Teth and during the second Battle of Geonosis. He took part in numerous operations, such as the escape of Jedi Master Even Piell from the Citadel on Lola Sayu, and the taking of Umbara's capital after the betrayal of Jedi Master Pong Krell. He was also present during the hunt for General Grievous on Utapau. Despite his loyalty during the Clone Wars, he mercilessly executed Order 66, given by Chancellor Palpatine, and shot down Kenobi while the Jedi was climbing a wall on his varactyl.

Commander Willard

See Vanden Willard

Conan Antonio Motti

This native of the planet Seswenna was an officer in the Imperial fleet whose career as admiral came to an explosive end when the Death Star was destroyed with him aboard.

During the emergence of the Rebel Alliance and the advent of the Galactic Civil War, the Empire turned a corner when it came to its enslavement of the systems fighting its dictatorship. Two opposing sides formed inside the Imperial command: those who advocated the development of a sentry fleet that would guard the galaxy, and those who were in favour of the construction of a gigantic space station that had the ability to destroy whole planets. Motti was an enthusiastic member of the second faction and its mercilessly oppressive strategy.

Not only was the admiral confident in the abilities of the Empire's military technology, but also in his own power and capacities. He aggressively opposed Darth Vader during a discussion about the size of the rebel threat in the wake of the rebels stealing the technical plans of the space station. Motti openly ridiculed Vader and his use of the Force, condemning it as nothing more than the practice of dark magic from another age, adding that it would be ridiculous to compare it to the sheer power of the Death Star. But Motti didn't even have time to finish his sentence as he began to choke on his own words – Vader had decided to demonstrate the power of the Force by putting a stranglehold on the admiral. Motti only survived because Grand Moff Tarkin intervened, ordering the Sith Lord to release the suffocating admiral. Despite this near miss, Motti died shortly after, during the Battle of Yavin, along with a large part of the Imperial military elite, when the Death Star was defeated.

Cordé

A Naboo citizen and handmaiden of Senator Padmé Amidala, Cordé was just one of the senator's many loyal companions.

Brave and very devoted, she took Amidala's place in order to serve as a decoy and guarantee her security. Captain Typho used this tactic when the Naboo delegation arrived on Coruscant from Naboo. The senator was invited to play the role of a starfighter pilot, while Cordé wore the dress and traditional make-up of the senator. Unfortunately, the ship transporting the delegation was targeted, and it exploded while Cordé and the passengers emerged from it. Gravely hurt, Cordé died in Amidala's arms.

Corellia

A planet located in the central core of the galaxy.

Known for its ace pilots and the construction of leading starships, Corellia was the homeworld of Han Solo, Crix Madine, Wedge Antilles and BoShek. Solo's *Millennium Falcon* was built at Corellia's famous shipyards.

Coruscant

Believed to be the cradle of the human species, Coruscant was the seat of the Galactic Republic and the Imperial Empire, and was central to many important events throughout history.

Located in the Corusca sector, in the centre of the galaxy on the border of the Inner Core, the planet was densely populated with urban constructions. Its cities spread from the ground up to the thick layer of clouds that shrouded the towering skyscrapers. The huge height of the buildings reflected the social achievements of those who lived in them. Rich merchants earned profits from the fact that they lived on the crossroads of the most-frequented trade routes, while the partly corrupted political class and high commissioners of the different administrations occupied the tallest buildings, where the air was filtered and deemed to be far healthier than at ground level. The middle classes were forced to live some floors lower, while the poorest lived alongside the criminals on the ground floors, where the air was toxic.

A never-ending stream of vehicles navigated the air, although despite the density of traffic, there were surprisingly few accidents. Only the flying taxicabs and private crafts had the authorisation to take more direct routes. In this saturated urban landscape, many places were worthy of interest: the Galactic opera, the Square of the Monuments, the dome of the Senate and the imposing pyramidal structure of the Jedi Temple, which was later converted into the enormous Imperial Palace. After the Emperor's death, the New Republic transferred its powers to other planets, with the rule of the rotating seat of the Senate. This rotation of power was why Hosnian Prime was destroyed by the First Order, which used its new superweapon, Starkiller Base, to annihilate the Senate.

Coruscant Taxi

This passenger repulsorcraft, piloted by a driver, was the most common mode of aerial transport in the skies above Coruscant.

Owing to the congestion of the roads on the planet's surface, air taxis were the only vehicles able to get around quickly. Although at only 8 metres long they were relatively small, they benefited from having the unique authorisation to stray from the set aerial routes. Jar Jar Binks, Anakin Skywalker, Queen Amidala and her handmaidens took a taxi during their first visit to the planet.

Count Dooku

The former apprentice of Jedi Master Yoda, and himself the teacher of Qui-Gon Jinn, Count Dooku eventually defected to the dark side.

Dooku left the Jedi Order after the death of his disciple Qui-Gon Jinn on Naboo. Seduced by the dark side of the Force, he joined Darth Sidious and became his apprentice. In order to assist his new master and to help him, as Sheev Palpatine, reach the highest level of power within the Senate, Dooku urged numerous leaders to stir up a revolt against the Republic. The revolt soon gave birth to the Separatist movement. Still obeying Darth Sidious, and using the name Darth Tyranus, Dooku manipulated Jedi Master Sifo-Dyas to order a clone army from the Kaminoans. The Clone Wars, which were orchestrated in secret by the Sith Lords, finally erupted on Geonosis between the Republic's clone army led by the Jedi, and the droids of the

Separatists. Count Dooku defeated Obi-Wan Kenobi and Anakin Skywalker during the battle, but was beaten by Jedi Master Yoda. Dooku then fled the battle before he could be captured.

During the Clone Wars, Count Dooku led the droid troops of the Separatists alongside his new apprentice Asajj Ventress and the cyborg General Grievous. He tried to turn the Hutts against the Republic by kidnapping Jabba the Hutt's son, Rotta, but failed before briefly being taken prisoner himself by the pirate king Hondo Ohnaka. Darth Sidious ordered Dooku to eliminate Ventress, fearing that she was becoming too powerful. Dooku then took a new apprentice, a Zabrak warrior named Savage Opress. He faced the wrath of his old apprentice, who he eventually defeated by sacking Dathomir, the world inhabited by the Nightsisters, of which Ventress was a member.

When the Separatists attacked Coruscant, Dooku was ordered to trap Anakin Skywalker on the starship *Invisible Hand*. He beat Obi-Wan Kenobi, and then fought Skywalker for the last time, in front of Palpatine, who faked being a hostage to stir up the darker side of the young Jedi's personality. Count Dooku was eventually double-crossed by his master who, having planned everything, ordered Anakin Skywalker to execute Dooku.

Credit

A money value unit used within the Galactic Republic, and later the Galactic Empire.

The credit, which was sometimes referred to as the Galactic credit, Republic credit, or Republic dataries, could be used on many worlds. However, in some parts of the Outer Rim Territories, such as Tatooine, this currency was totally worthless. That was the reason the scrap dealer Watto refused to sell a hyperdrive generator to Qui-Gon Jinn for 20,000 credits. On the contrary, some years later, a desperate Han Solo immediately accepted an upfront payment of 2,000 credits from Obi-Wan Kenobi for passage to Alderaan.

Criden Valdas

A lieutenant posted at the Citadel Tower at Scarif, this manager was in charge of the schedule and management of the military technologies alongside General Sotorus Ramda.

The life of this perfectly organised and precise Imperial officer was cut short the day he confronted a clandestine group of rebels known as Rogue One.

Crix Madine

A general of the Rebel Alliance who took part in the Battle of Endor.

This former commando soldier was originally in the service of the Empire, but defected to join the rebels who were against the Imperial tyranny. After his defection, Madine acquired the rank of general thanks to his expertise in the infiltration of hostile territories. In fact, it was under his supervision that a team of rebels was sent to the forest moon of Endor with the objective to destroy the shield generator that protected the second Death Star. By destroying the shield, the rebels would leave the space station vulnerable to the assault by the rebel fleet. To lead this crucial mission, Madine chose a fellow Corellian, General Han Solo. In spite of some setbacks and a trap set by the Empire, Madine's plan succeeded, leading the Alliance to an enormous victory over the Imperial regime. Shortly after the Battle of Endor, the blue-eyed strategist was appointed head of the Special Forces of the New Republic.

Crokind Shand

Originally from the human colonies of Nar Kanji, Crokind Shand was a member of Kanjiklub and one of the companions of Tasu Leech.

A strange-looking warrior, in the purest tradition of the Kanjiklub, he had cybernetic legs that gave him great speed, and several customised weapons. His heavy rifle had a roggwart bone grip, and he possessed a handmade bayonet. He often followed Tasu Leech, the charismatic leader of the Kanjiklub, on his expeditions and didn't hesitate to get involved in combat, as his wounded right eye proved. Being present aboard the *Eravana*, Han Solo's freighter, to force the smuggler to pay his debts, he got into trouble when he came face-to-fang with a furious rathtar.

'Crusher' Roodown

Ex-wreck-raider Roodown, an Abednedo resident of the Niima outpost, had his arms cut off by Unkar Plutt's men after a misunderstanding.

He replaced his lost appendages with a freight lift system that had mechanical arms and he proceeded to offer his services as a carrier. He owned a sledge made from the hull of a water tank that allowed him to transport gear and other retrieved parts, which included an old propulsion system and some 12-CG droids.

Cybernetics

Cybernetic technology that was used to replace or improve the functions of a person's existing biology.

The Sith Lord Darth Vader, who was left for dead after his lightsaber duel with the Jedi Obi-Wan Kenobi, was almost entirely reconstructed with the help of prosthetic and artificial organs. Despite being rebuilt using cybernetic technology, he still required life-long mechanical assistance in order to breathe, which was why he used special breathing apparatus until his death. His son, Luke Skywalker, underwent the transplant of an artificial hand, a common operation during the Galactic Civil War, after his defeat to Vader at Bespin. Many initially argued about the ethics of using cybernetic technology to improve upon a person's natural limits and abilities, and so the use of the technology was at first illegal and clandestine, and used in secret for a long time.

Cycyed Ock

A member of Saw Gerrera's rebel militia, this long-armed, big-bellied Keredien had a cybernetic eye that gave him super sight.

This phenomenal skill meant he had an almost perfect aim when throwing his vibrorang, and was able to analyse kyber deposits and microcircuits with precision. He was seated with a glass in hand when Jyn Erso entered the den of the militia, and it was unknown whether or not his exceptional sight helped him to escape the Catacombs of Cadera when Jedha City was destroyed by the Death Star.

D-93 Flamethrower

A double-barrelled combat incinerator, this piece of equipment was integrated into the standard gear of the First Order's flametrooper units.

Using a reinforced, double-compartmented conduit, the D-93 flamethrower was connected to armoured, independent tanks that contained the extremely volatile and flammable gel known as conflagrine-14. Propelled using pressurised gas contained in an adjoining tank, the mixture was then ignited at the mouth of the barrel using a piezoelectric igniter. The strength of the flames could be adjusted up to a range of 75 metres using the pressure indicator. The whole unit was quite heavy, so a flametrooper using the D-93 had to be in very good physical condition.

D'Qar

This lush Outer Rim planet was partially hidden by an asteroid cluster and served as a secret base for the Resistance.

It was first listed by the Rebel Alliance as a potential base when Corona Squadron explored it, however, during a skirmish with the First Order the Resistance rediscovered the planet and decided to establish its main base of operations on it. The planet's mountainous geography lent itself to the construction of hangars and underground installations which couldn't be viewed from passing air patrols. It was from here that General Leia Organa and the Resistance prepared the assault on the First Order's Starkiller Base.

D4-R4B 'Arfob'

An astromech R4-unit allied with the rebels and was stationed on Yavin 4.

With white and charcoal grey stripes, this unit, nicknamed 'Arfob', was afraid of aerial flight owing to a programming glitch. Thanks to the bug, it was unable to fly in a starfighter, but its enormous guilt over the fact that it couldn't aid pilots during combat meant that it compensated by carrying out excellent maintenance work on the ground.

Dagobah

Located in the Outer Rim, this planet's surface was covered with thick forests and treacherous swamps.

Because it existed far from any known world, and therefore had no particular political allies, it was the perfect place for Jedi Master Yoda to go into exile when the Empire carried out its execution of the Jedi.

It would be difficult to find a better environment for meditation and isolation, as Dagobah was completely devoid of any sentient civilisation. It was a place where nature had run wild, and was home to numerous creatures, such as the birds of the swamps, sleen lizards and the dangerous dragonsnakes, which all lived in peaceful coexistence.

Yoda previously felt a very strong presence of the dark side of the Force on Dagobah, which seemed to be concentrated inside an underground cave close to where he had made his home. Yoda succeeded in remaining undetectable for many years, until he received a visit from Luke Skywalker, who found him on Dagobah shortly before Yoda's death.

The young apprentice travelled to Dagobah on the advice of Obi-Wan Kenobi, who had become one with the Force, but Yoda, knowing the link between Skywalker and Darth Vader, at first refused to have anything to do with young Skywalker.

Nevertheless, Dagobah served as the setting for Skywalker's training and under Yoda's watch, Skywalker entered the underground Cave of Evil and was confronted with his own fears. They materialised in the form of a vision in which he saw himself inside Darth Vader's armour. The terrifying vision gave Skywalker an early clue about his connection to the Sith Lord, and also showed him how the dark side tried to lure individuals who were overcome by fear and anger.

Dak Ralter

A pilot of the Rebel Alliance, Dak Ralter was born on Kalist VI and took part in the Battle of Hoth.

He was a young idealist who was overcome by enthusiasm when he learned he had been enlisted in Rogue Squadron to defend Echo Base on Hoth. He died during an assault on an Imperial walker.

Danbit Brun

This grizzled, middle-aged lieutenant, posted on the orbital shield gate of Scarif, wore the black cap and uniform of an Imperial technician.

His function was to observe the dynamics of the field and their fluctuations, in order to ensure that the system never got overloaded. He died during the Battle of Scarif when the Star Destroyers, the *Persecutor* and the *Intimidator* crashed into the shield gate.

Dantooine

An Outer Rim planet where the base of the Rebel Alliance was hidden before it moved to Yavin 4.

Located in the Raioballo sector, its remote location made it an ideal base for the rebels. When

Princess Leia Organa was being interrogated by Grand Moff Tarkin, she lied that the Rebel Alliance was still based on Dantooine.

Darth Bane

The Sith Lord responsible for the creation of a new philosophy dedicated to the dark side of the Force.

Living a thousand years before the Clone Wars, Darth Bane recognised the fundamental self-destructive nature of the Sith. He realised that the power the Sith possessed was actually being used in conflicts between the Sith Order, instead of helping them to eradicate the Jedi. The sole survivor of his Order, he established the Rule of Two, which meant that only two Sith could ever be together at the same time – a master and an apprentice. This rule allowed the Sith Order to survive in secret for a whole millennium before it attempted to take its revenge on the Jedi.

Darth Maul

The apprentice of Darth Sidious, this Dathomirian Zabrak was known for his deadly skills with his double-bladed lightsaber.

When his Force-sensitivity was detected at a very young age, he was removed from his mother by the Sith Lord Darth Sidious. He then began many long years of initiation into the dark side of the Force. Modelled after his mentor, he became a fierce servant of the Sith and a powerful fighter, longing to enter the battle against the Jedi.

Darth Sidious planned to use Darth Maul as part of his plot to overthrow the Republic, and orchestrated a crisis between Naboo and an ambitious trading corporation, the Trade Federation. When Queen Amidala escaped from Naboo with her Jedi protectors, Darth Sidious sent Darth Maul on their trail. Darth Maul succeeded in locating them by sending a false distress signal from Naboo governor Sio Bibble. Landing close to Mos Espa on the desert planet of Tatooine, Darth Maul then conducted meticulous research of his target. Using his personal starship, the *Scimitar*, as a base of operation, he sent his three DRK-1 probe droids to track Amidala and her comrades. At first, there was no result, but the hunter's patience was rewarded when one of his mobile spies detected Qui-Gon Jinn talking with Watto at the end of the Boonta Eve Classic Podrace. By following this target, he discovered the location of the Naboo starship, but it was readying for departure.

Arriving at full speed on his Sith speeder, he intercepted the Jedi Master, who protected a young boy called Anakin Skywalker. They engaged in a lightsaber duel, brutal in its technical execution, and Maul got the upper hand on Jinn with his ferocious assaults. The Jedi only escaped when the starship extended its ramp, and Jinn leapt to freedom aboard the craft. Furious that he had been deprived of his victory and failed the mission his mentor had set, Darth Maul had nevertheless achieved a psychological advantage over his enemy.

While Queen Amidala spoke with Senator Palpatine, who, unknown to her, was Darth Sidious, Darth Maul went to Naboo to observe his targets. Without delay, the Jedi and Amidala came up with a plan to recapture the planet. They fought in Theed and reached the hangar of the Royal Palace, where the tattooed Zabrak patiently awaited them. The duel between Maul, Jinn and Obi-Wan Kenobi coincided with a huge battle between the occupants of Naboo and the Trade Federation's droid army. Going up against the two Jedi, Darth Maul appeared outnumbered, but his double-bladed lightsaber meant he could easily take on two opponents.

With a combination of his acrobatic technique and his double-bladed lightsaber, Maul got the upper hand on the two Jedi. Whirling around his adversaries, he drew them to Theed's immense generator complex. There, while pretending to lose his footing, he drew them through the laser walls that protected the complex, effectively separating the two Jedi. With Kenobi unable to join the fight between Maul and Jinn, the Sith unleashed his full power in a whirlwind of energy, finally beating Jinn in battle and impaling him. The Jedi Master fell, severely wounded.

Satisfied, Darth Maul awaited Kenobi, confident that the young Padawan would be far less dangerous than his master. The laser walls finally lowered and the confrontation resumed, and Kenobi was now fuelled by anger and grief at the loss of his master. The Sith Lord was unable to fight back and was cut in two by the vengeful Jedi. Shocked by his failure to beat the Padawan, Darth Maul plummeted into the duct at the centre of the complex.

Darth Plagueis

The Legendary Sith Lord Darth Plagueis may have existed or not, but he was used by Chancellor Palpatine to stir up Anakin Skywalker's doubt, while giving an easy solution to his innermost fears.

Legend spoke of how this Sith Lord had succeeded, thanks to his mastery of the dark side, to save his loved ones from death. Darth Plagueis was then killed by his own apprentice, who had been taught all of Plagueis' secrets. Skywalker, troubled by his visions of Padmé Amidala's death, was intrigued by the story, and immediately asked Palpatine if it would be possible to become as powerful as Darth Plagueis. Palpatine told Skywalker that a Jedi Master would not be able to teach him how to use that kind of power, opening Skywalker's mind to the possibility of embracing the dark side of the Force.

Darth Sidious

See Sheev Palpatine

Darth Tyranus

See Count Dooku

Darth Vader

See Anakin Skywalker

Darth Vader's Castle

The personal residence of the Sith Lord on the volcanic world of Mustafar.

It was built on the planet where Anakin Skywalker was defeated by Obi-Wan Kenobi, a humiliation that Darth Sidious forced his apprentice to remember by constructing the fortress. Completed five years before the Battle of Yavin, the imposing building was previously a cave dedicated to the Sith. A solitary place of meditation, the castle also had space for Vader's bacta tank, and it provided a sanctuary where Vader rarely received visitors. Nevertheless, Director Orson Krennic gained an audience with the Sith Lord at his home, and was introduced by Vaneé, Vader's personal aide.

Dasha Promenti

A resident of the small village of Tuanul on the planet Jakku.

She lived an austere life within the colony, which established itself in the Kelvin Ravine. Following the spiritual values of the Force without being able to use it, she belonged to an underground movement of believers who revealed themselves after the fall of the Empire. Armed with a laser blaster that was equipped with a grip made of zaywar horn, Dasha Promenti was ready to take up arms to defend her beliefs against the malevolent influence of the dark side. She was killed along with all the villagers from Tuanul by the First Order's stormtroopers, under the command of Kylo Ren.

Dataries

See Credit

Datoo

Colonel Datoo was a Starkiller Base officer, who was in charge of the primary fire control station.

He was part of the first generation of exiled Imperials born and raised in the area of unknown space after the Galactic Civil War, and fantasised about the Empire and its fall. The heir to a glorious past, Colonel Datoo was guided by the heroic veterans who believed they had been robbed of their destiny by the Rebel Alliance and the New Republic. He became convinced that the First Order was the only force able to save the galaxy from chaos. Posted to the Starkiller Base fire control station, he showed boundless admiration and respect for the First Order's ultimate weapon.

Daultay Dofine

A Trade Federation captain, this Neimoidian dared to criticise Darth Sidious' tactics, declaring the Naboo blockade to be a failure.

In retaliation, the Sith Lord called him a 'stunted slime' and ordered him to disappear from his sight. The Battle of Naboo saw Dofine die inside the Droid Control Ship when Anakin Skywalker destroyed it with his Naboo Royal N-1 starfighter.

Dauntless, the

Acting as a symbol of Imperial occupation, this *Imperial I*-class cruiser could be seen stationed constantly above Jedha before the desert moon was attacked by the Death Star.

Although predominantly employed to protect the supply line of kyber crystals crucial to the performance of the new Imperial secret weapon, it also served to intimidate the many religious practitioners on Jedha, some of whom the Emperor considered to be similar to the Jedi Order.

Davits Draven

As a general, and part of the Intel Department of the Rebel Alliance, Davits Draven was in charge of the clandestine operations opposing the Empire.

Born on Pendarr III, he began his career in the secret services during the last gasp of the Galactic Republic, and the troubled period of the Clone Wars. Instead of fighting on the battlefield, he would obtain and share important information with strategists from the headquarters, as well as commanders of fleets and other high-ranking officers. With this impressive background, he was able to meet with and assess the worth of the soldiers who would remain in the army after the rise of the Imperial regime. He knew how they thought and acted, and what the soldiers would be capable of in the fight against the Empire.

His rallying of the Rebellion happened while the rebels were in a state of emergency. Too much time was being wasted, and the hostile Imperial power was about to reach a critical apex that could guarantee its absolute victory. Draven's analysis of the situation went some way to explain his sense of urgency. Contrary to his counterpart, Antoc Merrick, Draven didn't lead a group of chivalrous and dutiful pilots. His pilots were part of a shadow army, generally operating in small victories without glory, such as sabotage, theft and assassination.

Facing Jyn Erso after her escape from Wobani, he viewed her as an egoist who had led a life of petty thievery. After an important debriefing with Erso, he was seriously concerned about the integration of the young woman into Operation Fracture, which was intended to extract her father Galen Erso in order for him to testify in front of the Imperial Senate. Worried about Galen's loyalties, Draven ordered Cassian Andor to eliminate him on Eadu, a drastic change in the mission that Draven had kept secret from the members of the Alliance Council. For him, it was more important to stop the development of the Imperial scientist's military work. He was so sure about this directive that he gave a second unauthorised order to send in starfighters to bomb the base on Eadu to make sure Galen was neutralised.

After Galen Erso was killed, Draven had to justify his actions to Mon Mothma. While he lied to her about the fact he had ordered Andor to take Galen out, he tried to convince Mothma that Galen Erso's death was in fact a victory for the rebel camp. But Mothma had hoped that, through the scientist's testimony, she would be able to convince her allies to pass a senatorial motion that would demilitarise the Empire. Nevertheless, in the wake of Galen Erso's death, the Council of the Rebel Alliance gathered to inform Mothma's allies that the 'planet killer' was in fact already a reality.

While Draven was annoyed that Jyn Erso was called upon to speak at the gathering, his opinion of her changed during the stormy meeting. He discovered that she was committed to acquiring the information her father had referred to about a flaw in the Death Star, in order to destroy the superweapon. Unfortunately, there were objections to her plan, and the Council were unable to reach a unanimous decision to send Jyn Erso to Scarif. When Draven heard that she had gone anyway, leading the Rogue One operation on Scarif, he knew that she had made the correct move.

Death Star

Developed by the Geonosians and built by the Empire, this spherical space station had a diameter of 160 kilometres and could destroy a planet with a single superlaser shot.

Halfway between an artificial moon and a military base, the Death Star, under the command of Grand Moff Tarkin, boasted a wealth of impressive capabilities. In addition to the superlaser, the space station contained 5,000 batteries of turbolasers for close protection and almost 800 tractor beams. The crew was made up of more than one million people, including 25,000 stormtroopers and 27,000 officers. The Death Star, which became a symbol of tyranny, was the physical product of years of political manipulations by Sheev Palpatine, the Supreme Chancellor of the Republic Senate.

Following the end of its construction, which lasted around twenty years, a small group of rebels managed to lay their hands on the space station's technical plans during a mission to Scarif. They were able to transmit the plans to the rebel fleet before Tarkin destroyed the complex using the Death Star's superlaser. Princess Leia Organa, senator and rebel, retrieved the plans and fled, looking to give them to the Rebel Alliance on Yavin 4. However, she was caught and held prisoner by Darth Vader, who was trying to regain the plans and discover the location of the rebel base. To convince the princess to reveal the location, Tarkin threatened her homeworld of Alderaan with the Death Star, forcing her to watch as the planet was destroyed.

Set free by Han Solo and Luke Skywalker, Leia finally made her way to Yavin 4, but the Empire followed her and discovered the location of the rebels' base. As the Death Star prepared to turn its full might on Yavin 4, the rebels attacked, targeting the weak spot detailed on the stolen plans. It was Luke Skywalker who managed to launch a proton torpedo into an exhaust port, which then caused a chain reaction that led to the destruction of the Death Star and all its Imperial staff, leaving Darth Vader as the sole survivor.

Death Star II

This new spherical space station was constructed by the Empire following the destruction of the first one by the Rebel Alliance at the Battle of Yavin.

Although few details were known about the structure at the time of its existence, this Imperial military base was not identical to its first incarnation. In fact, the second Death Star had a diameter of 200 kilometres as opposed to the 160-kilometre diameter of the first 'planet killer', which meant that its lethality had increased. There were also other changes, including its main weapon, the superlaser, which had improved its time of recharging to only three minutes. Then, for its own defence, the combat base had been fitted with 30,000 turbolaser batteries, 7,500 laser cannons and 5,000 ion cannons. Finally it was provided with whole squadrons of thousands of TIE/LN fighters and their variants, and an immense reserve of All Terrain Armoured Transports and All Terrain Armoured Reconnaissance vehicles for effective ground operations. With 560 levels, it could accommodate almost 2.5 million personnel assigned to different tasks, which included combat units, technicians and civil servants.

The gigantic structure was maintained in a stationary orbit by a SLD-26 planetary shield generator installed on the moon of Endor, because it required an enormous force to counterbalance its gravity. However, this procedure had a secondary effect because it interfered with the stability of the planet and triggered groundquakes and flooding. Its construction was also a wager: to make it bigger than the original, and more quickly. Chosen by the Emperor himself, the Moff Tian Jerjerrod progressed quickly during the first phase of construction, but was soon caught up in the inherent problems of creating high technology on such a large scale, which included the lack of a qualified workforce, ruptures in the supply chain and even chaotic financing – regardless of the priority statute of the project in the Imperial budget.

In spite of the escalating threats of Darth Vader, one hemisphere of the station was still under construction when Palpatine arrived. However, the Emperor had devised a plan that would offer the Rebel Alliance an irresistible opportunity to get rid of him and his massive weapon of destruction, and so he voluntarily leaked the information of his arrival, the location of the second Death Star and the so-called inoperative status of its superlaser. In actual fact, the station was fully operational, with the shield generator guarded by elite troops and the Imperial fleet who laid in wait to ambush the rebels. However, the Battle of Endor saw the destruction of the second Death Star, which exploded after a rebel commando unit and an indigenous tribe of Ewoks destroyed the shield generator, which allowed Lando Calrissian in the *Millennium Falcon* to make his fateful attack.

The Emperor had also gone – thrown deep into one of the station's reactors by Darth Vader, who had become Anakin Skywalker once again. The combined disaster of his death and the loss of the second Death Star had serious repercussions for the Empire and the crucial rebel victory was celebrated throughout the whole galaxy, causing scenes of jubilation and revolt, particularly on Naboo – Palpatine's homeworld – and Coruscant, which had been the Empire's seat of power. Twenty-nine years later, strategic military similarities to the original Death Star could be detected in the design of Starkiller Base, the superweapon of the Empire's would-be successor, the First Order. It shared exactly the same fate as its destructive predecessors, and proved the lack of vision of the cruel new pretenders to power.

Death Stick

An addictive substance that was popular on Coruscant, the death stick was an illicit product that was covertly sold by dealers.

Just like the pickpockets sizing up potential victims under the garish neon street lights, death sticks were an important part of the nightlife in the seedy areas of the gigantic urban world. It wasn't unusual for a dealer to sell his merchandise in a tavern or a nightclub in the lower levels of the city. The Outlander, a famous club in the Entertainment District, was no exception, and welcomed a number of small-time crooks, who approached the patrons of the bar in order to sell them death sticks. While chasing the assassin Zam Wesell into the club, Obi-Wan Kenobi ran into one of the dealers. When the dealer wouldn't take no for an answer, the Jedi convinced him to go home and think about his future.

Death Trooper

Elite soldiers from the stormtrooper corps, trained to execute special operations and to defend some Imperial military dignitaries.

Death troopers had to meet superior physical and ideological criteria in order to be selected for the rigorous training on Scarif. They also underwent medical procedures designed to

enhance their natural capabilities and make them almost superhuman. They were skilled in many areas but particularly noted for their precision shooting, close combat guerrilla warfare and stealth. Equipped with a light SE-14r repetition blaster, a long-range E-11D and C-25 fragmentation grenades, they possessed better weapons than the traditional troopers. Their plastoid armour was covered by a new material, known as reflec, that offered partial stealth and was undetectable by passive radars. Their helmets contained built-in sensors that allowed them to be permanently informed of the enemy's whereabouts. The high cost of such sophisticated equipment ensured that the death troopers remained small in number.

These fearsome soldiers were preceded by their sinister reputation, which rumoured that they originated from a supposed Imperial project to resurrect the flesh of dead troopers. While the rumour remained unfounded, it certainly gave the death troopers, in their unmistakable black armour, a deadly reputation. Director Orson Krennic had a squad of death troopers at his disposal, for both personal protection and to use as necessary during his project within the Tarkin Initiative. They were deployed on the beaches near the end of the Battle of Scarif and demonstrated deadly efficiency against the rebel soldiers.

Decraniateds

The Decraniateds were a class of servant created by a rogue surgeon in Jedha City.

Going by the name of 'Roofoo', Dr. Cornelius Evazan was aided by his accomplice Ponda Baba (a.k.a. Sawkee). Evazan welcomed in the injured and invalid victims of war, and practised highly unethical treatments, callously combining medical techniques with cybernetic technology. The end result was the creation of mindless beings without will, and deprived of their identity, who could then be unscrupulously sold into servitude.

The ghastly servants earned their unusual nickname from their appearance. Sometimes it was just the top of the cranium that had been removed, but on others it was the entire head that was missing, as was the case with the humanoid soldier Caysin Bog. Several specimens served tea at Gesh's Tapcafe and unlike their fellow residents of Holy City, they didn't flinch when Saw Gerrera's partisans chose to ambush Tythoni Square.

Deflector

See Energy Shield

Defstat

The Imperial alert procedure that indicated varying levels of threat, used by the different military forces of the Galactic Empire.

For example, 'Defstat Three' indicated that an intrusion had been spotted, as was the case on Scarif when the rebels infiltrated the area surrounding the Citadel Tower. The response was a swift intervention from the resident garrison.

Dejarik

A holographic game that was very popular throughout the galaxy, and was played on the unmistakable dejarik table.

The table consisted of a circular chequerboard split into three concentric rings with black and white spaces converging towards the centre of the board. The aim was to move the small, aggressive holographic projections of various alien species, and make them fight each other. Han Solo had a table on board the *Millennium Falcon* and during one of many games, R2-D2 learned that when it came to dejarik, it was always best to let the Wookiee win.

Delta-7 *Aethersprite*-class Light Interceptor

A ship built by Kuat Systems Engineering and specially designed for the Jedi Knights, this one-man recon starship was equipped with laser cannons, twin secondary ion cannons and a powerful deflector shield.

However, its size didn't allow room for either a navigation computer or hyperdrive system, which meant that the pilot had to be assisted by an astromech droid directly linked to the port side of the ship in some models, or via a traditional astromech socket in others. The droid managed the diagnostics and repairs of the craft, the secondary sensors and the communication tools, and also stored the navigational data. For hyperspace travel, a booster ring, built by TransGalMeg Industries, was necessary. This model of ship was used by the Jedi Order for stealth missions. Obi-Wan Kenobi flew to Kamino in the Delta-7, before going on to hunt down the bounty hunter Jango Fett on Geonosis.

Delta-class T-3c Shuttle

This type of shuttle, developed by Sienar Fleet Systems, was used by Director Orson Krennic.

Originally created as a side project, Krennic was fascinated by its design, so much so that the Imperial army's long-time supplier eventually took it into production. Featuring a geometric hull and retractable, bat-like wings upon which were mounted laser cannons, the austere shuttle looked like a bird of prey. Despite its lack of comfort, Krennic kept it for more than a decade.

Dengar

This Corellian-born bounty hunter began his career under the protection of Jabba the Hutt – a position which saw him regularly work with the notorious Boba Fett.

Offering his services from the beginning of the Clone Wars, Dengar grew rich during the years of the Imperial regime, which frequently employed bounty hunters to take care of some of its more questionable business. After the Battle of Hoth, Dengar was one of the bounty hunters employed by Darth Vader to track a team of rebels, however, he narrowly missed out on the prize when Boba Fett captured Han Solo and his friends. Dengar was also present when Luke Skywalker infiltrated Jabba's Palace on Tatooine, however, he managed to avoid the memorable showdown at the Great Pit of Carkoon.

Dengue Sisters

The insectoid figures of the three Dengue sisters, a group of Culisetto, were a common sight at Maz Kanata's Castle on Takodana.

With their chest shells and traditional pink travelling overalls, they could often be seen at the gambling tables of the castle, enjoying a drink while playing their favourite board game – Deia's Dream. They played using gambling chips that could only be exchanged at Maz's establishment.

Depa Billaba

A Jedi Master and member of the Jedi High Council, this Chalactan was present when Qui-Gon Jinn first presented Anakin Skywalker as the Chosen One.

She later assisted the other Jedi Masters on Naboo with the funeral preparations for Jinn.

Derek 'Hobby' Klivian

A Rebellion pilot who distinguished himself during the Battle of Hoth as part of the famed Rogue Squadron.

Answering to the call sign Rogue Four, Klivian was just one of many pilots who defected to the ranks of the Rebel Alliance from the Imperial academy. He took part in all of the Rebellion's main battles against the Empire.

Destroyer Droid

Also known as a droideka, this combat droid model was quick and lethal.

It was used by both the Trade Federation during the invasion of Naboo and the Confederacy of Independent Systems during the Clone Wars. It worked most effectively on the large, smooth surfaces of starships and buildings where it was able to reach speeds of up to 75 kph by transforming into a rolling ball. It would then revert and deploy itself onto three feet, generate a defensive shield and start firing repeatedly with its twin cannons. Rune Haako and Nute Gunray used these droids in an attempt to eliminate the Jedi ambassadors Qui-Gon Jinn and Obi-Wan Kenobi when they came to discuss the end of the blockade of Naboo.

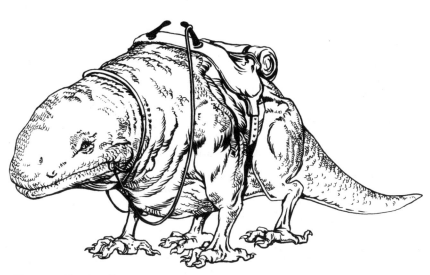

Dewback

These peaceful, four-legged reptiles, each around 2 metres in length, were native to the planet of Tatooine.

Imperial soldiers on dewback were a common sight on the planet, not just because the beasts were easily tamed, but because they were able to withstand the dramatic temperature drop that occurred at night in the desert.

Dexter Jettster

This four-armed Besalisk from the planet Ojom was the owner and chef of Coruscant's popular restaurant Dex's Diner.

Despite his greasy appearance, Dexter was a favourite among those who came to visit his Coco Town District establishment to enjoy his famous food and a tasty Jawa juice. Before settling on Coruscant, Dexter travelled the galaxy and saw many things, which often made him an invaluable source of information. It was Dexter who famously identified a Kamino dart for his old friend, Obi-Wan Kenobi, which eventually led the Jedi Knight to discover the clone army on Kamino.

DF.9 Turret

An anti-infantry battery manufactured by Golan Arms, this piece of equipment was comprised of a tower mounted with a heavy, rapid-fire laser cannon.

Manned by three people, a gunner and two operators who were in charge of the electronic targeting and power, the DF.9's impressive operational range of between 20 and 16,000 metres made it the ideal weapon for the defence of strategic positions. Nevertheless, during the Battle of Hoth, these capabilities were not enough to repel the assault of the five AT-ATs the Empire had dispatched to destroy the energy generator that powered the shield protecting the Rebel Alliance's Echo Base.

DH-17 Blaster Pistol

Mass-produced by BlasTech Industries during the Galactic Civil War, these blasters were predominantly used by Rebel Alliance soldiers.

Designed for close combat and lighter than the E-11 blasters, they were also preferred among Imperial officers, who were less exposed to direct confrontations.

Dianoga

A sprawling tentacled creature that was native to the planet of Vodran, and could grow up to 7 metres in length.

They lived mainly in watery sewers or swamps, but have also been found in starship trash compactors. Luke Skywalker was almost drowned by a dianoga during the rescue mission to free Princess Leia Organa while aboard the Death Star.

Dioxis

A deadly gas used by the Neimoidians during an assassination attempt on Qui-Gon Jinn and Obi-Wan Kenobi.

At the time of the attempt the two Jedi were aboard the Trade Federation's droid control ship, the *Saak'ak*, to begin diplomatic negotiations to halt the Naboo blockade.

Disciples of the Whills

Dedicated to worshipping the Force, the Disciples of the Whills was the oldest religion on Jedha and its supporters would assemble in the Kyber Temple, until the Empire forbade access to it.

The Disciples, who could be identified from their large, red dresses, were less showy than the Guardians of the Whills. Angber Trel, Killi Gimm and Silvanie Phest were all Disciples who died when the Death Star destroyed Jedha City.

Diva Funquita

This Theelin dancer with spiky, scarlet hair, was Gardulla the Hutt's assistant.

A gift from Jabba the Hutt, she could often be seen accompanying her mistress to events, such as the Boonta Eve Classic Podrace on Tatooine.

Diva Shaliqua

This half-Theelin, blue-haired singer was a particular favourite of Jabba the Hutt's, whom she belonged to.

She accompanied him to events including the Boonta Eve Classic Podrace and could often be seen wearing the revealing outfits the crime lord was so fond of.

DL-18 Blaster

Produced by BlasTech Industries after the Clone Wars, the DL-18 was commonly used throughout the galaxy.

It was inexpensive, could be easily customised and offered a good weight–power ratio that made it especially desirable among smugglers and bounty hunters. This model of blaster was used by Kanan Jarrus, one of the rare Jedi to survive Order 66.

DL-21 Blaster

These blasters, the product of BlasTech Industries, were specially chosen to equip the rebel infantry during the Battle of Hoth.

The DL-21 could be customised in order to make it suitable for use by many different species. Aqualish smuggler Ponda Baba possessed a modified model that had been adapted especially to suit his hand shape. Although this model could cause serious damage, there was also an element of the unknown to it owing to the triangular-shaped cannon mouth which discharged multidirectional energy shots.

DL-44 Heavy Blaster Pistol

Produced by BlasTech Industries, not only was this handheld weapon regarded as the most powerful of its type in the galaxy, it was also known to cause the most damage at close range.

These distinctive characteristics meant that it was just as likely to be used by the most dangerous bounty hunters of the Outer Rim as it was by military organisations, such as the Empire. Among the most famous owners of this weapon was Han Solo, who, from roguish smuggler to Alliance general, had relied on its efficiency throughout his many adventures.

Doallyn

This Geranite hunter was in the service of the Tatooine crime lord Jabba the Hutt.

Easily identified by the black helmet that covered his whole head, Doallyn was present when Boushh the bounty hunter delivered Chewbacca to Jabba the Hutt. He got a bit too close to the action and was shoved out of the way by the captive Wookiee.

Dobias Cole-Truten

A modest hunter and dealer in Jedha City, Cole-Truten hunted and sold silichordate worms to local restaurants as a way of making a living.

However, digging close to the kyber crystal mines and inhaling the ore left him with a serious breathing problem, which resulted in him having to use a large respirator. With his turban on his head and his basket full of prey across his shoulder, he was a regular sight in Jedha City, but was killed when the Death Star destroyed the city.

Docking Bay 94

A boarding port at the Mos Eisley spaceport that was famous for being the place were Obi-Wan Kenobi, Luke Skywalker and the droids R2-D2 and C-3PO joined Han Solo and Chewbacca on the *Millennium Falcon*.

Docking Bay 94 was a pit used by starships to land on Tatooine and required the use of vertical repulsorlifts. Just before his journey to Alderaan, the bay was the scene of a tense meeting between Han Solo and Jabba the Hutt, to whom the smuggler owed a debt.

Doda Bodonawieedo

This professional Rodian musician was a member of the Max Rebo Band, the group that played at Jabba's Palace when the dancer, Oola, met her terrible fate.

Bodonawieedo and the band also witnessed the arrival of the bounty hunter Boushh with the captured Chewbacca.

Dondebus Blaster

Typically used by the Nar Kanji colonies, the dondebus blaster was a handcrafted short barrel weapon made from an assembling of flexocord.

The distinctive feature of this model of blaster was in its finishing, in particular its grip, which was made of kintian hiker. Creating grips or bayonets using bones from creatures, such as gundarks or roggwarts, was common practice within the criminal organisation known as Kanjiklub.

Dopheld Mitaka

Dopheld Mitaka was a First Order officer assigned to the *Finalizer*, under the command of Kylo Ren and General Armitage Hux.

Top of his class at the academy, it was Mitaka's talent for efficiently carrying out orders that won him his place on the First Order's flagship. Despite his youth, his command experience made him the perfect fit for the *Finalizer*'s crew, and won him the respect of his men. However, all his training couldn't prepare him for the bursts of anger that Kylo Ren often directed at his crew, particularly those delivering bad news. Like every other officer, he had code cylinders attached to his uniform and wore a rank armband displaying the name of a famous Imperial fleet admiral.

Dr. Cornelius Evazan

Condemned to death in twelve systems, Dr. Cornelius Evazan, also known as 'Roofoo', was once a promising surgeon.

However, Evazan became notorious for his cruel medical experiments, such as the creation of the Decraniateds on the moon of Jedha. He later turned to smuggling with his partner, Ponda Baba. Obi-Wan Kenobi and Luke Skywalker encountered an angry Evazan in the Mos Eisley Cantina on Tatooine, when they were looking for passage to Alderaan.

Dragonsnake

These large predators lived in swampy, stagnant water and were most commonly found on the wilder planets throughout the galaxy.

Their survival hinged on their ability to detect the smallest movements in water, which in turn alerted them to the presence of a possible prey. During his time on Dagobah, Luke Skywalker fell into a swamp inhabited by a dragonsnake, alerting it to his presence. However, it was R2-D2, Skywalker's astromech droid, who was snatched by the creature. When the dragonsnake realised that R2-D2 was not a tasty meal, it spat him back out, ejecting the little droid from the swamp.

DRK-1 Probe Droid

This scouting droid was often used by the Sith for reconnaissance missions.

Darth Maul deployed three DRK-1s on Tatooine to locate Queen Amidala and her two Jedi bodyguards in Mos Espa. However, it wasn't until the end of the Boonta Eve Classic Podrace that one of the DRK-1 droids finally spotted Qui-Gon Jinn talking to Watto.

Droid Capital Ship

Placed under the command of Captain Daultay Dofine during the invasion of Naboo, this command vessel of the Trade Federation was also the scene of the attempted assassination of Jedi Master Qui-Gon Jinn and his Padawan learner Obi-Wan Kenobi.

Along with the other warships orbiting the peaceful planet of Naboo, the Droid Capital Ship, the *Saak'ak*, was a modified *Lucrehulk*-class LH-3210 cargo freighter. To tell it apart from the other warships and to signify its bearing as the fleet's capital ship, the *Saak'ak* had an array of additional antennas. Using the central computer installed on the vessel, these antennas then relayed orders to every part of the droid army. However, this technological vision soon turned into a nightmare for the Trade Federation when the young Anakin Skywalker destroyed the flagship. With no orders being relayed, the battle droids on the Naboo surface became disorientated and useless.

Droid Interceptor

See Vulture Droid

Droideka

See Destroyer Droid

Droopy McCool

The Kitonak soloist flute player in the Max Rebo Band.

He was best known under his stage name, Droopy McCool, but was also called Snit. He specialised in playing a flute called the chidinkalu.

DSS-02 Shield Generator

This military defence installation was manufactured by the Kuat Drive Yards.

Owing to its high cost, the equipment was mainly only used by the Imperial regime, however, the Rebel Alliance obtained one of the shield generators to protect its Echo Base on Hoth. Because of its crucial tactical importance, the generator on Hoth was protected by multiple combat towers and other heavy artillery. During the assault of the Imperial troops at the Battle of Hoth, the shield generator gave the Rebel Alliance enough time to evacuate its main base. When it became necessary for the shield to be temporarily disabled in order to allow the transports to escape, cover was provided by an ion cannon.

Dud Bolt

This predatory podracer pilot was placed in the second row at the start of the Boonta Eve Classic Podrace, which was won by a young Anakin Skywalker.

Nicknamed 'the Great Dud Bolt' by the announcer, he was considered one of the favourites to win. However, Bolt was unable to win the race on that occasion, but continued competing in events throughout the galaxy. Several years later, when Anakin Skywalker and Obi-Wan Kenobi visited a Coruscant nightclub, Bolt could be seen on a holonet screen, competing in a podrace on a snowy planet.

Dug

A species native to the planet Malastare, which was easily identifiable by its 'reversed' appearance.

In a break from biological convention, Dugs used their hands to walk while their feet were kept up in the air, like a second pair of hands. The most well-known representative of this species was Sebulba, the podracer pilot famed for his vicious and underhand tactics.

DUM-4

This pit droid was allocated to the team working on Ody Mandrell's podracer at the Boonta Eve Classic Podrace.

Sucked up by a turbine, it destroyed both the engine and Mandrell's chances of winning the race, but luckily DUM-4 survived the incident and was flung out from the other side of the engine.

DUM-series Pit Droids

These droids, produced by Serv-O-Droid, were about 1.2 metres high and specialised in the mechanical repairs and maintenance of podracers.

Aside from its affordability, a DUM-series pit droid had the added attraction of being able to fold itself into a compact shape, then return to form with just a simple knock to its 'nose'.

Dune Sea

The Dune Sea was a vast desert plain on the planet of Tatooine.

The Mos Espa Arena, which was the starting point of the Boonta Eve Classic Podrace, was situated on its west side, while on the southwest border, the modest home of Obi-Wan Kenobi and the opulent palace of Jabba the Hutt could be found. The Great Pit of Carkoon, in which lurked a notorious sarlacc, was also located in this area.

Dwarf Spider Droid

This spider-like DSD1 combat droid, built by the Baktoid Armor Workshop, was characterised by a globe-like head equipped with a cannon and was mounted on four mechanical legs.

Frequently used by the Commerce Guild, the dwarf spider droid was deployed by the Separatist forces for many different uses during the Clone Wars. Its main cannon, able to shoot in quick bursts or in high-intensity blasts, provided good cover on the battlefield. Its mechanical legs were able to attach themselves to walls or cliffs, enabling the droid to move easily across many types of terrain. The dwarf spider droid was notably used during the Battle of Teth to contain the walkers of the Republic, and on Kashyyyk to defeat the Wookiees.

E-11 Blaster Rifle

Produced by BlasTech Industries, this model was a popular choice among the Imperial infantry.

Derived from the DC-15A blaster used by the Republic army during the Clone Wars, it was designed to be quickly modified into a rifle with the help of a mobile crosier, fixed on an axis close to the barrel. This weapon offered impressive features, was extremely flexible and could be easily adapted depending on the combat situation. The attack level of the E-11 could be quickly set to one of three different preprogrammed settings: paralyse, counter-attack or lethal.

E-5 Droid Blaster

This light gun based on an original design by BlasTech was produced by the Baktoid Armor Workshops.

It was modified to fit the mechanics of the B1 battle droids, and was prized for its ability to function even when its repeated shooting raised its temperature, making it severely hot. The E-5 was such a perfect match for the B1 battle droids that it became the Trade Federation's standard weapon.

E-web Heavy Repeating Blaster Cannon

A heavy weapon that was composed of a laser cannon standing on a fixed support.

The E-web cannon was anchored to the ground by its three powerful legs, which absorbed the kinetic energy it unleashed while firing. The cannon was charged using a portable generator, which could take some time to install before engaging the enemy.

Eadu

This mountainous planet, located in the Outside Border of the Bheriz sector, was the setting of secret Imperial experiments on the powerful kyber crystals.

Inhabited by a rare population of breeders in its southern hemisphere, Eadu was constantly battered by rain, wind and lightning, to the point that its thick, cloudy cover gave the impression of permanent night. It was the perfect place for the Empire to hide two secret installations. The first, created by Director Orson Krennic, was the High Energy Concepts and Implementations Lab that employed a team of highly qualified researchers, one of whom was Galen Erso, to solve the challenges of converting volatile crystalline energy. The second was the Imperial Kyber Refinery, which was devoted to a different purpose – the fusion of kyber crystal shards into larger forms.

Aside from the planet's natural defences, this strategic part of the Tarkin Initiative was protected by the 975th garrison, an anti-aircraft defence battery and a squadron of TIE fighters. However, following the annihilation of Jedha City by the Death Star, none of these elements would be enough to prevent the destruction of the facilities and the death of Galen Erso during the rebels' Operation Fracture, launched by General Davits Draven.

Ebe E. Endocott

A podracer pilot who competed in the Boonta Eve Classic Podrace on Tatooine.

Discreet but efficient, this Triffian was able to avoid the mechanical carnage and ended up in a satisfactory fourth place behind Aldar Beedo, Gasgano and Anakin Skywalker.

Echo Base

Built inside a glacier on the planet Hoth, Echo Base was the military installation of the Rebel Alliance.

The Alliance's victory over the Empire at the Battle of Yavin proved disastrous for the Imperial regime, but it also made the rebels a prime target for the remaining Imperial forces. In the wake of the Battle of Yavin, Mon Mothma's organisation needed time to recover and regroup. The rebels knew that they needed a new base from which to conduct their assaults, which should be focused on more strategic targets – a new development, given that the Alliance had previously utilised predominantly space-set assaults.

The planet Hoth was chosen to shelter the new rebel base. It was selected because it met a similar set of criteria as Yavin 4 – it had a harsh climate and it was difficult to access. While Yavin 4 benefited from an impenetrable jungle, which provided valuable cover, Hoth's snow-covered plains and imposing glaciers made it difficult for enemies to navigate.

It was inside one of the planet's glaciers that the rebels installed their facilities, and they benefited from the glacier's naturally vast caverns, which were perfect for creating hangars to shelter the rebel fleet. In the face of the extreme cold weather, the rebels used tauntauns – bipedal creatures that were native to Hoth – for patrols and reconnaissance missions.

Other facilities included troop and staff barracks, a medical bay with its own bacta tank, and a command centre where discussions and strategic briefings were held. Echo stations were arranged strategically around the base in order to increase the patrol's perimeter and the base's surveillance. The base's external defences included a V-150 ion cannon, while a deflector shield generator helped protect the base. It was the destruction of this shield generator during the Battle of Hoth that tipped the conflict in the Empire's favour.

Echo Station

These rebel outposts were situated around Echo Base on the planet of Hoth.

The Rebel Alliance installed more than a dozen of these surveillance stations to detect both native creatures and any strategically hostile presences.

Edcel Bar Gane

This Roonan official was a representative in the Galactic Senate during the Clone Wars.

Hailing from the planet Roona, Senator Edcel Bar Gane's most distinguishing feature was his bulging, ice-blue eyes.

Edrio

A Tognath mercenary pilot who became one of the partisans of Saw Gerrera.

Following the invasion and subsequent rule of his homeworld Yar Togna by the Empire, Edrio became a refugee alongside his brood 'brother', Benthic. Known as 'Two Tubes' because of the respiratory equipment that allowed their physiology to survive a 'human' atmosphere, Edrio and Benthic also shared a thirst for vengeance against the Imperial forces, which made Gerrera's extremists the perfect allies.

Eeth Koth

This Iridonian Zabrak Jedi Master sat on the Jedi High Council when Mace Windu tested young Anakin Skywalker.

During the Battle of Geonosis, he was sent, along with the other Jedi and clone troopers, to save Obi-Wan Kenobi, Anakin Skywalker and Padmé Amidala.

EF76 Nebulon-B Escort Frigate

This Rebel Alliance cruise ship was manufactured by the Kuat Drive Yards company.

An escort ship not designed for direct combat, it served as a medical frigate in the rebel fleet. It was on board this ship that Luke Skywalker received emergency care following the lightsaber duel with Darth Vader that left him seriously injured. A 2-1B droid conducted the delicate but successful operation of a cybernetic transplant on Luke's hand and forearm.

Eirtaé

The blonde-haired, blue-eyed handmaiden of Queen Amidala, who accompanied her sovereign to Coruscant after her homeworld was invaded.

A brave fighter during the invasion of Naboo, she was present at the funeral of the Jedi Master Qui-Gon Jinn, who fell during the conflict.

EL-16HFE Blaster

A laser rifle developed by BlasTech Industries.

The EL-16HFE blaster was an assault rifle that was very common throughout the galaxy. Popular with the Resistance forces, it was prized for its durability and handiness. It was also a favourite of gangsters operating within the Outer Rim.

Elan Mak

A podracer pilot who participated in the Boonta Eve Classic Podrace.

This Fluggrian from Ploo IV finished the race in a respectable fifth place.

Electrobinoculars

This electronic optical device enabled the onlooker to observe faraway items while adding supplemental information, such as their distance and height.

Unlike the macrobinoculars, the electrobinoculars had built-in processors to rework and improve the picture.

Electrostaff

A two-handed weapon developed by Holowan Mechanicals for the IG-100 MagnaGuards.

Made from a conductive material that was able to deflect lightsaber blows, it was the weapon of choice for the droid bodyguards developed by the same corporation. Equipped with an electromagnetic module at each end that could produce energy jolts of adjustable intensity, the electrostaff had the ability to stun or kill most living organisms. These weapons were a real challenge for the Jedi Knights as they were extremely difficult to ward off.

ELG-3A Blaster

A simple and elegant weapon, produced by SoroSuub Corporation.

With a chrome finish and a grip made of wood, the ELG-3A was a much more reasonable size than the heavy S–5 blaster. This weapon was most notably used by Padmé Amidala during the battles inside the Royal Palace of Theed.

Ello Asty

This brave X-wing Resistance pilot from Abednedo was a member of Red Squadron, call sign Red Six, and took part in the attack on Starkiller Base under the command of Poe Dameron.

Ello Asty wore a customised helmet, which was printed with the logo of the old Cobalt Squadron. As with many members of the Resistance, Asty's devotion to the cause cost him his life. During the attack on Starkiller Base, he covered his squadron leader as they plunged into the trench that led to the oscillator – the Resistance's primary target. He was shot during the manoeuvre and died as his starfighter crashed.

Elyhek Rue

This Rebel Alliance pilot had the call sign Red Seven and was a hero of the Battle of Yavin.

After having valiantly obtained his rank of pilot, Rue was part of the legendary Red Squadron during the attack on the Death Star. Under the call sign Red Seven, he was one of twenty-seven pilots killed during the assault.

Emperor's Advisers

These high-ranking bureaucrats were advisers to Emperor Palpatine.

Instantly recognisable by their purple robes and extravagant headgear, they were feared throughout the Empire and could sometimes be seen accompanying the Emperor on visits. The eldest of these dignitaries were also responsible for training the Imperial Council, which was the governing body of all Imperial moffs, generals and admirals.

Endor

A forest moon situated in the territories of the Western Reaches, Endor was covered in primitive forests, savannah and mountains.

The moon was home to various species and creatures including the Ewoks, Duloks, Yuzzums and the gigantic predator, the gorax. A real sanctuary for the nature found on the moon, its ecosystem was heavily disturbed by the arrival of the Empire and before long the songs of the churi and lantern birds were replaced by the throbbing of speeder bikes. More serious, though, was the fact that Imperial forces had constructed a new Death Star in its sky. A stationary space station that required an immense amount of power in order to counter the gravitational pull of the moon. To create the necessary anti–gravitational field and maintain the second

Death Star's position, Imperial forces constructed a shield generator on the surface of the forest moon. In reaction, the strength generated by the immobilised artificial satellite triggered many ecological disruptions on Endor, including groundquakes, tidal disturbances and geological distress. The moon later became the setting for a colossal battle in which the Ewoks fought alongside the Rebel Alliance to bring about the ultimate destruction of the second Death Star.

Energy Ball

Also referred to as 'booma', this blue, exploding energy sphere was used by the Gungans, most notably during the Battle of Naboo when thousands were launched against the Trade Federation's droid army.

This fearsome weapon varied in size and was made of plasma. It could be launched by hand or propelled by a cannon, a catapult, a slingshot or a Gungan atlatl.

Energy Shield

Technology that generated an impenetrable force field around ground armies, buildings, vessels and even immense space combat stations.

Several types of shields were available according to the kind of combat they would be up against. The beam deflectors were able to withstand and disperse any energy rays being targeted at them, while the particle shields could absorb the impact of high-speed projectiles and proton weapons. Meanwhile, protective fields could repel space debris and other objects. To ensure maximum defence optimisation, some starships combined several of the energy shield systems.

Eopie

A quadruped herbivore from the planet Tatooine, theses creatures had a trunk and were often used for transport or as beasts of burden owing to their ability to adapt to the desert climate.

Despite being domesticated, they could be headstrong and sometimes uncontrollable if their cargo was too heavy. Anakin Skywalker and Kitster used two eopies to transport Padmé Amidala and Shmi Skywalker to the Mos Espa Arena hangar for the podrace.

Ephant Mon

This Chevin was a member of Jabba the Hutt's close circle of comrades.

Recognisable by his peculiar appearance, he was among those laughing and making fun of Princess Leia when she believed she had discreetly freed Han Solo. He was very perceptive, especially about the danger that Jedi Luke Skywalker represented, so much so that unconfirmed rumours suggested that despite his friendship with the Hutt, Ephant Mon deliberately chose not to be aboard Jabba's sail barge on the day it was destroyed, and therefore escaped death.

Eravana, the

This heavy *Baleen*-class freighter was made by the Corellian Engineering Corp. and owned by the famous smuggler, general and Alliance hero, Han Solo.

A makeshift ship, the *Eravana* was a bulk freighter more than 400 metres long that Solo used to transport merchandise, which was sometimes stolen, but often just of doubtful origin. The ship was comprised of a large, main loading zone combined with a huge network of gridded corridors, which provided an incredible storage capacity. It was also equipped with a tractor beam to immobilise smaller crafts before bringing them back inside the loading bay. Despite attempts to update the ship and improve its capabilities, Solo was forced to compromise on what it could achieve, particularly because of a hole in the vortex warp stabiliser.

Nevertheless, the *Eravana* was the ideal tool to provide deliveries and complete contracts, and needed just a minimal crew of Han Solo and Chewbacca to be operational. After years of searching, Solo was finally reunited with the *Millennium Falcon*, and following a run-in with the Guavian Death Gang and the Kanjiklub, he was forced to abandon the *Eravana* and flee in the *Millennium Falcon*, along with Chewbacca, Rey and Finn.

Escape Pod

An emergency evacuation ship present aboard most starships.

This small vehicle held a modest number of passengers. Some were equipped with thrusters, but most of them were simple pods designed to protect passengers who had fled their starship. The droids C-3PO and R2-D2, who was carrying the technical read-outs of the Death Star, escaped from the *Tantive IV* and landed on Tatooine by using an escape pod.

Eskro Casrich

This corporal from the rebel special forces unit volunteered to be part of the Rogue One mission.

Despite his adventurous past, which included rappelling from the peaks of Scipio, exploring the Utapau gulfs and sailing through the dunes of Ingo, it was the clandestine mission to Scarif that was to be his last adventure.

Essie

See SE-2 Labour Droid

ETA-2 *Actis*-class Interceptor

Following on from the Delta-7B starfighter, the ETA-2 was a smaller and easier to handle *Actis*-class light interceptor, developed by Kuat Systems Engineering.

It was armed with two laser cannons and two ion cannons, but navigation, repairs and various flight diagnostics were still assisted by an astromech droid, placed on the port-side wing of the ship. The twin ion engines, coupled with the very compact design, allowed this starfighter to take very sharp bends during combat. Nevertheless, as with its predecessor, the vehicle's size did not allow for the installation of a hyperdrive, meaning that it still required an external hyperspace ring in order to make use of that technology. Many of its design elements, like the octagonal windshield and the retractable panels at the end of the wings to prevent overheating, would later be reused for the creation of the infamous Imperial TIE fighters.

The ETA-2 Jedi starfighter participated in many campaigns, notably on Cato Neimoidia and during the Battle of Coruscant, where Anakin Skywalker and Obi-Wan Kenobi were able to infiltrate the Separatist flagship the *Invisible Hand*.

Euwood Gor

A native of the planet Alderaan, Euwood Gor spent his life fighting the Galactic Empire, first with the Rebel Alliance, then alongside Saw Gerrera's partisans.

During his time with the Rebellion, Gor became an accomplished soldier in the Special Forces. However, while serving in the control room on Onderon, events forced him to reconsider his role in the fight against the Imperial forces. Abandoning everything, Gor joined Gerrera, who promised apocalypse to the enemy. Becoming more radicalised and extremist in his views, Gor survived many battles while his partisan comrades fell around him. He followed his charismatic chief into the Catacombs of Cadera on Jedha, where he also witnessed the arrival of Jyn Erso, shortly before his death during the Holy City's destruction by the Death Star.

EV-9D9

A female, EV-series droid supervisor owned by Jabba the Hutt.

The EV-series droids manufactured by MerenData suffered from a recurring problem – a programming defect that deprived them of all empathy towards other droids. Jabba, always looking to bring out the worst in his employees, paired EV-9D9 with a partner that was just as ruthless, the sinister 8V8. With the help of its fellow droid, EV-9D9 established a torture chamber inside Jabba's Palace, dedicated to traumatising disobedient droids.

Even Piell

This Lannik Jedi Master bore a punctured left eye and large scars as a mark of his bravery, giving him an appearance which, for the faint-hearted, made him the most frightening of all Jedi Council members.

An expert in telekinesis, Piell was present when the young Anakin Skywalker's Force potential was tested, and could later be seen at the funeral of his peer, Qui-Gon Jinn and the victory parade on Naboo.

Ewok

A primitive species native to the forest moon of Endor, the Ewoks were fur-covered, omnivorous bipeds who grew to about 1 metre in height.

Although their fur was usually all one colour, some Ewoks possessed streaks of a different colour. They had hands with two fingers and an opposable thumb, and were physically strong to the point of even being able to beat a human in a fight. At the time of the Galactic Civil War, the species had evolved to the point of being able to create fire and had mastered techniques in hunting, pottery and even primitive flight using hang-gliders. They were also civilised, with an appreciation for artistic expression and an interest in medical, religious and political activities.

Most of their time was devoted to gathering food and although they lived mainly in trees, the Ewoks would descend to the ground to pick berries, collect herbs and to hunt. In their society, although hunter-gatherers were fundamental for survival, there were also many other important roles including the chief, the shaman and the sages who, together, formed the Council of the Ancients. Deeply spiritual, Ewoks revered the immense trees in which their villages hung, and their faith brought them to believe that they were descendants of the 'Big Tree', a sacred tree situated in a holy place in the forest. The Empire hugely underestimated the Ewoks. Believing them to be little more than primitive savages who could never pose any threat against the will of the mighty Empire. This underestimation cost the Empire dearly, as it discovered during the Battle of Endor.

Ewok Hang-glider

Despite its primitive appearance, the Ewoks' hang-glider was actually an astonishing technical achievement.

Constructed from large, dried beast hides stretched across a skilfully-made wooden chassis, it showcased the Ewoks' technical expertise. Although used primarily for transportation and hunting purposes, the vehicle was also used to great effect against the Imperial stormtroopers during the Battle of Endor.

Ewok Village

See Bright Tree Village

Executor, the

This *Executor*-class Star Dreadnought, also known as a Super Star Destroyer, was one of the biggest warships that Kuat Drive Yards constructed for the Empire.

Following the Battle of Yavin, the *Executor* became Darth Vader's flagship, from where he commanded Death Squadron, which was assigned to track the rebels throughout the galaxy. The destruction of the Death Star gave those who had opposed the space station's construction the opportunity to recapture the Emperor's attention, which many believed had previously been monopolised by Grand Moff Wilhuff Tarkin. Instead, it was now the time of the supercruisers, with their impressive features that would intimidate any opponent, and at almost 20 kilometres long, carrying more than 5,000 turbolasers and propelled by 13 motors, the *Executor* was chief among them.

The *Executor*'s involvement in Death Squadron's task was a strong indicator of the mission's importance to the Emperor, reinforced by the fact that its supervision had been assigned directly to Darth Vader. With financial cost of no concern, the Empire launched thousands of probes throughout the galaxy, one of which led them to the planet of Hoth. A mistake by Admiral Ozzel allowed the rebels time to raise their shield, and forced the Imperial troops to conduct a ground assault. Unable to attack them from space, the powerful Imperial fleet was forced to watch as the rebel transports escaped from Hoth. However, the subsequent pursuit of the *Millennium Falcon* led Death Squadron to the planet of Bespin, where Vader was given a new mission – find and capture Luke Skywalker.

One year later, during the Battle of Endor, the *Executor*, under the command of Admiral Piett, was subjected to a concentrated attack by the rebel forces. Aware that the destruction of the Empire's ship could topple the balance of force in favour of the Rebellion, Admiral Ackbar ordered the destruction of its deflector shields. In an attempt to defend the ship, Piett requested additional firepower, but Arvel Crynyd, the pilot of a damaged rebel A-wing, sacrificed himself by flying into the main bridge of the Super Star Destroyer. The impact caused the *Executor* to crash into the surface of the second Death Star and explode.

Executrix, the

This ship of the Imperial fleet was synonymous with one of the most eminent military dignitaries of the Galactic Empire – Wilhuff Tarkin.

Already under the command of Tarkin eighteen years before the Battle of Yavin, the cruiser had served in the victorious campaign against Saw Gerrera on Salient I and II. Four years later, after the theft of Tarkin's personal corvette, the Emperor awarded the *Executrix* to Tarkin as compensation for his loss and reward for his services. Besides the crew, Tarkin received a security detail composed of thirty-two stormtroopers to use as however he saw fit. Following his promotion to Grand Moff and Governor of the Territories of the Outer Rim, Tarkin conducted a tour of that part of the galaxy aboard the Star Destroyer. From his command bridge he regularly supervised the construction progress of the new Imperial space station and witnessed the superlaser's placement from aboard the *Executrix,* as it emerged from the Death Star's imposing shadow.

Exogorth

See Space Slug

Ezra Bridger

An orphaned street boy, Ezra Bridger found a family in the Spectre team, along with a name for the powers he possessed.

Full of raw talent with the Force, Bridger not only discovered his own Jedi abilities when joining the crew of the *Ghost,* he helped his Master Kanan Jarrus sharpen his own powers too. Bridger's traumatic childhood left deep scars of fear and anger, making his connection to the light side worryingly unstable. Having unwillingly channelled the dark side to summon an enormous fyrnock creature during a battle on Fort Anaxes against Jedi hunter the Inquisitor, Bridger retreated to a hidden Jedi temple on Lothal to search his feelings. After being tested by troubling visions of his teammates' deaths, Bridger was able to shed the negativity weighing him down. His choice resulted in a kyber crystal, which he used to build his own lightsaber, uniquely modified with a blaster. Aided by his new weapon, Bridger and the Spectres continued to fight against the Empire. The Emperor took a particular interest in Bridger, sensing his connection to the Force, and he tried to tempt him to the dark side with a promise to resurrect his parents and alter the course of his life. However, Bridger resisted and escaped the Emperor's clutches, then helped to liberate Lothal and save his friends. His whereabouts, after this final encounter with the Empire, are unknown.

Fambaa

This tall quadruped, native to the swamps of Naboo, was employed by the Gungan Grand Army during the battle of the Great Grass Plains.

Four fambaas were used in total, two at the front of the army, carrying the Gungan shield generators on their backs, and two at the back, carrying a projector drum. The energy transmitted from the shield generators at the front would strike the projector drum at the back, therefore deploying a giant, defensive bubble that acted as a shield to repel blaster fire.

Farns Monsbee

A rebel pilot who used the call sign Blue Five during the Battle of Scarif.

As the only fighter pilot at the outpost on Cassidode VI, he had accrued many more solo flight hours than any other member of his squadron. An essential part of Blue Squadron on Yavin 4, he frequently led reconnaissance patrols from the Massassi Great Temple.

Farseein

Gungan optical device used to see remote items.

These big, heavy binoculars needed support from a stand fixed to the chest of the user.

Farsin Kappehl

A ranger who volunteered for the clandestine Rogue One operation on Scarif.

This bearded reconnaissance specialist mounted a targeting laser on his DH-17 blaster that made it easier for him to shoot his intended targets. In order to get the best possible aim, this first-class soldier had to be as close as possible to the hostile front line. He died during the violent battle on the beaches surrounding the Citadel Tower.

Fassio Ablund

Once a Jedha-based informant for the Galactic Empire, Fassio Ablund obeyed only one rule – self preservation.

To guarantee his own survival, Ablund sold information about the activities of Saw Gerrera and his partisans to his Imperial contacts. However, he fell from grace following his attempt to steal armour from the corpse of a dead trooper. Considered a criminal, his protection was immediately stopped and he was forced to keep a low profile in the Holy City in order to avoid either of the two parties he had betrayed. Without allies, his fate following the destruction of the city by the Death Star was unknown.

Felucia

This planet in the Outer Rim Territories was the seat of the Commerce Guild.

With its lush vegetation and tropical climate, the planet played host to the Pyke Syndicate and the Weequay pirate Hondo Ohnaka. Felucia was one of the conflict zones of the Clone Wars, and was also the last home of Jedi Master Sifo-Dyas, whose shuttle was shot down while on a diplomatic mission long before the war against the Pykes. Jedi Master Aayla Secura also met her end on the planet when she was killed by her own clone troopers of the 327th Star Corps after Chancellor Palpatine issued Order 66 at the very end of the Clone Wars.

Feyn Vann

This scientist was attached to the Tarkin Initiative under the regime of the Emperor.

A recognised specialist in shield technology, Vann had previously been a researcher for the Nordoxicon Unlimited company. However, his precious skills were retained by the Empire and he was forced to work in captivity at the secret facility in Eadu's mountains. It was there where he solved the problem of how to create a beam at the end of the energy bombardment of kyber crystals, by creating a set of deflectors that would drive the hypermatter flow of the main reactor to the shooting crystals. As a reward for his hard work he was shot down, along with the rest of his captive colleagues, on Director Krennic's orders, despite the confession of Galen Erso, who was the source of the security leaks.

Finalizer, the

This *Resurgent*-class Star Destroyer was the flagship of the First Order and was under the joint command of General Hux and Kylo Ren.

Based on the Republic's *Venator*-class cruisers used during the Clone Wars, the ship underwent various improvements to become a new, versatile type of cruiser, able to adjust to different situations. The First Order made use of the ship in many capacities, but primarily it was used as a transporter and was capable of housing several interceptor squadrons, more than one hundred assault and deployment vehicles and an entire legion of stormtroopers. The tremendous transport capacities of the *Resurgent*-class ships afforded the First Order's armies both mobility and stealth, and the First Order's tacticians considered them a huge advantage in their ongoing campaign to recapture the galaxy.

Its heavy weaponry also made it a formidable war machine and the ship possessed a fearsome amount of firepower, including turbolaser turrets, ion cannons, retractable missiles, turrets and several batteries installed on each side of the bow. Defence improvements were also made, which included the addition of powerful shields, as well as a highly integrated and protected command bridge. Designed in secret, and travelling mainly out of sight on the verge of the Unknown Regions, the full extent of its power was largely unknown, which gave it a definite advantage in battle.

Finis Valorum

Unable to control the bureaucracy-infested, corrupt administration the Galactic Senate had become, politician Finis Valorum was the second-to-last Supreme Chancellor of the Galactic Republic.

During the Naboo blockade, Valorum sent two Jedi to negotiate its end with the Trade Federation viceroy, Nute Gunray. To Valorum's great surprise, Qui-Gon Jinn and Obi-Wan Kenobi returned from the mission, having avoided an assassination attempt, with the Queen of Naboo, Padmé Amidala, whose planet was occupied by the Trade Federation. Wishing to appear benevolent, he summoned a special session of the Senate to discuss the problem. However, when a commission was the only proposed solution, Amidala realised that it had all just been a show and moved for a vote of no confidence against Valorum, in condemnation of his inaction. The other senators supported this motion, which led to the sudden end of Valorum's career as Supreme Chancellor. Left totally bewildered by this unpredictable turn of events, matters were made worse with the election of his successor – Senator Sheev Palpatine of Naboo. Valorum had always considered Palpatine his ally, but was completely unaware that he had been one of the first pawns to be manipulated and swept away in Palpatine's master plan, which had been laid out a decade earlier.

Firmus Piett

This Imperial officer from the planet Axxila began a promising military career under the orders of Grand Moff Wilhuff Tarkin and made it to the rank of admiral as commander of the dreaded Super Star Destroyer, the *Executor*.

Three years after the Battle of Yavin, the Empire had reorganised its headquarters and replaced the numerous leaders killed during the explosion of the Death Star, making the Imperial fleet stronger than ever. Endowed with terrifying cruisers that were often used for intimidation, the Empire had the means to conduct patrols and carry out surveillance to an extent that it had never done before. During these important times in the Imperial fleet, Piett was named First Officer on the *Executor*, Darth Vader's flagship. Its objective was to locate and destroy the rebel base. At the end of a routine data analysis, Piett alerted Admiral Ozzel to a signal emitted by one of their probe droids in the Hoth system. Ozzel ignored the suppositions of Piett, but Darth Vader, present on the bridge, ordered them to head for the location, convinced that they would find the rebel base there.

It was a costly strategic mistake by Ozzel that then led to Piett being promoted to admiral. While Vader was entrenched in his private quarters, Ozzel allowed the fleet to materialise from hyperspace too close to the planet, giving the rebels time to activate the base's protective shield and so avoid a merciless attack from orbit. In punishment, Vader used the Force to strangle Ozzel, then promoted Piett from captain to admiral. Aboard the *Executor*, during the Battle of Endor, Piett was killed when an A-wing crashed into the ship's bridge, causing the impressive supercruiser to plummet to its destruction against the surface of the second Death Star.

First Order

This organisation, established in the Unknown Regions from the ashes of the Galactic Empire, was opposed to the New Republic.

After the fall of the Empire, the last Imperial forces went into exile at the end of the galaxy, colonising unknown worlds and secretly preparing their comeback. Under the command of the mysterious Supreme Leader Snoke, who was adept in the dark side of the Force, the First Order developed new technologies and trained a new generation of soldiers who had been conditioned since childhood and were faithful to the regime.

Members of the First Order were fanatical about the Empire and spread their ideologies using false stories that demonised the Rebel Alliance as terrorists and celebrated the Imperial forces as great heroes. Under the command of such emblematic new figures as General Hux and Kylo Ren, they travelled through the galaxy on gigantic *Resurgent*-class cruisers on a mission to bring a permanent end to the Jedi, as well as engineering the fall of the New Republic. The First Order was responsible for building Starkiller Base, which was able to destroy a whole star system.

Only the Resistance, an independent organisation led by veterans of the Rebel Alliance, attempted to thwart the First Order's plans and warned the New Republic of the danger the First Order posed. Unfortunately, their warnings were ignored and the First Order, using its ultimate Starkiller Base weapon, entirely destroyed the Hosnian system, where the Galactic Senate presided.

The Resistance hit back, decimating Starkiller Base, but the attack left them dangerously vulnerable to retaliation. The First Order responded in kind, attacking the Resistance base on D'Qar, before pursuing the fleeing Resistance fighters using a hyperspace tracker to an old, disused Rebel Alliance base on Crait. With the Resistance seemingly backed into a corner, the First Order assumed victory was a foregone conclusion. But a powerful Force projection trick by legendary Jedi Master Luke Skywalker created a chaotic diversion, allowing the few remaining Resistance fighters to escape on the *Millennium Falcon*.

Flametrooper

These First Order troopers, who also went by the nicknames of 'roasters', 'hot heads', or 'burnouts', were specialised in using a D-93 flamethrower.

Dispatched as one unit to each squad, flametroopers supported assault troops on the battlefield by methodically destroying all spaces of withdrawal. They were equipped with double-barrelled D-93 incinerator flamethrowers connected to autonomous

armoured tanks containing conflagrine-14, an extremely volatile flammable liquid. While stormtrooper armour could easily withstand heat, flametroopers wore an adapted outfit that featured a reinforced heat protector suit, which enabled them to stay around the zones they were destroying. Their helmets were also equipped with a reduced visor to minimise the glare from the flames and had an additional attachment to supplement oxygen reserves. The strategic advantage the flametroopers provided during the First Order's ground assaults was undeniable.

Fleet of the Alliance

See **Rebel Fleet**

FN-2187 'Finn'

This First Order stormtrooper was raised to be a killing machine that obeyed orders, but before joining the assault squad, he was in charge of bathroom maintenance on Starkiller Base.

FN-2187 possessed physical capabilities that sent him to the top of his class, but he lacked zeal and was more concerned for teammates than the First Order's objectives. It was during a violent raid on the planet of Jakku, where the order was to massacre the villagers of Tuanul, that he realised his moral sense had survived his stormtrooper training. Unable to open fire on innocents, FN-2187 was told by his superior, Captain Phasma, to submit his blaster for inspection. Destined to undergo further conditioning, he made the decision to leave the First Order. He freed Poe Dameron, the Resistance pilot who had been captured during the assault on Jakku, to help him escape from the Star Destroyer *Finalizer*.

After their escape in a stolen TIE fighter, Dameron renamed FN-2187 'Finn', which was the former stormtrooper's first step towards becoming a true individual. Although Finn wished for nothing more than to put his stormtrooper past behind him and lead a peaceful, normal life, he was devoted to the companions he had shared his early adventures with – Poe Dameron, Rey, Han Solo and the Resistance. Although fiery and a bit naive, Finn was also brave and very resourceful, and his experience of the First Order was invaluable in helping the Resistance combat the First Order's superweapon, Starkiller Base.

It was Finn's loyalty to Dameron and instinct to protect Rey that informed his next endeavour after the Resistance successfully destroyed Starkiller Base. Accompanied by Resistance maintenance worker Rose Tico, Finn accepted Dameron's unauthorised mission to disable the First

Order's hyperspace tracker. Unfortunately, the plucky pair were discovered and imprisoned on Supreme Leader Snoke's flagship, the *Supremacy*, and needed to be rescued by BB-8. However, Finn enjoyed one triumph on the mission – he defeated Captain Phasma in combat.

Fodesinbeed Annodue

This popular sports announcer was better known under the names of Fode and Beed.

Annodue was a Troig with one body and two heads that could speak two different languages at the same time. Fode, the red-haired, thinner face, spoke Basic, and Beed the thicker, green-haired head, spoke Huttese. This unusual broadcaster was always popular with the large, diverse crowds that attended the Mos Espa Arena, who appreciated his wit and knowledge.

Force, the

The energy that surrounded all things, the Force was contained and passed on in midi-chlorians and maintained the cosmic balance of the galaxy, where mind and matter coexisted in harmony.

Some people were sensitive to the Force and could use it to interact with their environment. However, in order to do this, the user had to first be able to control and feel their own energy within the Force, which took extremely high levels of concentration. Once in contact with the Force, the user could then influence it to their will, eventually to the point of being able to move items without touch, influence the mind of another being, or, on a more global scale, be able to sense distress in the universe through disruptions in the Force. This profound mastery of the Force also enabled the wielder access to premonitions and knowledge unbound by the constraints of space and time.

Practitioners in the Force were mainly the Jedi and the Sith who, although both adept in their mastery, used it for very different reasons. The Jedi believed that the Force had very specific purposes and should only be used for limited reasons, which included the acquirement of knowledge, in service to others and for protection and defence, but only when it was necessary to bring justice and peace to the galaxy. It was obvious to them that in order to be able to use the Force correctly, the user should already be predisposed to the necessary qualities required to wield it. Therefore, a Jedi worthy of using these powers needed to have complete devotion to and respect for the discipline required by the Jedi Code, and possess a very strong inner peace. This last point was crucial as it often determined the path that the apprentice would choose in the ways of the Force, dedicating themselves to either the light or the dark side.

For their part, the Sith were born of the light side but chose to divert from it in search of personal gain and power. Use of the Force, when fuelled by the dark side, gave access to vast powers and offered instant gratification, which seduced many young apprentices. However, this choice didn't come without a price. Irrevocably, the dark side would consume the spirit of the Sith by way of a slow and evil corruption.

Some locations and planets presented powerful connections with the Force, especially with the dark side, such as the Cave of Evil on Dagobah, where Luke Skywalker once faced a terrifying premonition. Over 5,000 years, the Jedi's and Sith's differing interpretations of the Force sparked conflicts of varying scale, often leading to the temporary extinction of one of the two Orders.

Forest Moon of Endor

See Endor

Fozec

A human guard at Jabba the Hutt's Palace on the desert planet of Tatooine.

Fozec threw Han Solo into a palace cell after the Corellian smuggler was released from carbonite by the disguised Princess Leia Organa.

FreiTek Respiratory Unit

This standard respiratory assistance device was incorporated into the outfits of Rebel Alliance pilots and was also later used by the Resistance.

Developed by FreiTek Incorporated, this little box, which was positioned on the front of a pilot's main protection vest, could be very useful if the starfighter's oxygen generator failed or was damaged, or the cockpit depressurised after coming under fire.

Frobb

This second lieutenant was in charge of Platform 9 of the Imperial complex on Scarif.

As landings supervisor, he sent technician Kent Deezling, an officer and two stormtroopers to inspect the cargo shuttle registered as SW-0608, unaware that he had sent them to a fateful end. Unknowingly, he had also provided two precious Imperial uniforms for Jyn Erso and Cassian Andor to use, which enabled them to infiltrate the Citadel Tower.

FX-7 Medical Assistance Droid

This adaptable medical droid was designed to supply medical support in conflict zones.

Equipped with up to twenty arms, the FX-7 had the ability to manipulate multiple tools at the same time, imitating the effect of several physicians working together. The Rebel Alliance used it at Echo Base on Hoth. It was the perfect companion for the 2-1B series.

G2-1B7

A 2-1B surgical droid that worked in Saw Gerrera's lair on the moon of Jedha.

This 2-1B unit was white, silver and yellow and it took care of the partisans wounded during their missions. Its most essential task was to keep the partisan leader, Saw Gerrera, alive. Gerrera's poor health and his particular medical demands forced him to make modifications to G2-1B7's programming, which allowed the droid to provide him with drugs at more frequent intervals than were usually allowed. However, even this reprogramming wasn't always enough to bypass the code of conduct set down by Industrial Automaton in the droid's original programming, which frequently led to G2-1B7 being deactivated in order to prevent it automatically stopping treatment that contradicted its medical ethics. Usually amazed by Gerrera's will to survive, the droid could only note the grim resolution with which its master faced his final fate in the Catacombs of Cadera, as they prepared to meet the deadly onslaught of the Death Star.

GA-97 Droid

This simple, battery-operated service droid worked at Maz Kanata's Castle on the planet of Takodana and was also an informer working for the Resistance.

Thanks to its unremarkable appearance, the droid roused little suspicion as it roamed between the gambling tables and patrons, catching intel and rumours spread by the various smugglers and pirate-ship crews. Directly wired into the Resistance intel network, GA-97 alerted the rebels to the arrival of Han Solo, Rey, Finn and BB-8 at the castle.

Gaderffii

A primitive, hand-to-hand weapon used mainly by the Tusken Raiders on Tatooine.

It usually featured a spike or blade on one end and a curved club on the other, which could be used to inflict non-lethal injuries. Particularly useful for stealth attacks, the discreet and silent gaderffii was the perfect weapon for the Tusken Raiders, as opposed to a blaster or any other energy weapon that would signal their presence. The gaderffii's association with the Tusken Raiders was so strong, that when the Imperial troops searching for the droids C-3PO and R2-D2 killed the Jawas that had captured them, they used this weapon to make people believe the Tusken Raiders were the perpetrators of the massacre.

Gaffi Stick

See Gaderffii

Galactic Emperor

Galactic Empire

The Galactic Empire was a political administration organised according to the model of a constitutional monarchy.

It ruled for twenty-four years, from the end of the Clone Wars to the Battle of Jakku. The end of the Republic, and the rise of the Empire, happened when Sheev Palpatine, also known as the Sith Lord Darth Sidious, took control of the Galactic Senate. By secretly playing dual roles, as the Sith Lord and the Senate's leader, he was able to engineer a vast political power play, which took more than ten years to complete.

The first step was the invasion of the planet of Naboo by the Trade Federation. This weakened the Senate and provoked a political crisis that led to the appointment of Palpatine as Supreme Chancellor. The second major step consisted of building up political tensions, which led to the creation of a secret secessionist movement. This Separatist faction was soon at war with the Republic, a war that had huge repercussions as the Jedi, loyal peacekeepers of the Republic, were soon the victims of a carefully planned purge.

Soon after, Darth Vader was sent to assassinate all of the Separatist leaders on Mustafar, and the money stolen from the Trade Federation was used to implement the economic structure of the Empire. All the political and military systems of the Republic were converted and received Imperial denominations. The Imperial Palace on Coruscant replaced the Jedi Temple that had stood on the same spot for thousands of years.

The Empire also benefited from an unparalleled industrial support. Many companies signed exclusive contracts with the Empire, including Sienar Fleet Systems who built TIE fighters, and the Kuat Drive Yards who built Star Destroyers and the AT-AT walkers. The day Emperor Palpatine announced the birth of the Empire soon became a holy day, known as 'Empire Day'. An outwardly popular celebration, it was nothing more than a spectacular assertion of the all-encompassing reach of the Imperial army, where the inhabitants of the dominated planets were forced to cheer pompous parades and recorded speeches from the Emperor.

The Empire was at its strongest during the first fifteen years following the fall of the Republic, and opposition to its rule was only tentative. Some internal dissents nevertheless planted the seeds of the decline of the Empire, and the first signs of the Galactic Civil War began to show. The rise of the ambitious Grand Moff Tarkin provoked political changes that were not approved of by everyone, and his presumed influence over the Emperor led to a radicalisation of the methods of the Empire. This tougher stance, which should have led to the second phase of the Imperial deployment in the galaxy, saw the Imperial Senate, the last semblance of democracy, dissolved, and the construction of the Death Star commenced. The Empire believed that the threat of the space station would help them quickly convince the last unconquered systems to join their side. Believing that he could terrify and subdue the galaxy by destroying the planet of Alderaan with the Death Star, Tarkin only managed to galvanise the Rebel Alliance against the Empire and increased the number of its supporters. The rebel forces went into action against this symbol of Imperial tyranny and the ensuing battle was the first large-scale conflict of the Civil War. The Battle of Yavin was won by the Alliance after its attacking fleet destroyed the Death Star.

The following four years were marked by the Empire's obsession with hunting the rebels and the Emperor's desire to locate the hero of the Battle of Yavin, Luke Skywalker. The boy, whose extreme sensitivity to the Force, was part of Palpatine's new plan. He wanted Skywalker to replace Vader, believing that with Skywalker at his side, he could strengthen the might of the Empire even more, and make his victory a permanent one. In less than a year, the Empire and the Alliance fought several battles, with the Empire tasting a bittersweet victory on Hoth, before Vader failed to capture a wounded Skywalker on Bespin.

The conflict that signalled the beginning of the end for the Empire was the Battle of Endor. In mere hours, following the destruction of the second Death Star and the death of the Emperor at the hands of Vader, who had turned back to the light side to save his son, Skywalker, the Empire had become an organisation on the brink of extinction. After this unprecedented defeat, celebrations erupted throughout the galaxy and the weakened Empire lasted just one more year before being dissolved after the Battle of Jakku. The Imperial remnants retreated into the Unknown Regions of the galaxy, where they settled, awaiting their moment to return.

Galactic Republic

A democratic union of independent star systems, whose representatives sat at the Galactic Senate.

Before the rise of the Empire, the Galactic Republic had governed the galaxy for centuries. It received the help of the Jedi Order, whose Jedi Knights were the keepers of peace and justice, and together they managed to avoid widespread conflict. However, it finally fell victim to increasing bureaucracy and rampant corruption, two evils that helped Senator Palpatine achieve his goal of toppling the Republic. Palpatine had infiltrated the Republic by presenting a respectable, reassuring and benevolent face to the public, while all the time hiding the fact that he was actually a Sith Lord.

Palpatine began his plot by creating a seemingly benign crisis on the planet of Naboo, which eventually enabled him to be democratically elected to the highest office of the Republic – Supreme Chancellor. He then devised an enemy, the Separatist movement, whose aim was to weaken the Republic. He stirred up fear, creating a need for a Republic army by allowing Separatist attacks to multiply at the heart of the Republic. He then manipulated the conditions of an imminent war in order for the Senate to give him absolute power over the Republic. He militarised the Republic and the Jedi, thereby fundamentally transforming the image of the two traditionally peaceful institutions, which in turn allowed him to discredit and destroy the

Jedi with Order 66. This signalled the end of the Clone Wars and he used his new apprentice, Darth Vader, to dispose of the no longer needed Separatist Council. When Palpatine declared himself Emperor during a special session of the Galactic Senate, the Republic died and the Galactic Empire was born.

Galen Erso

This well-known pacifist and scientist was forced to help build the Death Star – the greatest war machine the Galactic Empire had seen.

Born on the agricultural planet of Grange, this boy from modest beginnings showed such exceptional talents that he was chosen to take part in the 'Futures of Brentaal' programme – a project designed to develop the most brilliant students into the next generation of the elite to serve the Republic. It was during this project that Erso became friends with Orson Krennic. Krennic would defend the shy Erso when other students harassed him, and after their diplomas, it was Krennic who helped Erso get a chair in the institute of applied sciences of Coruscant, where he specialised in crystallography.

Thirty years later, Erso, fell in love with geologist Lyra, his guide on an expedition to Espinar. They married the following year on Coruscant and Erso accepted a research position working for Zerpen Industries, choosing not to enter the service of a government that he feared would use his work for military ends. Erso was a pacifist and philanthropist, and dreamt of discovering a way to make almost unlimited energy for everyone using kyber crystals.

A few months before the Clone Wars, Erso and a pregnant Lyra moved to Vallt – a planet where synthetic kyber crystals were produced in cooperation with Zerpen Industries. Following a coup supported by the Separatists, the couple were detained and the scientist was arrested under the deceptive pretext of spying for the Republic. It was during these dramatic events that Jyn Erso was born. A few months later, Erso and his family were liberated by Krennic during an exchange of prisoners with the Confederacy of Independent Systems. But Erso didn't know that Krennic had, in fact, been aware of his situation for some time, choosing instead to let him suffer for a year before intervening on his behalf, in the hope that Erso would then be indebted to his 'saviour'. In truth, having gained access to the Death Star project during his time with the Special Weapons Group of the Republic, Krennic knew that sooner or later, Erso would be essential to the development of the gigantic combat station.

However, Erso held true to his belief of not working for the government. So, Krennic placed his former friend into a scientific community that ostracised him for his pacifism and placed Erso's family at great risk during one of the final battles of the Clone Wars. Having faced so many trials, the shaken researcher was ready to accept the proposition of working on the Celestial Power project, which Krennic presented as the new Emperor's dream for rebuilding the ravaged galaxy using renewable energy. Believing that he was working for the common good, Erso threw himself wholeheartedly into the work, neglecting his wife and child in the process. He never guessed that it was Krennic, anxious to distance the more suspicious Lyra from her husband, who arranged her absence on a six-month mission to Alpinn. Ironically, it was this mission that opened Lyra's eyes to the reality of the Empire. After returning to Coruscant, Lyra was able to convince Erso of the treachery of their 'friend' and the real military use the Empire had in mind for his genius. With the help of the rebel Saw Gerrera, they escaped from the planet and began a new life in hiding on Lah'mu.

Having left his research career behind, Erso spent an idealistic four years living a simple, but happy life with his wife and young daughter. However, Krennic and his death troopers finally tracked the scientist to his hiding place. Ignoring their plan to hide, Lyra challenged Krennic, threatening him with a blaster. After wounding him she was shot and killed in front of her family.

Unaware that Gerrera had rescued his daughter from her hiding place, the widowed and captive Erso was left with little room for manoeuvre. Driven by his hope of one day seeing Jyn again, he joined the kyber crystal research team inside the Tarkin Initiative at Eadu and tricked his jailers by playing the role of a resigned researcher taking refuge in his only compensation – to achieve the scientific masterpiece of his life. Erso made himself essential to the cause and managed to create a fatal flaw in the Death Star's design, a module which, when shot, would launch a chain reaction that would destroy the station. As a reference to his daughter, he gave the complete structural schematic the name 'Stardust', the nickname he had given to Jyn as a child. To make the rebels aware of his actions, Erso turned a sympathetic Imperial pilot named Bodhi Rook to his side, then charged him with delivering a holographic message to Gerrera and Jyn, which fully explained his sabotage plans.

Following the pilot's departure, Erso could do little but bide his time on Eadu. Meanwhile, inside the Rebellion, rumours of the construction of a 'planet killer' were rife. Erso had been identified as the reluctant creator of the weapon and became the objective of a rebel recovery mission. Mon Mothma, always in search of a political resolution against the Imperial regime, wished for Erso to be rescued so that he could testify to the Imperial Senate about the existence of the superweapon. However, General Draven took it upon himself to change the objective of the mission and planned to eliminate Erso as a traitor. Cassian Andor, the rebel agent who was working with Jyn Erso to locate her father, was charged with the task, alongside a squadron of rebel starfighters that were ready to supply aerial back-up.

When Krennic discovered the leak about the superweapon, he returned to Eadu to identify the traitor. Gathering together Erso's team of researchers, he asked the informer to identify himself. Not wanting anyone else to suffer, Erso confessed to his actions, but Krennic proceeded to shoot the researchers down anyway, then angrily slapped his former friend. Meanwhile, Andor witnessed this scene from afar. He detected the conflict between Krennic and Erso, which gave credence to Jyn's story of her father as a saboteur. Despite Andor's decision not to assassinate Erso, the second part of the operation was already in place. As Erso and Krennic stood on the platform, a proton torpedo was launched by a Y-wing. Severely wounded and in his last moments, Erso was joined by Jyn, who had been hiding close by. She just had time to reveal herself to her father and exchange a few words before he died in her arms. Erso was a genius crushed by a political agenda, but thanks to his sabotage, the man in the Imperial uniform died a rebel.

Gamorrean

A porcine humanoid species with olive skin from the planet of Gamorr.

Muscular and skilful at handling the axe, the Gamorreans were commonly seen as the foot guards of Jabba the Hutt's Palace. Although they possessed an intimidating physique, they could be rather slow and demonstrated relatively limited intelligence. They also had little empathy for their own kind. On one occasion, some Gamorrean guards were delighted to watch one of their comrades being eaten by a rancor after he fell into the creature's lair.

Gamorrean Guard

See Gamorrean

Garazeb 'Zeb' Orrelio

A brave, muscle-bound warrior from the planet of Lasan, Zeb was an integral member of the rebel team known as the Spectres.

Having witnessed the brutality of the Imperial stormtroopers on his homeworld, during which nearly all of his species was wiped out, Zeb came to sympathise with all those oppressed by the Empire, and joined the Spectres to fight for freedom throughout the galaxy. Tough, strong, gruff and quick-tempered, he had a tendency to act first and ask questions later – a trait that often landed him in trouble. However, having formerly been a member of the Lasan Honour Guard, Zeb possessed strong military training, which made him a valuable strategist and fearsome warrior, particularly with the Bo-rifle, his weapon of choice. As the only member of the rebel team aboard the *Ghost* to have military experience, he became invaluable to their operations. His Lasat physiology meant that he was able to move more quietly, run faster and jump higher than humans, which, combined with his determination for revenge against the Empire, made him a fearsome adversary.

Gardulla the Hutt

A female criminal of Tatooine, Gardulla the Hutt bought Shmi Skywalker and her son as slaves, but after losing a bet, she was forced to give them to the Toydarian junk dealer, Watto.

Years later, the female Hutt witnessed the victory of her old possession, Anakin Skywalker, at the Boonta Eve Classic Podrace, while seated in Jabba the Hutt's private booth.

Garindan

Born on the planet of Kubindi, this Kubaz worked mainly in the Mos Eisley spaceport on Tatooine and was an informer who offered his services to the highest bidder.

The Kubaz could be identified by their long snout and dark skin, but they were also known for their very acute ocular sensitivity. Therefore, in order to protect himself from the quite common sandstorms and intense brightness of Tatooine, Garindan wore protective goggles and a metallic helmet that covered his snout. When he heard the Empire was looking for two droids on Tatooine, he immediately offered his services and was soon on the trail of Luke Skywalker, Obi-Wan Kenobi, R2-D2 and C-3PO. Garindan saw Skywalker sell his landspeeder in order to hire a pilot that would take them to Alderaan. Garindan then led a stormtrooper patrol to Docking Bay 94, were the *Millennium Falcon* was docked. The fugitives barely escaped the ensuing Imperial assault.

Garven 'Dave' Dreis

Born on the planet Virujansi, Dreis was an experienced pilot with the Rebel Alliance.

Following his involvement in the Battle of Scarif he was chosen to take command of Red Squadron during the Battle of Yavin. It wasn't just his charisma and natural authority that marked him out as a leader, he also had a strong reputation as a smart tactician with courage and a sense of duty. During the assault on the Death Star, following the failure of Gold Squadron, he took the heavy responsibility of trying to start the chain reaction that would end in the destruction of the space station. His attempt failed and his torpedo exploded on the surface of the battle station. With Darth Vader on his tail, Dreis knew that he was condemned, so he quickly organised the attack of the third assault wave with the remaining starfighters. He was then shot down by the Sith Lord moments later.

Gasgano

A competitor at the Boonta Eve Classic Podrace, this Xexto could be found in the first row of the starting grid aboard his podracer named *Ord Pedrovia*.

Thanks to an excellent start that put him in first place, Gasgano spent the best part of the race in the lead, before being beaten in the last moments by the young human slave, Anakin Skywalker. This six-armed pilot, two of which were used as legs, had plenty of dexterity for driving a podracer and his second-place finish was well deserved.

Gavra Ubrento

This young mechanic was part of a team of technicians that offered their services to ship owners.

Despite not having state-of-the-art tools and facilities, she was still able to guarantee the smooth-running of the propulsion systems of all craft she was in charge of fixing. Dressed in dirty blue mechanic's overalls, she was among the crowd in the alleys of Jedha City before its destruction by the Death Star. It's unknown whether she escaped from the moon.

General Grievous

The Supreme Commander of the Separatist droid army employed by the Confederacy of Independent Systems, this old, widely-feared Kaleesh warrior had his vital organs transplanted into a mechanical duranium body in order to gain power and prolong his life.

A good strategist and excellent duellist, he learned the art of the lightsaber from Count Dooku and was a major opponent of the Republic and the Jedi Knights during the Clone Wars. He had a habit of keeping the lightsabers belonging to the Jedi Knights he had beaten and killed. Grievous participated in numerous battles and skirmishes, during which many Jedi were almost killed. He destroyed an entire fleet led by Plo Koon, and dominated Ahsoka Tano during a duel until her master, Anakin Skywalker, intervened and saved her life. He beat Jedi Master Kit Fisto and killed his Padawan Nahdar Vebb, and managed to kidnap Master Eeth Koth, who was later rescued by Obi-Wan Kenobi, Skywalker and Adi Gallia. Defiant by nature, he never hesitated to taunt his opponents and often masterminded elaborate, daring strategies that left the Republic's troops embarrassed.

During the Battle of Coruscant, Grievous managed to organise the kidnap of Chancellor Palpatine, which led to the Republic forces taking great risks to rescue their leader. Kenobi and Skywalker managed to infiltrate the Separatist's flagship, the *Invisible Hand,* and rescued the Chancellor. However, General Grievous evaded capture and managed to get away in an escape pod, joining the Separatist leaders in the Utapau system. Betrayed by Darth Sidious, who revealed Grievous' location to the Jedi, the general went on the run, hunted by Kenobi. In his final confrontation with the Jedi Master, it was the weak point in his cyborg armour that finally brought about Grievous' demise. Protected only by a synthetic skin sack, his vital organs were left dangerously exposed – an opportunity that Kenobi didn't hesitate to capitalise on.

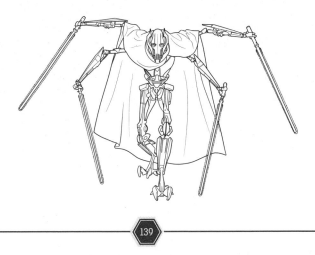

General Tagge

See Cassio Tagge

Geonosian Sonic Blaster

Built by the Gordarl Weaponsmiths, this sonic weapon was largely used by the Geonosians, including the troops of the Archduke Poggle the Lesser.

The sonic blaster used powerful oscillators to produce a destructive, single-direction sonic blast. Several transmitters were charged to channel the energy that was contained within the confinement sphere of the weapon. The blaster was a two-handed weapon, equipped with a grip for precision shooting.

Geonosis

Situated in the Arkanis sector of the Outer Rim, this planet was home to an insectoid species that specialised in the production of battle droids.

Geonosis, with its arid and inhospitable mountainous landscape, was a bastion of the Separatist movement under the rule of the Geonosian leader, Archduke Poggle the Lesser. It housed the droid-building factories that supplied soldiers and war machines to all supporters of the movement, including the Trade Federation, which used the droids during the invasion of Naboo.

Not far from the factories and the seat of Poggle the Lesser's government was the Geonosis Execution Arena, also called the Petranaki Arena. It was there that the unsuccessful execution of Anakin Skywalker, Padmé Amidala and Obi-Wan Kenobi heralded the beginning of the Battle of Geonosis and the Clone Wars. The planet and its factories then became major strategic locations. In order to prevent the Separatists from replenishing their forces as the war continued, the Republic strategists had no choice but to face them once again on the arid planet. The second Battle of Geonosis, in which Jedi such as Anakin Skywalker, Ki-Adi-Mundi and Ahsoka Tano took part, saw the capture of Poggle the Lesser and the Republic's hold on this sector of the galaxy increased.

With the coming of the Galactic Empire, Geonosis served as the initial construction site of the Death Star, before the battle station was moved to a more secure location to deter spies and saboteurs. To cover their tracks, the Empire eradicated nearly all native Geonosians using a deadly insecticide.

Geonosis Execution Arena

Also known as the Petranaki Arena, the Geonosis Execution Arena was a giant amphitheatre that hosted events to entertain the Geonosian people.

Situated on a desert plain next to the droid foundries on Geonosis, and not far from the seat of government of Archduke Poggle the Lesser, it was where many cruel executions took place. During executions, prisoners were gored, devoured or stabbed by wild creatures, such as the reek from Ylesia, the nexu from Cholganna and the acklay from Vendaxa. The arena was composed of a vast central space lined with high walls, where the viewing public were safely out of reach of the wild beasts. On the walls were several rows of seats and balconies, while high stone pillars were set in front of the main tribune. Prisoners were often fastened to the pillars and would await their execution by the giant beasts, which were herded by Geonosian picadors.

While they were held prisoner on Geonosis, Obi-Wan Kenobi, Anakin Skywalker and Padmé Amidala were sentenced to death in front of the cheering Geonosian crowd. They were chained to the central stone pillars, but used their dexterity, ingenuity and courage to free themselves of the chains and fought the beasts. When reinforcements arrived, the Geonosis Execution Arena became the setting of an even wilder conflict between the Jedi and the Geonosian droid army.

Ghoel

A resident of Jabba the Hutt's Palace, this Wol Cabasshite who looked like a mollusc, could be found glued to the walls and arches of the crime lord's Tatooine home.

With a prehensile tongue as long as his body, Ghoel liked to lick the occupants of the court, including C-3PO as he translated Jabba's condemnation of the rebels.

Ghost, the

A modified light VCX-100 cargo freighter manufactured by the Corellian Corporation, this ship acted as the mobile base of operations for the Spectre rebel unit during the Imperial era.

It belonged to the Twi'lek Hera Syndulla who, after becoming a general, was with C1-10P on Yavin 4 during the clandestine Rogue One mission. Her vessel took part in the orbital battle of Scarif along with the rest of the rebel fleet that engaged the Imperial forces.

Gial Ackbar

Commander of the rebel fleet during the Battle of Endor, it was this Mon Calamari who understood, just in the nick of time, that the orbital battle was an Imperial trap.

His swift reactions prevented disaster and when Lando Calrissian succeeded in destroying the second Death Star, Ackbar's relief was palpable. The Rebel Alliance had won, but it had also come very close to total annihilation. Promoted to Grand Admiral of the fleet of the New Republic, he led his troops to victory at the decisive Battle of Jakku, before retiring to his aquatic homeworld.

This brilliant tactician came out of restful retirement after twenty-nine years at the request of General Leia Organa, who asked him to become a member of the Resistance and join her in the fight against the First Order. On D'Qar, he helped her supervise the battle that destroyed the massive superweapon known as Starkiller Base.

Gian V-44 Landspeeder

The Gian V-44 landspeeder was a single-seater model of a vehicle produced during the Imperial regime.

Equipped with repulsors, this vehicle was fitted with two directional propulsion units that allowed it to reach a substantial speed. Galen Erso had one of these landspeeders on his property on Lah'mu, but it had rusted and fallen into disrepair.

Gian-211 Speeder

A dilapidated patrol speeder customised and used by the Resistance as a utility vehicle, the Gian-211 was a good example of the Resistance's philosophy of using everything it could in the fight against the First Order.

The New Republic's anti-militarist policy forbade the Resistance to develop new combat equipment, forcing it to recycle old craft in answer to its needs on the battlefield. The Resistance used the speeder to quickly transport maintenance equipment around its huge network of runways.

Giran

This male Kadas'sa'Nikto was assistant to Malakili, the rancor's guard at Jabba the Hutt's Palace on Tatooine.

After Luke Skywalker killed Jabba's rancor, Giran was the first on the scene. He grabbed the Jedi, but was pushed out of the way by Malakili who hurried to the fallen body of his favourite pet. Arm-in-arm and both consumed with sorrow, Giran guided the tearful Malakili away from the traumatic scene.

Glie-44 Blaster Pistol

A compact hand blaster, the Glie-44 was manufactured by Eirriss Ryloth Defense Tech and was a common weapon within Resistance forces.

An efficient weapon that benefited from having a barrel end with a short sight and its ammunition battery gave it great autonomy in the battlefield. It was the weapon of choice for many officers, including General Leia Organa.

Globe of Peace

A luminescent sphere, this relic symbolised the years of peace on the planet of Naboo.

After the parade celebrating the victory over the Trade Federation, Queen Amidala presented the globe to Boss Nass, who held it high for everyone to see, sealing the reconciliation between the Gungans and the Naboo.

Gold Leader

The leader of the Rebel Alliance's Gold Squadron.

At the Battle of Scarif and the Battle of Yavin this coveted role fell to Jon 'Dutch' Vander. In his final attack run the brave rebel pilot led Gold Squadron against the might of the Death Star, but he failed to launch the decisive torpedo before his starfighter was destroyed by Darth Vader. During the Battle of Endor, the role of Gold Leader fell jointly to General Lando Calrissian and Nien Nunb who, commanding the *Millennium Falcon*, lead Gold Squadron in its successful mission to destroy the second Death Star.

Gold Squadron

During the Galactic Civil War against the Empire, Gold Squadron was comprised of rebel starfighters who had taken part in the Battles of Scarif, Yavin and Endor.

Under the command of Jon 'Dutch' Vander, the Gold Squadron that attacked the Death Star was made up solely of Y-wing starfighters. Three of them, including Vander, attacked the trench and tried to launch a proton torpedo into one of the exhaust ports of the space station. The target was a weak point in the construction of the Death Star, a hit on which would trigger a chain reaction that would destroy the entire space station. Vander had an opportunity to launch a torpedo, but it exploded on the surface, causing only superficial damage. Instead, it was Luke Skywalker of Red Squadron who eventually led the victorious attack run.

Three years later, Gold Squadron was rebuilt as a ragtag fleet of starships led by Lando Calrissian and Nien Nunb piloting the *Millennium Falcon*, with a mission to launch an assault against the second Death Star. This time the attack aimed for the main reactor, but it required careful coordination with the ground troops on the moon of Endor, whose mission was to destroy the shield generator protecting the battle station. Once again, the assault was a gamble. Either the Empire would be decimated, or the Alliance would be wiped out. Following a huge space battle, the *Millennium Falcon* entered the reactor and successfully launched the torpedo that destroyed the second Death Star just moments later.

Graf Zapalo

Master of Sciences and adviser to the successive monarchs of Naboo, Zapalo stood side-by-side with Queen Amidala in the Theed Royal Palace throne room when the Trade Federation launched its invasion.

He was next seen with Queen Jamillia when she met with Senator Amidala and Jedi Knight Anakin Skywalker to discuss their fears concerning the growing conflict with the Separatists.

Grand Moff Tarkin

See Wilhuff Tarkin

Great Pit of Carkoon

This desolate place of execution was also the natural habitat of a sarlacc.

A sand basin located in the north part of the Dune Sea on Tatooine, the Great Pit of Carkoon was the den of an ancient and greedy creature that Jabba the Hutt favoured as a means of execution for some of his enemies. The sarlacc slowly digested its live prey over the course of a thousand years, offering the type of drawn-out, painful torture that the crime lord relished. The executions were often arranged as some kind of sadistic spectacle, with Jabba and his courtiers enjoying the show from a sail barge. The victims were brought on skiffs and were pushed into the pit where the hungry, tentacle-filled mouth of the sarlacc waited for them.

This lethal punishment was supposed to be the fate of Luke Skywalker and his friends, but they managed to escape. However, not wanting to deprive the creature of its meal, the rebels made sure that several of Jabba's henchmen, including the notorious Boba Fett, found their way into the pit.

Greeata Jendowanian

Greeata Jendowanian was one of the three singer-dancers of the Max Rebo Band that played at Jabba the Hutt's Palace.

With her orange crest and heavy gold jewellery, this Rodian watched on in horror as the Twi'lek dancer Oola met her terrible fate after refusing the advances of her Hutt master.

Greedo

Born on the planet of Rodia, Greedo was an impetuous bounty hunter who occasionally worked for Jabba the Hutt on Tatooine.

Greedo's most famous mission was also his last. He was sent to find Han Solo so that the Corellian smuggler could repay his debt to Jabba. Having tracked Solo to the Mos Eisley Cantina, where he was about to depart for Alderaan with Obi-Wan Kenobi and Luke Skywalker, Greedo finally had the smuggler in his sights. However, convinced that his quarry had no chance of escape, he became arrogant and let his guard down during an argument, which gave Solo just enough time to reach for his blaster and shoot his would-be capturer.

Green Four

See Attico Wred

Green Leader

See Arvel Crynyd

Green Squadron

A group of rebel starfighters who distinguished themselves during the famous Battle of Endor.

Composed entirely of very fast RZ-1 A-wing starfighters and placed under the command of the brave Arvel Crynyd, this squadron gathered to attack the terrifying *Executor* Super Star Destroyer. When Crynyd sacrificed himself to destroy the Imperial flagship, the mantle of Green Leader immediately fell to Lieutenant L'ulo L'ampar, and once the second Death

Star's shields were deactivated the primary objective of Green Squadron also changed. Rather than engage in battle they were charged with intercepting Imperial ships attempting to escape from the battle station.

Green Ten

See **Broan Danurs**

Green Twelve

See **Wion Dillems**

Grey Squadron

This group of starfighters served in the fleet of the Rebel Alliance during the Galactic Civil War.

The squadron, made up of both B-wing and A-wing starfighters, famously participated in the Battle of Endor and contributed to the victory of the Rebellion over the Empire.

Grummgar

A renowned hunter and mercenary, Grummgar was one of the regulars at Maz's Castle on Takodana.

Originally from Dowutin, he could be easily identified by his imposing figure, often nonchalantly slumped on one of the castle's sofas, and his intimidating face with its characteristic horns. Obsessed with trophies, he travelled the wild regions looking for rare animals to hunt using a rifle that was specially made for long-range shooting. Grummgar was also obsessed with women. He liked to be seen in the castle's main hall accompanied by beautiful creatures, and relied on his animal magnetism to attract them. Self-obsessed, he showed no interest in others or their motivations, so he completely missed the fact that his latest girlfriend, Bazine Netal, was a spy working for the First Order, using her position as his date as her cover.

GTAW-74 Welder Droid

This independent maintenance droid was from the Niima outpost on Jakku.

Equipped with a plasma soldering iron, GTAW-74, also known as 'Geetaw', roamed the tent encampment offering his services to wreck-raiders who needed to fix their pieces of machinery and components before trying to sell them on. Despite the often extensive damage from overexposure to the sand and desert winds, sometimes just a blob of solder could double their value. Geetaw worked in exchange for energy refills, gas containers or isolating metals that would allow him to continue his work. It was rumoured that even a good joke could be offered as payment, although it was impossible to tell his reaction from behind his protective face plate.

Guardians of the Whills

This ancient religious order of warrior-monks was built on a faith that worshipped the Force.

Contrary to the teachings of the Jedi, members of the Guardians of the Whills didn't deepen the existing antagonism between the dark and the light sides. Instead, they believed that by following a less dualistic approach, the mortal spirit of the believer could more easily embrace the entire cosmic energy field that was the Force.

Compared to the Disciples of the Whills, the Guardians were reputed to be concerned with a more supported mysticism and a more discreet clothing. Their members had the honourable task of protecting the Kyber Temple until the Empire finally forbade access to it and threw the Guardians out into the Jedha City streets. Uncertain of their fate and not knowing how to best resist the oppression, they became a source of disruption in the city, at least, that was Captain Cassian Andor's explanation upon meeting Chirrut Îmwe, a blind monk of the Guardian of the Whills. He was accompanied by Baze Malbus, who declared that he was no longer part of the religion after losing his faith.

Guavian Death Gang

Formerly based in the Core Worlds, the Guavian Death Gang had to relocate following the decline of the Hutts and the fall of the Empire.

Operating in the Outer Rim and the colonies, the gang carried out its illegal activities under the supervision of Bala-Tik and were invested in numerous trafficking and smuggling operations from which they earned interesting profits. The gang's power lay in its enhanced soldiers, killers who swore to be faithful to the gang in exchange for cybernetic and chemical improvements that made them stronger and faster. These soldiers wore a faceless red mask that featured a central disc that allowed them to share data. Their specific blood-red outfits and their total lack of expression reinforced their powers of intimidation.

Equipped with the best weapons that could be found on the black market, such as percussive cannons and grenade launchers, they represented a serious threat to anyone who tried to interfere in gang business. Always interested in a fruitful operation, the Guavian Death Gang sometimes funded skilled pirates or smugglers and would use force, if needed, to recoup its money when things didn't go as planned. As Han Solo was well aware when they showed up on his freighter, the *Eravana*.

Guch Ydroma

A travelling, mystical water seller in Jedha City.

Guch Ydroma claimed that during a pilgrimage in the desert he acquired the miraculous power of making water appear from thin air, and that this phenomenal ability came from the god of his Phirmist faith. He bottled the precious liquid and carried dozens of sealed bottles between the numerous temples of the Holy City, selling them to believers and to those who were simply thirsty.

Gundarks

These ferocious and strong creatures lived in caves on the planet of Vanqor and could grow to an average size of 2 metres.

The gundarks did not like to be disturbed and when Anakin Skywalker and Obi-Wan Kenobi crashed on Vanqor, they found themselves facing this particularly aggressive species. The Jedi only managed to survive thanks to their deep knowledge of the Force, and after this mishap, Skywalker would never cease to remind his master that he saved him from a nest of gundarks.

Gungan

The indigenous, amphibious species from the planet of Naboo.

The colour of Gungan skin varied greatly, from orange to brown, and green to pink, and their ears ended in very long, characteristic growths known as 'haillu'. Endowed with four fingers on each hand, three toes and a prehensile tail, they were adapted to both terrestrial and aquatic life. Nevertheless, on solid ground they had a gangling style that could appear comical, owing to the flexibility of their skeleton.

This secretive people, who lived in submarine cities in remote swamps, were, for a long time, considered by the Naboo as primitive. A misconception that was mainly due to the assumption that their society operated at a lower technological level. However, this was a big mistake. The Gungans had actually succeeded in developing numerous advanced technologies, including bongos, underwater habitats, hydrostatic bubbles and plasma weapons. The difference was that they created them using organic materials and cultivated techniques that worked in harmony with their ecosystem. This misconception resolved itself when the Gungans and Naboo were united in the war against the Trade Federation and got to know each other better.

Gungan Grand Army

This gigantic military force on Naboo was exclusively made up of Gungans.

Mainly focused on a defensive strategy, it employed relatively rudimentary war technology and relied heavily on the use of animals, such as kaadu, falumpasets and fambaas. While the kaadu served as cavalry, the fambaas carried the protective shield generators. Gungan soldiers were armed with traditional spears, or catapults called atlatls, which could be used to hurl exploding balls of energy. Nevertheless, this army was of fundamental strategic importance during the Battle of Naboo. It created a diversion 40 kilometres from Theed in order to attract the main part of the Trade Federation's droid army. Despite being outclassed on every level except courage, it was through this sacrifice that the Gungans contributed to the eventual victory.

Gungan High Council

Located in the underwater city of Otoh Gunga on Naboo, this government body represented the Gungan people and was presided over by Boss Rugor Nass.

Nass held this post during the invasion of Naboo, while Jar Jar Binks later joined the Council, and became a close ally of Padmé Amidala when she rose to become a senator close to the central power on Coruscant.

Gungan Shield

Also known as a Gungan shield generator, this defensive bubble used the same basis as other Gungan plasma technology.

This two-part device, used to generate protective shields around a segment of the battlefield, was transported by large war beasts called fambaas. The shield was capable of deflecting energy weapons, including shots from AATs, but its weakness was that it could be breached by the Trade Federation infantry, made up of thousands of B1 battle droids that easily penetrated it by moving slowly through its barrier wall.

Gwellis Bagnoro

This Onodone forger specialised in transit documents.

A mysterious character and a regular at Maz's Castle on Takodana, he never spoke much about where he came from or his past. Possessing skills that were essential to every pirate and smuggler in the galaxy, he saw the main hall of the castle as the ideal place to meet customers. Bagnoro was accompanied by Izby, his domesticated barghest that possessed strong jaws and sharp teeth, and would quickly jump to his master's defence whenever a difficult customer disagreed on prices.

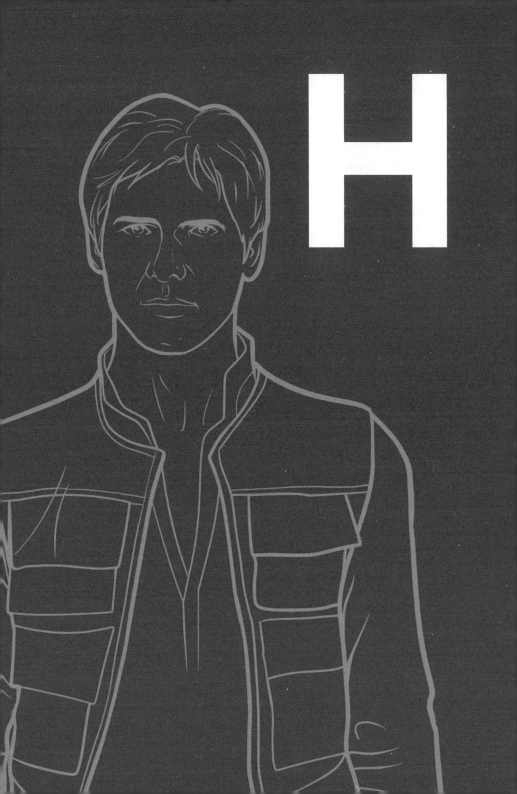

Hailfire Droid

This tank-type droid, developed by Haor Chall Engineering, was also known as the 'Wheel Droid' because of its locomotion system that was characterised by two giant, hoop-like wheels.

Primarily, the hailfire droid was a manoeuvrable and fast, missile-launching platform, capable of holding two launchers that could each contain up to fifteen missiles. The Intergalactic Banking Clan ordered IG-227 hailfire droids in anticipation of conflict, and used them against the Republic troops during the Battle of Geonosis.

Han Solo

Born on Corellia, Han Solo was a mercenary and smuggler, and a key member of the Rebel Alliance. Often accompanied by his life-long friend and co-pilot Chewbacca the Wookiee.

After winning a game of Sabacc against Lando Calrissian, Han Solo became the owner of the *Millennium Falcon*, a ship that proved to be instrumental in his professional future. Thanks to the modifications he made to the *Millennium Falcon*, Solo gained access to more lucrative smuggling deals, which often also proved to be more dangerous.

Solo's path towards joining the Rebellion began when he accepted a seemingly simple commission from Obi-Wan Kenobi in the Mos Eisley Cantina. The job was to fly the Jedi, his young friend Luke Skywalker and two droids, C-3PO and R2-D2, to Alderaan, without attracting the attention of the Empire. For this straightforward task the smuggler negotiated a fee of 17,000 credits, with which he planned to pay off his debt to Jabba the Hutt. After shooting and escaping the clutches of Greedo, the bounty hunter, who had been sent to recover the debt, Solo discovered Jabba waiting for him at the *Millennium Falcon*. However, he managed to negotiate a new deal with the crime lord that allowed him to leave, unaware of the adventure he was about to become embroiled in.

Upon emerging from hyperspace to find nothing but an asteroid field where Alderaan should have been, the mission suddenly took on a new focus and Solo unwittingly joined the Rebel Alliance. While in pursuit of a single TIE fighter, the *Millennium Falcon* was caught in the pull of a powerful tractor beam belonging to the Death Star. The droid R2-D2 carried the stolen plans of the gigantic space station for the Alliance. The *Millennium Falcon*'s secret compartments, usually used for hiding contraband, proved to be extremely useful for concealing Solo and his associates when the ship was boarded by Imperial inspectors. After reluctantly agreeing to help free Princess Leia Organa, who was imprisoned on the space station, Solo and Skywalker disguised themselves as stormtroopers, while Kenobi went to deactivate the tractor beam.

After battling their way through the Death Star, exchanging blaster fire and encountering extreme danger in the space station's gigantic trash compactor, the rescue team and Leia finally succeeded in getting back to the *Millennium Falcon*. However, it was only Kenobi's sacrifice during his lightsaber duel with Darth Vader that created a diversion long enough for them to escape. The Empire sent their TIE fighters in pursuit, but Solo and Skywalker were able to destroy them.

After safely transporting Leia, Skywalker, R2-D2 and C-3PO to Yavin 4, Solo was paid handsomely for his services. He decided to return to Tatooine to repay Jabba the Hutt, leaving the Alliance as its ships prepared for the assault on the Death Star. But Solo soon turned back and his timely intervention allowed Skywalker to launch the torpedo which started the chain reaction that destroyed the space station. By shooting down one of the two fighters that

escorted Darth Vader, Solo had created a distraction that caused the second pilot to crash his fighter into Vader's, sending the Sith Lord whirling into space at the very moment he had locked Skywalker in his sights and was preparing to fire.

While the Rebellion was searching for a new base, Solo decided it was time to repay his debt to Jabba. But, once again, events involving the Alliance prevented him from doing so and he ended up at the rebels' Echo Base on the ice planet of Hoth. When Skywalker didn't return from a routine patrol, it was a concerned Solo who mounted a tauntaun and went in search of him, despite the dangers of being outside the base at night. Luckily, he found Skywalker, unconscious and wounded by a wampa, and was able to get him to safety.

It was Solo and Chewbacca's subsequent encounter with an Imperial probe droid that led to the rebels' need to evacuate Echo Base. Leia, as one of the last rebels to leave, was forced to escape with Solo aboard the *Millennium Falcon*, but owing to the hasty exit the Corellian and his Wookiee co-pilot had been unable to complete any of the essential repairs to his ship, which resulted in more Imperial entanglements.

Needing to escape the Imperial fleet but unable to use the damaged hyperdrive, Solo followed a course of action which, according to C-3PO, was deadly – Solo flew into a particularly dense asteroid field. Seeking refuge, Solo headed for the planet of Bespin and Cloud City, which was managed by his friend Lando Calrissian. Unknowingly, they were being tracked by Boba Fett, a bounty hunter who had succeeded in negotiating an arrangement with Darth Vader – Solo would act as a decoy to attract Skywalker to Bespin – and at the same time be a test subject for the viability of carbon-freezing on human beings. Captured soon after his arrival at Cloud City, Solo survived the process of being frozen in carbonite. He was then given to Boba Fett, who transferred him to Jabba the Hutt, who in turn used him as a decoration in his palace on Tatooine. The ensuing rescue mission staged by Skywalker, Leia and Calrissian, led to the destruction of Jabba and his organisation, and finally freed Solo from his debt. Now, Solo could fully commit himself to the Rebel Alliance.

Later, promoted to the rank of general, Solo led the perilous mission to destroy the shield generator on the forest moon of Endor. It was a vital piece of equipment that powered the protective shield surrounding the second Death Star. Help came in the unexpected form of the moon's indigenous species, the Ewoks, who formed an alliance with the rebels. Their support proved to be invaluable and Solo eventually succeeded in destroying the generator, which allowed the rebel fleet to attack the second Death Star, and to secure a victory that became the first step towards the fall of the Empire.

One year later, following the Battle of Jakku, the Empire was over and the New Republic was declared. Han Solo and Leia Organa married and had a child named Ben Solo, who demonstrated great sensitivity to the Force. However, Leia detected a tumultuous inner conflict in her son. When Ben developed a fascination for his grandfather, Darth Vader, Leia and Solo gave their son to the care of his uncle, Luke Skywalker, who was training a new Jedi Order of young Padawans. However, they failed to understand that the young apprentice had also been influenced by Snoke, the Supreme Leader of the First Order, and was being tempted by the dark side of the Force. Having taken the name of Kylo Ren, Ben slaughtered his uncle's apprentices, and Skywalker, believing that he had failed, went into exile.

Unable to cope with the loss of their son, Solo and Leia's marriage struggled and the former smuggler returned to his previous occupation, eventually losing the *Millennium Falcon* during a clandestine operation. Thirty years after the creation of the New Republic, Solo intercepted his former ship while on board his current one the *Eravana* – a large cargo freighter. Upon inspecting the *Millennium Falcon* he found scavenger Rey, and the reformed First Order soldier Finn, accompanied by a droid called BB-8. After listening to their epic tale and the revelation that BB-8 was carrying a map that could lead to Skywalker, Solo found himself drawn back into the Resistance's fight.

Solo led Rey and Finn to the planet of Takodana to meet Maz Kanata, who discerned that Rey had a strong sensitivity to the Force. This prompted Maz to give Rey Luke Skywalker's old lightsaber, which had been lost during his battle with Darth Vader in Cloud City. However, the First Order had managed to track BB-8 to Takodana and organised a blitz attack, during which Solo, Chewbacca and Finn were captured. They were soon freed when the Resistance forces, led by pilot Poe Dameron, launched a counter-attack. Solo witnessed the retreat of the First Order fleet, and saw his son, Kylo Ren, carrying an unconscious Rey aboard his ship.

Later, it was Solo who undertook the mission to destroy Starkiller Base, the First Order's gigantic combat station on an unknown planet. It had the capability to decimate whole star systems. Finn's prior knowledge of the base and its operations was essential when it came to planning the mission. The superweapon drew the vast energy it needed from a nearby sun and that energy was stored in a thermal oscillator. The Resistance's research indicated that the destruction of the oscillator and the subsequent release of the stored energy would be enough to destabilise the planet, and cause it to implode at its core. Leia also entrusted Solo with another, more delicate mission – to find their son and try to convince him to return to the light side of the Force.

The first part of the mission was a total success. The infiltration of the base combined with the assault by the Resistance fleet succeeded in the destruction of the superweapon. But the second part was not. Han Solo was killed by his son, Kylo Ren, as he attempted to convince him to leave the First Order and return to his family.

Happabore

A draft animal that could be found on several planets.

These impressive creatures, with very thick skin and a prominent muzzle, were sought for their robustness and remarkable docility. Able to withstand the harshest climates, happabores could be seen at the Niima outpost on Jakku, where they quietly drank from special troughs. Despite their calm nature, they could sometimes softly push away a troublemaker. Happabore leather was also a widely used material, and Jakku scavenger and future Jedi Rey owned a wallet made from the prized hide.

Harb Binli

This Rebel Alliance pilot took part in the orbital combat at the Battle of Scarif.

A newcomer to Red Squadron, the moustached cadet from the planet of Eriadu could be seen in the front line, just behind Jyn Erso, during the heated debate of the rebel council that took place on Yavin 4. A specialist in the destruction of anti-aircraft defence units, he participated in the Battle of Scarif using the call sign Red Seven. Despite his expertise, Binli was unable to prevent his teacher and teammate, Pedrin Gaul, from being shot down.

Harter Kalonia

A Resistance medical officer who served with General Leia Organa in the conflict against the galactic threat of the First Order, Harter Kalonia took care of the wounded and supported them during their recovery.

Promoted to the rank of major, she was responsible for overseeing initial diagnoses and providing adequate care for each patient at the Resistance's secret base on D'Qar. Her cheerful mood combined with her ability to listen encouraged a positive attitude among her patients that helped their recovery. Some of them, such as Chewbacca after the raid on

Takodana, couldn't wait to recount their adventures in order to catch her attention.

Heff Tobber

A rebel pilot who held the rank of lieutenant during operation Rogue One.

Based on the abandoned Rebellion outpost of Crait, this carrier pilot was transferred to Blue Squadron on Yavin 4. Although he was at ease flying an X-wing, he turned his skills to piloting U-wings and, owing to his good humour, soon became extremely popular among the soldiers that he escorted. He took part in the Battle of Scarif under the command of General Antoc Merrick, but was unable to follow the general through the shield gate. Instead, determined to play his part, Tobber helped Green Squadron during the orbital combat with the Imperial fighters.

Hela Brandes

A member of the Naboo Royal Advisory Council.

This Council member from Naboo served as Music Adviser under the reign of Queen Padmé Amidala.

Hera Syndulla

One of the first, and greatest, commanders to lead the rebel fight against the Empire, Twi'lek Hera Syndulla was also an exceptional pilot and the captain of the *Ghost*.

The planet of Gorse was the setting for Syndulla's life-changing encounter with Kanan Jarrus. Together, Syndulla and the young Jedi formed the Spectre team, picking up Ezra Bridger and Sabine Wren en route as they fought back against the Imperial forces on the planet of Lothal. Undoubtedly a highly talented pilot, Syndulla's ultimate strength lay in her ability to lead others – sometimes by following them. When the Empire captured Jarrus, Syndulla listened and followed her teammates' unorthodox plans to send C1-10P to track Jarrus down. This humility led to Jarrus being discovered aboard Grand Moff Tarkin's Star Destroyer, and to Syndulla and Jarrus being reunited once more.

Syndulla led the Spectres on many dangerous missions to undermine the Empire and fight against their occupation of the planet Lothal. One such mission, to rescue her from the clutches of Governor Pryce, ended in the sacrifice of Kanan Jarrus, but the Spectres were ultimately successful. Following Jarrus' death, Syndulla gave birth to their son, Jacen Syndulla. She was later promoted to General in the Rebel Alliance and fought at the Battle of Endor.

Hermi Odle

One of the many gangsters on Jabba the Hutt's payroll and was often present at the crime lord's palace on Tatooine.

This massive Baragwin, who wore a tattered cloak and clothes, was more than 2 metres tall. His head and lips fell to the level of his throat, which gave the impression he was a hunchback.

High Priest, the

The religious leader of the Brotherhood of the Beatific Countenance, this Lorrdian willingly abandoned his name to complete his renouncement of all individuality, as was his faith's belief.

The Brotherhood's other important dogma was the vow of silence, and its followers could only speak to their leader by producing a moaning sound. The High Priest could be identified by his Blue Gown of the Sullen Moon and a Lorrdian Cowl of Quiescence. He was leading his congregation on a pilgrimage to the Holy City of Jedha at the time of the city's cataclysmic destruction. It was unknown whether he survived the attack.

Holocron

This information storage device was mainly used and built by the Jedi and the Sith.

It generally took the form of a harmoniously designed polyhedron, usually a cube or a dodecahedron. It stored knowledge or important information, often about the nature of the Force, which was meant only for the Jedi. When a holocron was in use, the crystal material that it was made from would glow and the information that it contained was projected as an interactive hologram of the Jedi Master who recorded it. The use of a holocron sometimes required a specific memory crystal.

The holocrons were essential artefacts for the Jedi Order, as much because of the data stored in them as for their historical value. They were kept in the Jedi Archives and the less common models were stored behind laser motion sensors, in a vault equipped with a heavy, armoured door. The memory crystals needed for the activation of some of the holocrons were stored in a different secure location.

Sith holocrons also existed and, generally taking the form of a pyramid, they worked in the same way as their Jedi counterparts. These objects, which contained many secrets about the dark side of the Force, were regarded as being among the most dangerous items in the galaxy. To activate a Sith holocron, the user normally had to have mastered the dark side of the Force. Ancient lore specified that if a Sith and Jedi holocron were combined, they could, via the Force, answer even the deepest, most burning questions.

HoloNet

A communication system that transmitted holographic content.

The HoloNet was practical for both simple communications between a receptor and an emitter, and for the mass broadcast of content from an emitter to all receptors connected to the HoloNet network. This system became a very efficient mass propaganda device and was frequently used to spread the Imperial doctrine throughout the galaxy.

Holoprojector

A recording, transmitting and receiving device of three-dimensional images, designed for information, communication and leisure.

It came in many sizes, and the technical quality of the picture was noticeably different according to the model. For example, astromech droids were equipped with a very convenient holoprojector, but its recording and projecting functions had rather poor, bluish colours – as demonstrated by the recording of Princess Leia Organa by R2-D2. On the other hand, the pocket holoprojector used by Jedi Master Qui-Gon Jinn to show Queen Amidala's ship to junkyard dealer Watto, possessed a high-quality projector unit that created an ultra-realistic hologram.

Home One

Admiral Gial Ackbar's flagship within the rebel fleet during the Battle of Endor.

Originally a civil exploration starship, this MC80 star cruiser was customised for military use. Armed with turbolasers and ion cannons and measuring 1,200 metres in length, it was the biggest ship in the fleet. It became the Alliance's mobile command centre following the destruction of the rebel headquarters on Hoth and remained so until the Battle of Endor. Between its white walls, Mon Mothma, Crix Madine and Ackbar briefed troops on the eve of the crucial battle, in hope that the Mon Calamari admiral could guide his forces to victory.

Hookah Pipe

Favoured by Jabba the Hut, this pipe, fitted with a long, flexible hose, was a smoking device that allowed its user to inhale the vapour of a percolating liquid.

Jabba, whose hookah pipe was connected to a liquid-filled, sphere-shaped smoke tank, was often seen using it in his palace throne room on Tatooine, where it rested on a bowl of Klatooine frogs, which the infamous Outer Rim crime lord liked to snack on.

Horox Ryyder

This Anx senator represented several thousand worlds that formed the Raioballo sector.

A wise member of the Galactic Senate, he was particularly recognisable at a distance owing to his great height, standing at over 4 metres tall, as well as his yellow, crescent-shaped head, which was embellished by a long beard.

Hosnian Prime

A cosmopolitan planet located in the Core Worlds region and part of the affiliated worlds, Hosnian Prime was, before its destruction, the most recent capital of the New Republic.

With its dense, busy urban zones, the planet was reminiscent of Coruscant, the historic capital of the Republic and the Empire. Following the introduction of a new electoral system, designed to give better representation to worlds that had joined the New Republic after the fall of the Empire, Hosnian Prime had also become the new home of the Senate. However, this was only an interim measure as the electoral reform also decreed that, in the spirit of fairness and equality, the Senate building should regularly be relocated among the planets of the New Republic. Hosnian Prime was among the planets targeted by the First Order and was destroyed after being fired upon by Starkiller Base.

Hoth

The sixth planet of the Hoth system, this icy world was completely made up of glaciers and snowy plains.

Although absolutely inhospitable during the night-time when temperatures could plummet to -60°C, this world was still home to some animal species. Most notable among these creatures were tauntauns, biped lizard-mammals that could be tamed, and wampas, their main predator.

The planet's huge, icy wastes were the setting for the historic Battle of Hoth, during which the Empire sent ground troops to destroy Echo Base, where the Rebel Alliance had regrouped after the Battle of Yavin. The battle was a stinging defeat for the rebels, who, following its conclusion, were reduced to a single, retreating fleet.

Hovercam

See Cam Droid

Hrchek Kal Fas

Born on the planet Durkteel, Hrchek Kal Fas was a male Saurian who made a living from trading droids.

He was present in the Mos Eisley Cantina when Obi-Wan Kenobi met Han Solo, and spotted the droid, C-3PO, who accompanied the old Jedi Master. However, after witnessing the brawl that left Dr. Evazan for dead and saw Ponda Baba lose an arm, he quickly decided that it would be unwise to try to steal the droid from its owner.

Hugo Eckener

Chief architect and member of the Royal Advisory Council of Naboo under the leadership of Sio Bibble, during the reign of Queen Amidala.

He was present in the Theed Royal Palace throne room when Senator Palpatine's communication was interrupted, which heralded the Trade Federation's invasion of Naboo.

Humidity Vaporator

This device was used by the owners of moisture farms to collect water contained in the atmosphere.

Even though different models were in existence, the general principle was always the same. They used one or several refrigerated tubes that when they came into contact with the atmosphere produced a condensation that allowed pure water to be collected in the vats located at the base of the device.

HURID-327

This maintenance droid was employed at Maz's Castle on Takodana.

Its tall stature required repulsor supports that generated a counterweight, and the high position of its main receptors suggested that it also had a gyrostabilisation unit. Equipped with strong, prehensile handlers and reinforced articulations, this droid was responsible for any kind of heavy-weight work. Han Solo, Finn and Rey encountered the red HURID-327 returning to its ship when they arrived at Maz's Castle.

Hurst Romodi

This Imperial general was a veteran of the Clone Wars.

Wounded during the time of the Republic, he gladly welcomed the birth of the Galactic Empire, and, following the restructure of the army in order to guarantee its allegiance to Emperor Palpatine, he was one of the first to be promoted to the rank of general. Romodi became close to Wilhuff Tarkin and served at his side during the pacification operations in the western territories. After his retirement, he was formally asked to return to serve as aide to Grand Moff Tarkin during the completion of the Death Star.

It was Romodi who informed Tarkin of General Sotorus Ramda's message, warning of the rebel attack on Scarif. Tarkin's response was to find Darth Vader and warn him of the situation. Romodi's suggestion of using the superlaser against the rebel fleet was rejected by Tarkin, who instead chose to leave the matter to the Sith Lord. Always faithful and disciplined, Romodi then transmitted his superior's order to fire on Scarif, even though it housed a non-evacuated Imperial base on its surface. Shortly after this battle, General Romodi attended the meeting during which the Grand Moff announced the dissolution of the Imperial Senate.

Hutt

This species from the planet of Nal Hutta had the appearance of a gigantic slug.

With the ability to live for several hundred years, the Hutts were gangsters on many planets. The most famous of their number was Jabba the Hutt, who controlled his criminal empire from his palace on Tatooine.

'Huttsplitter' Blaster Rifle

A customised blaster rifle owned by Tasu Leech, Kanjiklub's symbolic leader.

This partially handmade weapon was typical of the creations made by the Kanjiklub and an example of the craftsmanship of the human colonies of Nar Kanji. Tasu Leech's gun had a gundark bone grip and a vibro-spike bayonet made of narglatch task. Its name served as a reminder of the conflicts that saw the power and the influence of the Hutts decline after the fall of the Empire.

Hyperdrive

A propulsion system that enabled ships to reach light speed in order to travel through hyperspace – the distance between stars.

This technology had far-reaching consequences for the exploration of the galaxy, as well as trade development, politics and military strategies. It was interesting to note that the Rebel Alliance's X-wing starfighter was equipped with a hyperdrive, but its natural enemy, the Imperial TIE fighter was not, which meant it was necessary for the Empire to carry its ships in transporters to wherever they were required.

Hyperspace

This alternative space dimension was accessed through molecular displacement, which was achieved by travelling at a velocity equal to or greater than the speed of light.

Using hyperspace, starships that were equipped with a hyperdrive had the ability to travel to any part of the galaxy. Hyperspace travel required a calculation that worked out the empty distance between stars and planets. Folds in space could hugely reduce the time it took to travel between these bodies, but they could only be accessed by the molecular displacement that occurred by travelling faster than the speed of light. The dangers of attempting to calculate a hyperspace trajectory led to the creation of maps detailing known and secure routes, but new routes, often faster or more secure, were constantly being found, and could offer their discoverer benefits, particularly when used for military advantage during a conflict.

Although hyperspace travel allowed users to move between two planets in a flash, there were certain criteria that had to be in place before a ship could make the jump. In order to avoid the likelihood of the ship disintegrating, it was essential to be in space at both the start and finish point of the jump. It was believed to be theoretically impossible to enter hyperspace when still in the gravitational pull of the departure planet, and incredibly risky to exit the jump in the atmosphere of the arrival planet. However, during the conflict between the Resistance and the First Order, Han Solo succeeded in the impressive feat of making the jump to hyperspace in the *Millennium Falcon* from inside the hangar bay of a cargo ship. He also exited another hyperspace jump when already in the atmosphere of Starkiller Base. Previously, the Empire had succeeded in developing a system that enabled its interdictor cruisers to activate a tractor beam that could extract a ship from hyperspace, even during its jump.

IG-100 MagnaGuard

These droid bodyguards were developed by Holowan Mechanicals and were generally assigned to important Separatist military leaders, such as Count Dooku or General Grievous.

Distantly related to IG assassin droids, the MagnaGuards specialised in close combat. Excellent duellists, they were armed with two-handed electrostaffs that were able to compete with the Jedi lightsabers and were also very effective when outnumbered by opponents. Their programming enabled them to continue fighting even after the loss of a limb, which made them even more dangerous.

Present alongside General Grievous on the Separatist flagship the *Invisible Hand*, they tried to stop the Jedi Anakin Skywalker and Obi-Wan Kenobi. On the planet Utapau, they were beaten by Kenobi, who crushed them under a metallic structure he ripped from the ceiling through the use of the Force.

IG-88

IG-88 was an IG-series droid manufactured by Holowan Mechanicals.

The IG-series, nicknamed 'assassin droids', had originally been designed to accompany the galaxy's gangsters and mafia members, but some among them became mercenaries and worked as freelancers with a relentless determination. This was the case with IG-88, whose reputation had caught the attention of Darth Vader. Vader included IG-88 in a group of bounty hunters to whom he offered a contract for the capture of the crew of the *Millennium Falcon*. It was Boba Fett who successfully captured Han Solo in Cloud City at Bespin, where Solo was taking refuge with his friend Lando Calrissian. IG-88 was destroyed during his mission by his successful competitor in the Mandalorian armour.

Igar

This Imperial army commander, stationed on the forest moon of Endor, was based at the strategic shield generator protecting the second Death Star.

Igar oversaw the surrender of one of the most famous personalities of the Rebellion – Luke Skywalker. He delivered this precious prisoner to Darth Vader in person, and asked for permission to search the forest moon for other rebels, which the Sith Lord granted him.

Ilco Munica

An Abednedo citizen from the small village of Tuanul on the planet of Jakku, Ilco Munica lived an austere life as part of the colony that established itself inside the Kelvin Ravine.

Although unable to use the Force, he followed the spiritual values of it and became part of the underground movement of believers who revealed themselves after the fall of the Empire. Like the majority of his fellow villagers, Ilco Munica was ready to take up arms to defend his beliefs against the influence of the dark side. Out of respect for the values of his community and to avoid giving money to the big armament corporations, Munica made his own weapons, which explained how he came to be the owner of a mass blaster made from a used industrial frame. He was killed along with the rest of the Tuanul villagers by First Order stormtroopers under the command of Kylo Ren.

Imperial Academy

A military training and recruitment programme set up by the Galactic Empire after the fall of the Republic.

The Imperial Academy's main training facility was based on Coruscant, but dozens of additional branches were created all over the galaxy. After passing the core curriculum, the best cadets went on to advanced academy training. The elite graduates were then assigned to specialised training according to their strengths: the Imperial army, the Imperial fleet, or the stormtrooper corps, which included a Special Forces commando division.

Imperial Guard

This elite corps was dedicated to the close protection of the Emperor. Armed with vibro-active spears and fully covered by red dresses and helmets that allowed them to remain anonymous, the Imperial guards were silent, imposing and lethal.

The corps was founded at the time of Sheev Palpatine's nomination as Supreme Chancellor, and took only the best and most obedient members of the Senatorial Guard, transforming their blue uniforms to red. The guards were originally intended for the protection of the Chancellor's offices, rather than exposure to the public, but their existence was confirmed at the start of the Clone Wars as Palpatine's power increased. After his auto-proclamation to the title of emperor and the advent of the Galactic Empire, the Imperial guards permanently replaced the dissolved Senate Guards. Officially endorsed by the regime, the guards continued to receive complete training in all forms of combat and remained faithful to the Emperor, carrying out Palpatine's every law and order without a moment's hesitation, even when it implied the death of one of their own. The knowledge of their master's secret Sith nature was kept in absolute silence, even between themselves. In spite of their levels of expertise, Palpatine, confident in his own power, didn't feel he needed protection from the Imperial guards, but kept them to impress his visitors. However, he would come to regret his rejection of them. After requesting to be left alone with Darth Vader and Luke Skywalker during the Battle of Endor, Palpatine paid the ultimate price for his overconfidence, and perished.

Imperial Kyber Refinery

This secret Imperial research centre was part of the Tarkin Initiative and was located on Eadu.

Under the leadership of Galen Erso, a team of scientists and specialists was assigned two closely related projects during their twenty years of captivity. Within the refinery they were tasked to find a way to merge crystal shards in order to make larger crystals, while those in the High Energy Concepts and Implementation Labs investigated how to create and direct the crystals' chain reaction. The aim was to succeed where the Geonosians had failed: to produce a controllable laser beam by bombarding kyber crystals with energy. In other words, to equip the nearly constructed superstructure of the Death Star with a superlaser.

The researchers achieved both objectives, but were executed shortly after by Director Orson Krennic's death troopers. Erso himself perished when the facility was bombed by rebel starfighters during Operation Fracture. The loud explosions heard by Captain Cassian Andor, who was near the site, proved that the research centre had been destroyed.

Imperial Officer

A member of the controlling elite of the Imperial regime established by Emperor Palpatine.

At the end of the Clone Wars, the Emperor decided to abandon mass cloning and instead founded the basis of his new regime on recruits supplied by a recruiting army, which excluded nearly all non-human species from the drafting process. The Imperial officers, who were in charge of commanding the different military forces, were therefore almost exclusively male humans. Their primary task was to form and direct the stormtroopers, the elite of the Imperial infantry. All officers shared the same 'qualities', which consisted of being ambitious, being willing to use military force and, of course, an indisputable loyalty to the Emperor, his projects and the means used to achieve them.

Imperial Palace

See Temple of the Jedi (Coruscant)

Imperial Security Complex

The Empire's secret base on Scarif, this vast installation included a huge main building known as the Citadel Tower.

The main tower consisted of a command room and a secure vault where sensitive data was stored. The complex was connected by a system of repulsor rails, on which wagons travelled along a network of U-shaped routes. The network ran from the landing pads and barracks located on tropical islets around the main base. The research centre served as a base for the development of the Death Star, with important research, structural engineering and partial construction taking place there.

Its tropical climate, remote location and high degree of security made the fortress a highly valued station for Imperial officers. Officers were often transferred there by gaining the favour of their superiors, or by influencing important decision-makers. But the fortress's high level of security meant that officers were often lax in their own security, and became complacent about securing the complex.

This relaxed attitude was blown apart as the rebel infiltration team named Rogue One detonated explosive devices around the beaches of Scarif. During the Battle of Scarif, the Imperial base was targeted for destruction by Grand Moff Tarkin, who made the controversial move in order to prevent the rebels from stealing the Death Star plans from the Citadel Tower. Tarkin ordered the attack on the complex, and after the Death Star shot a ray into the planet, the entire research centre was utterly destroyed.

Imperial Senate

The Imperial Senate was the legislative apparatus of the Galactic Empire once Supreme Chancellor Sheev Palpatine proclaimed himself Emperor of the galaxy.

At the end of the Clone Wars, which had been orchestrated by Palpatine, the Supreme Chancellor called a special session of parliament where he presented himself to the Senate as the galaxy's saviour from the political decay, decadence and corruption that had infiltrated the heart of the Republic. His speech was greatly helped by the fact that he used his Sith Lord appearance – his face had been wounded by the use of the dark side of the Force – and he attributed his injuries to the Jedi. Once Emperor, he initialised the second part of his plan, which gave the illusion of a democratic assembly. This facade gave him time to finalise a weapon that had originally been conceived by the Geonosians to enslave all systems of the galaxy by force: the Death Star, a space station the size of a small moon that had been constructed in total secrecy.

Over the years that followed, the Senate was transformed into a mockery of democratic deliberation. Although laws were still debated and voted on, Palpatine applied none of them. The Imperial Senate was dissolved nineteen years after its creation, during the emergence of the Rebel Alliance, which had begun to win some sympathisers within the assembly. Crucially, the construction of the Death Star had also finished and all senatorial powers were transferred to the army and the regional governors, who from then on had complete authority over their territories. It was the rise of a dictatorship and only the Rebel Alliance carried the new hope of liberty in the galaxy

Imperial Shock Trooper

A division of high-class stormtroopers selected from the Empire's regular stormtrooper corps.

Imperial shock troopers were the successors of the clone shock troopers and continued to wear the same distinguishing red and white armour as their predecessors. They specialised in heavy weapons and routinely used DLT-19 heavy blaster rifles, DLT-20A laser rifles and rocket launchers, as opposed to the standard E-11 blaster carried by regular stormtroopers. An elite force, they were even known to act as bodyguards to the Emperor himself.

Imperial Shuttle

See Lambda-class T-4a Shuttle

Infrablue Zedbeddy Coggins

Along with Taybin Ralorsa, Ubert 'Sticks' Quaril and Sudswater Dillifay Glon, this musician was a member of the quartet at Maz Kanata's Castle on Takodana.

Coggins played the hypolliope horn cluster, a large wind instrument linked to a tube equipped with keys that allowed the player to direct their breath around a complex network of brass pipes. The instrument produced a soft sound that became part of a background music that merged with the natural ambient noise of the castle, namely the sound of glasses, laughter and altercations.

InterGalactic Banking Clan

A powerful organisation that specialised in loans and credit, the InterGalactic Banking Clan was based on Scipio.

Representing the union of several great banking powers, the InterGalactic Banking Clan was one of the main financing sources of many organisations and institutions, such as the Trade Federation, and even the Republic itself.

During the crisis that saw the Separatist movement develop, the InterGalactic Banking Clan quickly became an alternative financing source for those who wanted to escape the influence of the Republic. The banks attempted to remain neutral in the ensuing Clone Wars, even though high-ranking clan members, such as San Hill, secretly backed the Separatists. The Sith Lords Darth Sidious and Darth Tyranus engineered the rise of a malleable leader of the clan, a human named Rush Clovis. They engineered a Separatist invasion of Scipio that forced the Republic to take over the banks, putting huge amounts of money directly into the control of soon-to-be Emperor Palpatine.

Invasion of Naboo

An apparently minor conflict between the invading Trade Federation and the planet of Naboo that created fundamental political repercussions for the ten years that followed.

The crisis of Naboo took place in three acts: the blockade of the planet, its invasion and, finally, its liberation – commonly known as the Battle of Naboo. The second phase, the invasion, consisted of the occupation of the capital city, Theed, and its adjacent regions by the Trade Federation's droid army. This disproportionate attack, which met only little resistance, forced Naboo's sovereign, Queen Padmé Amidala, to flee and request the help of the Galactic Senate. She then returned to her planet in secret to forge an alliance with the Gungans, who lived in underwater cities in the waters of Naboo.

The liberation of Naboo took place on three fronts. The Gungan army created a diversion by facing the Trade Federation's droid army head on, while a squadron of starfighters struck at the Trade Federation's control ship in orbit. Meanwhile, Queen Amidala and the Jedi infiltrated the Royal Palace of Theed and captured Viceroy Nute Gunray, the Trade Federation's leader. Following Anakin Skywalker's destruction of the control ship, the Gungan army was victorious and Gunray was taken prisoner. Owing to the indisputable victory, Naboo's senator, Sheev Palpatine, who was actually a Sith Lord and had secretly orchestrated the whole conflict, fulfilled his goal of being elected as Supreme Chancellor of the Republic. A Republic that he would continue to undermine and ultimately destroy from the inside out by triggering the Clone Wars, allowing Palpatine to form the Galactic Empire.

Invisible Hand, the

This *Providence*-class dreadnought, built by the Free Dac Volunteers Engineering Corps, was the flagship of the Confederacy of Independent Systems.

Under the command of the cyborg General Grievous since the loss of the *Malevolence* during a battle against the Republic, the *Invisible Hand* was the spearhead of the Separatist navy. This heavy carrier, which was around 1,000 metres long, could transport 20 droid starfighter squadrons and more than 400 ground assault vehicles. Its arsenal comprised of 14 quad turbolaser cannons, 34 twin laser cannons, 12 point-defence ion cannons, 2 heavy ion cannons and more than 100 proton torpedoes. Its impressive firepower enabled it to easily bombard the surface of a planet from the safety of space. Its control bridge, raised in a sensor pod far above the hull, enabled a clear view of the whole operation. During the Battle of Coruscant, General Grievous kidnapped Chancellor Palpatine and took him aboard the *Invisible Hand*. Obi-Wan Kenobi and Anakin Skywalker were able to save him and forced the Separatist general to abandon his ship and flee in an escape pod. Eventually, the *Invisible Hand* ended its course on the surface of Coruscant, where Skywalker managed to safely crash-land the battered ship.

Ion Cannon

A heavy weapon that delivered devastating ionized blasts.

Ion cannons used ionic technology to produce electronic blasts that could freeze or temporarily disrupt electrical systems. It was able to neutralise the protective shields and weapon platforms of hostile buildings and ships, rendering them susceptible to attack or infiltration.

Used in planetary defences, the ion cannon was ideal for disabling large capital ships. The Rebel Alliance used a V-150 ion cannon to assist their evacuation from Echo Base on Hoth as the Imperial army attacked. Its disrupting blasts temporarily nullified the Imperial threat in orbit, allowing the fleeing rebel transports to escape.

Ion Pistol

A weapon that projected ionic energy instead of the laser blasts of the classic blasters.

The main characteristic of this kind of energy was that it could neutralise electrical systems, from droids to starships. This pistol was known to be the preferred weapon of Jawas, the scavengers from Tatooine. Ion pistols were generally old blasters reconditioned for this use. Some Ion pistols contained a restraining bolt, which locked or shut down a droid for a determined duration.

IT-0 Interrogator Droid

Secretly developed by the Imperial Department of Military Research, the IT-0 series continued the Imperial tradition of illegal devices and weapons.

These interrogation droids were equipped with repulsors to give them advanced mobility and the ability to act in a variety of ways on their victims. Spherical in shape and fitted with a sinister, eye-like red sensor, each droid was covered with syringes containing uninhibiting serums. But the most frightening and feared of their torture weapons was the mental probe, which had the ability to inflict a tremendous amount of pain without ever physically touching the victim. Only trained Jedi were able to resist the orders of an interrogation droid, however, Princess Leia Organa showed extraordinary courage and self-control when she faced an IT-0 while being interrogated by Darth Vader, who was trying to discover the location of the rebels' secret base.

IT-000 Interrogator Droid

The IT-000 interrogator droid specialised in interrogation torture methods and was developed by the First Order in violation of the laws and treaties signed with the New Republic.

Inspired by medical droids, the IT-000 was equipped with a medical telemetry transmission system, which assisted the First Order officers aboard the Star Destroyer the *Finalizer* during interrogations by communicating the physical limits of the prisoner.

Ithor

This Mid Rim planet was known for its luscious, sacred jungles and was home to the Ithorians, who were famous for their remarkable farming technology.

The exiled informant Momaw Nadon, also known as 'Hammerhead', and Old Jho, the owner of a cantina on Lothal, were two well-known Ithorians.

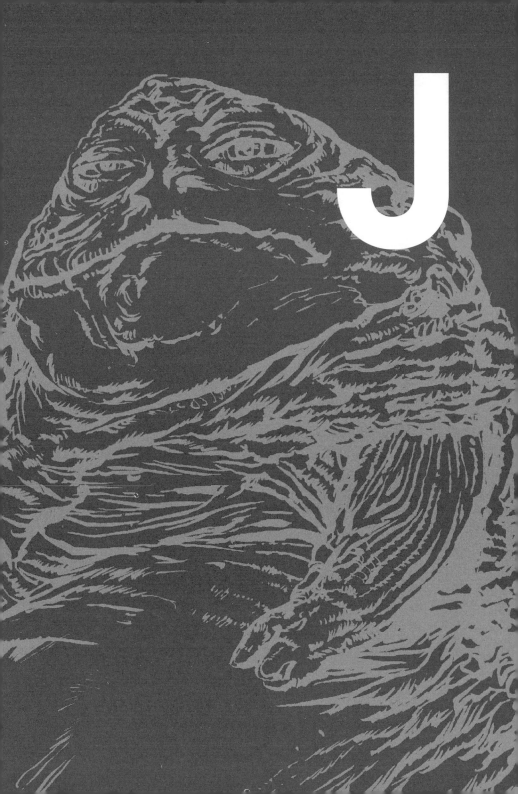

J

J-type 327 Nubian Starship

This model of craft was manufactured by the Nubian Design Collective, which used its own sublight drive and T-14 hyperdrive generator in the ship's construction.

The Naboo Royal Starship was modelled on the J-type, but its structure and interior were entirely modified by a group of engineers and local craftsmen. Its interior was therefore very different from the original J-type 327 Nubian starship.

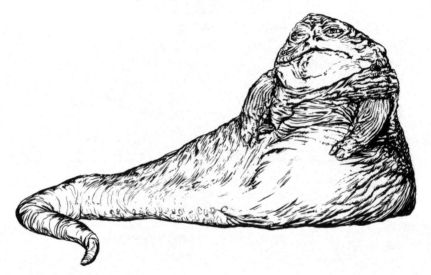

Jabba the Hutt

Jabba Desilijic Tiure, known across the galaxy as Jabba the Hutt, was an imposing crime lord based on Tatooine.

He made huge profits from a variety of criminal activities that included gambling, piracy, slavery and dealing in illegal products, such as weapons and narcotic substances. Thanks to a network of smugglers, informants, assassins and generally villainous and corrupt individuals, his influence spread far beyond the boundaries of Tatooine to encompass all of the Outer Rim Territories.

Jabba was regarded by many as an important public figure, a reputation he liked to promote, particularly at his palatial home and notably in the Mos Espa Arena where he owned the biggest private stall. This privilege was awarded to the crime lord not only because of his local stature, but more because he paid for the construction of the stalls – in order to control the concessions and the betting on the arena's many podraces.

The most famous of these podraces was the Boonta Eve Classic and the popular crime lord was present at the event that took place shortly after the invasion of Naboo, opening the spectacle to the cheer of the 100,000 spectators gathered in the arena. With little interest in the podraces themselves, he mainly dozed during the event, he therefore gave little attention to the victory of a nine-year-old slave boy named Anakin Skywalker.

Ten years after the events in Naboo, Jabba's power had increased to the point that he had become a valuable stake between the two opposing political forces of the Clone Wars, with both the Confederacy of Independent Systems and the Galactic Republic both hoping to win his good favour. Liaison with a criminal may have been the idea of Chancellor Palpatine, a Sith secretly devoted to debasing the Republic ideal from inside the system, but it was also the result of the consequences of conflict. In such a turbulent time, each party needed to find the most efficient allies, even if it meant having to lower their standards.

The Galactic Empire which emerged at the end of the Civil War was not exactly the antithesis of the Republic, but more a changed version of it, subtly altered by years and years of the Sith's manipulations. Under the new totalitarian administration, the slug-like crime lord was able to continue his illegal activities on a scale that was almost unchanged. However, one incident was to have dramatic repercussions for the Hutt. One of his best smugglers, Han Solo, lost his cargo when his vessel, the *Millennium Falcon*, was stopped for an Imperial inspection. Unable to recoup the loss for the value of the lost merchandise, Jabba assigned Greedo the bounty hunter to capture Solo, but the smuggler shot and killed his would-be capturer in the Mos Eisley Cantina. During a meeting at Docking Bay 94, Solo and Jabba agreed on a new deadline for the payment in exchange for a higher debt. However, when the news came that Solo had rallied to the side of the Rebellion, the crime lord's patience had worn thin and he put a bounty on the smuggler's head.

After the destruction of the Death Star, to which Solo contributed, the Empire was in urgent need of important resources for its machine of war and opted for a realistic solution. They went directly to the underground economy of the Hutts, who established a market in supplying raw materials direct to the Imperial regime. The crime lord benefited hugely from this arrangement, winning both the protection of the regime and assurance that the Empire would crack down on the criminal activities of his competitors.

Three years later, thanks to the efforts of Boba Fett, Darth Vader offered Jabba another gift – Han Solo frozen in carbonite. Captured during the hunt for Luke Skywalker, the frozen Corellian was put on display in Jabba's court, where he became a favourite decoration. Jabba's belief that he was untouchable was the beginning of his end. Having ignored Luke Skywalker's message conveyed by R2-D2 and C-3PO, he next unmasked Princess Leia in her disguise as Boushh and put a stop to her rescue attempt. Finally, he tried to eliminate Skywalker by pitting him against a rancor. Convinced of his power and anxious to put an end to the whole situation, Jabba then condemned Solo, Skywalker and Chewbacca to death – they were to be consumed by the Sarlacc at the Great Pit of Carkoon. This excursion was supposed to be an entertaining spectacle for the Hutt, but instead it became his last journey. After Skywalker freed himself with his lightsaber he caused chaos on the skiffs and Jabba's sail barge, the *Khetanna*. Meanwhile, Leia, the daughter of Anakin Skywalker and now herself enslaved to the crime lord, used the symbol of captivity, her slave chain, to strangle Jabba and escape.

Jabba's Palace

The operational base for the criminal activities conducted by Jabba the Hutt, this palace was located on the fringes of Tatooine's Dune Sea.

Access was strictly controlled through its one entrance, which was located at the end of a single ruined road; visitors would then be identified by an ocular droid that served as a doorman. This electronic eye moved on its axis and was built into the main door. It would cross-examine anyone who wished to enter and would then decide whether or not to let them pass.

The palace was composed of different architectural elements: the main building was round and domed and was accompanied by a smaller round building and a few towers. The structure was originally a monastery of the B'omarr Order, one of whose followers still roamed the halls and could be seen when C-3PO and R2-D2 first arrived. In order to protect Jabba's physical safety and improve his quality of life, the structure was fortified, which saw an update to both the palace's technology and its interior amenities. For instance, a throne room was created, under which there was a pit that housed a rancor. It also had prison cells to hold the crime lord's enemies and a room dedicated to the torture of droids, which was run by the unwavering 8D8 and its superior, EV-9D9. At Jabba's court, business and pleasure always mixed with a combination of good music, deals, dancers and summary executions.

Jabba's Sail Barge

A luxurious vehicle with orange sails that was manufactured by Ubrikkian Industries, Jabba the Hutt's sail barge was named the *Khetanna* by its owner.

It boasted three bridges, making it ideal for the crime lord's many pleasure trips. The second bridge included a banquet room that offered guests fantastic views of the surrounding landscape through the shutters in its hull. The shutters also protected them

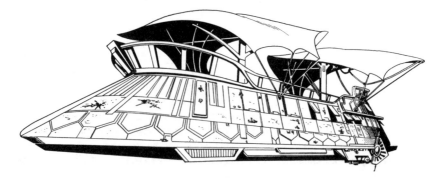

from the blinding twin suns of Tatooine, while the openings also served like arrow slits, through which Jabba's bodyguards could shoot their enemies in the event of an assault. Jabba also used his barge to transport his prisoners towards certain death in the stomach of the Sarlacc at the Great Pit of Carkoon. One such trip went wrong when Jabba attempted to execute the heroes of the Rebellion. After freeing themselves, Luke Skywalker and Princess Leia Organa set the bridge cannon to automatic mode and, after they had fled, the cannon set off a chain reaction that resulted in the sail barge violently exploding.

Jakku

This desert planet in the Outer Rim was the last base of the Galactic Empire before its fall, and it continued to bear the scars of the last battle of the Galactic Civil War for many years.

The planet's stratosphere was set on fire by the conflict, which saw many starships from both sides crash onto the planet's sandy surface. A countless number of gigantic wrecks could be seen jutting out from the planet's many dunes, particularly in the area known as the 'Starship Graveyard', where wreck-raiders were often at their happiest. Jakku welcomed a diverse population composed of peddlers, mechanics, scrap merchants, bounty hunters and droids of any kind that would work in transport, catering, or even the sale of parts collected from the war relics. The planet's commercial activity mainly took place in old outposts that could be identified by their specific porches where groups made camp and set up their stalls for trade.

Jaldine Gerams

Jaldine Gerams was a Rebel Alliance pilot who participated in the Battle of Scarif under the call sign of Blue Three.

Before getting involved in real combat, this programmer, who was around sixty years old, tirelessly immersed herself in flight simulators. The day she crossed paths with the Rebellion on her native planet of Fresia, she grabbed the opportunity to put her intensive practice to use and finally became a pilot of a real X-wing starfighter. In the first moments of the Rogue One support operation, her skills were put to the test when she managed to save herself from crashing into the closing Scarif shield gate. It was Gerams who then went on to sound the alarm when swarming TIE fighters emerged from the ring surrounding the shield.

Jalice Andit

A mercenary known for her courage, Jalice Andit was wife to Joali and lived with her husband in Jedha City.

The pair took full advantage of the permanent chaos that prevailed in the Holy City under the occupation of the Imperial army. Their passion for violence and openness to bribery saw them lend their skills to Saw Gerrera's partisans. Paid in credits for their services, they were a hired workforce as opposed to allies, more interested in Gerrera's money than in his ideals. Andit participated and helped the insurgents in the Holy City shortly before it was levelled by the Imperial superweapon known as the Death Star.

Jamillia

As elected Queen of Naboo, Jamillia was the successor of Padmé Amidala.

Conscious of the popularity of Amidala, she asked her predecessor to represent Naboo in the Galactic Senate. A strong supporter of the Republic and democracy, she defended the values of the Royal House and those of the people of Naboo. She reigned for four years and was succeeded by Queen Neeyutnee.

Jan Dodonna

Born on the planet Commenor, Jan Dodonna was a general of the Rebel Alliance and commanded the base installed in the Massassi Temple on Yavin 4.

The decisive moment in his military career was the part he played during the Battle of Yavin, when he organised the tactical assault against the first Death Star. Having carefully analysed the stolen plans of the space station, he discovered the tiny flaw in its design that offered a slim, but tangible chance of success, and made the tactical choice to use small, one-man starfighters in the attack. Dodonna understood that the space station had been designed to repel huge-scale assaults and that the Empire, certain of the terror the Death Star would instil throughout the galaxy, would never consider that a small fleet of starfighters would be foolish enough to attack a space base defended by hundreds of turbolasers. However, Dodonna's briefing just before the assault left many pilots bewildered by the fact they had to fire a torpedo into an exhaust port no more than 2 metres wide.

After the Death Star exploded, Dodonna accompanied Princess Leia as she awarded Medals of Bravery to Han Solo, Luke Skywalker and Chewbacca during a military ceremony that celebrated the historic victory of the Alliance. After supervising the evacuation of the Yavin 4 base, Dodonna gradually withdrew from the rebels' general staff.

Jango Fett

An accomplished bounty hunter and contract killer who allegedly hailed from Concord Dawn, Jango Fett accepted Darth Tyranus' offer to be the original model for a new clone army.

In addition to his payment, he asked for a non-altered clone that he would keep with him to raise as a son. For the sake of the cloning programme, Fett spent most of his time on Kamino, although he would sometimes fulfil a contract, either personally or through an acolyte, such as Zam Wesell. On Coruscant, when Wesell failed in her attempt to assassinate Senator Padmé Amidala, Fett was forced to intervene. He eliminated Wesell but left behind a Kaminoan dart, which enabled Obi-Wan Kenobi to track the bounty hunter to Kamino.

A great pilot and tactician, as well as an excellent sharpshooter, Jango Fett wore a tough, durasteel-alloy armour, a helmet with a built-in computer that enabled him to locate his targets, and a pair of blaster pistols. In the field, he regularly used a jetpack that gave him great mobility and enabled him to deploy a powerful remote-controlled missile. For his trips outside of Kamino he used his personal starship, *Slave I*.

Under contract with the Trade Federation to kill Amidala, he extended his collaboration with the Separatist movement and Count Dooku, and was present at the beginning of the Battle of Geonosis. He was responsible for shooting down Jedi Master Coleman Trebor, but was ultimately defeated by Mace Windu, who beheaded him in front of his 'son', Boba Fett.

Jar Jar Binks

General of the Gungan army and delegate to the Galactic Senate, the adventure that led Jar Jar Binks from his home on Naboo into the vast universe began with an act of courage.

Banished by the leader of his city for accidentally destroying a luxury submarine, Binks was strictly forbidden from returning to his home, but he ultimately risked his life by going against that ruling. After Jedi Master Qui-Gon Jinn rescued him from being run over by a multi-troop transport in the forest, then from the attack of droids on STAPs, Binks felt indebted to the Jedi Master. Despite the danger posed by ignoring his banishment, the Gungan led Jinn and his apprentice, Obi-Wan Kenobi to the underwater city of Otoh Gunga. Quickly intercepted by the patrol of Captain Tarpals, the travellers were taken before Boss Nass. However, the Jedi Master saved Binks from punishment by arguing that the Gungan owed him an eternal debt for saving his life, and therefore Binks was permitted to leave along with Jinn and Kenobi, in order to guide them to Naboo's capital, Theed. The impressive underwater journey aboard a bongo took them through the planet's watery core. The journey was full of terrifying encounters with the native opee sea killer and the colo claw fish.

Despite these attacks, Binks successfully guided them to Theed, only to find that the palace had already been occupied by the troops of the Trade Federation. After rescuing Queen Padmé Amidala, the Jedi decided to help her escape from the planet of Naboo. During this journey, Binks found himself face-to-face with Amidala, the monarch of a people that shared his planet, yet were unfriendly towards his species.

When the rescue ship broke down, the group unexpectedly found themselves on Tatooine. It was Jar Jar Binks' first journey out of his own world and in Mos Espa, his casual attitude almost cost him his life. He made an enemy of the vicious Dug podracer pilot, Sebulba, when he accidentally spat food at him. Anakin Skywalker, a young slave boy belonging to the scrapyard merchant, Watto, came to his aid and invited the Gungan and his companions to take shelter from an approaching sandstorm in his modest home. There, Binks glimpsed what the daily life of a slave was like, but above all, thanks to Jinn, learned to control his huge appetite.

If the Gungan considered Tatooine to be a disreputable place, he soon discovered that Coruscant was on a whole different level. The Gungan, with no taste for power and unable to grasp the concept, could not understand the world he found himself in. Following the Senate's

disappointing response to Queen Amidala's petition, Binks stood by the monarch and offered his support, understanding and counsel, and when all seemed lost, he was the spark from which the plan of liberation took place. Binks revealed the existence of the secret Grand Gungan Army.

Back on Naboo with Amidala and the Jedi, Binks noted during a scouting mission that Otoh Gunga had been completely evacuated. Unlike Captain Panaka, Binks was confident of the Gungans' survival and led the party to the sanctuary where they were hidden. There, Queen Amidala offered Boss Nass an alliance. Joined by Binks, she made the humble request on bended knee and was so full of humility that Boss Nass happily accepted her proposal and demonstrated that the bad blood between their two peoples was finally over. Nass also acknowledged Binks' important role as a peacemaker and unexpectedly rewarded him with a promotion to general. Although it was a title that probably didn't suit this particular Gungan, he nevertheless didn't hesitate to go to war, despite being terrified.

The droid troops of the Trade Federation eventually overpowered the Gungans and forced them to surrender, but Skywalker's destruction of the droid control ship handed a last-minute victory to the local forces. However, this victory was overshadowed by the death of Qui-Gon Jinn, whose empathy for others had allowed him to see the hidden qualities possessed by the clumsy Gungan, who was sometimes simple, sometimes casual, sometimes irritating, but also always without pretension or hate.

The pride of the Gungan people, Binks was the first of his species to become a representative in the Naboo delegation at the Senate. He was exemplary in the position, which even saw him, ten years after the crisis of Naboo, temporarily replace Senator Amidala, who had gone into hiding after several attempts were made on her life. In a cynical ploy, politicians encouraged him to believe that she would have been favourable to the formation of an army to counter the Separatist threat. Confident in Palpatine as a fellow native of Naboo, Binks suggested to the Senate that it give the Chancellor the full power necessary to create a Grand Army of the Republic. The Gungan's motion was adopted and it opened the way, after the Battle of Geonosis, for the Clone Wars. However, it was an act for which he could not be held personally responsible. The Sith's plan was so well conceived that if it had not been Binks who was manipulated, it would have been another.

Blind to a plot that no one had guessed and shocked by the turn of events, Binks was present at the funeral ceremony of his friend, Padmé – a considerate woman who had helped him achieve his ambition to live in the world, instead of leading the life of an unwanted outcast.

Jashco Phurus

A Tricorraan pirate famous in the Arrowhead region to the east of Coruscant, Jashco Phurus was a regular among the diverse clientele at Maz's Castle on Takodana.

Phurus could sometimes be seen talking with the ME-8D9 droid to get the latest information and, like every other customer, he was always vigilant and attentive to unusual events. He generally wore a traditional Tricorraan raider robes and seldom let his field-accelerated blaster rifle leave his side. While on Takodana, he witnessed the First Order's Starkiller Base attack against the New Republic.

Jav Mefran

This soldier of the Special Forces 4th Regiment of the Alliance was a member of the Rogue One mission to Scarif.

Identifiable by his imposing dark beard, this experienced adventurer's favourite environment was the jungle. When the Alliance chose Yavin 4 as its new base, he was one of the men in charge of the deforestation of the surrounding area and secured the Massassi Great Temple.

A specialist in combat in hostile environments, he was convinced by Jyn Erso's speech and declared his fidelity to the daring mission. Assigned to the protection of the SW-0608 shuttle along with other rangers and Corporal Stordan Tonc, he hid when the latter warned that hostile troops had begun to invade the zone, but before long confrontation became unavoidable. Along with his comrades, he gave the former Imperial pilot Bodhi Rook time to establish a communication link with Admiral Raddus, before being shot just seconds before Rook was killed when their shuttle exploded. For a soldier who had such a true affinity with the tropical climate, it was a fitting final resting place.

Jawa

A nomadic people from the planet of Tatooine, the origin and nature of the Jawas was always the subject of vast speculation.

Some believed that they were a species of rodent that had evolved and had huge technological capabilities, while others thought they were devolved humans. Whatever the answer, they were dangerous wreck-raiders, always hunting for the tiniest scrap or manufactured spare part. They travelled the desert and lived in huge vehicles known as sandcrawlers, which also served as their business premises. Although their body size was variable, the majority of them were no more than 1 metre tall, and all Jawas wore a large, hooded gown, which drew attention to their luminescent eyes.

Jawas were sometimes seen as helpful, their cleaning, scavenging and recycling restoring Tatooine's ecosystem to what it once was thousands of years ago. However, there were many more testimonies from unhappy customers of the Jawas', who often accused them of selling faulty droids or equipment that had been repaired well enough to work just long enough to allow the Jawas to sell their goods, collect their money and retreat.

Jawas were also fond of podraces – particularly the accidents that often occurred during them. They never hesitated to take tremendous risks to be the first to arrive at the still-steaming wreckage to recover as many spare parts as possible. Although they only lived on Tatooine, the Jawas were very popular throughout the whole galaxy and it was not uncommon to find them in bars, enjoying the famous Jawa juice.

Shortly before the Battle of Yavin, a tribe of Jawas recovered C-3PO and R2-D2, the two droids sought by the Galactic Empire. They proceeded to sell them to Owen Lars, but were killed shortly after by the Imperial patrols tracking the droids.

Jawa Juice

Jawa juice was the nickname given to Ardees, a very popular drink on Tatooine made from squashed bantha hide and fermented grains, which, apparently, the Jawas had a hand in creating.

Served in the cantinas, it had a distinctive sandy colour and was popular among the pilots and passing travellers. But its popularity didn't end on Tatooine, it was also possible to find it in the diners on Coruscant. Obi-Wan Kenobi was offered Jawa juice by a droid waitress at Dex's Diner, a popular establishment that belonged to Kenobi's old friend and informant Dexter Jettster.

Jawa Sandcrawler

Huge mobile fortresses that were around 40 metres long and used by the Jawa tribes on the planet of Tatooine.

The sandcrawlers served as both houses and workshops for the hooded Jawas. They travelled through Tatooine's deserts looking for droids and space debris. After a day's scavenging, they would often stop at moisture farms to sell their often mediocre cargo. R2-D2 and C-3PO spent some time aboard one of the sandcrawlers before they were sold to Owen Lars.

Jedha

Part of the Jedha system in the Mid Rim, this desert moon orbited the planet of NaJedha.

On the surface, its landscapes offered dunes as far as the eye could see, as well as large, eroded, rocky formations and mesas on which cities, such as Jedha City, were built. In addition, the ground was notably rich in kyber crystal deposits, which were used in the construction of both Jedi and Sith lightsabers. This old moon was the cradle of one of the first civilisations to explore the nature of the Force, to the point that some historians concluded that it had given its name to the Jedi Order. Others believed the opposite, but all agreed that the two were deeply bound.

Many other movements, schools of thought and religions also considered Jedha to be holy ground, and went there on pilgrimage or to officially establish themselves. The Disciples and the Guardians of the Whills; the Confraternity of the Beatific Countenance; the Clan of the Toribota; the Phirmists and the Church of the Force were just some of the names on the long list of those who had crossed the galaxy to find the truths buried in the moon's sand.

Steeped in history, some primitive structures stood out, such as the Catacombs of Cadera. This place, shortly occupied before the Battle of Yavin by the partisans of Saw Gerrera, reflected the increased resistance to the Imperial occupation, which had grown following the plundering of kyber crystal resources for a secret Imperial project. It was once that same project had finally taken shape as a combat space station that Grand Moff Tarkin decided to conduct a test. Director Orson Krennic wanted to use the Death Star at full power to destroy all of Jedha, but his superior preferred to 'just' annihilate the Holy City. The Imperial regime hid this destruction from the Senate and the rest of the galaxy, pretending instead that a gigantic mining disaster had caused the atrocity. However, days later, fighting on the beaches during the Battle of Scarif, 'For Jedha!' could be heard as the battle cry of some rebel soldiers.

Jedha City

The ancient Holy City, also known as NiJedha in the old texts, was located on the desert moon of Jedha in the Mid Rim.

Constructed on a rocky mesa and surrounded by high ramparts, it majestically overhung the surrounding landscape despite the Imperial occupation, which was symbolised by the presence of the Star Destroyer the *Dauntless*. In the architectural landscape of the Holy City, known for its numerous religious buildings, one was more visible than the others. The Temple of the Kyber, also known as the Temple of the Whills, was where the congregation of the Church of the Force gathered. Other religious places, including the immense Dome of Deliverance, the Holy Quarter and the Path of the Judgments also distinguished themselves. Because of its mystical treasures, the streets of Jedha City were constantly full of priests, pilgrims and other religious historians, who were not put off by the presence of the Empire.

Transportation to and from the Holy City remained a lucrative business, with only authorised space pilots allowed to reach the docks of the mesa. Deprived of its Jedi past, swarming with Saw Gerrera's partisans and robbed of its kyber crystals, NiJedha appeared to be living on borrowed time under Palpatine's regime. The Empire, intolerant of any display of spirituality judged to be too near the faith of the former Jedi Order, considered this knot of religions and insurgents problematic. The decision was reached to give the particular problem of Jedha City a definitive solution, and so the apocalyptic Death Star pulverised the city and its inhabitants.

Jedi Archives

The library of information collected by the Jedi Masters over many lifetimes.

Housed in a safe place inside the Jedi Temple on Coruscant, the archives were arguably the richest and most complete source of information about the whole galaxy. Jedi investigators and searchers constantly used the archives during their missions. As well as data records and holobooks, it housed the holocrons containing sensitive information, safely kept in a stronghold only accessible to the Jedi. The Jedi Archives were considered so complete that, when Obi-Wan Kenobi asked about the planet Kamino, Jocasta Nu, the chief librarian, told him that if that world wasn't mentioned in the Jedi Archives, it didn't exist.

Jedi High Council

The executive council of the Jedi Order was composed of twelve Jedi Masters, one of whom was designated as Grand Master – a position that was held by Yoda during the last decades of the Galactic Republic.

This experienced assembly, housed in the Jedi Temple on Coruscant, once sat in the council room located in the south-west tower of the building, but were relocated to the central tower at the end of the Clone Wars. While the High Council's area of expertise was everything related to the Jedi, it also worked closely with another ministerial organisation in the Galactic Republic, such as the office of the Supreme Chancellor. Of course, when it came to working with a democratically elected representative, the council of a religious order could only offer its opinions or contribute in an advisory capacity.

The first sign of Chancellor Palpatine's hostility towards the Jedi Order could be detected when he destroyed the balance between the two institutions by promoting Anakin Skywalker to the High Council as his personal representative. It was an unprecedented appointment, but the council accepted it, and the young Jedi Knight became a spy for the intrusive politician.

Jedi Knight

A member of the Jedi Order elevated to a higher ranking by the High Council of the Jedi.

A Jedi could become a Jedi Knight after his or her training as a Padawan, and when they had successfully passed the nine Jedi tests. Once ordained, a Jedi Knight was no longer attached to their master and became independent, in charge of his or her own destiny. While many Jedi reached the rank of Jedi Master, and oversaw peace and justice within the Republic, it wasn't an automatic promotion. When the threat of the Sith arose at the start of the Clone Wars, Jedi Knights became generals and commanded the troops of the Republic army against the Confederacy of Independent Systems.

When Supreme Chancellor Palpatine, who was secretly the Sith Lord Darth Sidious, commanded the execution of Order 66, the Jedi Knights were betrayed and condemned as traitors, along with the rest of the Order. With the subsequent rise of the Galactic Empire, Jedi Knights became taboo, an almost entirely extinct part of society. Nevertheless, the symbolic power of the Jedi Knights was strong and despite the Imperial propaganda that sought to eradicate them from history, their legacy endured, demanding respect decades after their eradication. Their memory lived on in pockets of the population, particularly among those who had suffered under the rule of the Empire. At the end of the Galactic Civil War, Luke Skywalker was the last known Jedi Knight, and the former farm boy from Tatooine set out on a mission to resurrect the Order with complicated results.

Jedi Mind Trick

In this manipulation, an adept of the Force was able to influence somebody else's mind in order to make him or her act according to their wishes.

It was generally accompanied by a calm, but firm tone of voice and a hand gesture in front of the face of the manipulated. Used for various purposes, the trick could target one isolated victim or temporarily put a group of people to sleep. In Mos Eisley, Obi-Wan Kenobi managed to influence a patrolling stormtrooper officer without alerting the soldiers that accompanied him. The weaker the mind of the target, the better chance of success. However, some species were notably resistant to Jedi mind tricks and some were totally immune to them, like the Toydarians and the Hutts, as Qui-Gon Jinn and Luke Skywalker discovered when they respectively faced Watto and Jabba.

Jedi Order

This monastic society that gathered around the belief of a caring and selfless use of the Force appeared about 5,000 years before the rise of the Galactic Empire.

Under the governance of the Jedi High Council, members of this community displayed a political diplomacy devoted to the exercise of peace and justice during the entire era of the Galactic Republic. Previously, several thousands of years before the events of the Galactic Civil War, they had faced the Sith Order, the ultimate nemesis of the Jedi Order, whose members were skilled in the dark side of the Force. However, the Jedi won the fight and they became the devoted guardians of freedom and justice during the 1,000-year reign of the Galactic Senate, but, thirty years before the Battle of Yavin, the Sith Order reappeared in the form of Senator Palpatine.

Every action a Jedi performed had to be accomplished using humility, discipline and responsibility, which were the pillars of the Jedi Code. The course of progression and promotion within the Order followed four compulsory steps: the initiate, Padawan, Jedi Knight and, finally, Jedi Master. Children who were identified as being Force-sensitive were, shortly after their birth, transferred to the Jedi Temple where they became part of a communal group that learned about the ways of the Jedi, including kyber crystals, which they eventually used to build their own lightsabers. Those who wished to pursue their learning were then eligible for the position of Padawan and they became an apprentice under the responsibility of a Jedi Master. As a Jedi Master could only teach one Padawan at a time, this was an important stage and the correct pairing was vital.

At the end of this stage, the length of which could vary, the apprentice had to perform nine trials whose objectives were solidarity, isolation, fear, anger, treason, concentration, instinct, forgiveness and protection. If the Padawan passed all of the trials, the Council promoted the apprentice to become a Jedi Knight. The last phase was the ascension to the rank of Jedi Master, which only happened when a Jedi Knight had shown an exceptional capacity for teaching and developing their Padawans. Among the Jedi Masters, twelve were chosen to sit on the Jedi High Council and one of the twelve was promoted to the rank of Grand Master.

The main Temple of the Order was on Coruscant. The building was surmounted by five towers and acted as a religious complex, as well as an academy. Above all, it housed the numerous Jedi Archives, which were the most complete and precise in the galaxy. After the fall of the Republic, the temple was partially destroyed and Palpatine decided to install the Imperial Palace in its place. Having slaughtered nearly every Jedi, he also wished to humiliate them and his ultimate goal was to wipe out even the past existence of the Jedi Order.

Legend has it that in the beginning, a small circle of Force adepts gathered to preserve, develop and to be in charge of the beliefs that led to the ways of the Jedi. Together, they discovered the special power contained in kyber crystals that gave energy to the lightsaber. As the Jedi began to spread throughout the galaxy, one of them, shy and unpredictable, discovered new possibilities in the use of the Force by studying its dark side.

He opened a breach that was far beyond his control and having seen for himself the great power of the Force, he judged that the restrictions the Jedi imposed on its use were intolerable. He accused them of using the Force in a passive way, which restricted its potential power, and he thought that the Jedi had invented a code and discipline that actually concealed their fear of the almighty power the Force could offer. He soon formed a band of adepts who shared his fascination for what he called the true power of the Force and a short time later, the Sith Order was founded. Sith had a lust for power and they were fundamentally opposed to the Jedi, which led both sides to war.

The Jedi Order were eventually victorious because the Sith tore themselves apart with power struggles and infighting. The last surviving Sith, Darth Bane, created the Rule of Two, which worked on the principle that there could not be more than two Sith in existence at any one time – the master and the apprentice. When Bane died, the Jedi falsely believed that the Sith Order was finished.

At the end of this period, the Old Republic was replaced by the Galactic Republic, which was this time solidly anchored on a peaceful democracy and an institutional stability in which the Jedi helped to maintain law and order through non-military means. The Galactic Senate was created – presided over by a Supreme Chancellor – and there were no major conflicts for about 1,000 years.

Although the Republic was still all-encompassing, tensions began to rise in both the Senate and the Jedi High Council. Among them, a Jedi Master named Sifo-Dyas wished to furnish the Republic with an army that would be able to face a large-scale conflict that he foresaw in the near future. The Council absolutely rejected the proposition, but Sifo-Dyas managed to achieve his wish without their knowledge. He ordered an army of clones from the Kaminoans under the pretence that it was a demand from the Senate. On the other hand, he ignored that the Sith were preparing to return and that their first act would be to take care of their historical enemies, the Jedi.

The Jedi pursued their missions, not knowing that a gigantic plot was secretly afoot. It was about thirty years before the Battle of Yavin, during a diplomatic visit between the Trade Federation and the dignitaries of Naboo, that the Sith Order chose to show its face once more. The whole situation was a trap, with the negotiations having been initiated by Senator Palpatine of Naboo – the public identity of Darth Sidious. The two Jedi that had been dispatched on the diplomatic mission, Qui-Gon Jinn and Obi-Wan Kenobi, went on to Tatooine to provide protection to the Queen of Naboo, Padmé Amidala. There they encountered the young Anakin Skywalker, who Jinn believed was the Chosen One of the prophecy that proclaimed a Jedi would bring balance to the Force. Jinn survived the surprise attack by the mysterious Darth Maul and he subsequently reported his discovery to the Jedi Council, which was answered with scepticism. This news, associated with the discovery of Skywalker, generated some unrest in the balance of the Force and the Council refused Jinn's wish to take the young boy as a Padawan. It was only after the death of Jinn that the Council entrusted Kenobi with the training of young Skywalker, despite Grand Master Yoda's obvious reluctance.

The plan of Darth Sidious then entered its second phase with the involvement of Count Dooku. Dooku, now the apprentice of Sidious following the apparent death of Maul, became the incarnation of the opposition in the Republic. Over the next eight years, he lit the fires of unrest and attempted to convince the leaders of numerous systems to escape the control of the stifling Republic administration. He was mostly successful in these attempts and naturally took leadership of the Confederacy of Independent Systems. The Jedi didn't have the numbers to support a Republic so broken up and divided, so the Senate debated trying to find some additional means to protect itself from the Separatist threat. Sometime later, Kenobi discovered an army of clones was about to be delivered to the Republic. He announced his discoveries to the Jedi Council, which, although hesitant, welcomed the news.

The intervention of the Separatists' droid army drove the Senate, with the Jedi Council's approval, to deploy the clone army. Just as Palpatine had foreseen, all the factors that led to the first historic confrontation of the Clone Wars were in place. A group of Jedi, led by Jedi Master Mace Windu, accompanied by a detachment of clone troopers, led by Yoda, fought the Separatist army during the Battle of Geonosis, which ultimately opened the door to conflict on a galactic scale and therefore put an end to a millennia of peace.

In order to meet the demands of war, the Jedi Council was forced to reorganise its forces and the Jedi Masters and Knights became generals of the Republic's army, in which they commanded their Padawans. The war, which lasted for three years, held many important victories for the Jedi, but a lot of them were killed while others joined the dark side. The war ended shortly after the deaths of Count Dooku and General Grievous during the battles of Coruscant and Utapau respectively.

Meanwhile, the importance of Anakin Skywalker grew as his mastery of the Force increased. In turmoil over personal conflicts, he allowed himself to be manoeuvred towards the dark side by Palpatine. Skywalker had secretly married Padmé Amidala, against the Jedi Code. In order to save his wife from what he believed was imminent death, Skywalker renounced the Jedi and became the Sith Lord, Darth Vader. Under the name of Darth Vader, the former Jedi hoped to save Amidala, using the unlimited powers of the Sith, which Darth Sidious (Palpatine) had promised him access to.

And so Palpatine began the last phase of his elaborate plot to bring about the combined fall of the Republic and the Jedi Order. He declared that the Jedi were henceforth enemies of the Republic and gave Darth Vader the mission to kill all Jedi present in the Jedi Temple: Knights, Padawans, everyone. Having completed his mission, Vader then travelled to Mustafar where he eliminated the Separatist Council, who had been mere puppets in Palpatine's ascension to power.

Palpatine then issued Order 66 and in mere minutes, thousands of Jedi across the galaxy were killed by their own clone troopers. Kenobi, who had just left Vader for dead following their duel on Mustafar, was one of the survivors of the Order. The Jedi Knight had been entrusted with the safety of Skywalker and Amidala's children, and as such he delivered their daughter, Leia, to Bail Organa on Alderaan and their son, Luke, to Owen Lars on Tatooine. Yoda, who had fled to Dagobah, believed that in due time, these two children, sensitive to the Force, could be the future of the Jedi Order.

Nevertheless, the Jedi were extinct. Rare survivors were hunted down and all temples destroyed, but it was not sufficient for the Sith who wanted to completely eradicate the culture surrounding the Order and its history. As a result, Palpatine forbid any mention of the Jedi in any educational facilities. This brutal dictation turned the Jedi into the stuff of myth and legend, and over the next twenty years they became nothing more than stories.

It was on the planet of Lothal, about fifteen years after the fall of the Republic, where the first spark of hope for a renewed Jedi Order quivered. Kanan Jarrus, a former Padawan who had survived the Jedi cull, was sent to Lothal under the recommendation of Ahsoka Tano. Although Tano had kept her distance from the Jedi Council, she was still very active in the fight against the Empire and had coordinated the birth of a rebellion with the royal family Organa of Alderaan. On Lothal, Jarrus met Ezra Bridger, a young boy who was sensitive to the Force, whom he began to train in the ways of the Jedi. A network of rebels led by Organa and Tano united the scattered cells of the Jedi and the resistance, and they created the Rebel Alliance.

Some years later, Kenobi emerged from his exile to help the Rebellion recover the plans of the Death Star. It was a mission that provided him with the opportunity to offer the young Luke Skywalker his first training in the ways of the Jedi. Over the years, Kenobi had become certain that only Skywalker could become a Jedi powerful enough to destroy Vader and the Emperor. The young Skywalker then destroyed the Imperial space station, the Death Star, using an intuition that could have only been accessed by someone who had a powerful connection with the Force.

It was the exiled Yoda himself who continued young Skywalker's training, which eventually helped the young Jedi to destroy the Emperor and find redemption for his father who died to save him. The return of the Jedi, Anakin Skywalker, fulfilled the prophecy that had foretold he would one day bring balance to the Force. Before his death, Yoda entrusted young Skywalker with the responsibility of being the last Jedi of the galaxy and instructed that he must pass on everything he had learned to continue the Jedi Order.

Skywalker concentrated on this task after the Battle of Jakku and the subsequent fall of the Empire that followed. He began to train a new generation of Jedi, including his nephew Ben Solo, the son of Han Solo and Leia. Ben was a promising apprentice, but had developed a fascination with his grandfather and had been influenced by the mysterious Snoke, driving him towards the dark side. Henceforth named Kylo Ren, Ben slaughtered all of Skywalker's apprentices and joined the First Order, while Skywalker became a Jedi Master in exile.

Jedi Temple (Coruscant)

The headquarters of the Jedi Order under the Galactic Republic, the building itself was a massive rectangular, stepped tower, which sprang from one of the most elevated levels in the federal district of the city-planet.

It could be identified by what looked like a crown composed of five towers positioned on its top. Simple visitors had to make the symbolic climb up an immense staircase before they could rest their eyes on the huge pillars and statues that represented the four founders of the temple. In the majestic Grand Hall, the architectural design respected the size and nobility of the Jedi Order, but it also served as a practical operations base. Therefore dignitaries who arrived by air landed on platforms that were constructed on the thick walls of the building, and when leaving for missions the Jedi departed the temple's hangars from the same platforms.

The temple also housed a medical centre, analysis laboratories, dormitories and apartments, as it was also the place of residence for the Order. Meanwhile, interior courtyards and gardens were spaces for silence and peaceful meditation. Part monastery, part school, the construction housed the facilities necessary for the acquirement and mastery of knowledge. The Jedi Archives were the most complete information source in the galaxy and were stored electronically and holographically; scientists and researchers, Padawans and Knights, all used the data to study or prepare for their missions. The holocrons, which contained the teachings of the most famous and powerful Jedi Masters, were securely stored in a special section of the Archives. Offering multiple activities, the temple was the centre of the spiritual Jedi presence in the galaxy.

One of the temple's towers played host to the Jedi High Council, which would gather there to debate interesting and important questions. After the Jedi took command of the Great Army of the Republic, the whole conduct of the Clone Wars was discussed there. At the end of the conflict, Darth Sidious sent Darth Vader to the temple with the order to kill all the Jedi he found. Consequently the building was damaged and the Order destroyed. Sidious, having proclaimed himself Emperor, converted the defunct temple into the Imperial Palace some years later.

Jedi Testing Screen

This device was used by the Jedi Council to measure the abilities of an apprentice test subject.

The all-purpose screen displayed images mentally projected by a Jedi user: if the test subject was truly attuned to the Force they would be able to 'see' the hidden picture. Mace Windu used this process to test Anakin Skywalker in front of the Jedi Council. It confirmed that the Force was indeed strong in the boy who Qui-Gon Jinn claimed could be the Chosen One. Although the Council concluded that Anakin was too old to begin training, Windu decided that his future would still be considered after the resolution of the Sith mystery.

Jedi Training Remote

A technological device that was halfway between a drone and a droid, this equipment was used by the Jedi Order as a virtual sparring partner for Jedi Apprentices and Padawans.

These little spheres delivered electrical blasts that varied in intensity, frequency and power. The user had to parry them with his or her lightsaber. They could also be programmed to emit lethal blasts, which turned them into armed combat drones. The first Jedi lesson given by Obi-Wan Kenobi to the apprentice Luke Skywalker concerned this exercise in dexterity and intuition. The old Jedi Master asked Skywalker to parry the blasts while wearing a helmet with its opaque visor down, which completely blinded him.

Jek Porkins

Jek Porkins became a celebrated Rebel Alliance pilot after taking part in the Battle of Yavin.

A native of the planet Bestine IV, Porkins joined the rebels when his homeworld was brutally annexed by the Galactic Empire. As part of Red Squadron he participated in the assault on the Death Star under the call sign of Red Six. Porkins was shot and killed by a defence turbolaser, but thirty years later he gained immortality through a piloting manoeuvre the Resistance named in his honour – the Porkins Belly Run.

Jessika Pava

This strong-willed young woman was a Resistance X-wing starfighter pilot in Poe Dameron's squadron.

She passionately believed in the actions carried out by General Leia Organa against the First Order's forces and joined the Resistance on planet D'Qar as a pilot, where she rapidly proved her valour. As operational pilots inside the Resistance were scarce, Pava took part in all missions including the assault on the First Order's Starkiller Base under the command of Dameron. She wore the standard issue orange jumpsuit of the Resistance pilots, complete with a FreiTek breathing unit and Guidenhauser flight harness, and her flight helmet bore the emblem of the Tierfon Yellow Aces, whom she greatly admired.

Jimmon Arbmab

This first sergeant, designation HC-4120, commanded an Imperial tank used for the transportation of kyber crystal cargoes around the occupied Jedha City.

His first misfortune was to see his vehicle fall prey to one of the ambushes launched by Saw Gerrera's partisans in Tythoni Square. His second misfortune, which proved to be fatal, was to find himself in front of Captain Cassian Andor, rebel intelligence officer, who happened to be equipped with an A280-CFE blaster. Needless to say, Andor's shooting was as fast as it was precise.

Jira

An elderly, white-haired, green-eyed woman with tanned skin, Jira ran a modest booth at the Mos Espa marketplace in order to survive.

She was a good friend of the nine-year-old Anakin Skywalker and while he and Qui-Gon Jinn were sampling the pallie fruits she sold, Jira warned Skywalker of the imminent sandstorm, and advised him to take refuge at home.

Joh Yowza

A Yuzzum native to Endor, Joh Yowza was a singer with the Max Rebo Band.

He performed a duet with Sy Snootles, during the band's performance at Jabba the Hutt's Palace on Tatooine.

John D. Branon

A Rebel Alliance pilot who took part in the Battle of Yavin, John D. Branon participated in the assault against the Death Star under the call sign of Red Four.

He was one of the first rebel pilots to be shot down by the TIE fighters dispatched to defend the Imperial space station.

Jon 'Dutch' Vander

Born on the planet Onderon, Jon Vander was a Rebel Alliance pilot who took part in the Battle of Scarif and the Battle of Yavin as part of Gold Squadron.

Under the call sign Gold Leader, Vander led the group of Y-wings during the assault on the Death Star's equatorial trench. During General Dodonna's briefing, Vander was the first to express his doubts about the chances of the mission's success. Unfortunately, he never got to see Luke Skywalker make the successful shot that began the destruction of the Imperial space station, as he was destroyed by Darth Vader and his elite escort.

Jyn Erso

As a young rebel, Jyn Erso fought alongside Saw Gerrera, then later became a vital asset to the Rebel Alliance when she stole the plans to the Imperial superweapon, the Death Star, which had been designed by her scientist father.

The daughter of Galen Erso, Jyn was born in captivity on the planet Vallt during the Clone Wars. Her parents were being kept prisoner because Galen, a pacifist scientist, didn't want to work for either political regime. All three were liberated when Galen's old friend, Orson Krennic, arranged a prisoner exchange with the Confederacy of Independent Systems. The very young Jyn then spent some months on Coruscant before her father's new employer sent them to Lokori. There, they experienced the trauma of almost being killed by B1 battle droids during the last minutes of the Clone Wars. When the conflict finished and the Republic had given way to the Empire, Galen accepted Krennic's proposition of working for the new regime, trying to develop a source of renewable energy.

Concentrating on his research, Galen neglected his daughter, who he nicknamed 'Stardust', before she was finally sent to join her mother, Lyra, who had been assigned on a six-month archaeological mission on Alpinn. When the Ersos discovered that Galen's work on the dynamics of kyber crystals was to be put to military use, they fled Coruscant with the help of the rebel Saw Gerrera. Gerrera transported them to Lah'mu, a planet where they would be able to hide, and it was during this journey that the four-year-old Jyn and the Onderonian rebel first developed a bond. The next four years were spent in the wild landscapes of Lah'mu where Galen became a farmer.

Krennic and his death troopers finally discovered the family's whereabouts and landed on the planet. Galen went to meet Krennic to give Lyra and Jyn time to reach their hiding place, but after giving her daughter a small kyber crystal pendant, Lyra returned for her husband. Jyn lost both parents – her father who was escorted away – and her mother, who was shot down and killed by one of the elite soldiers on Krennic's order. Hidden, Jyn waited for rescue, which eventually came in the shape of the friendly giant of Saw Gerrera.

For eight years, Gerrera educated Jyn as if she was his own daughter in the field he knew best – warfare. As a child-soldier in his militia, she went through armed combat and faced many difficulties that a child should never experience. Even though Gerrera saved her from the hardest atrocities he committed in his 'over-resistance' to the Empire, in Jyn's eyes he committed the most incomprehensible act of all against her. Having given his ward a blaster and the order to hide until morning, when the sun rose the next day the teenager discovered that her second father had abandoned her. Her trust betrayed, and believing that she could rely on no one but herself, Jyn's next few years were spent driven by the urge to survive, while she raged against the inanity of the rebel cause.

On her own, she embraced a delinquent career that consisted of forgery, smuggling and spending time with criminals. Anxious to forget a life of grief, she got lost in false identities. At twenty-one years old, her police record mainly consisted of the possession of non-authorised weapons, forgery of Imperial documents and armed aggression against soldiers of the Empire. While on a ship under the name of Liana Hallik, she was captured and transferred to the work camp on Wobani to serve a twenty-year sentence.

After six months of imprisonment, Jyn was being transported by turbo tank when she was surprised to find herself the object of a rescue mission. Extremely mistrustful, she stunned Sergeant Ruescott Melshi and two other rebels before rushing outside to be stopped in her tracks by the droid K-2SO. Handcuffed and taken to Yavin 4, she appeared before General Davits Draven, Mon Mothma and intelligence officer Captain Cassian Andor, who were particularly interested in her. The Rebellion asked her to make contact with Gerrera on Jedha, as he had detained an Imperial deserter who alleged that he had been sent by Galen Erso to warn of the existence of a 'planet killer' starship. With no other choice and shaken by the mention of her long-lost father, she took off with Andor and K-2SO. Despite the rather icy atmosphere between them, in a demonstration of trust, the intelligence officer allowed Jyn to continue carrying the gun she had stolen.

Having left their ship and droid outside, upon entering Jedha's Holy City the two agents began the search for a trail to Gerrera's militia. Among the crowd, Jyn was disturbed by a blind man who sensed the kyber crystal around her neck. Andor quickly dragged her aside, where they noticed an Imperial tank under escort and also detected the first signs of an ambush. At that moment the confrontation between the soldiers and the insurgents exploded and Jyn noticed a young girl, Pendra Siliu, caught in the crossfire. Courageously, she saved the child and handed her to her mother, but the situation around them had deteriorated and Andor was forced to kill a partisan who, upon falling, triggered his explosive charge.

During the commotion that was taking place around them, the two rebels – with some assistance from K-2SO who had abandoned his post by the U-wing – eliminated several stormtroopers. The three of them were about to be captured by another squad of soldiers when Chirrut Îmwe, the blind warrior-monk who had previously spoken to Jyn, and his companion Baze Malbus, came to their rescue. K-2SO was sent back to the ship and the four fighters were left surrounded by Gerrera's men. Upon revealing her true identity, Jyn and her comrades were taken to the rebel chief's den.

Andor, Malbus and Îmwe were thrown into a cell, while Jyn was taken to Gerrera. The discussion that ensued between the two friends was a difficult one, full of resentment on Jyn's part and paranoia on Gerrera's, who justified his past actions by highlighting the danger that her status as the child of an Imperial scientist had represented for him. Unmoved, Jyn coldly explained her current role as a simple go-between, uninterested in any politics. Reassured for himself, but dismayed by her dismissal of the rebel cause, Gerrera played her the contents of her father's hologram, in which Galen expressed his love for his daughter, the despair of living his life in the employ of a system he hated and the sabotage he had carried out at the very heart of the Death Star.

It was at that very moment that the Death Star launched its terrible assault on the desert moon and turned its superlaser on Jedha City. Under its destructive beam, the ancient Catacombs of Cadera began to shake and only the interruption of Andor, having escaped from his cell, shook Jyn from her reverie and returned her to the urgent reality. Forced to abandon Gerrera when he refused to leave, Jyn and her comrades staged a last-minute escape aboard the U-wing piloted by K-2SO, also taking with them the Imperial deserter, Bodhi Rook.

During their journey to Eadu, where Galen was located, Jyn relayed the information contained in the hologram. Faced with scepticism and unable to provide proof of her tale, she was consumed by anger when no one believed her. After a rough landing, Andor left to go on reconnaissance with Bodhi, and it was only Chirrut's intuition and K-2SO's frankness about the sniper mode of his master's weapon that alerted Jyn to the real objective of Andor's mission – to assassinate her father. While trying to catch up with Andor, Erso deviated from her path and instead ended up next to a platform on which her father was standing. Severely wounded during a sudden rebel bombardment, Galen only had time to share a few words with Jyn before he died in her arms.

Shocked by this latest loss, Erso confronted Andor over his lies, but was unable to listen to any arguments the intelligence officer tried to make in his defence, especially not the fact that he hadn't pulled the trigger on his target as he had been ordered to do. Back on Yavin 4, Jyn felt the heavy weight of her mission to carry through her father's plans and do everything necessary to achieve the sabotage for which he had given his life. However, her conviction was not shared by the Alliance Cabinet, who unanimously ruled against further action.

Disheartened, Jyn was therefore surprised to discover that she had the support of Andor, who had gathered together a band of rebel soldiers determined to support her on her mission. Having stolen, destroyed and killed for the Rebellion's cause, if there was any chance that they could recover the secret plans from the Citadel Tower at Scarif, they were willing to take it. The crew hastily named their unauthorised mission 'Rogue One' and took off aboard a stolen Imperial shuttle with a course set for the tropical world of Scarif. Promoted to the rank of sergeant by Lieutenant Taidu Sefla, Jyn addressed the men regarding the mission, while Andor reminded them of the strategy they would follow.

Upon landing, Jyn, along with K-2SO and Andor, infiltrated the base disguised in the stolen uniforms of an inspection team. The tactical diversion, created by the remainder of the rebel soldiers, drew the attention of the majority of the base's garrison, which allowed the trio to reach the secure vault where the plans they were looking for were stored. Leaving the droid outside the vault so that it could guide them through the console, Jyn gave K-2SO her blaster so that he could defend himself if necessary. Once inside, the young rebel focused the search on the Structural Engineering section following K-2SO's advice, and having reviewed many enigmatic filenames she eventually discovered one titled 'Stardust', which she instinctively knew her father had left there as a personal message.

Unfortunately, before Andor could use the electronic system to retrieve the file, K-2SO was unmasked as an impostor and had to sacrifice himself in order to save them. He locked them in the vault and destroyed the console, delaying the Imperial troops. Without power, Jyn and Andor began climbing the databank wall in order to retrieve the file by hand, but came under fire from Director Krennic and two death troopers who had accessed the vault via an auxiliary door. Covered by her partner, Jyn managed to reach the roof of the Citadel Tower, but Andor fell after being shot by Krennic.

Her first attempt at broadcasting the plans was aborted because of poorly aligned transmission equipment and the aerial attack from a TIE striker. Then, before she could try again, Jyn came face-to-face with Krennic, who demanded to know her identity. In response, Jyn proudly declared that she was Galen and Lyra's daughter and that her father had sabotaged the object of his pride, as she had just revealed to the whole galaxy. Unmoved, Krennic remained confident of his victory, convinced that this was a lie and that the planet's shield had prevented the file's transmission to the rebel fleet in orbit. Krennic prepared to kill Jyn, but was deprived of his opportunity when Andor appeared behind him and knocked him out.

When the planet's shield was deactivated, the two rebels successfully transmitted the structural plans of the 'planet killer'. Despite this victory, Jyn, full of years of rage, wanted to take revenge on the unmoving Krennic, but was stopped by Andor who helped her to the lift that would take them back down to the beach. Once there, they discovered that the recently materialised Death Star had already fired on the planet, just a few kilometres away from them.

Resigned to their fate, but reassured by the unexpected success of the Rogue One mission, the pair looked at the approaching fireball and embraced as they became one with the Force.

K-23

See Relby K-23 Blaster Pistol

K-2SO

Originally an Imperial security droid of the KX-series, K-2SO was reprogrammed by Cassian Andor and put into the service of the Rebel Alliance.

He became part of the extraction team aboard, *Bravo One*, who rescued a prisoner from a work camp on Wobani. The operation would have been a fiasco had it not been for the presence of the droid, who stopped the primary target, Jyn Erso, from fleeing after her liberation. Shocked by events, she had resisted and stunned three of her liberators, but was stopped in her tracks after being grasped by the throat and brutally thrown to the ground by K-2SO. As it offered her a dry congratulations on her escape attempt, it appeared that

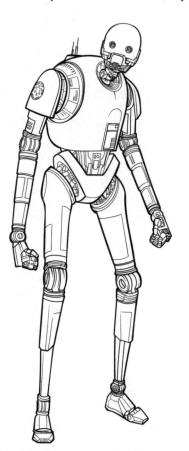

reprogramming the droid from its factory setting had introduced the concept of sarcasm into its personality. Thereafter, fully conscious of himself, the droid exhibited other such character traits as cynicism, stoicism, a brutal, often awkward, honesty and even the ability to disobey minor orders. Equipped with these qualities, the droid embarked with its master, Andor, and Jyn on a U-wing for Jedha in order to find Saw Gerrera and to locate Galen Erso, a scientist working on the Empire's 'planet killer' superweapon.

For K-2SO, the mission got off to a disappointing start when he was ordered to remain with the ship while Jyn and Andor began their investigation in the Holy City. However, with the capacity to ignore any commands he judged counterproductive, K-2SO decided to join them in order to prevent any trouble. Attracted by the noise of an armed confrontation between Imperial and partisan forces, he just managed to avoid being shot by Jyn, who instead shot down one of his fellow KX-series droids. Moreover, the droid saved the two rebel agents when he intercepted a grenade, which he then threw back into a squad of stormtroopers. Ordered to return to the ship by his master, the droid remained in contact with Andor, Jyn and their new allies, Chirrut Îmwe and Baze Malbus, as they were taken to the den of Saw Gerrera. However, events took a different turn when the Empire decided to test its new superweapon, the Death Star, by annihilating Jedha City. K-2SO was able to warn his comrades of this destructive shock wave and, at the very last minute, managed to save them from the Catacombs of Cadera and they escaped to the planet of Eadu.

Bodhi Rook, a deserter and former Imperial pilot, whom the team had saved from Jedha, maintained that Eadu was where Galen Erso was located. In spite of difficult weather conditions, K-2SO managed to land not far from the Imperial base. As Andor left to eliminate Jyn's father, the droid, with shocking frankness, confirmed the secret objective of the mission by talking about the sniper mode of his master's weapon. After Galen Erso's death at the hands of a proton torpedo, launched by a Y-wing during a rebel raid, K-2SO succeeded, along with Rook, in stealing an Imperial cargo shuttle and proceeded to save Jyn and Andor who were being pursued.

Back on Yavin 4, following the rebels' lack of consensus regarding what to do about the Empire's new combat station, the droid joined his comrades for a clandestine operation to go to the Citadel Tower on Scarif and steal the plans for the space station. Borrowing the vessel stolen on Eadu, he and Rook were in contact with air control for take-off. The ex-Imperial pilot named their mission 'Rogue One', and it was K-2SO, once again demonstrating his cool sense of humour, who told the protesting controller that if the mission name didn't exist before, then it did from that point on.

They successfully landed on Scarif at Platform 9 of the Imperial Centre of Military Research and K-2SO soon infiltrated the Citadel Tower alongside the disguised Jyn and Andor, while the remaining rebel soldiers staged an explosive diversion. The droid quickly located and pirated another KX-series droid in order to find the path that would lead to the databank. Once the ruse had worked, the three agents arrived at the secure vault and, having stunned the security officer, K-2SO took control of the console panel. In a moment that took the droid by surprise, Jyn, as a mark of confidence and respect, offered him her blaster. A symbolic gesture, it was enough to convince K-2SO that in addition to Andor, Jyn was another person who deserved his protection in any circumstance, until the very end.

For a while, the droid successfully avoided confrontation with the passing stormtroopers, while attempting to guide the two rebels through the files. However, his cover was blown when Andor's voice was heard on the intercom. Aware that it was his last chance to help his friends, and with little expectation for their survival, K-2SO succeeded in finding the 'Stardust' file and suggested that they retrieve it manually and attempt to climb to the top of the Citadel Tower where there was a slim chance that they would be able to transmit it to the rebel fleet in orbit.

After one last goodbye, the droid destroyed the console, sealing the vault's access door and his own fate. He then collapsed to the ground and finally succumbed to the multiple laser shots he had endured. Just before dying out, as proof of his attachment to Cassian Andor and simply to comfort himself, K-2SO simulated a scenario he knew was impossible, in which his friend got out of Scarif alive. Sometimes, even droids dreamt of survival.

K-3PO

This protocol droid was in the service of the Rebel Alliance during the Galactic Civil War, where he was used at the rebel base during strategic briefings and operational manoeuvre debriefings.

As its databanks were mainly filled with tactical data, it took part in the Battle of Hoth and was stationed in the Echo Base command room to help the rebels identify possible flaws in the progress of the Imperial assaults, both from space and on the ground. It was destroyed when the Imperial troops finally invaded the base.

K-OHN

This L-1 tactical droid was an inhabitant of Jedha City.

Being one of the rare free cybernetic units, the droid made a living by exchanging its expertise for spare parts, power charges, or even sometimes credits, which it then shared with a band of streets kids. When Jyn Erso and Cassian Andor first encountered the droid, it was in conversation with the children. The droid's generous spirit combined with its curiosity about something else that could be found in abundance in the city, spirituality. K-OHN hoped to be able to grasp the concept of spirituality once it had saved enough to buy an update for its processors. However, its humanoid, grey silhouette could be seen in the Holy City just before the city's destruction by the Death Star, so it was unlikely that K-OHN survived to ever make the upgrade.

Kaadu

A biped creature native to the planet of Naboo, the kaadu was able to breathe underwater and was used for patrols in the underwater Gungan city of Otoh Gunga.

The domesticated kaadu were also used by the Gungans for war during the Battle of the Great Grass Plains. Decorated with huge feathers, they were mainly ridden by officers. They were marvellous mounts on the battlefield, being impervious to the sounds of warfare and able to achieve great speeds.

Kabe

This female Chadra-Fan was a biped who measured about 1 metre in length.

This brown-haired, furry native of the planet Chad, was a regular customer at the Mos Eisley Cantina on Tatooine.

Kachirho

Designed in the classical style of Wookiee architects, this coastal city on the planet of Kashyyyk had its houses peppered around the trunks of the majestic wroshyr trees.

Kachirho's particular status as a central hub of Wookiee hyperspace traffic, paired with its open position, made it one of the strategic targets of the Clone Wars. Under the leadership of Chief Tarfful, Kachirho was one of the rare cities not to be protected by dense vegetation, which made it a prime target for the invading Separatist troops.

Kalit

A Jawa from the desert planet of Tatooine in the Outer Rim Territories.

Kalit was present at the palace of Jabba the Hutt when the heroes of the Rebellion arrived to save their friend and comrade, Han Solo.

Kamino

A planet beyond the Outer Rim, Kamino was an oceanic world inhabited by the Kaminoans – a tall, slender people that had mastered the art of genetic manipulation.

Its capital, Tipoca City, was built on stilts in order to protect it from the violent waves and storms. The tilted roofs of the buildings, equipped with lightning rods, allowed the rain to flow freely and housed large spaces ideal for the maintenance of large numbers of clones, as well as the equipment necessary to make them.

Tipoca City harboured the most efficient laboratories on the planet and immediately after the Battle of Naboo, the master geneticists were hired by Jedi Master Sifo-Dyas, himself manipulated by Count Dooku, to create a clone army to be used by the Republic. This army would become one of the key elements that would enable Darth Sidious to eliminate the Jedi Order and take complete control of the galaxy. A suitable genetic donor was required to create the clones, so Dooku negotiated with the bounty hunter Jango Fett who agreed to take part. Dooku then erased the coordinates of the planet from the Jedi Archives in an attempt to hide it from the Jedi Order.

However, it was the Kaminoans' activities on bordering planets, like the mining world of Subterrel, that enabled Obi-Wan Kenobi to eventually find it. By conferring with old friends, and using a Kaminoan dart that Jango Fett had left embedded in the neck of one of his associates, the Jedi was able follow the trail back to the ocean world. Kenobi then met with Lama Su, the prime minister of Kamino, and discovered the clone army.

Kamino became a vital strategic target during the Clone Wars, with the Separatists wishing to cut off the production of new Republic troops at the source. The capital was then attacked by droid troops, but was bravely defended by the clone troopers themselves, who were determined to protect their 'homeworld'.

Kamino Saberdart

Only a few specialists that had already seen the technology of Kamino could identify the unique design of this handmade metallic Kaminoan dart that contained a dose of lethal poison.

Extremely rare, the saberdarts were used to administer their deadly dose of poison from a distance. Jango Fett, who lived on Kamino as the genetic model for the clone army, was equipped with this type of toxic dart, which he used on Zam Wesell, a fellow bounty hunter and former accomplice, to prevent her from talking when she was captured by Anakin Skywalker and Obi-Wan Kenobi after her failed attempt to kill Senator Padmé Amidala. Kenobi's old friend, Dexter Jettster, subsequently identified the dart, which enabled the Jedi to find the bounty hunter.

Kanan Jarrus

A survivor of Order 66, young Jedi Kanan Jarrus lived in exile until a chance meeting with Hera Syndulla led him to face his Imperial enemy once more.

Although unable to live openly as a Jedi, the Force remained strong in Jarrus. So much so, he was capable of sensing Ezra Bridger while in Lothal's Capital City with Syndulla. Jarrus discretely began training the boy in the ways of the Force, only to be tricked into revealing his true identity by ruthless Jedi hunter, the Inquisitor. Many battles ensured, in which Jarrus narrowly escaped deadly defeats at the hands of the Inquisitor. After being captured and held captive on Grand Moff Tarkin's Star Destroyer, Jarrus' fate seemed sealed, until he was finally able to embrace his Jedi past and defeat the Inquisitor. Jarrus was openly, and proudly, a Jedi once more.

After facing and fighting many of the Empire's high command, in various confrontations across the galaxy, Jarrus and the Spectres returned to Lothal to liberate it from Imperial occupation.

It was there, that after successfully rescuing Syndulla, who was being held captive by Governor Pryce, that Jarrus sacrificed his life to protect the lives of his friends. He was unknowingly survived by a son, Jacen Syndulla.

Kanjiklub

An Outer Rim criminal gang originally from Nar Kanji, this group mostly consisted of human ex-settlers who had risen up against their Hutt masters following the Galactic Civil War and the fall of the Empire.

Led by Tasu Leech, Kanjiklub specialised in extortion, acts of piracy and stealing ships. It gathered together the most violent fighters and warriors under the command of a chief who could be challenged and overthrown at any time. Motivated by the law of the strongest and its members' greed, Kanjiklub, despite its erratic nature and constant internal power struggles, was a very dangerous enemy, distinctly set apart from other gangs by its unique appearance. Their weapons, body armour and jumpsuits were all customised and adorned with both practical and ornamental elements made of organic material, such as roggwart or gundark bones. This particular skill, which descended from the uprising against the Hutts, allowed the gang's members to make strange and efficient weapons.

Often at war with its rivals, particularly the Guavian Death Gang, Kanjiklub knew when to put its disagreements aside in order to protect its interests. After having lent a lot of money to the smuggler Han Solo, they were willing to do anything necessary to get their investment back.

Kashyyyk

A forest world in the Mid Rim region of Mytaranor and the native planet of the Wookiees, Kashyyyk remained loyal to the Republic and fought alongside the Jedi and the clone troopers against the Confederacy of Independent Systems.

Represented in the Galactic Senate, the Wookiees were fierce fighters, fond of peace and justice. Their culture was rich and respectful of the environment and their towns, with their unique architecture, were built in trees. Even their vehicles, such as the ornithopter, took their lead from nature.

When the Separatist droid troops landed on the beaches of Kachirho, the Wookiees joined the clone troopers in order to defend the Republic, under the leadership of Master Yoda. Using their knowledge of their surroundings and their powerful bowcasters, the Wookiees helped to inflict heavy damages on the Separatist forces, and when Order 66 was issued, they helped Yoda safely flee Kashyyyk.

The Wookiees paid dearly for their opposition to the new Galactic Empire and many of them were enslaved or deported to the spice mines of Kessel.

Kaydel Ko Connix

A junior controller within the command centre of the Resistance, Kaydel Ko Connix was part of the new generation of rebels fighting the First Order.

Brave and committed, Connix placed her trust in General Leia Organa, hero of the Alliance, and joined the Resistance on the planet of D'Qar to offer her support. Efficient and faithful, she followed the deployment of the Resistance troops and squadrons on her control screen and notified the command team when any problems occurred. During the assault against the First Order's Starkiller Base, she kept General Organa informed of the operation's progress and the number of Resistance casualties suffered.

Kelvin Ravine

A remote place in the very heart of Jakku's desert, the Kelvin Ravine sheltered the small village of Tuanul.

The ravine's topography saw it surrounded by rocky mounds, which offered villagers a discreet haven far from the wreck-raiders who pillaged the Starship Graveyard. In this seclusion they were able to quietly practise the cult of the Force, which had driven them to that remote place.

Kendal Ozzel

Born on the planet Carida, Kendal Ozzel was a superior officer in the Imperial fleet, and was one of the commanders of Death Squadron – a dangerous detachment of the Imperial navy spearheaded by the Super Star Destroyer, the *Executor*.

After a military career that began within the fleet of the Republic during the Clone Wars, Ozzel didn't miss the opportunity to satisfy his personal ambitions during the rise of the Empire. Irrespective of his unpopularity within the Imperial ranks, his incredible self-confidence, greatly unjustified according to his equals who considered him arrogant and incompetent, was sufficient to put him in charge of the fleet assigned to locate and destroy the new rebel base. In addition to the terrifying *Executor*, the squadron was composed of five other standard Star Destroyers. Darth Vader was present aboard the squadron's flagship to supervise the operation that led them to the planet of Hoth. Although the Sith Lord issued the main orders, he left Ozzel and his officers in charge of deciding the best strategy for attack.

Having opted to launch a surprise attack, the admiral made a disastrous mistake when he ordered the fleet to emerge from hyperspace too close to Hoth. After an Imperial probe droid had been sighted on the ice planet, the rebels had already guessed that the Empire wouldn't be far behind. The arrival of the fleet confirmed this, and the rebels were able to activate the energy shield that protected them in time to avoid any attempted attack from space. Ozzel, who had previously rubbished the idea that the rebel base could be on Hoth, had committed his final mistake. Forced to issue a ground assault in an effort to destroy the shield generator, which would finally allow an attack from space, Vader didn't wait to hear Ozzel's status report. Instead, the Sith Lord used his Sith powers to strangle him to death in front of Captain Piett, who found himself swiftly promoted to the rank of admiral as Ozzel hit the floor.

Kent Deezling

Jyn Erso borrowed the uniform of this Tech agent in order to infiltrate the Citadel Tower on Scarif.

Dressed in an Imperial flight jumpsuit and a black helmet with removable visor, Deezling helped pilots manoeuvre their ships when landing by instructing the vessels using luminous guidance sticks. It was also his job to inspect the recently landed ships, accompanied by an officer and two stormtroopers. Posted on Platform 9, Deezling had no idea that this routine operation would end in tragedy for him with the arrival of the *Zeta*-class Imperial cargo shuttle, SW-0608.

Kessel

This name was designated to a planet of the Outer Rim and a commercial trade route known by smugglers all across the galaxy.

Under Imperial jurisdiction, the planet of Kessel was administered by the Pyke Syndicate, which controlled the spice mines that represented the main wealth of the planet. Administered, however, was a loose description, given that the Empire's power was strong on Kessel, and the Syndicate did not appear to oppose it. In fact, it was nothing more than a slaving operation, known and feared throughout the entire galaxy. The harvesting of the crop notably required a strong Wookiee labour force.

The Kessel Run is a legendary navigational route through the chaotic space that surrounds the planet Kessel. The local Si'Klaata Cluster and the Akkadese Maelstrom are shifting systems of interstellar gas, carbonbergs, ice chunks, and other debris that makes hyperspace travel treacherous.

Khetanna, the

See Jabba's Sail Barge

Ki-Adi-Mundi

A Cerean Jedi Master with an elongated head and a distinguished white beard.

Ki-Adi-Mundi was a well-known sceptic, which partly explained his lack of belief concerning the possibility of the re-emergence of the Sith. When Qui-Gon Jinn described his duel on Tatooine with a warrior he believed to be a Sith Lord, Ki-Adi-Mundi was not convinced. Some years later, in the private chambers of Chancellor Palpatine, he spoke with Padmé Amidala, who had just escaped an assassination attempt she suspected Count Dooku was behind, to assure her that Dooku was just an old Jedi and a political idealist who could never be a killer. However, his blindness to the treacherous schemes of the Sith didn't detract from his many

Sent to Geonosis with 200 Jedi in order to save On Geonosis, Ki-Adi-Mundi infiltrated the Petranaki Arena and entered a deadly fight against a coalition of enemies. In a matter of minutes, many of his Jedi companions were dead and he found himself surrounded by the Separatist forces of Count Dooku. Saved at the last minute by Yoda and the clone army, Mundi was one of the few Jedi to survive the Battle of Geonosis.

When Palpatine issued Order 66, Ki-Adi-Mundi, who was by then a Jedi General, was charging into battle on the icy planet of Mygeeto. The clone Commander Bacara ordered his execution, but the Jedi's extremely sharp reflexes enabled him to retaliate and he was able to temporarily fend off their treachery with his lightsaber. He deflected the fire of two clones before he was shot in the stomach and fell to the ground, unable to defend himself any longer from the torrent of laser shots lashing down on him.

Killi Gimm

A Disciple of the Whills and a resident of the Holy City, Killi Gimm was in Jedha City when the Empire ordered its destruction.

She managed an orphanage with her sister, not far from the Temple of the Kyber, and when she left her young wards she increased her anonymity by wearing an optic visor and an air-filter mask. Her traditional, homespun red dress featured a hood that was of a distinctly dark purple. Her deep faith and her devotion to the abandoned children wasn't enough to save them from the annihilation delivered by the brutal Imperial regime.

Kitster Banai

A close friend of the young Anakin Skywalker, this young, black-haired slave boy was part of Skywalker's team during the Boonta Eve Classic Podrace.

He intently followed the developments of the race and cheered for Anakin alongside fellow friend Wald and the droids, C-3PO and R2-D2.

Klaatu

This green-skinned gambler was one of the many Kadas'sa'Nikto on Jabba the Hutt's payroll.

He had a gift for being able to repair the skiffs that belonged to the notorious slug-like crime lord. He also enjoyed watching Jabba's rancor devour its unlucky victims. Present on the bridge of the *Khetanna* during the expected execution of the rebels at the Great Pit of Carkoon, he beat a hasty retreat when Luke Skywalker landed just metres in front of him with his lightsaber drawn. This cowardly henchman was then pulverised when Jabba's sail barge subsequently exploded.

Klatooine Paddy Frog

This species of frog was particularly appreciated by Jabba the Hutt.

The Tatooine crime lord kept a jar filled with these frogs within reach of his chubby fingers, and would savour them with a lick of his lips. A small delicacy, Jabba notably enjoyed one just after witnessing Oola being devoured by his rancor.

Korr Sella

A young commander within the Resistance, Korr Sella was the official representative of the Resistance at the Galactic Senate of the New Republic.

Aware that she had lost respect in the Senate, and preferring to fight the First Order, General Leia Organa appointed Korr Sella as the Resistance's representative to reinstate legitimacy to their actions after the manipulations of some corrupt senators. The Resistance hoped to gain political support from the New Republic, as well as military support on the battlefield, in order to eradicate the threat represented by the First Order. Commander Sella was with Chancellor Lanever Villecham when Hosnian Prime was destroyed by Starkiller Base. She died during the attack, as did every living being on the planet.

Kouhun

These extremely venomous arthropods, around 30 centimetres long, hailed from the planet of Indoumodo.

Equipped with stingers at both its front and back, its sting could kill in mere minutes. Its deadly nature and its ability to stealthily reach its victims made it a weapon of choice for assassins that wished to stay far away from their targets. The assassin Zam Wesell employed kouhuns in an attempt to eliminate Padmé Amidala and used a probe droid to place two of the creatures in the senator's room. Having thwarted R2-D2's surveillance, at the very last minute they were finally killed by a stroke from Anakin Skywalker's lightsaber.

Krayt Dragon

There were several species of krayt dragon on Tatooine, all of which could be categorised by their habitat.

A large, carnivorous, four-legged reptile, the physical differences between the species were minimal and were largely linked directly to whether or not they were cave dwellers. The most feared species was that which could be found in the canyons at the edge of the deserts. These giant predators preyed on banthas, whose natural slowness made them an easy target. The unique scream of the krayt dragon was known and feared by everyone on the desert planet.

Kullbee Sperado

This enigmatic Meftian gunslinger with a face as white as a sheet, was a member of Saw Gerrera's partisans.

He was recruited by Gerrera himself based on the merit of his valuable actions on Serralonis, and although he didn't voluntarily join the group, he was obviously relieved at the opportunity to escape his past, which he never spoke about. Although part of the team, he was secretive and retained an aura of mystery and often disappeared for long periods of time. On Jedha, during those weeks of absence, some of his comrades would glimpse him praying with devotion in the Holy City at the Kyber Temple. Fortunately for him, when the city was obliterated by the Death Star, he was in the Catacombs of Cadera, contemplating the hologram of a Twi'lek dancer, which gave him a chance to attempt to escape from the shock wave.

KX-series Security Droid

This model, which carried the stamped symbol of the Imperial cog on its shoulder as an identifier, was produced by Arakyd Industries as a solution to the Senate's orders prohibiting the production of combat droids.

Designed to serve the Empire, the droids' programming combined the obligation of obeying Imperial officers with the command of not attacking any living people. The KX-series droid was equipped with a communication relay and an amplifier for Imperial frequencies, gyro-balance systems to achieve athletic mobility, a charging socket and a data needle in its fist that could act as a computer interface. Some cognitive modules were also installed to allow it to carry out such tasks as escorting dignitaries, defence of facilities and piloting craft. Although very difficult, reprogramming them was possible, as Cassian Andor demonstrated with K-2SO.

Kylo Ren

A leading figure within the command of the First Order and the only son of Han Solo and Leia Organa, Kylo Ren had a familiarity with the Force from a young age owing to his ancestry.

As Ben Solo, he followed the teachings of his uncle, the Jedi Knight Luke Skywalker, but during his apprenticeship he fell under the influence of the mysterious Snoke, a powerful being adept in the dark side of the Force. He betrayed his master and killed a whole new generation of Jedi apprentices, which earned him the nickname 'Jedi killer'. As Kylo Ren, he then joined the First Order, an organisation born from the ashes of the Empire, under the supervision of his new master. A member of the Knights of Ren, he was neither Jedi nor Sith, but personified something new; adept in the dark side, but constantly torn between the two opposite sides of the Force.

Kylo Ren used his great sensitivity to the Force to feed his powers and to crush or manipulate

his enemies. With the ability to stop a blaster shot in mid-air, paralyse his adversaries or read their minds, he was the archetypal ultimate warrior. However, this power also had a downside: he suffered from great emotional instability that drove him into violent, shocking fits of rage, during which he would destroy whatever was around him. His greatest fear was that he would fall to the light side of the Force and fail as he believed his grandfather, the powerful Darth Vader, had done. He possessed the charred helmet of Vader, and often spoke to it.

Ren wore the black habit common to the acolytes of the dark side and an old cape, which hid his helmet beneath its hood. His outfit indicated a past that had seen many violent battles, while the coarse design of Ren's lightsaber, inspired by an ancient style that dated back to the Great Scourge of Malachor, exhibited his lack of experience and tutelage. Its power, provided by a chipped kyber crystal, generated a fiery and unstable red plasma blade that echoed its user's inner turmoil. Part of the flux was channelled perpendicularly through lateral slots, which created two points that were used as a hilt and stabilised the weapon.

Ren was outside the hierarchical structure of the First Order, which gave him the authority to act as he saw fit. He could launch any operation he felt necessary to successfully achieve his assigned missions. He led interrogations and could modify mission objectives as he thought necessary, depending on the circumstances. Those objectives generally had priority over the military objectives of the First Order, which became a frequent source of tension between himself and other members of the First Order's command team, in particular, General Hux. Supreme Leader Snoke ordered that Kylo Ren's true name was never to be revealed, even though he knew that his apprentice would have to one day confront his past in order to finish his training.

On Takodana, Ren quickly sensed an outstanding sensitivity to the Force in the young Rey and, when he realised her potential, he took her back with him to the First Order's Starkiller Base. This potential was rapidly confirmed when, having killed his own father – Han Solo – Kylo Ren confronted the young woman in the snowy forest that surrounded the base. Extremely diminished by their duel, he was left for dead when Resistance forces finished their mission and totally destroyed the First Order's superweapon.

After a steady recovery, Ren was unable to shake off his encounter with Rey and manipulated their Force connection to bring her aboard the *Supremacy*. There, Ren killed Snoke as an invitation for Rey to join him and dominate the galaxy together. Rey's refusal left Ren more confused than ever. At the old Rebel Alliance base on Crait, Ren was unable to recognise his confrontation with his uncle and old master, Luke Skywalker, as the Jedi Master's clever use of Force projection. Luke's trick and Ren's distraction allowed the few remaining Resistance fighters to flee from the advancing First Order forces.

Laboratory of Conception and Implementation of the High Energies

See Imperial Kyber Refinery

Lah'mu

A planet of the Outer Rim sector of Raioballo, Lah'mu became the shelter of the Erso family owing to its distance from the main hyperspace routes.

Characterised by its surrounding rings that were the vestiges of a previously destroyed moon, the planet's grounds were especially rich as, during its first geological era, the terrestrial crust had split open and minerals and fertile earth had been pushed to the top. Its landscape was made up of grassy plains, saltwater seas with beaches of black sand, mountainous peaks, geysers and volcanic zones. In spite of the necessity to purify the water and sift the soil, this planet still held enough attraction that the Republic Ministry of Economic Development encouraged some citizens to settle there by offering parcels of land.

During the Clone Wars, this haven of peace, which took its name from a Neimoidian word meaning prosperity, attracted those who were anxious to escape the conflict. Nevertheless, it was estimated that there were only 500 colonists, who had mainly settled in the northern hemisphere. Anxious to escape the Empire, Galen, Lyra and their daughter, Jyn, hid in the eastern zone, where they lived the life of self-sufficient farmers with no desire to trade with the outside. However, even this relocation to a remote area of the galaxy did not stop Galen's old 'friend', Director Orson Krennic, who eventually discovered their sanctuary.

Lake Country

The most remote region on the planet of Naboo, the Lake Country consisted of peaceful valleys, waterfalls and lakes.

Inhabited by farmers, shaak herders and glass-blowers, the area was regularly flooded by the rivers that ran through it, which resulted in extremely fertile soil. The Festival of Glad Arrival, which took place during springtime, radically transformed the valleys with its colourful parades and jovial music. In the summer, the area was pleasantly dry and the surrounding lakes were not connected to the underwater network of Naboo, which meant that no sea monsters lived in them. It was in Lake Country that Senator Padmé Amidala, took shelter with Anakin Skywalker following the assassination attempts against her. It was also in this area, in the family house on Varykino Island, that she married the young Jedi.

Lake Paonga

This seemingly ordinary body of water was located near the swamps on the planet of Naboo.

The lake enabled Jar Jar Binks, Qui-Gon Jinn and Obi-Wan Kenobi to access the underwater capital city of the Gungans, Otoh Gunga.

Lama Su

As prime minister of Kamino, Lama Su was the planet's main spokesperson to the Republic, and he also looked after the interests of Kamino and the Kaminoan geneticists.

When Jedi Master Sifo-Dyas requested the creation of an entire clone army for the Republic, Su wholeheartedly accepted the commission. Proud of the work they had accomplished and unaware of the Jedi Master's death, he presented the finished army to Obi-Wan Kenobi, whom he had personally welcomed to Tipoca City, the capital. The clones had been grown from the genetic model supplied by Count Dooku – the bounty hunter, Jango Fett. Prime Minister Su was assisted by Taun We, the coordinator of the clone-army project.

Lambda-class T-4a Shuttle

This Imperial transportation vehicle could be easily identified by its triangular shape created by the shuttle's three wings.

Developed by Sienar Fleet Systems and equipped with a hyperdrive, these 20-metre long shuttles were particularly elegant compared to the usual raw and industrial Imperial designs. In fact, they were often used by high-ranking officers and such dignitaries of the Empire as the Emperor and Darth Vader. However, their more common mission was to transport troops or freight and their ability to answer an attack resided in the five laser cannons that could be found placed at the front and rear of the ship.

The ship could be flown by just one pilot if necessary, although it was often more comfortable to have a navigator as well, especially for the always delicate journeys through hyperspace. The three wings that brought such elegance to this ship were the dorsal, stationary and stabilising wings, the last two of which were collapsible, which reduced the shuttle's silhouette. To prove that the crew on board worked for the Empire, the T-4a shuttles were equipped with transponders that emitted secret codes to the Imperial cruisers assigned to control them. Decades later, the First Order was inspired by the design of this vehicle when it created the new *Upsilon*-class command shuttle, once again proving its will to copy the style of its ideological heir, the Empire.

Lando Calrissian

A human male from the planet of Socorro, Lando Calrissian had tried many careers – more or less legal – before he became a general in the Rebel Alliance and a hero of the Battle of Endor.

The paths walked by Calrissian in his life were atypical, to say the least. Nevertheless, he knew how to make a profit from the many situations the galaxy found itself in during the Imperial regime. He spent his youth alternating between two activities: smuggling and professional gambling. However, his natural charisma alone wasn't enough to save him from every delicate situation. Instead, he owed a lot to his modified cargo ship, the *Millennium Falcon*, which had rescued him from many dangerous and unexpected encounters. However, one game of Sabacc changed Calrissian's life – and that of his opponent's – forever. Carried away by the excitement of the game, Calrissian lost the *Millennium Falcon* to a young Corellian named Han Solo. After that, Calrissian decided to become a business man.

His first foray into the business world took place on Lothal, a planet of the Outer Rim. There he met a local outlaw named Cikatro Vizago, through whom he acquired lands that were eligible for mining. However, the Empire was also very interested in this planet and its natural resources,

which would meet some of the enormous demand for raw materials that were necessary for it to continue spreading its hold across the galaxy. As a result, Calrissian quickly found himself in trouble while attempting to mine his land and was forced to change his method and go in search of a puffer pig, known for its ability to discover valuable mining deposits. To achieve this he had to escape the Imperial blockade.

Once again, Calrissian found himself back at the Sabacc table, where he met one of the crew of the *Ghost*, a vessel belonging to a small group of rebels opposed to the Empire. He won a droid, but negotiated its return in exchange for a favour from the *Ghost's* crew. Lando had made a deal with the crime lord Azmorigan for a puffer pig, a deal which meant he had to 'exchange' Hera Syndulla, Twi'lek captain of the *Ghost*, for the pig. He managed to recover the animal while helping Syndulla escape - fooling Azmorigan. He later had the opportunity to help those same rebels by assisting them in their escape from Lothal where they had become hunted, notably by Darth Vader himself.

Calrissian then tried other businesses with varying degrees of success before seizing the opportunity of his life, when he took charge of the administration of Cloud City, a floating complex that mined tibanna gas, located in the atmosphere of the gas planet of Bespin. He prospered, creating a commercial tourist attraction and mining colony that did not attract the attention of the Empire.

Three years after the Battle of Yavin, Calrissian met his old friend Han Solo and welcomed him to Cloud City. Solo needed to repair his hyperdrive, but was careful not to mention the Empire, which was on his tail. However, Calrissian had already reached an agreement with the Empire to deliver the rebels in order to retain the city's mining privileges. Darth Vader then changed the terms of the contract and ordered Calrissian to keep Leia and Chewbacca forever in the city, while Solo would be entrusted to Boba Fett. After the smuggler was frozen in carbonite, Vader changed the agreement once again and informed Calrissian that Leia and Chewbacca were now prisoners of the Empire and would instead accompany him. The administrator of the city, more and more sickened by the agreement, prepared a plan to save Leia and Chewbacca. After they were successfully freed, they embarked with Calrissian aboard the *Millennium Falcon*.

Next, Calrissian accompanied the rebels and participated in a plot to save his friend Solo from the claws of Jabba the Hutt. After finalising a plan that he aimed to infiltrate the palace of the Tatooine crime lord, Calrissian was one of Solo's 'guards' and participated in the battle that took place above the Great Pit of Carkoon. A battle that ended with the death of Jabba the Hutt and the liberation of Solo. After these events, Calrissian committed himself to the rebels and it was his participation in the Battle of Taanab, where here repelled a fleet of pirate vessels, which earned him the rank of general in the Alliance.

He later undertook the immense responsibility of leading the attack of rebel fighters on the second Death Star during the Battle of Endor. This historic confrontation mobilised a fleet of cruisers commanded by Admiral Ackbar and a ground assault party whose mission was to deactivate the shield generator that protected the space station. The ground mission, led by Solo, required perfect coordination with the orbital assault. Piloting the *Millennium Falcon*, Calrissian finally succeeded in passing through the Imperial defences and entered the tunnels of the second Death Star's central reactor, where he launched the torpedoes that started the chain reaction that destroyed the space station.

Lanever Villecham

This New Republic senator, eventually elected to the position of Chancellor, was born on Tarsunt and represented his native planet at the Senate.

Once he had ascended to supreme responsibilities, even if the word 'supreme' had been removed from the Chancellor's title, he devoted much of his time to the development of trade treaties with neutral worlds from the Trans-Hydian border and was generally uninterested in the First Order's activities, as long as they respected the principles of the Galactic Concordance. He was in the second year of his first mandate when he died in the explosion of Hosnian Prime, after the planet was targeted by Starkiller Base.

Laren Joma

A rebel pilot who used the call sign Blue Eleven, Laren Joma was responsible for escorting reinforcements to the Scarif beaches and showed remarkable composure in the most difficult of circumstances.

She piloted her U-wing starfighter with Lieutenant Taslet Colb at the Battle of Scarif. She had a stern nature that was reflected in her physical appearance. However, she was happy in the company of characters completely different to her, as long as they were professional, so she fully accepted all the youthful exuberance demonstrated by the youthful Bistan, who was an ace when it came to using his left flank machine gun. Joma, Colb and Bistan all died in a crash after their ship took a hit to the lower left motor.

Leevan Tenza

This defiant Sabat warrior was a member of the Rebel Alliance before leaving to join Saw Gerrera's partisans.

Although not the only one to have followed this course of action, Leevan Tenza's motives were somewhat different to those who usually made the move to be more radical in their resistance of the Empire. Five years before the Battle of Yavin, Tenza served under the respected General Jan Dodonna. However, he disobeyed orders and attacked an Imperial target far too early, which saw him placed under arrest by the rebels. Facing a court martial, he escaped and joined Saw Gerrera's group.

Better suited to this troop and its more casual organisation, he proved to be very efficient, especially when it came to using his DH-447 sniper rifle. When Jyn Erso was brought to the lair of the insurgents, the sniper was quietly seated at a table playing a 'homemade' variant of the dejarik game, but even his usual terseness was put to the test when he understood what was heading towards the Catacombs of Cadera on Jedha – an immense, destructive shock wave generated by the destruction of the Holy City.

Leia Organa

A stateswoman and military leader born nineteen years before the Battle of Yavin, Leia Organa was the twin sister of Jedi Luke Skywalker.

Leia Organa held the title of Princess of Alderaan, but her diplomatic and political responsibilities included membership of the Imperial Senate and a leader of the Rebel Alliance. She played a central role during the Galactic Civil War and, like her brother Luke, was unaware of her origins for a very long time and only much later discovered her predisposition to the use of the Force.

Two days after the proclamation of the Galactic Empire, Leia Organa was born minutes after her brother, Luke, in the medical facilities on the asteroid Polis Massa. Leia was the daughter of Padmé Amidala and Anakin Skywalker, and from the moment of her birth, she and her brother instantly became the last hope for freedom in the galaxy. The decision was taken to hide them from their father who had become a Sith Lord under the name of Darth Vader. Bail Organa offered to adopt Leia, while Luke was handed over to the care of his uncle, Owen Lars, a peaceful farmer on Tatooine.

As part of the royal family Organa of Alderaan, Leia had access to the education that her title required. Although respectful of her title, she very soon showed some 'unsuitable' traits and had to come to terms with her impetuous temperament – a common trait that ran in the blood of the Skywalker family. She learned how to control and moderate her feelings with the diplomacy that was required from a dignitary such as herself.

Before becoming a senator, she participated in some secret missions on behalf of rebel cells. About three years before the battle of Yavin, at the age of sixteen, she managed to acquire several combat corvettes for the rebels, following their losses suffered during the Battle of Garel. On this occasion, she met Kanan Jarrus and Ezra Bridger and sensed their sensitivity to the Force.

Once elected to the Imperial Senate, her fears that it had become nothing more than a complacent assembly for Emperor Palpatine, dedicated to serving his commands, were quickly confirmed. She started her ideological resistance by taking charge of humanitarian actions, and never hesitated to publicly highlight systems that had been forgotten by the Empire. Those actions brought her huge popular sympathy, but radically split the political world – and from there she joined the Rebel Alliance, which, at that moment, was only in its embryonic stages.

At the Battle of Scarif, the Rebel Alliance achieved its first victory when it succeeded in stealing the technical read-outs of the Death Star, the gigantic combat station that was almost complete after twenty years of secret construction. Its purpose was to threaten and subdue any rebellious systems into compliance with the Empire, and to compel the last few resistant systems to join its regime. Leia volunteered for the dangerous mission to transport the plans to Alderaan and to ask Obi-Wan Kenobi, secluded on Tatooine, to join the battle to come. But the diplomatic vessel, the *Tantive IV,* aboard which the princess and her delegation were travelling, fell into enemy hands and was boarded by Vader and his stormtroopers. Nevertheless, Leia managed to conceal the plans in the memory

unit of R2-D2, who fled in an escape pod, along with the protocol droid C-3PO, in the direction of Tatooine and in search of Kenobi.

Despite the heroic resistance of Captain Antilles, Leia was quickly captured and presented to Vader. Disbelieving the senator's justifications, he ordered her to be taken prisoner and had her vessel destroyed, to make it appear that there had been an 'accident'. Leia was transferred to the detention block AA-23 aboard the Death Star, and demonstrated great bravery as she endured numerous torture sessions from the Empire, which wanted her to reveal the location of the rebel base. Even when faced with the mental probe, she continued to display a mental strength that was usually only exhibited by Jedi.

As the Imperial Senate stood on the brink of dissolution, Grand Moff Tarkin, governor of the Death Star, ordered its beam to be directed on Alderaan. With the view to blackmailing the princess, Tarkin delivered her a terrible ultimatum, which, for the first time, weakened her resolve. He would spare the princess' homeworld if she revealed the location of the Alliance's

base. In an attempt to save both her loved ones and the rebels, Leia lied and pretended that the base was on Dantooine. However, she was still forced to watch in shock and horror as Tarkin went ahead and destroyed Alderaan. This act of terror provoked such a disruption in the Force that it was felt by Kenobi aboard the *Millennium Falcon*, which was heading for Alderaan to deliver the Death Star plans to Bail Organa. However, before the *Millennium Falcon* got much further, it was caught in the tractor beam of the Death Star and pulled inside the gigantic space station.

Aware that the princess was aboard the space station, the small group from the *Millennium Falcon* devised a plan to rescue her. Although this team, diverse to say the least, possessed none of the military knowledge usually essential to this kind of mission, Han Solo, Luke Skywalker and Chewbacca succeeded in freeing Leia, before falling into the station's garbage disposal system, from which they also had to escape in order to make it back to their ship. At the *Millennium Falcon,* they found Kenobi, who had successfully deactivated the tractor beam, in the middle of a duel with Darth Vader. There they witnessed the death of the old Jedi, whose sacrifice allowed them to escape and to head to the rebel base on Yavin 4 with the Death Star plans.

When they arrived at the Great Massassi Temple that

housed the rebels' headquarters, Leia was welcomed by Commander Willard who, with the help of General Dodonna, devised an assault strategy against the Death Star – made possible after analysis of the plans she had delivered. Leia watched the battle from the war room and feared the worst as she witnessed the slaughter of the rebel fleet. At the most crucial moment, just a few seconds before Yavin 4 was due to enter the range of the Death Star's superlaser, Skywalker succeeded in launching a proton torpedo into the exhaust port that constituted a structural weakness. His shot began a chain reaction that led to the destruction of the Imperial combat station. After the victory, Leia presented medals of honour to both Skywalker and Solo, while paying homage to her loved ones by wearing the traditional ceremonial dress of Alderaan.

The following months were spent trying to escape the Empire. For the next three years, Vader used considerable means to extensively search the galaxy for the Rebel Alliance, which had installed itself on the inhospitable planet of Hoth. When the base was finally discovered and attacked by the Imperial troops, Leia supervised the evacuation before fleeing with Han Solo aboard the *Millennium Falcon*.

During the flight Leia and Solo exchanged their first kiss, although it was abruptly interrupted by C-3PO. Having escaped the Imperial troops, Solo headed for Cloud City in order to repair his ship. As the city was managed by Lando Calrissian, a friend of Solo's, they hoped they would be able to take a short break there in safety. But Vader had arrived first and, after making an deal with Lando, the rebels were captured. Solo was interrogated, but before he was frozen in carbonite Leia declared her love for him. She then succeeded in escaping with Chewbacca and Lando, who had by this point joined them.

Leia next organised a plan to free Solo, who had become the prisoner of Jabba the Hutt. Dressed and armed as a bounty hunter, she pretended to have captured Chewbacca and demanded the bounty from the Hutt in return. Although she succeeded in freeing Solo from his carbonite jail, she was then captured herself and reduced to being the personal slave of Jabba. Skywalker then attempted to negotiate the release of his friends, but Jabba refused and instead sentenced the rebels to death. The Jedi later succeeded in freeing his friends and destroyed the sail barge owned by the slug-like crime lord, while Leia strangled Jabba with the thick chain that had bound her to him.

Aboard a frigate, Leia then attended the briefing of the most important battle in the history of the Alliance – the assault against the second Death Star. An operation that could strike a definitive blow to the enemy after intelligence learned of the Emperor's presence aboard the space station in order to supervise the last steps of its construction. Leia volunteered to participate in the mission to Endor, in order to destroy the energy generator that powered the protective shield around the second Death Star.

The scout team, which also included Skywalker and Solo, landed on Endor aboard a shuttle stolen from the Empire, which allowed them to clear the Imperial orbital blockade around the forest moon. When they were spotted by an Imperial patrol, Leia and Skywalker gave chase aboard speeder bikes, but during the pursuit, in which they travelled at speeds of

200 kph among the ancient trees, Leia fell from her vehicle into the thickets. While Solo and Skywalker both searched for her, it was actually Wicket, an Ewok, who found her first. After some initial distrust, the princess and Wicket worked together to fight off some Imperial scouts, before he led her to his village. There, she found her friends who had been taken prisoner by the Ewoks. Skywalker used his ability in the Force to convince the Ewoks that C-3PO had powers and, mistaking the droid for a god, the Ewoks freed the rebels. Later that evening, Skywalker confessed to Leia that he was the son of Darth Vader, and that she was his twin sister.

The following day, Leia was wounded during a blaster fight with Imperial troops as the rebels attempted to infiltrate the shield generator. As Solo helped her, they were captured and held at gunpoint by hostile soldiers. During this critical moment, Solo chose to express his true feelings and echoed Leia's sentiment from the carbon-freezing chamber. Helped by Chewbacca, they finally succeeded in infiltrating the defences of the Imperial bunker and blew it up. This allowed the rebels' orbital fleet to attack the second Death Star, and Lando Calrissian launched the torpedoes that destroyed it.

Following the end of the festivities that celebrated the destruction of the second Death Star and the Empire's fall to nothing more than a small, fragmented group with no leader, Leia was tasked by Mon Mothma to recruit a controlling elite who would be able to create the administrative, legal, legislative and ministerial basis of the New Republic. Total peace was finally achieved one year after the events on Endor at the Battle of Jakku, which put a definitive end to the existence of the Empire.

Shortly after, Solo and Leia were married and had a son named Ben Solo, who demonstrated a great sensitivity to the Force, but also showed, from an early age, a fascination with the dark side and the legend of his grandfather, Darth Vader. Leia entrusted his training to her brother, who at that time was trying to revive the Jedi Order, which had been extinct since the end of the Clone Wars. However, at the same time, Ben fell under the ominous influence of the mysterious Supreme Leader of the First Order, named Snoke. Skywalker failed to help Ben overcome his obsessions with the dark side and could not prevent his nephew slaughtering all of the Jedi apprentices and becoming Kylo Ren. After these events, Solo and Leia split up and Skywalker went into exile in a secret location.

Leia attempted to alert the Senate of the New Republic to the dangers of the First Order, but was not taken seriously by the institution that considered her an alarmist and an exaggerating warmonger. She then founded the Resistance, within which she held the rank of general. Leia sent a young pilot named Poe Dameron to Jakku in order to recover Lor San Tekka, a member of the community of Tuanul, who possessed a fragment of map that led to the location of Skywalker. The whole village was slaughtered by First Order troops and Dameron was reported missing. However, before his capture he had time to hide the fragment of map in his droid, BB-8. Leia recovered the trail of the droid on Takodana, which then became the setting for a battle between the Resistance and the forces of the First Order. It was at this point that she met Solo again, who informed her of the role that Finn and Rey had played since Jakku, and also of their son's presence during the battle.

Using information from Finn, a former soldier of the First Order, the Resistance constructed a plan against the First Order's Starkiller Base. Solo volunteered to lead the mission to infiltrate the base and promised Leia that he would return with their son. During the mission, Leia sensed a disruption in the Force and realised that Solo had died. Back at the Resistance headquarters, after the destruction of Starkiller Base, Leia, Finn and Rey activated R2-D2, who had been asleep since Luke Skywalker's departure. R2-D2 used the map fragment to locate Luke Skywalker's secret location.

With Rey dispatched to find Luke, Leia began evacuating Resistance members from the planet of D'Qar only to be interrupted by the First Order. In a desperate bid to escape, Leia gave the call aboard her flagship, the *Raddus*, to jump into hyperspace, but the First Order, using a hyperspace tracker, followed and launched a devastating attack. Leia was blasted out of the ship and into space, saved only by her dormant Jedi powers. Leia's connection with the Force later allowed her to see her twin brother Luke Skywalker one last time at the disused Rebel Alliance base on Crait. As Skywalker used a Force projection to distract Ren and the First Order troops, Leia fled the scene with her few, but faithful, Resistance fighters.

Liberty, the

A Mon Calamari starship that served the Rebel Alliance during the Galactic Civil War.

This 1,200-metre vessel became famous thanks to its part in the Battle of Endor, during which it was destroyed by the second Death Star. It gave its name to the MC80 *Liberty*-class star cruiser that was modelled after its design.

Lightmaker, the

See Battle of Scarif

Lightsaber

The weapon of the Jedi and the Sith, the lightsaber used a technology based on the projection of a plasma blade energised by a kyber crystal.

The ability to wield a lightsaber expertly required regular and meticulous practice and could be improved when used in conjunction with the Force. Lightsabers possessed the unique status of being manufactured by their owner, either Jedi or Sith, which made them the only weapons in the galaxy that were not produced by weapons factories and which were not subject to illegal trade. The possibilities of a lightsaber were many insofar as its blade could only be blocked by another lightsaber blade or by the Z6 baton. A lightsaber could therefore cut, destroy or pierce nearly any matter, including the hull of a spaceship. Used as a weapon of defence, it enabled its wielder to ward off and divert blaster shots, or even, for the most experienced users, to deflect it directly against the shooter. A few eminent Jedi and Sith had succeeded in absorbing Force lightning with the help of their lightsaber, but it was a practice that required both an impressive technical mastery and an exceptional control of the Force.

Even though there was no particular significance concerning the choice of colour for their lightsaber, the Jedi avoided red, as it was historically connected to the Sith. Building a lightsaber was an extremely delicate operation, and one that constituted a very important initiation step in a Jedi's training. The smallest defect in the crystal alignment could result in a blade that activated only briefly before it died out, unreliable control, and, at worst, an explosion similar to the backfire on a deficient blaster.

It was technically possible to create numerous variations on the classic lightsaber design. For instance, the Sith Lord Darth Maul made a model equipped with two blades, while others made lightsabers with several rotary blades, which demanded extremely careful use. As for Kylo Ren, he took the risk to use unsteady crystals to create a model that featured a laser hilt in the shape of a cross. Naturally, owing to the lightsaber's long history and its use by innumerable cultures, multiple combat techniques existed for this weapon.

Lobot

This human from the planet Bespin had undergone a total cerebral cybernetic implant and was promoted to the role of Lando Calrissian's first deputy controller of Cloud City during the Galactic Civil War.

His increased mental faculties allowed him to operate as a liaison officer to the city's central computer with exceptional efficiency. He had access to the whole network and could grant any maintenance or security operation in an instant. He used these capabilities to aid the escape of Princess Leia and her friends from the city when Imperial troops invaded. While in the presence of the Imperial detachment intended to transport the rebel prisoners to Darth Vader's shuttle, Calrissian discreetly ordered Lobot to deploy the city's security agents. They succeeded in overpowering the rebels' Imperial escort, but could not prevent the Imperial siege that led to the evacuation of the floating city.

Logray

Shaman of Bright Tree Village on the forest moon of Endor, this Ewok, had brown fur striped with gold and he wore symbolic headgear.

He ordered the sacrifice of the captured rebels, Luke Skywalker, Han Solo, Chewbacca and R2-D2, in order to honour the 'golden god', C-3PO. Later, he hesitated on the tribe's involvement in the war against the Empire. Fearing for the security of the villagers, he was instinctively afraid that the conflict was far too big for them. However, the Ewoks' entry into the war was finally decided and Logray took part in both the fight and the subsequent victory celebrations.

Loje Nella

This shadowy Riorian was a member of Jabba the Hutt's court and was present when Leia Organa was caught in the act of trying to help Han Solo escape.

Hidden behind a curtain, standing between Droopy McCool and Max Rebo, she laughed heartily when Leia and Solo were discovered and captured.

Lor San Tekka

Lor San Tekka was an old explorer and follower of the Church of the Force who worked for the New Republic.

Having witnessed Force manifestations everywhere in the universe during his travels, San Tekka had always had a solid faith in the essential principles that were once defended by the Jedi Order. He maintained his beliefs throughout the Emperor's reign and could never believe the Imperial lies that made traitors of the Jedi. He secretly hoped, along with the other followers of the Church of the Force, that the light side would return and shine over the galaxy one again.

On the request of the New Republic following the fall of the Empire, he participated in recovering and restoring archives that had been destroyed by the fleeing Imperial officers. Lor San Tekka then travelled to the most remote regions of the galaxy to make notes and provide accounts of what he had discovered. This tedious work of compiling reports and gathering information gave him the opportunity to prove his worth and his faith to the values of the New Republic, and he was able to help the Resistance several times.

Always in search of spirituality and hoping for a well-deserved rest, San Tekka retired to the village of Tuanul, which was hidden in the Kelvin Ravine on Jakku. There he joined a community who also worshipped the principles of the Force. From then on he led the austere life of a pilgrim, but he was soon asked by Poe Dameron, the Resistance pilot, to help him find Luke Skywalker. The old man gave the pilot an essential piece of information to help him find the trail of the missing Jedi Knight. San Tekka was then killed by Kylo Ren when the old explorer refused to cooperate after Tuanul was attacked by the First Order's stormtroopers.

Lorth Needa

Lorth Needa hailed from Coruscant and served in the Republic army during the Clone Wars, before going on to become part of the Imperial fleet under the reign of Emperor Palpatine.

The massive restructure of the Imperial forces that followed the destruction of the Death Star represented a unique opportunity for career progression. Needa was just one of the many young officers who found themselves propelled to the highest echelons of the Imperial regime to fill the positions left vacant by the near-extinction of the previous elite command.

While tracking the rebel fleet after the Battle of Yavin, Needa was made captain and took command of the *Imperial*-class Star Destroyer the *Avenger*. This ship was part of Death Squadron, a group of vessels led by the menacing *Executor*, which was under the supervision of Darth Vader. This squadron had one mission, to track and capture rebels, particularly those responsible for the defeat at Yavin, one of whom had caught the Emperor's attention having revealed a great sensitivity to the Force.

Once the Alliance had been located on Hoth, Needa participated in the attack on the rebel base and pursued the fleeing transports. Among those ships was the *Millennium Falcon*, which drew the attention of Vader who had witnessed its departure from Echo Base. The rebel vessel was tracked by the *Avenger* but disappeared into an asteroid field. Needa presumed that the rebel vessel had been destroyed, but the Sith Lord ordered him to intensify his search. The *Millennium Falcon* came face-to-face with the *Avenger* after escaping the jaws of a giant space worm that inhabited one of the asteroids. It flew over the main bridge and landed lightly on the surface of the ship, instantly disappearing from the cruiser's radar screen. Needa, unable to explain the sudden disappearance, presented himself to Darth Vader to offer his apologies, which the Sith Lord accepted before he strangled Needa using his Force powers.

Lott Dod

This Neimoidian senator was a lobbyist for the Trade Federation who, while addressing the Senate, denounced Queen Amidala's testimony about the invasion of Naboo and lied to the other delegates in order to sow the seeds of doubt.

Lott Dod then skilfully convinced his peers to remain inactive by requesting the creation of a commission. Some years later he continued to confuse issues by asserting that not all members of the Trade Federation had joined forces with the Separatists and was therefore able to hide the subversive, anti-Republic actions of the trade conglomerate.

LPA NN-14 Blaster

A practical and handy blaster, the LPA NN-14's reinforced central body shell ensured it was an incredibly durable weapon.

Equipped with a compact grip, a safety catch, a stabilising barrel and a large battery, this weapon boasted impressive firepower. Its specs made it a weapon perfect for scavenger Rey, who was given the LPA NN-14 by Han Solo when they landed on Takodana. Solo considered the emerging Jedi capable of looking out for herself, and gave her the blaster to ensure she would be well-armed during combat.

Lucrehulk-class LH-3210 Cargo Freighter

A gigantic ship shaped like the letter 'C', the LH-3210 was used as a warship by the Trade Federation and the Confederacy of Independent Systems.

Manufactured by Hoersch-Kessel Drive, these huge cargo ships boasted an enormous diameter of over 3 kilometres, and were originally conceived for the transportation of goods. Rather cleverly, the Trade Federation modified a part of its fleet into warships, while retaining their outwardly civil appearance, which kept any suspicions from the Galactic Senate at bay. The most famous *Lucrehulk*-class LH-3210 military freighter was the *Saak'ak*, the Droid Capital Ship, which played a key part in the crisis of Naboo. The Trade Federation's plan to camouflage a warship as a cargo freighter proved remarkably effective, so much so that when Qui-Gon Jinn and Obi-Wan Kenobi boarded the *Saak'ak*, they had no idea it was in fact a warship. The Jedi delegates survived an attempt on their lives while aboard the freighter, before escaping to the surface of the planet of Naboo.

Lufta Shif

A blonde-haired, female member of the Royal Advisory Council of Naboo under the reign of Queen Amidala.

Lufta Shif was present in the Theed throne room during the dramatic first moments of the Trade Federation's invasion of Naboo.

Luggabeast

This cybernetically-customised draught beast was designed to adapt to the most extreme environmental conditions.

The front part of the creature was entirely hidden under thick armour and numerous invasive mechanical systems that gave it increased endurance and stamina, while its forehead device was equipped with air and water purifying tanks. Generally used by Teedos who were able to stay in the desert for a long time, the luggabeasts offered complete self-sufficiency. Sometimes, their owners would equip them with additional armour so they would be able to withstand attacks from other looters.

Luke Skywalker

This Jedi Knight and twin brother of Leia Organa, was born nineteen years prior to the Battle of Yavin and played a decisive role in the fall of the Galactic Empire.

Having helped weaken the Empire's grip on the galaxy, Luke also destroyed the Sith Order with the help of his father, Anakin Skywalker. The destruction of the Emperor brought balance to the Force and allowed Anakin to fulfil his role as the Chosen One.

Luke Skywalker was born on the asteroid Polis Massa a few minutes before his twin sister Leia, during what was possibly the darkest period in galactic history. Their mother, Padmé Amidala, died in childbirth just after giving them their names, while at the same moment their father, Anakin Skywalker, who became Darth Vader, was undergoing heavy medical treatment after being left for dead by Obi-Wan Kenobi following their duel on Mustafar. The twins were separated to protect them from the Emperor, who would probably have been very interested in any Skywalker offspring if he had ever learned of their existence. Luke was trusted to the care of Obi-Wan Kenobi who took him to Tatooine where Luke was raised by the Lars family, with Kenobi keeping watch from a safe distance.

Skywalker lived his first nineteen years on his uncle's farm, but was tortured by the call of adventure. He dreamt of joining the academy and becoming a pilot, but his Uncle Owen did his best to stop such zealous ambitions. Owen thought that Luke was too much like his father for his own good, but young Skywalker's destiny fell into place when Owen Lars acquired two droids, unaware that one of them contained a message to Kenobi. While searching for R2-D2, who had left to deliver the message, Skywalker was ambushed by Tusken Raiders, but was then rescued by Kenobi and followed him home. The old Jedi spoke to Skywalker about his father, before presenting him with his lightsaber. Kenobi then offered to start Luke's Jedi training. The young man hesitated, but when he discovered that the Imperial troops had tracked the droids and killed his aunt and uncle, he made the decision to follow Kenobi.

Skywalker, Kenobi and the droids went to Mos Eisley in search of a pilot to fly them to Alderaan, but the group drew some unwanted attention upon entering the city's main cantina, during which Kenobi was forced to draw his lightsaber and reveal his identity as a Jedi. It was in this cantina that they made the acquaintance of Han Solo, who accepted the job because its payment would enable him to repay the debt he owed to Jabba the Hutt. During the journey aboard the *Millennium Falcon*, Skywalker received his first training in the ways of the Force, in which Kenobi taught him that the senses could sometimes provide the wrong information, and only the Force could reveal the true reality of things.

When they arrived at Alderaan's coordinates, they found nothing but asteroids and quickly understood that the planet had been destroyed. They then came across a TIE fighter that led them to the Death Star, the Empire's gigantic combat station fitted with weaponry that had the ability to destroy a whole planet. Caught in the pull of one of its powerful tractor beams, they had to quickly hatch a plan, which saw Skywalker and Solo succeed in infiltrating the base wearing stormtrooper armour. Needing to deactivate the tractor beam they plugged R2-D2 into the Death Star's database and discovered the location of Princess Leia, who was a prisoner aboard the station.

While Kenobi disengaged the tractor beam, Skywalker succeeded in convincing Solo to conduct an emergency mission to save the senator of Alderaan and, still dressed as stormtroopers, they acted as a detachment assigned to the transfer of a prisoner, Chewbacca, in order to reach the detention quarters where the princess was being held. Once free, Leia took them into a trash compactor in order to escape a group of Imperial soldiers. While inside, Skywalker nearly drowned after becoming entangled in one of the tentacles of a dianoga – a creature that lived in the trash compactor's stagnant waters. They eventually escaped the crushing walls of the compactor and made it back to the *Millennium Falcon*, where they discovered Kenobi in the middle of a lightsaber duel with Darth Vader. The old Jedi attracted the attention of the Imperial guards, which gave the rebels a chance to escape. In order to give Luke and Leia a chance to escape, Kenobi sacrificed himself to Darth Vader. Kenobi's body disappeared and young Skywalker heard Kenobi's distant voice instructing him to run away.

Once Leia had guided them to Yavin 4, home of the Rebel Alliance, Luke joined the rebel fleet and became a member of Red Squadron, under the command of Garven Dreis and alongside his childhood friend from Tatooine, Biggs Darklighter. Luke attended the briefing given by General Dodonna who explained the details of the assault to be led against the Death Star. Then, having failed to convince Solo and Chewbacca to lend their skills to the Alliance, Skywalker embarked on his mission.

Eventually, it was Skywalker, under the call sign of Red Five who succeeded in making the shot that destroyed the space station. After witnessing almost the entire rebel fleet being shot down, Skywalker received assistance in two unexpected ways. The first came in the form of Solo, whose appearance served to divert the attention of Vader. The second came from the spirit of Kenobi, who advised him to abandon all electronic aids and shoot using only his intuition generated from the Force. It was a direct hit and a victory for the rebels, but Vader, who had managed to escape the destruction of the Death Star, detected the extraordinary sensitivity to the Force in the young rebel pilot, and began a restless pursuit to discover his identity.

During the following three years, Skywalker was assigned to numerous missions for the Alliance but, at the same time, he participated in more personal quests in order to pursue his Jedi training and to discover his origins. It was on Hoth, where the rebels decided to install their base, that he took a large step forward in his progression in the ways of the Force. At the end of a routine patrol he was attacked by a wampa that killed his tauntaun, but he succeeded in escaping from the cave of the dangerous creature. However, Skywalker quickly lost consciousness through the cold weather and exhaustion, but before his collapse he saw a vision of his mentor, Obi-Wan Kenobi, who directed him to the Dagobah system in search of a Jedi Master called Yoda, from whom Luke would receive the rest of his Jedi training. Rescued by Solo and despite the fact that his injuries hadn't completely healed, Skywalker took leadership of Rogue Squadron to permit the evacuation of the base while protecting its ground defences from the attack of the Imperial AT-ATs.

Luke boarded his X-wing and took off for Dagobah, but when he arrived on the planet he was forced to crash into one of its many swamps. He soon encountered Yoda, but never would have dreamt that the small, exasperating creature was the greatest Jedi Master of all time. Yoda concealed his identity to test Skywalker's patience and soon drew his conclusion – the son of Anakin was too old to start his training. He believed that so much impatience and temper were faults that invariably led to fear and therefore to the dark side of the Force. It was Kenobi's presence – or, rather, his voice – that defended Luke's case and convinced Yoda to finish his training. However, it proved to be difficult. Even though Skywalker was a hard-working apprentice, his physical, psychological and spiritual practice was full of anger, discouragement and resignation, and Yoda criticised him for being too emotional.

As part of his training, Yoda took Skywalker to an underground cave that manifested an extremely strong presence of the dark side. Skywalker, anxious to prove that he had mastered his fear, entered the cave, making sure to take his weapon with him, even though Yoda had explained that it would be of no use. The Cave of Fear, with its malevolent aura, made real the nightmarish visions of those who visited it and realistically projected the images into the cave's surroundings. For Skywalker, his terrifying vision took the form of Vader, who advanced towards him, lightsaber in hand. The young Jedi took part in a brief duel and decapitated the hallucinated Sith Lord, but then discovered his own face inside the helmet. This step marked the beginning of Skywalker's many visions and premonitions that affected not only the acuteness of his judgment, but also the balance required in the reasoning of a Jedi Knight.

After experiencing a vision of Solo and Leia in terrible suffering, Skywalker halted his training and was determined to rescue them, despite his master's numerous warnings. Although

Skywalker swore that he would return to finish his training, Yoda was sceptical of the abilities of the young man. He lamented the fact that he was their last hope, before the spirit of Kenobi reminded the old Jedi Master that there was another one.

Upon his arrival in Cloud City on Bespin, Skywalker immediately sensed the presence of Vader and was drawn towards the carbon-freezing chamber, where the Sith Lord was waiting to encase the young Jedi in carbonite in order to take him to the Emperor. Believing himself to be ready, Skywalker began the duel for which he had prepared, but Vader was a formidable opponent. Having cut off the hand of the young Jedi, Vader then revealed himself to be Skywalker's father.

When Vader offered the young Jedi the opportunity to join him and establish order in the galaxy, Skywalker threw himself from the top of the reactor shaft, where their fight had reached its climax, opting for death over the dark side. But his fall was stopped when he was sucked into the mouth of a ventilation duct, which ejected him outside of the city. As he clung to a meteorological antenna, overwhelmed by both physical and psychological suffering, he called on the Force to implore Kenobi for help, but with no success. However, another person then crossed his mind – Leia. Princess Leia heard his plea and was able to visualise the location of Skywalker. Eventually rescued by Lando Calrissian aboard the *Millennium Falcon*, Skywalker heard a new voice through the Force – the one of Vader, his father.

Reunited with the rebel fleet, Skywalker replaced his lost hand with an artificial one that was fitted in the medical facilities aboard the frigate, the *Redemption*. Meanwhile Chewbacca and Lando headed for Tatooine aboard the *Millennium Falcon*, where Skywalker soon joined them, having left the responsibility of Red Squadron to Wedge Antilles in order to concentrate on the mission to save Solo.

It was planned that if the first rescue attempt, which involved Leia and Calrissian infiltrating the court of Jabba the Hutt, failed, Skywalker would intervene. He had returned to Tatooine conscious of the fact that he would soon be entering the final phase of his Jedi training, which was marked by the symbolic – but crucial – action of making his own lightsaber. The one that had belonged to his father had been lost on Bespin, so Skywalker created a replacement in the shape of the one that had belonged to his former master, Kenobi, which encouraged a two-handed fighting style. Nevertheless, to symbolically liberate himself from two imposing inheritances, the young Jedi chose a green blade for his lightsaber.

The first rescue plan failed, so Skywalker entered Jabba's Palace, where he attempted some delicate mental persuasion using the Force. Although he didn't have any problems in his first encounters, notably with Bib Fortuna, who submissively took the Jedi to his master, he soon made the bitter discovery that Jabba was completely impervious to the use of the Force. Thrown into the rancor's pit, Skywalker faced the enormous creature that Jabba kept in captivity. He soon took the upper hand and killed the monster by making the heavy portcullis, which guarded the entrance to its lair, crash down upon its head.

Mad with anger at having lost one of his pets, Jabba sentenced the rebel group to death. He ruled that they should be devoured by the Sarlacc at the Great Pit of Carkoon, with the exception of Leia, who had become his personal slave. To satisfy the cruelty of the members of his court, Jabba invited them all aboard his imposing sail barge and transformed the execution into a spectacle. At that moment, Calrissian was the only rebel who had not been unmasked and it was thanks to him and R2-D2, who was concealing Skywalker's lightsaber, that the rebels succeeded in escaping, killing Jabba the Hutt and destroying his barge in the process.

After this mission, Skywalker parted with the group and flew back to Dagobah to honour the promise he had made to Yoda. Ready to finish his training, he found the old Jedi dying. Yoda managed to tell him that only a new confrontation with Vader would mark the end of his training. Yoda explained that Luke's destiny was to cross his father's and that Vader, the Chosen One who was supposed to bring balance to the Force, must come back from the dark side to achieve the prophecy. He confirmed that Vader was his father and after one final pause revealed that there was another Skywalker. These were his last words before his body disappeared and his mind joined the Force.

Flooded by questions and emotions, the spirit of Kenobi materialised in front of his eyes. The old Jedi felt the need to justify his lie about the identity of Skywalker's father and also revealed to him that he had a twin sister – Leia. Kenobi warned the young Jedi about the danger that he could put his friends in if the Emperor ever learned this information.

After his return from Dagobah, Skywalker accompanied Solo and Leia on their mission to Endor, which consisted of destroying the energy generator that powered the protective shield around the second Death Star. Once on the forest moon, he joined Leia in the pursuit of an Imperial patrol on speeder bikes, but they were soon separated. They were reunited later in the village of the Ewoks, where he was prisoner, along with Solo, Chewbacca and the two droids. As they were supposed to be the dinner during a banquet given in honour of C-3PO, Skywalker used the Force to convince the Ewoks that the droid had divine powers, and they were saved.

Later that evening, having heard the history of the Rebellion, the Ewoks decided to join the rebels in their fight against the Empire. Believing that the moment had come to answer the call of his personal quest, Skywalker decided to meet Darth Vader, who was on Endor awaiting his son. But before he left, Skywalker met with Leia and revealed to her the tie that not only bonded the two of them, but which also united them with Vader, so that she could understand what he was about to do.

Skywalker surrendered to the Empire while the rebel fleet prepared to lead the attack on the second Death Star. This apparently mad gesture was motivated by the intimate belief that he could bring his father back to the light side of the Force. Vader presented him to the Emperor, who used all of his cunning to provoke the anger of the young Jedi. When Palpatine finally revealed the trap that he had prepared for the rebel fleet and his friends on Endor, Skywalker seized his lightsaber, planning to strike the Emperor, but Vader countered. This time, the final fight between the Sith Lord and his son was even, as Vader no longer faced an impetuous young apprentice. Despite countering Vader blow for blow, Skywalker fell victim to a terrifying inner struggle as he was conscious of the enormous risk that his anger represented in the fight against the Sith Lord.

After a few minutes of intense combat, Skywalker decided to stop fighting and instead went into hiding in order to calm himself. While Vader used the Force to probe Skywalker's mind he discovered the existence of a sister, which evoked the possibility that she could be converted to the dark side. Driven by fear of the revelation, Skywalker went straight for his father. For the first time, Vader moved back and was quickly overwhelmed by the fury of his adversary, who even managed to cut off his hand.

The Emperor, delighted by the turn of events, congratulated Skywalker and ordered him to kill Vader, so that he instead could take his place at the Emperor's side. As the young Jedi looked down at his own artificial hand, he understood that he was already becoming like Vader. In response to the command, Skywalker threw down his lightsaber and challenged the Emperor by reminding him that he was a Jedi, as his father was before him. Enraged by the response, the Emperor used his terrifying Force lightning against Skywalker. Vader, unable to stand by and witness his son's agony at the hands of Palpatine, gathered the last of his strength and killed the Emperor by hurling him down a shaft leading to the second Death Star's central reactor. Palpatine didn't foresee that the personality trait that turned him into Vader – the refusal to lose his loved ones – was what would also eventually turn him back into Anakin Skywalker.

As Skywalker hurried to help his father he noted that the armour that had kept him alive for more than twenty years had suffered irreparable damage during his struggle with Palpatine. Anakin then asked his son to remove his helmet so that he could look at him one last time, with his own eyes, before dying. Skywalker returned his father's remains to Endor, where he conducted a cremation as dictated by the Jedi funeral ceremony rituals. In the glow of the funeral pyre he saw the spirits of Kenobi, Yoda and his father, united in the Force.

After those events, Skywalker participated in the setting up of the constitution of the New Republic. Nevertheless, he was conscious that, contrary to the former Republic, this one could not benefit from the protection of the Jedi Order. It was mainly for this reason that he decided to recreate the Order from its ashes, and hoped to reproduce the model that once allowed peace to reign for more than a thousand years. It was necessary to prepare a generation of future Jedi for the battles that would happen, and so he chose Ben Solo, the young son of Solo and Leia, as his apprentice. The boy required special attention because he had developed a strong attraction to the dark side and a strange fascination for his grandfather, Darth Vader. Skywalker failed in his ambitious enterprise and was unable to prevent Ben Solo from becoming Kylo Ren and slaughtering all of Skywalker's apprentices.

As a result, Skywalker decided to go into exile and hoped to find the site of the first Jedi temple with the help of Lor San Tekka, who had managed to steal some precious information from the First Order that dated back to the beginning of the Imperial era. After the Jedi cull, the Galactic Empire wanted to make sure that every trace of the Jedi Order had disappeared, so it destroyed all of the Jedi temples and the knowledge held within them. The Empire, followed by the First Order, kept star charts that indicated the positions of all places known to have sheltered the Jedi Order, and it was fragments of these maps that San Tekka possessed.

Thirty years after the Battle of Endor, the elderly explorer received a visit from Poe Dameron, who had been sent by Leia, now general of the Resistance, to recover the star chart that possibly contained information on Skywalker's location. Over the years, the Jedi Master had become something midway between history and legend, and some even believed that Skywalker was nothing more than a myth, invented by the former rebels to glorify their victory and used by the nostalgic followers of the Empire to justify its defeat.

The fragments of the map reached Leia who, at this time, also met Rey, a young wreck-raider from Jakku, who had discovered her own sensitivity to the Force when she came across Skywalker's first lightsaber, which had been lost on Bespin. Leia entrusted Rey with the mission to recover her brother and convince him to return to help her fight the First Order. The combination of the information held by Dameron's droid, BB-8, and that which had been contained in the memory of R2-D2 for many years, allowed them to discover the location of the planet Ahch-To, on which they believed the Jedi was exiled.

Rey found Skywalker on this aquatic planet and presented his lightsaber to him, only to be stunned by Skywalker's refusal to accept it. After Rey's relentless insistence, Skywalker agreed to become the Jedi Master she had been lacking. That very process opened painful wounds for Skywalker, particularly his failed attempts to make a Jedi Knight of his nephew, now Kylo Ren. After much contemplation, Skywalker confronted Ren via a Force projection, and disrupted the First Order's attack on the Resistance. Exhausted by such a powerful feat, Skywalker perished on Ahch-To, becoming one with the Force, and leaving behind only his simple Jedi robes.

Lyn Me

A backing singer and dancer, along with her two colleagues, in the Max Rebo Band.

Her art of choreography married itself perfectly with her Twi'lek beauty. This was a dangerous asset in the court of Jabba the Hutt, since it previously sent the Twi'lek dancer Oola to her death after she resisted Jabba's advances. It was a horrible and traumatic destiny for her colleague and Me subsequently feared for her life, even though she wasn't a slave and was part of a group that did not belong to the vile crime lord. This agonising uncertainty was quickly replaced by the chaos caused when the heroes of the Rebellion arrived to rescue their friend, Han Solo.

Lyra Erso

The brilliant wife of Galen Erso and mother of Jyn, her life was turned upside down by the birth of the Galactic Empire, which eventually led to her tragic end.

Born on Aria Prime, she then excelled at the University of Rudrig. She later worked as a guide for an expedition of researchers and accompanied them on the planet of Espinar to discover and map out a layer of crystals. Her knowledge of the cave network meant she worked closely with a scientist named Galen Erso. Six months later they were married on Coruscant and shared the vision of a life solely devoted to research.

Three years later, Lyra became pregnant and the couple transferred to Vallt, where they worked for Zerpens Industries. Unfortunately, on the brink of the Clone Wars, it was an uneasy time. Before long a coup placed an ally of the Separatists as the head of the world. Hoping to be repatriated, the couple were arrested and Galen was falsely accused of spying for the Republic. Jyn was therefore born in captivity and was only months old when the three of them were liberated by Orson Krennic in a prisoner exchange with the Confederacy of Independent Systems.

Ostentatiously installed in an isolated property on Coruscant, the Erso family seemed to have put its problems behind it. Galen was immersed in exciting work on energy creation and Lyra was offered a position on Alpinn. Despite her confusion at Krennic's interference, she accepted the position on her husband's advice and took their young child with her. She made two stops during the return trip, on Samovar and Wadi Raffa, which were two worlds the Empire had devastated for their ore. Once she had seen the devastation, the scales fell away from her eyes and she understood the brutality of this new regime, that seemed to only get worse under the permanent presence of Palpatine.

Lyra's interest in spirituality increased as a direct result of the political turmoil happening around her. In contradiction with the Imperial beliefs, she was interested in the history and the philosophy of the Jedi Knights, outcasts who had been eliminated throughout the galaxy. Perhaps it was that ideological proximity that led her to become a member of the clandestine Church of the Force, in the depths of Coruscant. No obvious proof demonstrated her involvement, but there was a certain clue in her clothing as she regularly wore scarlet ceremonial dresses, such as the red scarf of the scholars typical to Jedha, one of the last places that continued to demonstrate its faith in the Force.

From that moment, Lyra was clear on the nature of the Emperor's regime and on the fact that her husband actually worked for the Imperial military. She was also clear on the point that Krennic was not their benefactor and that they lived in a gilded cage. When she explained to her husband that his knowledge was going to serve to unleash a major destructive power, she convinced him to escape his terrifying responsibility. Posing as a family that was still part of the elite, they successfully fled and found shelter on the rough and barely inhabited world of Lah'mu. After escaping from that difficult life, she felt the immense relief of no longer being in the clutches of their 'friend' Krennic, and no longer contributing to the Imperial war machine.

Four years later, the thing she feared most occurred in the shape of an elegant Imperial shuttle. They had been found by their old acquaintance, Krennic, who arrived with a squad of death troopers. In spite of a plan that would allow Lyra and her daughter to remain undetected in a secret bunker if Galen was captured, she refused to abandon her husband. She gave instructions and a small kyber crystal pendant to Jyn, then returned to challenge Krennic, armed with a blaster. Determined to not let him kidnap her husband, nor even to benefit from any Imperial leniency, she shot and caught her adversary with a glancing blow to the shoulder. In a fraction of second, she was shot down by one of the elite troopers, in front of her daughter who was hidden nearby. Galen Erso hugged her lifeless body one last time before he left for his long captivity in the exclusive service of the Empire.

Mace Windu

One of the most powerful Jedi, Mace Windu rose to become a Jedi Knight, then member of the Jedi High Council and finally Jedi Master during the last decades of the Republic.

Mace Windu was also the only one to defeat Darth Sidious in a duel, a short-lived victory that was ended by a terrible betrayal. Born on the planet Haruun Kal, Windu was identified as being strongly connected to the Force and he underwent a long and extensive training in the different Jedi arts. He was part of the Jedi Council when Qui-Gon Jinn and his apprentice, Obi-Wan Kenobi, went to settle the minor matter of a blockade between the Trade Federation and the peaceful planet of Naboo.

The news that the two emissaries returned with was far more disturbing than expected. Jinn had been attacked on Tatooine by a Sith, a member of a dark Order committed to the destruction of the Jedi, but presumed extinct. Windu's scepticism, which was shared by Ki-Adi-Mundi, rejected this possibility, but he still promised to do everything possible to discover the identity of the mysterious warrior. His scepticism was also evident on another sensitive topic. Jinn had discovered a young boy, Anakin Skywalker, with no father, but whose cells showed the highest midi-chlorian count that had ever been seen. Deducing that his birth had been brought about by these organisms, which were bound to the Force, Jinn presented Skywalker as the Chosen One of Jedi Prophecy – the one that would return balance to the Force and destroy the Sith.

To be prudent, Windu himself conducted a test of the boy's sensitivity to the Force, which proved to be strong. Nevertheless, Windu thought the child was already too old to detach himself from his fears, notably his relationship to his mother, which was a necessary part of a Jedi's training. After the death of Jinn at the hands of Darth Maul, this time identified with certainty as a Sith, the Council finally agreed to allow Kenobi to train Skywalker. However, Yoda and Windu had been left facing a riddle: was it the Sith Master or the Apprentice that Kenobi had killed? It was with that heavy threat in mind that Windu attended the celebration of the victory on Naboo, where he met the understated and innocuous former senator and now newly elected Supreme Chancellor, Sheev Palpatine.

During the decade that followed, a Separatist movement formed itself within the Republic and started to make ripples that led to war. Windu warned the Chancellor that if war broke out the Jedi Order could not protect the regime alone, as the Jedi were keepers of the peace, not soldiers. The leader of the Separatists was Count Dooku, whom Senator Padmé Amidala suspected of financing an assassination attempt against her. Windu refused to believe the accusation and argued that Dooku was a Jedi and therefore not capable of such things. However, he was forced to face the brutal truth when Kenobi, who had been spying on Dooku and the Separatist Council on Geonosis, revealed that they had no intention of negotiating and had gathered an army ready for war.

Windu left for Geonosis with a Jedi intervention team and saved Kenobi, Skywalker and Amidala from certain death. In the Petranaki Arena he fought the Separatists' battle droids and killed the bounty hunter, Jango Fett, in front of his horrified son, Boba. Nevertheless, Windu's team were outnumbered and Dooku demanded their surrender. The Jedi Master's bold refusal would have led both him and his team to a quick execution, were it not for the arrival of Yoda and an army of clones, which changed the outcome of the battle. Wielding his purple-bladed lightsaber, Windu took command of the five commando units and charged to victory in the Battle of Geonosis. Dooku managed to escape and Windu was left to face the obvious: his old friend had turned to the dark side of the Force. For this reason, he regarded the incredible revelation made by Dooku to Kenobi – that a Sith Lord named Darth Sidious controlled more than a hundred senators – as nothing more than bait and a psychological trick designed to sow doubt. However, he still decided to keep a discreet watch on the Republic Senate.

During the ensuing conflict with the Separatists, known as the Clone Wars, the Jedi Master and his compatriots accepted the positions of generals in command of the Grand Army of the Republic. Windu fought on all fronts: he led his troops on the battlefields; on Coruscant he offered counsel to the Chancellor and supervised the war effort of the Republic; and he also served as a diplomat.

For a long while the incredibly intense mix of missions and activities prevented Windu from seeing clearly what had been going on, but suddenly things fell into place. He had been suspicious of the intentions of Palpatine, who had become, politically, almost all-powerful. When Anakin Skywalker revealed that the real identity of Darth Sidious was Sheev Palpatine, the last veil fell away and Windu discovered the brutal truth. Determined to arrest Palpatine before any further damage could be done, he went to the Chancellor's offices with Jedi Masters Kit Fisto, Agen Kolar and Saesee Tiin, who were slain by Palpatine's lightsaber in mere seconds. However, the toughest confrontation was between Windu and Palpatine. At one point Windu turned the duel in his favour and demonstrated why he deserved the title of 'Champion of the Jedi Order'. Having disarmed his adversary, he threw him to the ground and pinned him at the end of his lightsaber, but he was interrupted by Anakin Skywalker's arrival.

The drama unfolded in a terrifying misunderstanding between the two Jedi. When Windu realised that the Chancellor would never face justice because he controlled both the Senate and the Supreme court, his only chance to stop the Sith's evil was to execute him there and then. What Windu didn't understand was that Skywalker was traumatised by his vision of Amidala dying in childbirth and needed Palpatine to save her. All he needed was a pretext to distrust the Jedi, and Windu provided him with it when he asked him to carry out an act that was completely at odds with the Jedi Code – to kill a disarmed man on the ground instead of allowing him a trial.

Shouting 'I need him!', Skywalker raised his lightsaber, but Windu didn't realise it was the sign of the young man surrendering to Palpatine's influence. Skywalker cut off Windu's arm. In a state of shock, he was then struck by the Force lightning of Palpatine, who no longer feigned weakness, but instead revelled in his power. Just seconds earlier, Windu had almost extinguished the Sith threat, which would have avoided the terrible years that followed for the galaxy. Instead, he was violently projected through a broken window and fell to his death among the towering buildings of Coruscant. Imperial propaganda later described Mace Windu as the leader of a criminal gang, responsible for the illegal interruption of executions on Geonosis, which led to the Clone Wars.

Magva Yarro

A member of Saw Gerrera's extremist troop on Jedha, Yarro experienced a deep trauma on her homeworld of Ghorman.

An naive idealist, Yarro believed she was able to counter the Imperial oppression through non-violent means and joined a political demonstration on her planet. The peaceful protest turned into a massive bloodbath, of which she was one of the few survivors. This massacre, which happened two years before the Battle of Yavin, showed her the relentless determination and the true face of the evil regime, and it triggered a psychological reaction in her to search for the fiercest faction against the Empire, and join it.

She rejected the Rebel Alliance of Mon Mothma, which she thought wasn't fierce enough, despite the fact that Mothma was the only senator to openly condemn the slaughter at Ghorman. Instead, Yarro joined Gerrera's partisans where she became one of the pilots in the six-strong X-wing squadron known as the Cavern Angels. Based in the Catacombs of Cadera, she nonchalantly looked Jyn Erso up and down as the young girl was taken to Gerrera. That moment was quickly followed by the need to evacuate the lair owing to the risk of being buried under tons of rock and rubble created by the shock wave from the annihilation of the Holy City of Jedha by the Death Star.

Malakili

The keeper of the creatures in Jabba's Palace, this Corellian was once a trainer of animals, but became a slave after one of his circus beasts went on the rampage and killed some spectators.

Bought by the slug-like crime lord, he was put in charge of the menagerie that contained a rancor, which he became particularly attached to. When Luke Skywalker fell into the cave of the immense creature, Malakili had no doubt of the fate that awaited the young man in black. However, it was the Jedi that came out victorious against the towering rancor. Mad with pain and unable to believe what had transpired, the keeper rushed into the underground cave only to have his worst fears confirmed. Utterly shocked by the loss of his beloved pet, the tears began to flow and Malakili had to be comforted by his assistant, Giran, who was also saddened by the rancor's death.

Malastare

A planet mentioned by Qui-Gon Jinn as a place where particularly dangerous and fast podraces took place.

It was also the homeworld of the Dugs, and one of the best podracers ever, Sebulba. However, at the Galactic Senate, this world was generally represented by the Gran. In fact, Malastare's senator, a Gran named Ainlee Teem, opposed Palpatine for the title of Supreme Chancellor during the events on Naboo.

Mark IV Sentry Droid (IM4)

This line of drone droids was developed by the Imperial Department of Military Research. Equipped with highly efficient sensors and able to fly at a low altitude, the droids were often used for military scouting missions.

However, their ability to record holographic images also led to them being used as mobile surveillance cameras. After the Empire followed the droids C-3PO and R2-D2 to Tatooine, it was a small fleet of these patrol drones that were sent to track them, assisting the sandtroopers already on the ground.

Mark Omega

This was the name of a secret project briefly exposed by two rebel agents in the vault of the Citadel Tower on Scarif.

While desperately looking for the Death Star plans among the thousands of data cartridges in the Imperial databank, Jyn Erso and Cassian Andor had a glimpse of the atrocious hidden face of the Empire. This codename carried a denomination which seemed to designate an outcome (Omega), but it was not possible to deduce its nature. The Rogue One operation didn't have the time to retrieve this file in order to send it to the Rebel Alliance.

Mars Guo

Mars Guo was a podracer pilot in the Boonta Eve Classic Podrace in which Anakin Skywalker participated.

It was the first time this Bardottan had taken part in the event, as mentioned by the commentator Fode. He did an acceptable job and even managed to reach the second position in the pack behind the favourite, Sebulba. It was Sebulba that destroyed Guo's chances when he intentionally threw a metallic item behind him. It hit one of his enormous engines, which caused a technical problem that caused Guo to crash. One piece of Guo's podracer almost decapitated Skywalker, while another cut through one of his steel cables, which caused him to almost lose control of his podracer.

Mas Amedda

This Chagrian was vice chair and speaker of the Galactic Senate during the Supreme Chancellor Finis Valorum's tenure, and continued to mediate debates and oversee senatorial votes under Sheev Palpatine.

During the events on Naboo, he presided over the vote of no confidence against Valorum, which had been requested by Queen Amidala and slyly suggested by Palpatine following the Senate's inaction over the occupation of their homeworld by the Trade Federation. On the day the senators demanded that this vote take place, the natural authority of the blue, horned resident of Champalla came into play. Amedda soothed the uproar in the chamber having used only the power of his voice. He retained his post when Palpatine was elected new Supreme Chancellor and become a member of his entourage. He then presided over the session that saw Naboo's delegate, Jar Jar Binks, propose to give full powers to Chancellor Palpatine to counter the Confederacy of Independent Systems.

Massassi Temple

Built on the moon of Yavin 4 by the Massassi, the Rebel Alliance welcomed the use of the temple as their base and headquarters after they abandoned the one installed on Dantooine.

The Great Temple had been erected by the Massassi 5,000 years before the Battle of Yavin, when the Massassi was submitted to the slavery of the Sith. Surrounded by thick, lush jungle, the temple met all the criteria for the absolute discretion necessary to make it a military base. The set-up was relatively simple: although specific facilities were necessary for the control room and the chamber destined to hold martial ceremonies, the temple offered a large space that was used as a hangar for the fleet. The rebels evacuated the temple and Yavin 4 at the end of the Battle of Yavin, and settled three years later on the planet of Hoth.

Massiff

A small, four-legged, growling hunter found on desert worlds like Tatooine or Geonosis, the massiff was around 1 metre tall and was usually used as a guard beast.

It had a powerful set of jaws and its bite was very dangerous. A network of spikes on its back reinforced its natural defences, and its large eyes allowed it to see in the dark. The creatures were popular among the Tusken Raiders, who used them to hunt and kept them as pets. They were also used by the Weequay pirates and the clone troopers of the Republic.

Mawhonic

Mawhonic was a large-eyed Gran pilot who participated in the Boonta Eve Classic Podrace.

At the beginning of the race, he was placed on the right of the grid, which gave him a great start and enabled him to place himself just behind the race favourite, Sebulba. Unfortunately for him, he became Sebulba's first victim. Mawhonic didn't take the necessary care against such a vicious opponent, and, having driven too near a rock wall, he gave Sebulba the chance to send his green podracer spinning off the track during the first round.

Max Rebo

This very popular Ortolan musician was the leader of the Max Rebo Band.

He could be identified from afar by his blue skin and his calm, laid-back manner. Nevertheless, this gifted musician knowingly worked mainly for criminals and other doubtful clientele and it was quite common to see him play for Jabba the Hutt, one of the biggest crime lords of the galaxy.

Max Rebo Band

A popular music group that contained no less than twelve members, that could be seen playing for Jabba the Hutt at his palace on Tatooine.

Its members included singers Sy Snootles and Joh Yowza; singers and dancers Greeata Jendowanian, Lyn Me and Rystáll Sant; and musicians Ak-rev, Doda Bodonawieedo, Barquin D'an, Droopy McCool, Rappertunie, Umpass-stay and Max Rebo. Under the guidance of their leader, the blue organist Rebo, they never hesitated to play for dubious customers or even gangsters. In fact, they had become accustomed to playing their repertoire in shady venues. However, their music didn't always calm the spirits of their criminal clientele.

On one occasion, in front of the band's very eyes, Jabba the Hutt threw his most beautiful slave girl into a pit to be eaten alive after she refused his advances. Later, several members of the band joined Jabba's courtiers to surprise Princess Leia Organa as she tried to free Han

Solo. The destiny of the band seemed to follow the unhealthy downward spiral of the Hutt and, after being engaged to provide the musical background to the executions at the Great Pit of Carkoon, it was a miracle that they all escaped the destruction wrought by Luke Skywalker and his friends.

Maximillian Veers

This general of the Imperial army who hailed from the planet Denon, was famous for his exploits during the Battle of Hoth.

Following the destruction of the Death Star, Veers was assigned to the armed forces sent in search of the rebel base and was placed at the disposal of Death Squadron, a Star Destroyer detachment led by the *Executor*, the dreaded flagship of Darth Vader. When a probe droid reported from the planet of Hoth, Vader took the decision to attack the planet without delay and planned to conduct an orbital bombardment that would give the rebels no chance of escape. Admiral Ozzel's mistake, which brought the Imperial fleet out of hyperspace much too close to the planet and therefore revealed its presence to the rebels, allowed Veers to show the extent of his efficiency in combat. The ground troops were used to destroy the generator of the protective shield so that an assault on the base could be launched.

Veers deployed five four-legged AT-ATs that came under fire from Rogue Squadron, a group of rebel snowspeeders. Although Veers lost two units, he destroyed the generator as planned. As a result, the rebels sustained heavy human and material losses and had to improvise a delicate evacuation, with the last vessels of the fleet no longer protected by the shield. The Imperial troops were then able to invade the base very quickly and, thanks to Veers, Darth Vader's army was able to inflict a historic military defeat on the Alliance.

Maz Kanata

The mysterious manager of Maz's Castle on the planet Takodana was also a legendary pirate.

For over a millennium, Maz Kanata's frail figure welcomed travellers from everywhere in the galaxy to her castle – a haven of peace that offered strict neutrality so everyone could relax or talk business. Despite her fragile appearance, this strong-willed, generous innkeeper hid a huge power. Having born witness to some of the universe's great upheavals, she had acquired the capacity to read people's spirits and to understand the world around her. Aware of the balance of power and the successive shifts of the Force between light and dark, she resolutely stood against the dark side and offered help to all those who fought malevolent forces of any nature. Although she had a privileged bond with the Force, she had never felt the need to develop her sensitivity and used it only when she needed to prevent danger.

She kept numerous treasures and antiquities in an old crate made of wroshyr wood, among which were many artefacts that had been decisive in the struggle against the dark side of the Force. Kanata had the lightsaber that had belonged to the legendary Jedi Knight, Luke Skywalker, in her possession. When Han Solo, accompanied by Rey, Finn and BB-8, arrived at her castle, she welcomed Solo with a surly face that belied her fondness for the famous smuggler. She also had a special affection towards Chewbacca, who she jokingly called her 'boyfriend'. Maz tried to help the small group, allowing Rey to keep the lightsaber and showing her the path of the Force. After the First Order's troops raided the castle, she fled and disappeared.

Maz Kanata's Castle

This famous ancient inn was built on the banks of one of the numerous lakes on the planet of Takodana in the Tashtor sector.

As Takodana had stayed neutral throughout its entire history, Maz Kanata's Castle served as a haven for all kinds of people with different goals (and sometimes with doubtful morality). Decorated with Maz's statue, the building stood on the edge of a forest and the bank of a quiet lake where, legend had it, Sith and Jedi had once fought. To Maz, this contrast represented a cosmic balance. A tasteful mix of ancient and contemporary, the castle was full of sensors and communication devices that connected it to the outside world. Located at the crossroads of the trade routes between the Inner and Outer Rim, Maz's Castle was on the cultural line that separated the Core and the border. Maz's rules were simple: there was to be no discussion about politics or war; no one received special treatment; and business always came first. Diplomacy and protocol weren't welcomed at the castle, where each disagreement could be solved by a good old-fashioned brawl.

The inn provided many services, including loans, medical assistance and navigational updates, as well as a whole host of expertise on various subjects, but it was also a gambling den, where it was possible to play numerous games of chance like Sabacc, pazaak or dejarik. The games were the perfect outlet for pirates, smugglers, crooks and warriors to clash or prove their worth instead of letting their fists (when they had fists) do the talking. Gambling chips, which could only be exchanged at Maz's, chance cubes and spheres, and a Deia's Dream table were all available for the clientele, as well as a combat arena where bets were placed on games of droid-ball fighting. Han Solo, accompanied by Rey, Finn and BB-8, found shelter here while waiting for the Resistance. The smuggler knew Maz well, and also knew that her castle was the perfect place to hide from law-enforcement officers.

MB450 Macrobinoculars

An electronic optical device that allowed users to conduct observations from afar, these binoculars benefited from an aid that provided additional information relating to the distance and altitude of the objects being watched.

The MB450 could also be used at night, and some models possessed optics equipped with a recording system that allowed selected pictures to be saved.

MC75 Star Cruiser

A transport ship designed and constructed by the Mon Calamari.

Aware of the fate the Empire had in mind for them, the Mon Calamari anticipated its exodus and constructed immense star cruisers camouflaged among the buildings of their submarine cities. When the day came, they utilised the vessels to safely transport their people to the borders of space. The ships' hulls were reinforced and were equipped with weapons that ensured the vessels were not to be messed with. The space in the public atrium was modified to become a docking bay and a repair shop. Compared to the MC80, the MC75 was distinguished by its long ventral and vertical fin, at the end of which was the command bridge. Admiral Raddus' MC75 star cruiser, the *Profundity*, played a crucial part in the Battle of Scarif.

MC80 Star Cruiser

An assault ship designed and constructed by the Mon Calamari.

Notable for their organic design, which was made of circular shapes, these command or assault ships couldn't look any more different from the angular, sharp and aggressive appearance of the Imperial Star Destroyers. Despite the MC80's appearance, it was heavily armed with dozens of turbolasers and ion cannons, and the MC80 had the capacity to deliver ten fighter squadrons. Several MC80s took part in the Battle of Endor, including the *Liberty* and *Home One*.

ME-8D9 'Emmie'

This mysterious droid was a regular to Maz's Castle on the planet of Takodana.

Little was known about this droid, except that it seemed to have been there forever and was certainly part of the castle's old population – it could have even been as old as Maz herself. Its systems were still operational and it had a pelvic servomotor that guaranteed perfect balance, as well as an armoured, data-storage unit that held who knew what information. Its vision was based on a multi-spectrum photoreceptor and its bronzium-enriched finish gave it an elegant, coppery look.

Mechanic Droid

See DUM-series Pit Droids

Meditation Chamber

A room used by Force-sensitive people to commune with their energy.

Whether used by a Jedi or a Sith, a meditation chamber came in many different forms, and was often very austere in appearance. It was designed to mirror the internal emptiness essential to the practice of the Force.

Darth Vader's meditation chamber aboard the *Executor* flouted the typically sombre appearance of such chambers, twinning as a medical room. It was also a pressure cabin in which he could breathe without the aid that his sophisticated armour. The chamber was equipped with several monitors and computers that scanned his body and analysed the results, which the computer then reported back to the Sith Lord.

Melee

A resident of the desert planet of Tatooine, her path crossed with the slave boy Anakin Skywalker before he was freed from slavery.

As a small child she followed Skywalker around on Tatooine, and asserted that his podracer would never work. She was proved wrong when Skywalker won the very next Boonta Eve Classic Podrace.

Midi-chlorians

Midi-chlorians were intelligent, microscopic life forms that were contained in every living being at a cellular level.

Those who had developed a particular sensitivity to the Force were able, through meditation, to hear the Force speak to them, and by listening to these inner life forms they could gain an understanding of its will. The level of midi-chlorians inside a person could be determined by a blood test. At more than 20,000, Anakin Skywalker's level was the highest ever seen, and contributed to the theory, strengthened by his mother's confirmation that he had no father, that he could have been conceived by the midi-chlorians themselves to be the Chosen One.

Millennium *Falcon*, the

Indisputably the most famous Corellian YT-1300 light freighter, initially manufactured by the factories of the Corellian Engineering Corporation, this vessel became the property of Han Solo after he won it from Lando Calrissian in a game of Sabacc.

Saying that the *Millennium Falcon* was a modified ship would be nothing short of a huge understatement, given that it was nearly impossible to keep track of all the improvements Han Solo made to it. However, if there was one thing for certain, it was that none of the modifications were of a cosmetic nature. In fact, its sorry-looking appearance cleverly disguised its true capabilities.

The basic features of the YT-1300 model included a circular shape of about 35 metres in length, which featured two powerful mooring arms, and an unusually placed flying deck that allowed direct visibility when the ship was used as a tug. It could carry six passengers, as well as two crew members, and a maximum cargo of 100 tonnes. Of the known modifications made to the *Millennium Falcon*, many were influenced by the nature of the activity of its successive owners. Solo pushed the class of its hyperdrive to the impressive level of 0.5 and reinforced its armament by upgrading two shooting turrets using a four-cannon battery, two missile tube carriers and a small cannon blaster that could be used in the event of a ground attack. The vessel was also fitted with five escape pods, scanner-resistant smuggling compartments and a dejarik game table.

The *Millennium Falcon*'s involvement in operations proved decisive on numerous occasions. It participated in the assault on the Death Star, intervening at just the right time to help Luke Skywalker make the successful shot that eventually led to the space station's explosive destruction. Then, three years later, Solo arrived on Hoth – where the Rebel Alliance was taking shelter – with the *Millennium Falcon* in need of repair. However, before repairs could be completed the base had to be evacuated after coming under attack from Imperial troops, and Solo, Princess Leia, C-3PO and Chewbacca were forced to escape aboard the *Millennium Falcon*. After being chased into an asteroid field and landing in the mouth of a giant space worm, Solo made for the Anoat system and Cloud City, which was under the stewardship of his old friend, Lando Calrissian. There he hoped to finish making the necessary repairs to the vessel, but was instead captured by the Empire who handed him over to Boba Fett, who in turn delivered Solo to Jabba the Hutt. With Solo gone, the *Millennium Falcon* fell into the hands of its previous owner, Lando Calrissian, Leia, Chewbacca and the droids.

After the rescue of Han Solo, the *Millennium Falcon* became part of the rebel fleet and officially joined the assault against the second Death Star. Once again, its involvement was decisive. With Lando Calrissian at the helm, the *Millennium Falcon* launched the missile that destroyed the unfinished space station, then victoriously shot out of the flames just seconds after the explosion.

About twenty years later, the *Millennium Falcon* was stolen from Han Solo. Having passed through the hands of several owners it fell into abandonment, and was the property of Unkar Plutt at the Niima outpost on the planet of Jakku when Rey and Finn, accompanied by the droid BB-8, stole it to escape a First Order raid. A short time after leaving the orbit of the planet, they were boarded and searched by none other than Han Solo and Chewbacca, who were at the controls of a huge cargo ship. Having returned to his former career as a smuggler, Solo inspected his old ship and quickly discovered Rey and Finn. They explained they were on an important mission to reach the Resistance and safely deliver the droid who carried a star map showing the location of Luke Skywalker, who had for many years been in exile.

Following the First Order's attack on Takodana, Solo used the *Millennium Falcon* to infiltrate Starkiller Base where he found Rey, who had been captured during the attack. But it was down to Chewbacca to finish the mission as the new captain of the *Millennium Falcon* following Solo's death during his confrontation with his son, Kylo Ren. The Wookiee saved Finn and Rey by taking them back to the Resistance's base. Having recovered the coordinates of Luke Skywalker's location, Rey, accompanied by Chewbacca and R2-D2, boarded the *Millennium Falcon* and made her way to Ahch-To to find Skywalker.

Milton Putna

This Imperial lieutenant was in charge of the strategic controls that allowed access to the secure vault of the Citadel Tower on Scarif.

After his career as a librarian, he was recruited for this position of trust because of his mastery of database organisation and his unwavering commitment to Emperor Palpatine's regime. A large figure behind his console, the security officer was stunned by K-2SO during the rebel infiltration during the Battle of Scarif. Having been dragged, unconscious, across the floor by Jyn Erso and Cassian Andor, his last action was to unknowingly open the armoured main door for them, with his right hand, which was used for digital recognition.

Mochot Steep

A trading hub on the desert planet of Tatooine in the Outer Rim.

Mochot Steep was a site where traders would come to trade, barter and exchange goods and wares. It was a popular haunt of the Jawas of Tatooine.

Moisture Farm

An agricultural operation that produced water on arid and hot planets by extracting water vapour from the humid air via the use of vaporators.

On Tatooine, these farms were usually rather big, notably that of the Lars family, where Luke Skywalker was raised.

Momaw Nadon

A male from the planet of Ithor who was nicknamed 'Hammerhead', Nadon was a Rebel Alliance sympathiser who lived in exile on Tatooine to escape the Empire.

He witnessed the argument between the old Jedi Knight Obi-Wan Kenobi and Dr. Cornelius Evazan in the Mos Eisley Cantina.

Mon Calamari Star Cruiser

See MC80 Star Cruiser

Mon Mothma

Mon Mothma was a memorable politician, originally from the planet Chandrila, who served during three different regimes: the Galactic Republic, the Empire and the New Republic.

As one of her planet's representatives to the Senate, Mothma was at first indistinguishable from the other politicians that could be found in the institution. However, as the Separatist crisis increased she began to emerge as a predominant face on the public stage. Along with other well-known figures in the Senate, such as Bail Organa and Padmé Amidala, she created a group known as the 'Loyalist Committee' in order to support the actions of Supreme Chancellor Palpatine.

Mothma wanted to establish a dialogue with the Confederacy of Independent Systems as part of her objective to achieve peace, but it was overshadowed by military strength when the Clone Wars was declared. Meanwhile, the Supreme Chancellor continued to grow in power and the once pro-Palpatine Loyalist Committee paradoxically became the core resistance against the powerful politician, although even then they never suspected his secret intentions.

When Palpatine founded the Galactic Empire, Mothma retained her position within the new Imperial Senate, but, undercover and with the help of Bail Organa, she began to plant the seeds of a rebellion against the autocratic regime that eventually led to the creation of the Rebel Alliance. However, it was two specific events that finally pushed her to join the rebels. First, the dissolution of the Senate and secondly, the tragic disappearance of Organa during the destruction of Alderaan.

She became the main political rebel leader during the Galactic Civil War, and among her numerous interventions within the Alliance was the briefing aboard the command frigate, where she unveiled the construction of the second Death Star and predicted the Emperor's arrival aboard it. Those two pieces of information drove the Rebellion to engage in the Battle of Endor, although it was a conflict that Mothma did not physically attend as the Alliance wished to ensure her safety.

The death of Palpatine brought the partial disintegration of the Empire, which allowed the Rebellion to form the New Republic and a new Galactic Senate on Mothma's homeworld of Chandrila. Her election as the first chancellor saw her strip the role of all the powers it had accrued under Palpatine's tenure during the Clone Wars. After the Battle of Jakku, the Republic and the Empire signed a peace treaty, known as the Galactic Concordance, which gave the Senate the opportunity to pass a military disarmament law that was one of Mothma's most profound wishes.

As a result, the Republic armed forces were reduced to the minimum in favour of local defence units dedicated to every world. The Chancellor also reformed the way the New Republic worked, in order to modify it and distinguish it from its predecessor. From then on, the Senate sat in a capital that was established on a rotating basis between the different worlds that had regrouped as the New Republic. Mothma, although still strong in her vision, became weakened by illness and was forced to withdraw from office. She left behind the legacy of an unforgettable career.

Monarch of Naboo

The queen, or king, of Naboo was elected by the citizens of the planet and was assisted by the Royal Advisory Council, who kept them informed of events and helped them make decisions.

It was therefore a democratic monarchy, with no hereditary dynasty. The citizens of Naboo believed that the young had more wisdom and purity than adults and as a result, often elected young women to the role. Padmé Amidala was just fourteen years old at the beginning of the first of her two mandates, and the young age of her successors, Queens Jamillia and Apailana, was also striking.

Moons of lego

The orbiting moons of the planet of lego.

According to the belief of the young and naive Anakin Skywalker, these moons were inhabited by angels who looked like Queen Padmé Amidala.

Moroff

A mercenary gunslinger that joined Saw Gerrera's troops on Jedha.

This huge Gigoran with long white hair was not an idealist, but sold his services to anyone who was willing to pay for them. His weapon of choice was his dangerous 'Blastmill' Vulk TAU-6-23 rotary cannon blaster. The pay and the company of the partisans suited the grouchy giant, and he carried a vocoder to enable him to speak Basic with his comrades. He was part of the first patrol that, along with Two Tubes, captured the deserting Imperial pilot, Bodhi Rook and took him to Gerrera. He also participated in the assault at Tythoni Square and nimbly carried away an orange container of kyber crystals before the arrival of the AT-ST. However, the Gigoran wasn't among the troops that stopped and transported Jyn Erso and her friends to the Catacombs of Cadera.

Mos Eisley

This town was best known for accommodating the biggest spaceport on Tatooine and held the accolade of being one of the most wretched hives of scum and villainy in the whole galaxy.

Located in a craggy, rolling area, Mos Eisley spaceport was one of the nerve centres of trade – both legal and illegal – in the Outer Rim Territories. The colourful, buzzing activity of Mos Eisley offered a striking contrast to the desolate wasteland that surrounded it, and proof of its importance in the galaxy could be found in the spontaneously organised ceremonies and huge celebrations following the fall of the Empire that were held in its streets.

The wreckage of an ancient starship stranded in the middle of the town gave birth to a legend about the creation of Mos Eisley, which suggested that the original settlers had been the survivors of the crash.

Mos Eisley Cantina

Most famously, this was the place where Luke Skywalker and Obi-Wan Kenobi first met Han Solo and Chewbacca during their hunt for a pilot to take them to the planet of Alderaan.

The Mos Eisley Cantina was popular with criminals and smugglers, and attracted an almost exhaustive variety of different species from across the known systems. The numerous fights that erupted in the bar were usually met with indifference – and a few seconds after a fight broke out, things would return to normal. It was here that the bounty hunter Greedo discovered and confronted Han Solo, and hoped to turn the space smuggler over to Jabba the Hutt. But Greedo didn't leave the cantina alive. As he feigned a pleasant chat with Han Solo, the smuggler discreetly aimed his blaster under the table and killed the green-faced bounty hunter.

Mos Espa

This Tatooine city was home to a spaceport and also a well-known sporting event.

Located near the Dune Sea, the city, which regularly experienced sandstorms, was especially famous throughout the galaxy for its podrace – the yearly Boonta Eve Classic that took place in the Mos Espa Arena. This type of mechanical competition had always been known for its element of danger, but on Mos Espa it could be lethal as the rules were very simple and even a nine-year-old child could participate 'legally'. Of course, this race led to illegal gambling, of which Jabba the Hutt took his share.

Another pillar of the economy was slavery. Although the squalid trade had been forbidden by the laws of the Republic, they hardly had any impact on a planet of the Outer Rim, which was known to provide cheap labour. Slavery was also a source of profit itself in the city, which resulted in a population of slaves so important to Mos Espa that a district of modest dwellings had been reserved for them.

One of these dwellings was home to the young Anakin Skywalker and his mother, Shmi, and it was here that they welcomed Jedi Master Qui-Gon Jinn and Queen Padmé Amidala. It was the starting point of an epic tale that went on to have many consequences for the galaxy. In economical terms, the spaceport of Mos Espa was less important than that of Mos Eisley, but it still attracted many, from well-off scrap merchants like Watto to the stalls of poor storekeepers, which included Jira, the humble fruit seller.

Mos Espa Arena

Located at the north point of the Dune Sea in Tatooine's Mos Espa, this arena hosted the annual Boonta Eve Classic Podrace.

Formed of several buildings, the arena included a hangar for the podracers, an observation platform used by the officials of the race, plus the commentators' studio and the private stalls – the largest being reserved for Jabba the Hutt. Most impressive by far were the arena's open terraces, which could hold up to 100,000 spectators. The terraces were curved in a similar shape to the amphitheatre, following the natural curve of the Mos Espa canyon, and offered spectacular views of the all-important start and finish line.

Mosep Binneed

A small creature from the planet Nimban, Binneed, like most other representatives of his species, had big ideas about becoming a bureaucrat.

He lived on Tatooine at the beginning of the Galactic Civil War and worked for Jabba the Hutt alongside numerous other accountants and henchmen. Like all patrons in the Mos Eisley Cantina, he witnessed the two arguments that followed Obi-Wan Kenobi's arrival in the bar: Kenobi's disagreement with Dr. Evazan and the fight between Han Solo and Greedo that ended in the death of the Rodian bounty hunter.

Binneed perished four years later during the battle at the Great Pit of Carkoon, which was supposed to see the death of Luke Skywalker and his friends. However, they succeeded in turning things around and put an end to the reign of Tatooine's crime lord, Jabba the Hutt.

Mospic High Range

The frontier between Mos Espa and the Dune Sea.

This rocky region was made up of some of the highest mountains in Tatooine.

Mouse Droid

The MSE-6 repair droid, better known as the Mouse Droid, was developed and produced by Rebaxan Columni for the Empire.

Small in size, it was less than 30 centimetres high, this four-wheeled model was used for basic maintenance and cleaning tasks.

Muftak

A male Talz from the planet of Orto Plutonia, this species had the peculiar feature of possessing two pairs of eyes of different sizes.

Muftak had made a career as a successful pickpocket on Tatooine, despite two major handicaps that would have normally impacted on his chosen line of work. At a height of more than 2 metres he was very tall and his body, covered with white fur, would have been more useful as camouflage on Hoth. Both of these physical attributes didn't lend themselves to the stealth required by a pickpocket. He was in the Mos Eisley Cantina when the famous smuggler, Han Solo first met the Jedi Knight Obi-Wan Kenobi.

Multi-troop Transport

This armoured repulsorlift vehicle had the capacity to transport 112 B1 combat droids in the battlefield.

It was used by the Trade Federation during the invasion of Naboo, and the Confederacy of Independent Systems during the Clone Wars, when it was adapted to transport B2 combat droids. It was this type of vehicle that nearly ran over a distraught Jar Jar Binks in the first minutes of the ground invasion of Naboo.

Mustafar

An Outer Rim planet situated in the Atravis sector, Mustafar was a molten world with a scorched crust, lava landscapes, ashen skies and a wasteland that was littered with volcanic rocks.

This world possessed an array of valuable minerals, which were mined by the Techno Union that had installed several mining facilities on the planet. Although the fiery conditions on the planet's surface made mining on Mustafar costly, it was still profitable, which led the Techno Union to maintain its hold on the inhospitable world. During the Clone Wars, the bounty hunter Cad Bane was asked by the Sith to kidnap Force-sensitive children and to take them to Mustafar. However, the Jedi thwarted this plan.

After the Battle of Coruscant, General Grievous escorted the leaders of the Separatist movement to Mustafar. The leaders were then killed by Anakin Skywalker, who had become Darth Vader, ending the Clone Wars. Vader then engaged his old friend and master Obi-Wan Kenobi in an epic battle that left Vader scorched and near death. Vader was rescued from a fiery death by the Sith Lord Darth Sidious, who took him back to Coruscant.

Mynock

These silicon-based, parasitic flying creatures could be found throughout the galaxy.

Mynocks were attracted to all technology that used energy – be it a device or a vehicle – and could often be found feeding from generators, cables, batteries and converters. They were able to drain a starship of all its energy in just a few minutes. Their physical make-up allowed them to live in both the atmospheric layers of a planet and the emptiness of space, and they could even sometimes be found in asteroids, where they lived as parasites in the gigantic exogorths (space slugs).

Mytus Adema

An ambitious lieutenant serving under the orders of General Sotorus Ramda at the Imperial Centre of Military Research on Scarif, Mytus Adema was stationed in the command centre located in the Citadel Tower.

He was present when Director Orson Krennic disembarked and requested all of the communications made by Galen Erso that were held on site. The huge task that his superior, Ramda, seemed to dread was a gift for the young soldier who was eager to discredit the general in order to get promoted. However, when the series of explosions triggered by the Rogue One rebel group began, he shared the same reaction as his superior – a stunned silence.

It was Krennic who shook everyone from their stupor when he demanded the garrison to be mobilised. To make matters worse and believing that he was doing the right thing, Adema then uselessly sent troops to locations where there was no fighting, after falling for the trap that pilot Bodhi Rook and Corporal Tonc had created. However, he was also responsible for supplying Krennic with the critical information that there was an intrusion in the secure vault.

Naboo

A planet situated in the Chommell sector, Naboo was the homeworld of some of the great, emblematic figures of the Republic, such as Padmé Amidala, Jar Jar Binks and Sheev Palpatine.

The small planet possessed a peculiar geological attribute in that it had no molten core, but was essentially made of a rocky aggregate full of underwater tunnels and galleries. This make-up also affected the landscape, which consisted of rolling plains and grassy hills with swampy areas full of different-sized lakes that were connected by numerous waterways. Naboo possessed a rich ecosystem, as much in its depths as on the surface.

The people of Naboo were divided into different species and classes. On the surface, the peaceful Naboo made a living from their handmade items that were traded between the great river cities and Theed, the capital of the planet and seat of royal power. The rest of the population was made of farmers who lived in the great green spaces of Naboo or in the Lake Country. Underwater, the Gungans lived in great aquatic cities made of hydrostatic forcefield bubbles that they could pass through at will. Their capital, Otoh Gunga, was at the bottom of the great Lake Paonga.

Naboo became the target of an aggressive blockade and was then invaded by the Trade Federation, who had been secretly manipulated by the Sith Lord Darth Sidious. The conflict ended after the Battle of Naboo, which saw the birth of an alliance between the Naboo and the Gungans, which strengthened their bonds both for the battle and the future.

Naboo Crisis

See Invasion of Naboo

Naboo N-1 Starfighter

Used by the Royal Security Forces of Naboo during escorts, patrols and defence missions, this elegant one-seater starfighter represented a fusion of beauty and technology typical of the planet's elegant society.

The hull of the fighter was painted a vivid yellow, while its nose was chromium-plated in a way that recalled Queen Amidala's royal vessel. It was constructed at the Theed Palace Space Vessel Engineering Corps. On the technical side, it had two J-type engines and a Nubian Monarc C-4 hyperdrive that gave it incredible speed, while its firepower was assured by two laser cannons and a proton

torpedo launcher. The pilot was assisted by an astromech droid, which would also conduct minor repairs and other helpful tasks.

These starfighters took part in the final orbital raid against the Trade Federation control ship during the Battle of Naboo. Additionally, they escorted the royal cruiser to Coruscant when an attempt was made on the life of Senator Padmé Amidala, and they were glimpsed soaring through the skies of Theed during the galaxy-wide celebrations following the destruction of the second Death Star.

Naboo Pilot

Members of the Naboo Royal Space Fighters Corps, these pilots were in charge of protecting the air and space around the planet.

During the Battle of Naboo they took part in the assault on the orbiting Droid Capital Ship that was destroyed with the help of an unexpected pilot in the shape of Anakin Skywalker. In addition to Skywalker's natural talents, he was taught how to pilot a Naboo ship by the most famous of their aces, Ric Olié.

Naboo Royal Security Forces

Although it was comprised of the Space Fighter Corps, the Security Guards and the Palace Guards, this law enforcement organisation of the planet of Naboo was not a real army.

Being mainly made up of trained volunteers, the Royal Security Forces were no match for the Trade Federation droid army, which outclassed them on every military level. However, under the command of Captain Panaka, they were able to help Queen Amidala escape from the occupied planet aboard the royal ship, piloted by Ric Olié.

Naboo Royal Space Fighter Corps

This division of the Naboo Royal Security Forces was dedicated to the aerial protection of the planet.

Under the command of Captain Panaka, the corps counted the veteran pilot Ric Olié among its members. During the Battle of Naboo, this squadron led the assault on the droid control ship of the Trade Federation and contributed to its destruction with the help of the young Anakin Skywalker.

Naboo Royal Starship

A prestige starship that was normally reserved for the transportation of Queen Padmé Amidala on her official trips, but was also used as an escape vessel during the invasion of Naboo.

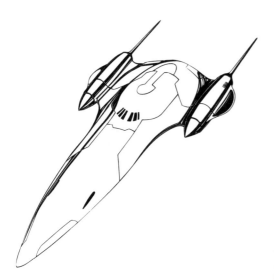

The starship had no offensive weapons but was equipped with a powerful shield and a hyperdrive. Alongside those two features, its T-14 generator was the only one manufactured by the Nubian Design Collective. The sublight drive was therefore that of a J-type 327 Nubian vessel. The rest of the ship's construction was executed by the Theed Palace Space Vessel Engineering Corps. The reflective hull was fashioned in chromium, and was a decorative sign of royalty. It was entirely hand-polished by meticulous craftsmen. The interior of the starship was created with the same care, though the creation of a throne room in the ship was mainly for reasons of protocol than of comfort. Mixing grace and beauty, this technological work of art could be considered as a crowning achievement for the society that prevailed during the last peaceful years of the Galactic Republic.

Naboo Speeders

These militarised terrestrial vehicles with repulsors were used by the Naboo Royal Guards.

The speeder was a light device capable of high speed and great manoeuvrability. It was designed for the simple use of patrolling during peace times. However, in more dramatic circumstances, the cannon built on the rear turret allowed the vehicle to be used in combat. The usual missions given to the Naboo speeder were along the lines of crowd control and urban defence. To achieve that, the speeder featured heavy armour, as well as two lateral laser cannons. Some had even been modified to increase their firepower with the addition of a heavy cannon on the front hood. During the invasion of Naboo, Queen Padmé Amidala and Captain Panaka used the speeders to infiltrate and free the capital of Theed from the occupation of the Trade Federation troops.

Nahani Gillen

Nahani Gillen was the planet of Uyter's emissary to the New Republic Senate.

Like her fellow senators, Gillen followed the alternative movement created after the Galactic Civil War regarding the Senate seat and therefore lived on Hosnian Prime, the latest capital elected to house the New Republic's institution. She usually wore a traditional robe of the assembly that gave her a simple and elegant look. She died when Hosnian Prime was destroyed by the First Order's Starkiller Base.

Neimoidian

This humanoid species had no nose, and could be identified by their orange eyes with a horizontal pupil and their green-grey skin.

The Neimoidians, who hailed from the planet of Neimoidia and its colony Cato Neimoidia, were well known all over the galaxy for being skilful, greedy merchants. They ran a powerful guild known as the Trade Federation and were masters of double-dealing. At the same time their viceroy, Nute Gunray, aggressively invaded the planet of Naboo, their senator, Lott Dod, tried to look innocent in front of the Galactic Senate. The double-dealings of the Neimoidian consortium continued when it secretly joined the Confederacy of Independent Systems, while officially remaining a member of the Republic.

Nesta Term

A female member of a morbid religious sect, Nesta Term was the self-proclaimed Lens of the Central Isopter.

Fascinated by death in all its forms, this religion took its followers to the most dangerous places in the galaxy. Term followed her beliefs to Jedha City with two of her fellow practitioners. When Jyn Erso and Cassian Andor arrived in the city, Term and her colleagues were standing in front of a market stall while an AT-ST was on patrol. Draped in their large, thick shawls and their masks, these followers studied the chaotic disharmonies of the Holy City. Asking for death herself, Term proved to be in the best place to see her wish granted a short time later, when the city was annihilated by a superweapon that offered her what she craved.

Neva Kee

The most mysterious of the podracers who competed in the Boonta Eve Classic Podrace.

This Xamster tried to take a shortcut during the second lap, but completely disappeared. Neither he nor his podracer were ever seen again.

New Republic

The New Republic was the institution that replaced the Galactic Empire at the end of the Galactic Civil War.

Since the historic signing of the treaty known as the Galactic Concordance with the vanquished Empire, there had been concerns about establishing a durable peace in the galaxy. To recoup the confidence of the numerous peoples and planets that had been destabilised by the change of regime, the New Republic launched a vast campaign of political reforms to balance powers and to retrieve some kind of effective form of representation.

The most spectacular reform was the 'adaptable' status of the Senate, which regularly moved its seat according to the elections, to symbolically and successively integrate worlds and systems in which it had established itself. The Hosnian system was the last seat of the Senate to gather under the guidance of its Chancellor, Lanever Villecham. The New Republic had also started a progressive demilitarisation programme to prevent further armed conflict. The Republic's fleet remained under its command, but was by this time just a small fraction of the forces it had gathered before the rise of the Empire.

More focused on signing commercial treaties and ensuring the proper functioning of institutions than it was on indistinct and far-fetched threats, the New Republic did not heed the warnings of General Leia Organa about the First Order, a faction that was born from the ashes of the Empire and whose power continued to grow. That carelessness was paid for when the First Order entirely destroyed the Hosnian system with its new superweapon – Starkiller Base.

Newland

A major of the Imperial army, Newland carried out reconnaissance missions aboard an AT-ST on the forest moon of Endor.

During one mission, not far from the planetary shield generator, he discovered, along with his pilot, Blanaid, an Ewok on the roof of his scout walker. He sent his pilot to resolve the incident, but he was snatched by the Wookiee, Chewbacca, who then knocked out Newland and turned the AT-ST's firepower against the Imperial troops.

Nexu

A feline predator from the forest world of Cholganna, the nexu was an agile and very aggressive creature.

It was around 2 metres long and 1 metre tall and had multiple eyes, a hairless tail and sharp claws. Popular because of its fighting abilities, the nexu could be found on many worlds, but mostly on Geonosis where it was used for the execution of prisoners in the Petranaki Arena. It was in this situation that Anakin Skywalker, Obi-Wan Kenobi and Padmé Amidala had to face the creature. After attacking the Geonosian picadors in charge of controlling it, it chose to hunt down Amidala, whom it wounded before being killed by the violent charge of a reek mounted by Skywalker.

Nien Nunb

Once a gunrunner and smuggler, this Sullustan pilot – with his protruding ears and large jowls – became part of the Rebel Alliance and a member of the Resistance after joining the fleet when it regrouped close to his native world of Sullust.

Nien Nunb was very gifted when it came to piloting a vessel and he was personally chosen by General Lando Calrissian to be his co-pilot aboard the *Millennium Falcon* during the Battle of Endor. His reactions, calmness and insight contributed to their success and it was their vessel that dealt the decisive blow to the main reactor of the second Death Star, starting a chain reaction which would destroy the space station. Twenty-nine years later, Nunb was a member of the Resistance created by Leia Organa and fought the First Order in a X-wing starfighter. Always a gifted pilot, he was among the seven survivors of the victorious assault against Starkiller Base and returned to celebrate the event on D'Qar.

Niima Outpost

An outpost on Jakku established at the centre of an enormous starship graveyard, Niima outpost boasted a mixed population of travellers, fugitives, bandits, droids, bounty hunters and wreck-raiders.

Founded sometime after the Battle of Jakku by a Hutt named Niima, the outpost was intended to provide the backbone of an industry in which collectors salvaged precious materials from the huge starships that had crashed on the planet during the last battle of the Civil War. While her outpost operated far from the influence of the Hutts, Niima was eventually killed by a bounty hunter, but the outpost retained her name.

Combining a number of buildings with a vast flat field that was used as a dock for passing vehicles, the Niima outpost gathered together several posts under a huge awning, creating an improvised marketplace where travellers met to exchange information and wares. Niima was also the place of business for corrupt scrap merchant Unkar Plutt. He orchestrated a food shortage by building his monopoly on survival rations found in the stocks of the crashed Alliance and Imperial ships, which Plutt exchanged for spare parts brought to him by wreck-raiders. Rey regularly spent time at Niima Outpost to sell her scavenged goods.

NiJedha

See Jedha City

Nik Hepho

An independent bounty hunter who specialised in tracking members of the Church of the Force, this bald Britarro with bluish-grey skin and an almost non-existent nose was very successful at his job.

As the Empire had declared the Church of the Force illegal, Nik Hepho was able to make financial profit by pursuing its followers. His time on Coruscant was extremely profitable as he 'cleansed' the planet-capital of his religious targets. He next went to Jedha City. There, equipped with his A300 rifle with punctured barrel and a black list compiled by the Imperial intelligence, but purchased on the black market, Hepho pursued his task. On his back he carried a powerful emitter so that he could maintain contact with the intelligence droid that controlled his ship, the *Apostate*, which was left orbiting the moon. It's possible that his instincts and the visible signs of an evacuation may have allowed him to escape before the Death Star annihilated his new hunting ground.

Niles Gavla

This lieutenant of the Imperial army was posted on Scarif and represented the pure product of the Palpatine regime.

The Galactic Empire had opened schools of excellence to form a generation of military elite who would manage the galaxy. As a graduate of the Academy of Carida, Niles Gavla had been assigned to the Imperial Centre of Military Research. His role was as a liaison officer and his counterpart was in charge of the Death Star defences. Gavla's career and life were brutally stopped by the Rebel Alliance attack and the cataclysmic consequences of the shot that was issued from the Empire's new combat station.

Nippet

Nippet was a baby Ewok from Bright Tree Village when the Battle of Endor occurred. Before the combat began, C-3PO relayed the epic adventures of Luke Skywalker to the whole tribe.

As part of this audience, Nippet was fascinated by C-3PO's engaging story, which was full of adventure, heroism and sound effects.

Nower Jebel

A member of the Imperial Senate and Minister of Finance in the secret government of the Rebel Alliance, Nower Jebel represented his agricultural homeworld of Uyter, and favoured political solutions that rejected violence.

Horrified by the terrorist activities of Saw Gerrera's militia, he advised a dialogue with the Empire, even though he couldn't guarantee that it would be willing to make any concessions. During the meeting on Yavin 4, Jebel was one of the members of the Alliance Cabinet that rejected the option put forward by Jyn Erso, as he did not believe in the 'planet killer' ship and thought the rebel forces should be disbanded. However, his absence of courage and vision didn't stop the politician from being promoted to Minister of Finance when the Rebellion was reorganised into the New Republic, five years after the Battle of Yavin.

Nozzo Naytaan

Nozzo Naytaan was a rebel pilot who took part in both the Battles of Scarif and Yavin.

Previously employed by the Corellian Engineering Company, the lieutenant abandoned his position when it became obvious that he would have to test, and therefore help to manufacture, the TIE fighters for the Empire. Some years later he was based at the Massassi outpost as part of Red Squadron, where he maintained a mischievous rivalry with another Corellian from Green Squadron named Attico Wred. Under the call sign Red Nine, Naytaan participated in and survived the orbital combat above Scarif. Some days after, he took part in the assault on the Death Star and was shot down during the famous rebel victory by the escort of Darth Vader.

Nuna

These small-sized bipeds, reminiscent of wingless birds, originally lived in the swamps of Naboo but they soon spread throughout the galaxy and were often cooked in delicious meals.

One of their other involuntary functions was to amuse the crime lord Jabba the Hutt. He started the Boonta Eve Classic Podrace by spitting the head of a freshly decapitated nuna at the gong, and cruelly pushed another one from the edge of his private balcony in the Mos Espa Arena.

Nute Gunray

This Neimoidian was viceroy of the Trade Federation and one of the Separatist leaders of the Confederacy of Independent Systems.

Acting on the advice of Darth Sidious, his involvement in the invasion of Naboo was driven by greed. Nute Gunray didn't understand that he had been manipulated by the Sith Lord until his humiliating defeat, and even then, having escaped jail in spite of four proceedings in front of the Supreme Court, he persisted in his alliance with Sidious and joined the Separatist movement driven by the Sith's new apprentice, the charismatic Count Dooku.

His only-driven-by-money nature didn't help Gunray to understand the political triangle that had been created by the Sith Lord between the Republic and his new puppet, the Confederacy of Independent Systems. Unaware of the real stakes, the Trade Federation's viceroy pledged allegiance to this organisation during a secret meeting on Geonosis. In front of his eyes the battle that followed gave birth to the Clone Wars, and the Republic and the Jedi underwent a huge transformation.

By the end of this war, Gunray's discomfort and lack of composure were there for all to see, especially after the deaths of the Separatist chiefs Count Dooku and General Grievous. The merciless leader of the biggest commercial guild became no more than the proverbial lamb to the slaughter, which was exactly what happened when he accepted an invitation to meet the Sith Lord one last time on Mustafar. Instead of peace, the Separatist Council was eliminated member by member by the new apprentice of Darth Sidious – Darth Vader. There was a poetic irony to the fact that as his former self, Anakin Skywalker, Vader had already once before executed the hopes of Gunray during the Battle of Naboo.

Nysad

One of the numerous Kajain'sa'Nikto in the service of Jabba the Hutt, Nysad faced Luke Skywalker during the battle at the Great Pit of Carkoon.

Nysad came face-to-face with Skywalker on Jabba's sail barge. He fired one shot at the Jedi, but Skywalker angled his lightsaber and the blast rebounded straight back into Nysad's chest.

Obi-Wan Kenobi

Sage Jedi, veteran of the Clone Wars and mentor to two Skywalkers, Obi-Wan Kenobi survived several duels with Sith Lords and became one of the few Jedi to achieve immortality within the Force.

Born on the planet of Stewjon, he was chosen during the first six months of his life to go to the Temple on Coruscant in order to become a Jedi. As a novice he began his practice under the guidance of Master Yoda, before passing to the guidance of Jinn as a Padawan. Shortly before he was due to take his nine trials, Supreme Chancellor Finis Valorum sent him and Jinn to settle a minor conflict, the blockade of Naboo by the Trade Federation, so that it didn't degenerate into something more.

The relationship between Kenobi and Jinn was so strong that they formed an almost symbiotic partnership, linked by serenity and a dangerous efficiency. It was this mastery of their skills and confidence that enabled them to escape the attempt that had been made on their lives by the Trade Federation. Then, on their way from Otoh Gunga to Theed, they succeeded in escaping from two deadly predators that lived in the oceanic depths. Once in Theed, Jinn and Kenobi saved the life of the Queen of Naboo and proceeded to help her escape the planet, despite the blockades.

During this adventure Kenobi met the Gungan Jar Jar Binks and two other people who would prove to be very important to him – Padmé Amidala and R2-D2. Stranded on the desert planet while waiting for repairs, Kenobi remained in the royal ship, where Jinn sent him a blood sample from a young slave boy of Mos Espa, named Anakin Skywalker. Kenobi was surprised to find that the concentration of midi-chlorians in the boy's blood was elevated beyond that shown by any Jedi. At the moment of their arrival at the vessel, Jinn and the slave boy were attacked by a warrior that appeared to be the heir of an Order that had disappeared a whole millennium ago – the Sith.

When Jinn made his report to the Jedi Council about the attacker and Anakin, it was received with scepticism. In contradiction with the Jedi Code, he was even ready to train the young boy himself, despite the fact that he already had a Padawan. Kenobi came to his aid and pleaded to take his trials to become a Jedi Knight and relieve Jinn from his duty as his mentor. At the end of this tight exchange, Kenobi kindly pointed out to his master that he could have been on the Jedi Council if he was more accommodating. Jinn explained that his actions were not motivated by pride or anti-conformism, but by an absolute necessity – if he thought that Skywalker was the Chosen One, he could not pretend otherwise.

Back on Naboo, Kenobi helped Queen Amidala to gain the indispensable support of Boss Nass and his Gungan Army. During the battle, Kenobi and Jinn protected Amidala until they once again crossed paths with the mysterious Sith. The duel between the Jedi and Sith was technical and merciless. Although they fought side-by-side, Master and Padawan were barely enough to counter the mastery of Darth Maul's double-bladed lightsaber. Very cleverly, the Sith managed to separate Kenobi from Jinn, and the Padawan had to witness the sudden impalement of his master by the blade of the Sith's red lightsaber. As soon as he was able, Kenobi swept down on Maul, but the Jedi landed in a bad stance and he was quickly disarmed and left clinging to a block in the shaft of a reactor duct. Eventually, Kenobi was able to use the pull of the Force to attract and grab his dying master's lightsaber and then sliced his adversary in two. He watched Darth Maul fall into the immense duct. Then, before Jinn died, Kenobi promised him he would train young Skywalker.

After this trials, the newly promoted Jedi Knight made a very reluctant Yoda endorse his oath. Kenobi confided the news to the young Skywalker during the funeral ceremony of the man to which they were both indebted – a small consolation in that painful moment.

Ten years later, Obi-Wan and his Padawan were assigned to the protection of Senator Amidala after an attempt was made on her life. They soon neutralised a second attempt and captured its perpetrator, Zam Wesell. However, before she could speak, the bounty hunter Jango Fett used a poisoned saberdart to kill her. Following these events, Skywalker was ordered by the Jedi Council to continue protecting Amidala by himself, while his master began a long investigation. Tipped off by his friend, Dexter Jettster, that the saberdart was Kaminoan, Kenobi headed to Kamino where he made a startling discovery. An army of clones, secretly ordered by the late Jedi Sifo-Dyas and based on the genetic code of Jango Fett, had been commissioned. Kenobi then trailed the bounty hunter to Geonosis, where he discovered a hidden plot against the Republic while spying on a meeting of the Separatist Council.

As he tried to contact Skywalker, Kenobi was taken prisoner and interrogated by the leader of the Separatists, Count Dooku, who stated that a Sith Lord by the name of Darth Sidious was corrupting the Republic. Although the revelation was actually true, Kenobi considered it a political manoeuvre as Dooku then tried to convince Kenobi to join the Confederacy of Independent Systems. Sentenced to death with Skywalker and Amidala, who had arrived to attempt a rescue, Kenobi was saved by Mace Windu's Jedi task force and a squadron of clone troopers commanded by Yoda. Although they caught up with Dooku, the Jedi Master and the Padawan were defeated and the encounter left Skywalker amputated, without his right forearm. Dooku managed to escape and the Clone Wars began.

Kenobi served as a general of the Grand Army of the Republic during what became a poisonous conflict for the Jedi Order and the Republic. Kenobi was often accompanied by Skywalker, who had become a Jedi Knight after achieving several important victories. During the Battle of Coruscant, the two Jedi were sent on a mission to rescue Chancellor Palpatine who had been kidnapped by the Separatist commander General Grievous. Aboard the Separatist's flagship they faced Count Dooku once more. The duel again turned to the disadvantage of Kenobi, who was stunned. He woke up to find Dooku defeated. Skywalker had executed him on a direct order from Palpatine.

The cyborg General Grievous fled, and the two Jedi safely returned the leader of the Republic to the Senate. Kenobi warned Skywalker about the politician, who seemed to be getting closer and closer to him. Before long, Palpatine had named Skywalker as his personal representative to the Jedi Council. The Order accepted the intrusion, but refused to promote Skywalker to the rank of Jedi Master. Instead, they asked him to keep an eye on the Chancellor, who they believed had a dangerous lust for power. Skywalker was reluctant to the task, but despite the tension in the Order, he and Kenobi parted as friends. Kenobi then left with a lighter heart for Utapau, where he victoriously confronted and killed Grievous with a blaster shot after a furious pursuit and battle.

Darth Sidious' activation of Order 66 forced the clone troopers to turn against the Jedi and their own generals. Kenobi survived the attack and succeeded in joining Senator Bail Organa and Yoda, who had also escaped. He returned to Coruscant with them in order to stop the signal of the Jedi Temple attracting any surviving Jedi into a trap. He then replaced it with a message of hope, before finding out that the massacre was committed by Skywalker who, having been renamed Darth Vader, was now in service to the new Emperor and Sith Lord, Palpatine. It was a painful moment that suggested the downfall of a prophecy, the mistake of a beloved Jedi Master, and the eradication of the Jedi Order.

Yoda convinced Kenobi to eliminate this new Sith Apprentice, who was no longer the man that he had trained and loved as a brother, but was now a tool of suffering focused towards the dark side. In the hope of finding Vader, Kenobi went to Amidala, who refused to believe his account and refused to tell him anything about her husband's location. He pretended to leave but instead hid in a compartment of Amidala's vessel, in which she then took off with C-3PO for Mustafar. There, Kenobi bore witness to the depths of Vader's paranoia and distrust. When Vader saw Kenobi, he believed that it was part of a deadly plot hatched by his wife, and attempted to choke Amidala using the Force. While Kenobi checked Amidala's vital signs, he tried to have a rational discussion with his former Padawan, but his answers proved to the Jedi Master that the only solution was confrontation.

The duel that followed, staged against an apocalyptic landscape, was brutal and merciless. Kenobi's despair violently clashed against Vader's pure hated, even in their verbal exchanges. The Jedi gained an obvious tactical advantage over his adversary when he was the first to reach the high ground of a bank that ran alongside a stream of lava. Still chivalrous after all that had passed between them, he warned Vader against making any further attempts, but his opponent, convinced of his infallibility, rushed at him. Kenobi swung his lightsaber and in a flash, the Sith lost his two legs and his remaining arm. Exhausted and broken-hearted, Kenobi then took his weapon from him and with tears in his eyes, overcome by anger and infinite sadness, blamed Vader for what he had forced him to do to the person he had loved

like a brother. Nothing more than a mutilated body on fire, Vader was left to his apparent death as Kenobi left the volcanic world.

Having attended the childbirth and the subsequent death of a broken-hearted Amidala, Kenobi agreed to take part in a plan to conceal the newly born twins from the unknowing Sith. Furthermore, Yoda confided in him the revelation that Qui-Gon Jinn had achieved immortality as a Force-spirit, and explained the training that Kenobi would have to undertake to communicate with him and to reach the same degree of knowledge.

On Tatooine, Kenobi handed the baby Luke to Owen and Beru Lars and, in order to watch over the child, he settled not far from their farm in the deserted grounds of the western Dune Sea. There, the former general and member of the Jedi, a man who had mixed with the galaxy's nobility, began an austere life in hiding. After taking the simple name of Ben to partially conceal his identity, Kenobi restricted his contact with the everyday world and soon became known as a crazy hermit. He avoided all visible use of the Force and stored away his lightsaber for years so as not to attract the attention of the Empire. His monotonous and lonely existence provided him with the opportunity to continue his exploration of immortality in the Force.

An apprehensive Owen Lars had kept Luke Skywalker away from Kenobi and ensured he stayed busy living the life of a farmer. However, after nineteen years had passed, Kenobi was forced to save the young man, along with two droids, from the Tusken Raiders. The young Skywalker told him that R2-D2 was anxious to find an Obi-Wan Kenobi. Kenobi's interest piqued by this unexpected reference to his past, and the old recluse welcomed the three of them into his modest home. As he handed young Skywalker the lightsaber that had once belonged to his father, collected on Mustafar, he briefly explained about their time together in the Jedi Order and the Clone Wars. Kenobi chose his words carefully in order to save the teenager from the terrible truth and split the two personalities – Jedi and Sith – into two separate people. He therefore told the young farm boy that Darth Vader had 'killed' his father, Anakin Skywalker.

Once Kenobi had watched R2-D2's message from Princess Leia Organa, in which she asked him to bring the droid, which carried the Death Star plans, to Senator Bail Organa, he proposed that Skywalker accompany him. After the discovery of the burnt skeletons of Owen and Beru, who had been attacked by stormtroopers searching for the droids, Luke resolved to go to Alderaan and learn the ways of the Force to become a Jedi like his father. As C-3PO and R2-D2 were being actively sought on Tatooine, Kenobi negotiated for a passage to Alderaan aboard the starship of the smuggler Han Solo. The journey gave him the opportunity to begin training the young Skywalker, but the old master was suddenly shaken by a disruption in the Force of a rare magnitude. He soon discovered the source of it when they emerged from hyperspace to find that Alderaan had been destroyed. The starship was then caught in the tractor beam of the Imperial superweapon, the Death Star.

After hiding in the smuggling compartments of the *Millennium Falcon*, they eventually arrived in the hangar's control room. Kenobi set off alone to locate the terminal that needed to be deactivated in order for them to release the ship and escape. Having successfully deactivated the tractor beam, Kenobi was on his way back to the ship when he met the man he had left dying on Mustafar. Having noted the old Jedi's weakness, Vader believed that Kenobi was easy prey. However, the former mentor warned the Sith that he could not win since, even in death, he would be more powerful than Vader could imagine. Seeing Skywalker and his companions about to escape, the wise Kenobi smiled enigmatically, took a last breath in and in the instant that Vader's lightsaber touched him, allowed his physical body to disappear and become one with the Force. Uncertain of what had transpired, Vader nudged the empty clothes that had slipped to the ground. It was the beginning of Kenobi's journey into immortality.

During the Battle of Yavin, it was Kenobi's voice that guided Skywalker in his X-wing and instructed him to trust his instinct on making the shot that would destroy the Death Star. Then, three years later, on Hoth, he reappeared to Skywalker while he was on the verge of death and persuaded him to seek Jedi training under the guidance of Yoda in the Dagobah system. It was there that the 900-year-old Jedi Master and the spirit of Kenobi argued over the young rebel's training and advancement. Having judged Skywalker on his first impression and the catastrophic attempts at training, Yoda appeared reluctant – a sentiment that was only strengthened when the young man hastily decided to leave to save his friends after seeing them in danger in a vision. However, anxious not to lose him as he had lost Anakin, Kenobi cautioned the young Skywalker against the Emperor and warned him that if he fought Vader he would not be able to help. He told him not to allow himself to give in to hate, which would lead to the dark side. Once the young Jedi had departed, Kenobi worried about this last hope but Yoda reminded him that there was another – Luke's twin sister, Leia.

After the death of Yoda, Kenobi communed for a long time with the young Skywalker on the danger that the Emperor represented and the necessity to confront Vader once more. He finally confided to him why he had not told him the whole truth about his father and the existence of Leia, his sister. After the Battle of Endor, the young Jedi was the only one to see the spirits of Kenobi, Anakin Skywalker and Yoda in communion in the Force, celebrating the victory that had come after twenty-three years of desolation, war and sacrifice.

Thirty years later, when Rey brushed against the lightsaber that had belonged to the two Skywalkers, she had a vision in which she heard the voice of Kenobi, who announced that she was taking her first steps towards the Force.

Ody Mandrell

A podracer pilot during the famous Boonta Eve Classic Podrace on Tatooine.

This pale, blue-skinned, thin-headed Er'Kit was announced by the double-headed broadcasters, Fode and Beed, who suggested that his team of pit droids were 'the most efficient of the moment'. Well placed in the pack, he managed to avoid the aggressive moves of Sebulba, but still had to stop at the pits at the beginning of the second lap, where a distracted pit droid was drawn into one of the podracer's engines. Although the droid escaped intact, the delicate machinery was destroyed and Mandrell was furious and disappointed that he was unable to continue in the race.

Omisha Joyo

A member of the Clan of Toribota, Omisha Joyo witnessed Chirrut Îmwe challenge the squad of stormtroopers that had taken Jyn Erso and Cassian Andor prisoner in Jedha City.

Joyo was part of the nomadic tribe of Isde Naha, which, thanks to the astronomical calculations of scientists, came to Jedha to settle themselves. They believed that the First Gleam, which was the primitive first star seen by their ancestors, was the same star that could be seen in Jedha's system. The very large, semi-circular helmet of Joyo was used as a receiver to the signal emitted by the primitive light, which was essential to his people, while the rest of his dark outfit also featured a water purifier. Unfortunately for its people, the mystical cosmology of the Clan of Toribota didn't foresee the arrival of the celestial body that would be responsible for the extinction of the Holy City.

Oola

Oola was a slave and dancer at Jabba the Hutt's Palace on Tatooine.

A Twi'lek with an olive green complexion who wore suggestive outfits made of netting, she performed her final dance just before the arrival of Princess Leia Organa, who was disguised as Boushh. Having finished a graceful dance with Yarna d'al' Gargan, her master suddenly felt the urge for much closer contact. To achieve his wishes, the immense slug-like crime lord pulled her brutally towards him using the chain that was fixed to the collar the young slave wore around her delicate neck. She openly resisted his advances and pulled against her leash, but the public humiliation of the disappointed Jabba didn't go unpunished and she was sentenced to death. The Hutt swiftly pushed a control on his throne, which opened a trapdoor and the dancer fell into the cave of the rancor. Despite her agility, she couldn't escape the beast and was devoured alive.

OOM-9

A battle droid commander that could be recognised by the yellow circle on its chest, OOM-9 led the Trade Federation droid army during the invasion of Naboo in the fight against the Gungan army.

From the rear of the battle, on its personal armoured tank, it oversaw the successful implementation of the battle plan using the B1 battle droids, and was even able to get the upper hand on the Gungans. Its success, however, was short-lived, as it was deactivated – along with all the other droids – when the Droid Control Ship in orbit above Naboo was destroyed.

Opee Sea Killer

This 20-metre-long, half-crustacean, half-fish possessed two rows of teeth and dwelt in the depths of Naboo's watery core where it searched for prey.

It was during their trip in a bongo that Qui-Gon Jinn, Obi-Wan Kenobi and Jar Jar Binks were hunted by an opee sea killer. It pulled the submarine into its jaws using its massive tongue and caught the vehicle between its teeth. However, they escaped when the opee sea killer itself was attacked by another sea monster, the huge sando aqua monster, which devoured the smaller creature.

Operation Fracture

The objective of this rebel mission was the extraction of the Imperial scientist, Galen Erso.

Initiated by Mon Mothma, the plan was conceived to extract the scientist so that he could testify to the Imperial Senate about the existence of the 'planet killer' ship. Mothma hoped this testimony would provoke a senatorial motion from her allies to launch a demilitarisation of the Empire and a reconciliation with the Rebel Alliance. Believing it was political naivety, General Davits Draven took it upon himself to modify the mission objective and asked Captain Cassian Andor to eliminate Erso instead of bringing him back.

As far as Draven was concerned, the absolute necessity to completely stop the military works of Erso prevailed over any other consideration. In fact, it was so important to the general that, uncertain of whether Andor could shoot the target down, he also gave a second order without authorisation, to launch an aerial assault to kill the scientist. When he was informed by K-2SO that Jyn Erso and Andor were on the spot and could be killed by the air raid, it was already too late – Operation Fracture had begun. Jyn and Andor miraculously survived, unlike Galen Erso, and Draven had to justify himself to Mon Mothma. By lying to her about the fact that he had acted out of necessity and that he had been forced to order the execution, he convinced the leader of the Alliance to stop dreaming about finding a peaceful political solution against an enemy that had an apocalyptic weapon.

Oppo Rancisis

A Jedi Master and member of the Jedi High Council, this Thisspiasian possessed thick fur and only his eyes and mouth were visible.

A good strategist, he was present when the child that was potentially the Chosen One was presented to the Council and he remained a member throughout the Clone Wars.

Ord Mantell

Ord Mantell was a planet of the Bright Jewel system located in the Mid Rim.

Known to be one of the centres of illegal and criminal activity in the sector, Ord Mantell therefore became the operational base for many of the crime syndicates that were spreading throughout the whole galaxy. Shortly before the Battle of Hoth, Han Solo met a bounty hunter on this planet, who reminded him that Jabba the Hutt never forgot a debt and that the contract on his head was still valid.

Order 66

The objective of this command was to wipe out all of the Jedi, wherever they were in the galaxy.

The clone troopers of the Republic, created on Kamino before the Clone Wars, were built with an inhibiting chip in their brains. The chip was not activated until Order 66 was given when Sheev Palpatine effectively transformed the Republic into the Galactic Empire. When the order came, clone trooper units scattered all around the galaxy killed their Jedi commanders in a sudden and swift attack.

Orn Free Taa

This Twi'lek senator represented Ryloth at the Senate and his bulky blue frame was easily visible in the senatorial buildings, where he was often accompanied by an attractive assistant.

He was present at Chancellor Palpatine's office when Padmé Amidala arrived, having just survived an assassination attempt. He was also present when the delegate of Naboo, Jar Jar Binks, demanded that Palpatine be given full power over the Senate.

Orray

This creature from Geonosis served as a mount for the Geonosians.

An adult orray, around 3 metres long and 2 metres high, was an obedient animal that was easily tamed. Picadors often mounted them in the Petranaki Arena, where the orray's stature and mobility provided its rider with some safety while he guided the savage creatures that were destined to devour the condemned victims. However, some agile beasts, like the nexu, occasionally managed to dismount a picador and eat him. Orrays were also used as beasts of burden to pull heavy loads or carts. Tame orrays could be identified by their cut-off tails.

Orson Krennic

Rising within the Republic Corps of Engineers to become the architect of the Death Star, Krennic sacrificed friendship and civil society for the Empire.

Born in the city of Sativran on Lexrul, at fifteen years old Orson Krennic was selected for the 'Futures of Brentaal' programme that offered the most brilliant students the chance to become part of the Republic's scientific or political elite. There he met Galen Erso, little knowing that their destinies would be entwined for the next thirty-six years. Once he had received his diploma, Krennic's talent as an architect opened a door into the Republic Corps of Engineers. His capabilities as a leader allowed him to manage vast terrestrial and space construction projects and his numerous successes gave him influence enough to find a position for his friend, Erso, at the Institute of Applied Sciences on Coruscant.

When the Clone Wars began Krennic joined a secret Republic think-tank tasked with designing secret weapons for the army. During one of these meetings, he discovered the existence of the Death Star project, which had been obtained by the Republic regime at the end of the first Battle of Geonosis. Among the numerous problems raised by its construction was the issue of arming it with a weapon proportional to its enormity. From that moment, the ambitious Krennic used his friend Erso as an indispensable, and unwitting, pawn.

To achieve his ends, Krennic resorted to several techniques of manipulation. To begin, Krennic portrayed himself as Erso's saviour in order to make his friend feel indebted to him. When the scientist was taken prisoner on Vallt, a planet conquered by Separatists, Krennic, with the discreet support of Mas Amedda, liberated Erso and took him to his native planet of Barn, which had also been ravaged by the conflict. In the face of Erso's resolute pacifism, Krennic then allowed him to be disgraced during a reunion of veterans from the 'Futures for Brentaal' programme. The former students and colleagues considered Erso's neutrality a sign that he was complicit with the Separatists. Finally, to complete the conditioning, Krennic assigned Erso an uninteresting position working for a difficult employer in a conflict zone.

At the end of the Clone Wars and with the advent of the Empire, Galen was ready to work on a project that his benefactor presented to him – to bring renewable energy to the ravaged galaxy. The scientist became involved in the intense research of kyber crystals, and involuntarily aided the progress of a new superweapon. Following the successful test of a first prototype, Krennic was reassured that success was near. However, when Erso's wife told her husband about the militarisation of his research, he fled with his family for an unknown destination. It was a personal humiliation for Krennic and a huge setback for the Empire. Krennic had to pay a high price for the scientist's desertion as Amedda symbolically demoted him and instructed Wilhuff Tarkin, who despised Krennic, to supervise the project instead.

Although the four years that followed were difficult, Krennic was eventually rewarded when he discovered that Erso was on Lah'mu. Although unable to find Erso's daughter, Jyn, he did find Erso and his wife Lyra – and after Lyra wounded him – he took satisfaction in her execution at the hands of his death troopers. Still convinced that the delivery of an operational combat station would make him a hero of the Empire, he put all other thoughts and events aside and bound his destiny to the completion of the Death Star.

During thirteen long years of work, Krennic spent his time travelling between several secure sites of the Tarkin Initiative, including the Imperial Centre of Military Research on Scarif and the High Energy Concepts and Implementation Labs of Eadu. When his huge project was finally finished it was at a transitional point in his career. The completion was the zenith of a career spent in the service of the Empire, but his multiple delays, his inability to obtain an audience with the Emperor, his arrogant and changing moods and, more directly, his contradictory relations within his hierarchy, had left him vulnerable. When Tarkin set him a full-size test, he smelt a trap, but was sure of the deadly invention.

On the day of the test, the Grand Moff was present, but the Emperor and Vader were absent. According to Tarkin, they had stayed away in order to spare the director from any humiliation in the event of failure. Tarkin ordered Krennic to conduct the test on Jedha City rather than the whole moon of Jedha, in what appeared to be a strategic manoeuvre to restrict any spectacular display that would make Krennic appear overly successful. The destruction of the city was total and with a complete lack of empathy for the residents that had lived there – including the three per cent of Imperial forces who couldn't be evacuated in time – Krennic claimed the success and beauty of the weapon's awesome power as his own. However, his ecstasy was short-lived. Tarkin, superior to Krennic in both rank and his relationship with Palpatine, immediately took control of the Death Star. Flushed with rage, Krennic tried to oppose the Grand Moff, but was forced to accept the situation when the governor insinuated there were leaks in Tarkin's team on Eadu. Humiliated in front of the gathered military dignitaries, Krennic decided to personally address the traitor in his troops.

Prior to his arrival on Eadu, Krennic ordered that Erso and his six fellow scientists be gathered on the landing pad. He addressed the group and asked the informant to reveal himself. When no one came forward, he ordered their immediate execution, which resulted in the confession of Erso. Furious, Krennic ordered that the scientists be shot down and struck Erso, who he believed he had subdued and converted to his vision. At that moment, the Rebel Alliance's Operation Fracture starfighters appeared overhead and dropped a bomb that killed Erso and forced the director to board his ship and flee, after which he received a rare communication – Darth Vader required his presence at his personal residence on Mustafar.

Received on a balcony of the immense building, he faced an unnerving meeting with the Sith Lord who desired a clear explanation of what had happened – without any personal justifications or recriminations towards Tarkin. It was imperative that the Death Star remained secret and the Senate ignorant of its existence, and so a cover story was devised to explain the destruction of Jedha City, purporting that it had been down to a tragic mining accident. Emboldened by the briefness of the meeting – with no deadly consequences – Krennic decided to consider it a simple briefing, the purpose of which was to confirm his duties. Made overconfident by this incorrect interpretation of events he pushed his luck by repeating his demand for an audience with the Emperor. It was an arrogant move and a bad idea, and resulted in the Sith Lord turning his powers on the director. In a demonstration of his Force strangulation technique, Vader suggested that the director curb his ambitions so they didn't end up choking him. On his knees, Krennic finally understood how little room to manoeuvre he had.

Having been warned by Vader that the Emperor wanted a guarantee that the integrity of the combat station had not been compromised by Erso, Krennic immediately left for Scarif, where he demanded that General Sotorus Ramda hand over all of Erso's communications. Looking out through the immense window of the command room, it was there that Krennic witnessed distant explosions and realised it was a rebel attack. Scandalised by the ineffectiveness and reluctance of the Imperial staff around him – and conscious that his own head was at stake – he ordered them to deploy the garrison.

With the arrival of the rebel fleet, Krennic understood that the real objective would be the theft of the secret Death Star plans and ordered the complete shutdown of the base. When Lieutenant Mytus Adema notified him that the vault of the Citadel Tower had been breached, Krennic's worst fears were confirmed and he immediately departed with two death troopers to personally take care of the problem, while sending the rest of his elite soldiers to fight on the beaches. After entering the databank through an auxiliary door, he was confronted by a man and woman stealing the plans. Despite his escort being eliminated, Krennic succeeded in putting Cassian Andor out of action and continued to follow the other thief to the roof of the tower.

On the roof, the director confronted the intruder with his DT–29 heavy blaster. Confused and furious he demanded to know her identity, to which she proudly replied that she was the daughter of Galen and Lyra Erso, and that her father had sabotaged his life's work, which she had just revealed to the whole galaxy. Despite the two huge revelations, Krennic remained composed, he was certain that the shield had prevented any transmissions. As he prepared to kill the last of the Ersos, he was shot by Andor, who had attacked from behind. As he lay on the ground, he was unable to stop the two rebel agents transmitting the plans to the rebel fleet in orbit.

Alone and having regained consciousness, the first thing Krennic saw upon raising his head was the emergence of the Death Star from hyperspace, and he understood the irony that his creation would also be his own annihilation. Aboard the Death Star, Tarkin had already initiated the destruction of the Citadel Tower with the superlaser in a vain attempt to stop the theft of the plans. In a final burst of emerald light, the man who was so convinced of his own genius was no more.

Otoh Gunga

This Gungan underwater city was hidden at the bottom of Lake Paonga on the planet of Naboo.

Thanks to its remote location, the Gungans were able to avoid their surface-dwelling Naboo neighbours who they considered arrogant. The city was composed of numerous huge residential light-studded bubbles that were powered by hydrostatic force fields, while a portal system enabled inhabitants to go in and out while keeping the water on the outside. Among the buildings of the city was one that housed the Gungan Council, presided over by Boss Nass. This city of one million inhabitants was evacuated and abandoned when it came under attack from the Trade Federation's droid army led by OOM-9.

Outer Rim

A region of the galaxy located far from the Core Worlds on the borders of Wild Space. These territories were scarcely populated compared with the more developed regions of the Inner Rim.

During the time of the Old Republic, the planets of the Outer Rim were inaccessible to the first human colonists from Coruscant. With the establishment of longer hyperspace routes, those populations were able to look for new opportunities in the attractive and promising region. With the birth of the Galactic Republic, roughly a thousand years before the Clone Wars, trading expanded hugely between the various territories that formed the galaxy. Despite the fact that many known worlds were keen to monopolise the Outer Rim, Republic rule and the Jedi Order managed to resolve the majority of conflicts during the ten centuries that preceded the rise of the Galactic Empire.

Sheev Palpatine, the former Naboo senator and newly self-appointed Emperor of the galaxy, believed that by muzzling the territories of the Outer Rim it would be easier to control the Core systems. He attempted to coerce worlds like Lothal to accept his rule, a move that he hoped would encourage other worlds to do the same. The task proved to be easy in some worlds, many of which were already ruled by criminal organisations that the Empire had connections with. After the fall of the Empire following the Battle of Endor, and the destruction of the second Death Star, the planets of the Outer Rim benefited most as they were released from the crushing Imperial rule. During the constitution of the New Republic, the planet of Akiva became the first in the Outer Rim to ally itself with the former Rebel Alliance.

Owen Lars

Owner of a moisture farm on Tatooine, Owen Lars was the uncle of Luke Skywalker, whom he raised with his wife, Beru, after the fall of the Republic.

Following the death of his mother, Aika, Owen Lars followed his father, Cliegg, to Tatooine, where they established a moisture farm. During a visit to Mos Espa in search of help during the harvest season, Cliegg met Shmi Skywalker, a slave who belonged to a scrap merchant named Watto. After falling in love with her, Cliegg bought her from her master, set her free and married her. Although he had never met him, Owen Lars then became the stepbrother of Anakin Skywalker.

Owen met Beru and the Lars family lived happily and peacefully until Shmi was kidnapped by a tribe of Tusken Raiders. Cliegg planned to save Shmi with the help of the other farmers, but their expedition failed. The group was decimated during a violent fight and Cliegg lost a leg. Around a month later, Anakin Skywalker experienced terrifying visions and nightmares. Although he dreaded what they might mean, he went to Tatooine to recover his mother. He followed the tracks from the Lars' farm, determined to find her. When Skywalker found his mother, she died in his arms and in a rage he slaughtered the Tusken Raiders. The following day he returned to the Lars' homestead with his mother's body.

Cliegg died shortly after and left the responsibility of the farm to Owen, who had married Beru. About three years later, Obi-Wan Kenobi made contact with the farmer and entrusted him with Luke – Anakin Skywalker's infant son – in an effort to protect him from the Emperor. However, Owen Lars didn't realise that he would also need to protect the boy from his father – whom he believed was dead along with the other Jedi. Lars agreed to raise the child, but forbade Kenobi from interfering in his education in any way.

After nineteen years, watched over from afar by Kenobi, young Skywalker had become a talented pilot in addition to his career as a farmer, and had grown impatient and wanted to leave Tatooine. Lars' destiny changed the day he acquired two droids that the Imperial forces were searching for. Skywalker discovered a holographic message of a young woman in the memory of the astromech droid, R2-D2, in which she implored Obi-Wan Kenobi to help. Later that evening, R2-D2 escaped from the farm in order to find the old Jedi. While Skywalker was out looking for the disobedient droid, Imperial soldiers tracked the droids from the Jawas to the Lars' farm, and Owen and Beru were brutally killed. When Skywalker returned home he discovered the farm burnt to ashes and his guardians dead.

Padawan

A young apprentice who was trained by a Jedi in order to achieve the title of Jedi Knight.

Within the Jedi Order, a child detected to have a sensitivity to the Force was submitted first to a common education course in a class with a Jedi Master. A few years later, this Padawan became the unique apprentice of a Jedi Knight or, more rarely, a Jedi Master. The extensive training took place over an undetermined period of time, and often included dangerous field missions undertaken with their master. During the period known as the Clone Wars, Jedi Masters and Knights became generals of the Republic and their Padawan learners served as commanders. To become a Jedi Knight, the apprentice had to pass nine tests, which were based on their reactions to isolation, fear, anger, treason, instinct, concentration, forgiveness, protection and solidarity. The Jedi would then be knighted and their braid, which was the symbol of their status as a Padawan, was ritually cut with a lightsaber.

Padmé Amidala

A Galactic Republic stateswoman; secret wife of the Jedi Anakin Skywalker; mother of Leia Organa and Luke Skywalker; and Ben Solo's grandmother, Padmé Naberrie was born on the beautiful and peaceful planet of Naboo.

Fourteen years later, she took the name of Amidala after she was elected as queen. Despite her young age, her love for her people and the common good shone through. When the Trade Federation first blockaded, then invaded Naboo, her leadership skills were put to the test, but she dealt with the events and demonstrated a maturity that belied her years. Unwilling to give in to the demands of the Trade Federation, she was saved from being imprisoned in Camp 4 by two Jedi – Qui-Gon Jinn and Obi-Wan Kenobi – who had initially gone to the planet on a diplomatic mission to settle the conflict. They convinced her to seek the support of the Senate on Coruscant and together escaped from the planet.

They escaped aboard Amidala's damaged Naboo Royal Starship, and were forced to land on Tatooine. Disguised in the uniform of one of her maids, the queen visited Mos Espa with her new companions, and witnessed first-hand its burning suns, slavery and the dangerous sporting competitions. It was in this brutal underbelly of the world that Amidala first met Anakin Skywalker, a boy five years her junior, who would change her destiny. Although the young Skywalker was fascinated by her beauty, she only saw him as a charming – if somewhat unusual – child. Owing to a wager on his victory in the Boonta Eve Classic Podrace, Skywalker was freed and granted permission to leave the planet. Lost and alone without his mother, who had remained a slave, Skywalker followed his new companions and allowed Amidala to look after him.

Amidala headed to Coruscant to plead with the Senate to rescue her planet. The bureaucracy and corruption within the Republic's governing body meant Naboo went unaided. Counselled by her friend and senator of Naboo, Sheev Palpatine, she petitioned for a vote of a no confidence in Supreme Chancellor Valorum.

Amidala secretly returned to her occupied planet, where, for the first time in history, she succeeded in striking a military alliance with the Gungans. In a demonstration of her great courage the young monarch put her strategy into action across the different fronts and soon proved triumphant. She liberated her planet, gained the friendship of the Gungans, and Palpatine was elected Supreme Chancellor of the Galactic Republic.

As an elected rather than hereditary monarch – limited in time – Amidala's mandate ended and she was succeeded by Queen Jamillia. Amidala continued to represent the people of Naboo and their interests in the Senate – a place that had so bitterly disappointed her in the past. But the Senate had become dangerous. As a senator opposed to the Republic's militarisation and a member of the Loyalist Committee, she narrowly escaped an assassination attempt financed by Count Dooku, leader of the Separatist movement.

This key event had major consequences. Following a recommendation from Palpatine, the Jedi Council furnished Amidala with two bodyguards: Kenobi and Skywalker. The young Padawan had grown and the age gap between him and Amidala was barely noticeable. Following a second attempt on her life, Amidala and Skywalker escaped to Naboo, where the young Jedi confessed his love for her. Between her political responsibilities and his allegiance to the Jedi, which had strict rules regarding relationships, it was a useless situation.

Amidala accompanied Skywalker when he went in search of his mother, Shmi Skywalker, on Tatooine. By the time he found his mother she was on the brink of death. Consumed by hatred and rage, the Jedi slaughtered all of the Tusken Raiders in the camp. Despite this shocking revelation, Amidala comforted him as he mourned the loss of his mother and condemned himself for the monstrous act he had committed. Their relationship faced a new test when they faced their impending deaths on Geonosis.

Alongside Kenobi, Amidala and Skywalker found themselves prisoners of the Separatists on Geonosis, and were sentenced to execution in the Petranaki Arena. Faced with the threat of death pushed Amidala to confess her love for the young Jedi. Mace Windu and Yoda, at the head of the Grand Army of the Republic, arrived and saved them. The shocking events, which demonstrated that they could be separated at any time, convinced them of their love and they secretly married on Naboo.

During the Clone Wars, their individual duties often kept the pair apart. Just before the end of the conflict, following the Battle of Coruscant, Amidala told Skywalker that she was pregnant. Although it was happy news, it compromised the couple and their forbidden link even further. In addition, Amidala never realised that her pregnancy would be the catalyst of her husband's most traumatic fears. Consumed by visions of Amidala dying in childbirth, he fell once more into an uncontrollable panic – terrified that just as with his mother he would be unable to save the woman he loved. Only Palpatine promised that he could save Amidala, using the knowledge of immortality that had been discovered by the Sith Lord, Darth Plagueis.

Meanwhile, Amidala continued to oppose the growing powers of the Supreme Chancellor and 'close friend' of Skywalker – a situation that caused a widening gulf between the young couple. However, she did not know that Palpatine was secretly a Sith Lord working to turn Anakin to the dark side. He would not turn his back on the Chancellor, and worried that Amidala was starting to sound like a Separatist. It was Kenobi who revealed to her the worst news – Skywalker had succumbed to the dark side. Unable to believe his claims, Amidala departed for Mustafar to confront her husband, not knowing that Kenobi had hidden himself on her ship.

In the apocalyptic wastes of Mustafar, she instantly realised Kenobi was telling the truth. Skywalker's tenderness towards her was mixed with his delusions of omnipotence and paranoia, making him unstable. Amidala could not reason with him even though he thought he had done everything in order to save her life. As Amidala refused his proposal to destroy Palpatine and rule the galaxy together, Kenobi emerged from his hiding place. Skywalker, now known as Darth Vader, believed that Amidala was plotting against him with his old master. Traumatised by his transformation, Amidala's horror was only compounded as her husband, incensed by what he considered was her betrayal, turned his rage on her and used the Force to attack her.

Having defeated Vader, Kenobi took Amidala to the medical facility on Polis Massa, where two days later she gave birth to twins, Luke and Leia. Destroyed by the psychological shock of recent events and physically exhausted by the trial of childbirth, Amidala died. The last seconds of her short life were dedicated to sharing with Kenobi her ultimate belief that goodness still existed in Vader. The power of the Sith was so great that this final conviction of Amidala's was more hope than truth, but years later, having never heard his mother's last words, a young man was driven to prove the same conviction. Luke Skywalker, Jedi Knight, would restore the humanity of the man who was the love of Amidala's life.

Pamich Nerro Goode

A lead dispatcher at the Resistance base on D'Qar, Pamich Nerro Goode was part of the young generation that hadn't experienced the Civil War but was ready to defend the New Republic against the threat posed by the First Order.

Brave and committed, Goode placed her trust in General Leia Organa, Rebel Alliance hero, and joined the Resistance on the planet of D'Qar to put her talents to good use. She was working in the base control room, where she participated in the execution of the plans devised by the High Command to attack Starkiller Base.

Paodok'Draba'Takat

A Drabatan from Pipada, Paodok'Draba'Takat was an explosives specialist and a corporal in the Alliance Special Forces unit that took part in the Rogue One mission.

The fatigues of the dangerous commando hid someone that could have been an engineer if the Empire had not turned his life upside down, so instead he took his knowledge of structural dynamics and put his genius to use for demolition purposes. Consumed by his hatred of Palpatine's regime, the Drabatan didn't hesitate to join Jyn Erso's operation, where he proved himself with his blaster. Commonly nicknamed Pao, his complete name was Paodok'Draba'Takat Sap'De'Rekti Nik'Linke'Ti'Ki'Vef'Nik'Nesevef'Li'Kek. Screaming his people's battle cry of 'Sa'kalla!' he joined the Battle on Scarif, but died during the conflict on the Scarif beaches.

Paploo

A brown-furred Ewok from Bright Tree Village on the forest moon of Endor, Paploo helped the Rebellion commandos during the Battle of Endor.

By stealing a speeder bike, as ordered by Teebo, Paploo significantly contributed to the battle by creating a diversion that reduced the number of guards that surrounded the bunker of the planetary shield generator.

Paril Ritta

This rebel pilot answered to the Blue Twelve call sign during the Battle of Scarif.

Originally based in the Atrivis sector, Ritta, who piloted a Y-wing starfighter, was one of four Y-wings reassigned to protect and significantly reinforce the attack capacities of Admiral Raddus and the *Profundity*. It was a tactical transfer that was hugely important during the assault that supported the clandestine Rogue One operation.

Partisans

The partisans were one of the first groups of insurgents to arm themselves against the Empire, nineteen years before the Battle of Yavin.

Founded and led by the iron fist of Saw Gerrera, this rebel cell succeeded in destabilising the Imperial occupation on Gerrera's native world of Onderon. This led to a natural alliance with the newborn Rebellion. A controversial militia group, the partisans weren't afraid to use torture and sometimes civilian attacks in their deadly struggle against Palpatine's regime – a course of action that saw both Mon Mothma and Bail Organa keep their distance from the group.

After numerous fights, the partisans relocated to the consecrated moon of Jedha, in order to purge it of a heavy Imperial presence. Gerrera was unable to carry through this campaign and perished when his den was destroyed by the strong shock wave caused when the Death Star fired on the Holy City of NiJedha. However, some of his followers successfully escaped in the few starships the group possessed.

Passel Argente

A Koorivar senator who served as the Magistrate of the Corporate Alliance, Passel Argente could be recognised by his spiral horn at the top of his skull.

His career took a similar path to that of the members of the Trade Federation, and after starting in the Galactic Senate he joined the Confederacy of Independent Systems during the Clone Wars by becoming a member of the Separatist Council. Based on Utapau, he followed the Council to Mustafar were he was eliminated by Darth Vader.

Pateesa

See Rancor

Patrol Droid

This Starkiller Base surveillance droid possessed a long-distance antenna that it used to transmit data about its surrounding area, which in turn was used to detect intruders.

The patrol droid had a white surface, which allowed it to go unnoticed in the snowy landscape of Starkiller Base.

Pau City

Capital of the planet of Utapau, Pau City was inhabited by the Pau'ans and the Utais, its native species, and was situated in a huge open-cut sinkhole characteristic of Utapau's geology.

Although the planet of Utapau always tried to stay neutral in the conflict between the Confederacy of Independent Systems and the Republic, it was the setting of several events directly linked to the Clone Wars. The death of a Jedi Master in the city led Obi-Wan Kenobi and Anakin Skywalker to uncover a Separatist plot to acquire an enormous kyber crystal, whose power would annihilate the Republic's forces; the Jedi eventually destroyed the crystal. At the end of the Clone Wars, Pau City was the last sanctuary of the Separatists and General Grievous.

Pau'ans

Tall and slender inhabitants of the planet of Utapau, Pau'ans coexisted peacefully with the Utai in sinkhole cities.

They formed a kind of aristocracy and generally occupied administrative posts. Although Utapau remained neutral, the Pau'ans were rather in favour of the Republic, and it was the port administrator of Pau City, Tion Medon, who gave Obi-Wan Kenobi pivotal information about the whereabouts of General Grievous. Few Pau'ans were Force-sensitive, but there were some exceptions, notably in the ranks of the Sith, in the form of the Pau'an Grand Inquisitor.

Pax Aurora

A top-secret project developed by the Galactic Empire whose file was kept in the secure vault of the Citadel Tower on Scarif.

While in the Imperial databank searching for the plans of the Death Star, Jyn Erso and Cassian Andor notably came across this mysterious codename. Although this title could be translated to mean 'peace', it could be assumed that the file hid less-than-peaceful ideas coming from a regime that was willing to wage war against the galaxy.

Pedrin Gaul

This rebel pilot took the place of Red Five in the Battle of Scarif, before Luke Skywalker assumed the call sign for the assault on Yavin.

On his native planet of Denon, Pedrin Gaul was a peaceful transport pilot who carried freight and passengers through the skies of heavily populated cities. On one occasion, after helping fugitives tracked by the Empire to flee, a price was put on his head for treason and he was forced to quickly escape. That exile drove him to join the Rebellion, where he became a cadet in Red Squadron, posted at the Massassi Great Temple on Yavin 4. He jumped at the opportunity to support the Rogue One mission, but his X-wing was shot down in a burst of flames not far from the Scarif shield gate. The position left vacant by his death was filled a few days later by a young farm boy from Tatooine, Luke Skywalker, who, as the new Red Five, destroyed the Death Star.

Pendra Siliu

This little girl was saved by Jyn Erso during the ambush of Tythoni Square.

Owing to the density of the population in Jedha City and their radicalism, the partisans didn't concern themselves with the fate of the civilians during their operations. Siliu was separated from her mother in the panic generated when a tank transporting kyber crystals was attacked. Crying, shocked and in the middle of the chaos, she was noticed by Jyn Erso, who left her hiding place in order to protect her. After being reunited with her mother, Huika, she was quickly led away from the violence.

Percussion Cannon

Directly issued by the weapon industry, the percussion cannon, which used Tostovin ammunition, was an incredibly popular heavy blaster, as long as you didn't mind buying your weapons from the black market.

The weapon of choice for the Guavian Death Gang, its barrels had a reinforced kinetic driver that allowed it to contain the blaster's considerable power, while its impact range gave it a surprisingly low miss rate. Its recoil counterweight enabled the user to stay on balance despite the blaster's power.

Phasma

The chief commander of the First Order's stormtrooper army, Captain Phasma was the third member, along with Kylo Ren and General Hux, of the unofficial triumvirate in charge of the Starkiller Base operation.

Her chromed armour, fashioned from an old Naboo yacht once used by the Emperor, was a symbol of her authority and set her apart from the stormtrooper divisions. As a perfectionist, Captain Phasma paid special attention to discipline, which she enforced with an iron grip. Though authoritarian and a strong supporter of hierarchy, she stood close to her troops, both on the battlefield where she could often be seen participating in operations, or other areas under her command, where she knew each stormtrooper by its identification number.

Phasma had some disagreements with her immediate superior, General Hux, about what made a good soldier. She encouraged tenacity and courage, which she viewed as essential qualities in anyone who wore the First Order uniform, and did not like to see her troops' skills used for unimportant missions. A skilled weapons expert, she used a chromed laser rifle that matched her uniform.

Phirmists

Practised throughout the galaxy, the followers of this Force-based religion distinguished itself through its belief that there was only one god, the Phirmist god.

Among its many practitioners on Jedha was Guch Ydroma, who claimed to have received the gift of transforming air into drinking water from the divinity.

Plo Koon

A Jedi Master and member of the Jedi High Council, this Kel Dor, like all members of his species, wore a respiratory mask, because oxygen was lethal to him, and protective goggles, to avoid the evaporation of ocular moisture.

He was one of the survivors of the mission to rescue Anakin Skywalker, Obi-Wan Kenobi and Padmé Amidala on Geonosis and became a Jedi general during the Clone Wars. Shortly after the Battle of Coruscant, Plo Koon helped the Republic achieve victory on Cato Neimoidia. After the military victory, as he patrolled the skies above the planet in his starfighter with his clone pilots, Order 66 was given and he was shot down by the clones. He died in the resulting explosion, unaware of what had happened.

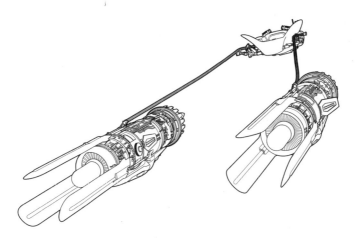

Podracer

This repulsor-fitted racing vehicle normally possessed between two and four highly powerful engines that were linked to the cockpit via cables.

In this sport, the podracers could vary greatly in shape or size, but they had to be able to go faster than 700 kph in order to compete and have a chance of winning.

Poe Dameron

A commander of the Resistance forces and an ace X-wing pilot, Poe Dameron was one of the iconic figures in the movement led by General Leia Organa against the threat of the First Order.

Born at the end of the Galactic Civil War that saw the fall of the Empire, his parents were both members of the Rebel Alliance. Dameron grew up on Yavin 4 in a new colony, not far from the ruins of Massassi. Having grown up listening to the stories of the great war heroes, he naturally joined the defence fleet of the New Republic where his skills saw him rapidly become a squad leader. Fully aware of the Senate's blindness regarding the rise of the First Order, he joined the Resistance.

Impetuous and charismatic, Dameron was a key element in General Organa's troops. He was both a squad leader, using the Black Leader call sign and an accomplished soldier. His inner strength and reliability ensured the High Command entrusted him with the most important and most dangerous missions. In the cockpit of *Black One*, a customised T-70 X-wing starfighter covered with ferrospheric anti-sensor paint, he travelled across the galaxy accompanied by his faithful astromech droid, BB-8.

It was on a mission to the Kelvin Ravine on Jakku where he met the honourable Lor San Tekka, who held the last clue for him to find the location of the legendary Jedi Knight Luke Skywalker. Captured by Kylo Ren and the First Order troops after a deadly raid, Dameron successfully hid the information given to him by Lor San Tekka in BB-8 and ordered the small droid to escape. Dameron was then taken aboard the *Finalizer*, the First Order's flagship.

With the help of FN-2187 (whom the pilot renamed Finn), a stormtrooper who was attempting to defect, Dameron managed to escape by stealing a TIE fighter and eventually reached Jakku. Having had to eject himself from the cockpit during the dangerous landing, Dameron was separated from Finn, but managed to rejoin the Resistance forces on D'Qar. He led the rescue mission on Takodana to help Han Solo, Rey, Finn and BB-8 and then led the assault against the First Order's Starkiller Base, during which he inflicted heavy damages on the enemy.

Poe was a brave pilot who rarely lost his temper, although occasionally he was guilty of provoking the enemy. His strong character helped him bear the worst tortures – although even he couldn't resist the tremendous power of the Force. Generous and faithful to his friends, he took his role within the command of the Resistance very seriously.

During a First Order attack, General Leia Organa was incapacitated and Resistance veteran Vice Admiral Holdo stepped up to lead the cause. However, Dameron was full of confidence in his own strategic capabilities and arrogantly undermined her orders. With the help of Finn and Resistance maintenance worker Rose Tico, Dameron hatched a plan to try and disable the First Order's hyperspace tracker – a plan that was unsuccessful, but fortunately for Dameron, Finn and Rose, the remaining Resistance fleet evaded capture as Holdo sacrificed her own life for the cause.

Poggle the Lesser

The leader of the Geonosians, Archduke Poggle the Lesser controlled the droid foundries of Geonosis, which made him a powerful ally of the Confederacy of Independent Systems.

It was the archduke who sentenced Obi-Wan Kenobi, Anakin Skywalker and Padmé Amidala to death on Geonosis in the Petranaki Arena – a sentence that triggered the intervention of the Jedi Order and, for the very first time, the Republic army. A leader of the Separatist movement in his own right, when Poggle the Lesser launched his droids into the battle it officially triggered the beginning of the Clone Wars. Along with Count Dooku, he was forced to flee the conflict zone, and as he escaped he took the plans for a future ultimate weapon, called the Death Star.

During the war, it was necessary for him to destroy one of his own factories to prevent the Republic seizing it. He was captured by the Republic when he unsuccessfully tried to take shelter with the Geonosian Queen Karina the Great. While being held in Republic custody, he agreed to divulge information about the Death Star project, before he escaped to join the other Separatist leaders on Mustafar. There, he was assassinated by Skywalker, who had become Darth Vader.

Polystarch

A synthetic food found inside the emergency rations looted by Unkar Plutt, the scrap seller, in the military kits found abandoned in the wrecks of the Starship Graveyard on Jakku.

Treated and freeze-dried in small vacuum portions, polystarch took the form of a grey powder that, when mixed with a measured amount of water and gently shaken, rapidly fermented and expanded into a small, fist-sized loaf of doughy bread. Polystarch contained the necessary nutrients to survive in hostile environments and was often supplied with a portion of veg-meat for a full meal.

Ponda Baba

This male Aqualish from the planet of Ando became a spice dealer on behalf of Jabba the Hutt on Tatooine, shortly after having formed a curious partnership with Dr Evazan.

The two met when Ponda Baba saved Evazan from a bounty hunter who had been tracking him on behalf of one of his former patients. They then decided to become associates, although their professional friendship was punctuated by the possibility that Baba would be tempted by the bounty on Evazan's head. Pragmatic, Baba always considered the profitable long-term gains he could generate from his associations.

The two partners were among the regular clientele of the Mos Eisley Cantina and frequently used their free time to provoke fights with those that appeared easy prey. On one occasion, Baba targeted a young farmer while he was ordering at the bar. He tried to intimidate him in his language using a powerful and guttural groan, which Evazan immediately translated. Unbeknown to the two brutes, the farmer was travelling with a Jedi Knight who carried the weapon of the Order. Obi-Wan Kenobi quickly came to the aid of Luke Skywalker and after he had tried to diffuse the situation calmly without drawing attention to himself, he was forced to draw his lightsaber in defence as the mad doctor drew his blaster. Two seconds later, Evazan lay on the ground having sustained a major slash to the chest while Ponda Baba lost one of his arms. Evazan's attempt to surgically repair his partner failed, and instead almost killed him.

Pote Snitkin

This Skrilling gunrunner was on Jabba the Hutt's payroll.

Aside from his commercial activity in contraband weapons, this sturdy green-skinned character also drove one of the two skiffs that escorted the Hutt's barge, the *Khetanna*. During the cursed expedition to the Great Pit of Carkoon for the execution of Luke Skywalker and his friends, Snitkin was thrown overboard into the mouth of the sarlacc after the Jedi managed to free himself.

Power Droid

The GNK-series power droid, commonly nicknamed 'Gonk', was the most popular model throughout the galaxy.

At its most basic model, the Gonk was, literally, a walking battery, designed for recharging vehicles and other machinery. Commonly found throughout the galaxy, it was able to adapt to many different climates, from the hot deserts of Tatooine to the ice of Hoth. Slow-moving and unremarkable, but highly dependable, the power droid was designed to stay in the background and just get on with its job.

Prashee and Cratinus

A pair of gambling enthusiasts, these two Ubdurian brothers were regular customers at Maz's Castle on Takodana and could often be seen in the main hall enjoying a game of Sabacc, pazaak or dejarik.

They visited the castle to relax and especially appreciated the music supplied by the resident bands. As with so many of the other regulars at the establishment, Prashee and Cratinus were of questionable moral character and took full advantage of their physical resemblance and similar Ubdurian travel gowns to swap identities and carry out ingenious and profitable scams.

Praster Ommlen

A regular customer at Maz's Castle on Takodana, Praster Ommlen was a repentant ex-weapons dealer of Ottegan origin.

Having left his criminal life behind him, Ommlen converted to the Sacred Order of Ramulus, an Ithorian religion, and searched for redemption by providing spiritual help to the bandits, criminals, pirates and crooks he lived among. His tall figure – dressed in worn-out simple robes – could often be seen near the entrance to the castle, where he welcomed the patrons he hoped to convert.

Probe Droid

Produced by Arakyd Industries, these droids were used for reconnaissance and spy missions.

One such droid was the Viper probe droid – used by the Empire for planetary exploration while searching for the rebel base. Spider-like in its appearance, this droid was equipped with manipulator arms, in addition to repulsors that allowed it to adjust its movement to suit any global surface. It was also fitted with a cannon blaster to combat light assaults and a self-destruct mechanism to protect any top-secret information it may have collected.

Profundity, the

See Raddus *and* MC75 Star Cruiser

Protective Screen

See Energy Shield

Proton Charge
A delayed-action magnetic grenade.

This weapon was used by Han Solo and Princess Leia Organa to destroy the global shield generator during the Battle of Endor.

Proton Torpedo

These military weapons functioned through a principle of combustion, which ignited an explosive that released clouds of high-velocity proton particles.

The torpedoes were used to create more serious damage than that caused by concussion missiles, but they also limited the risk of collateral or involuntary damages as advanced controls allowed a destruction perimeter around the target to be set. Some models of 'intelligent' torpedoes were able to lock on to moving targets and the most effective ones were able to make ninety-degree changes of direction in a radius of less than a metre. All these features made this weapon the best choice in confrontations that required precision and/or long-range shots.

This weapon marked the history of two famous battles. First at the Battle of Naboo, when the young Anakin Skywalker involuntarily destroyed the Trade Federation's warship engaged to control the blockade of the planet. And then at the Battle of Yavin, where Luke Skywalker destroyed the Death Star by creating a chain reaction created by the launch of proton torpedoes into one of the space station's exhaust ports.

Puck Naeco

This Rebel Alliance pilot took part in the Battle of Yavin as a member of Red Squadron.

He used the call sign Red Twelve and was designated to be part of the small group of X-wings whose mission was to escort Red Leader, Garven Dreis, during the assault of the Death Star's equatorial trench. The initial mission was to concentrate their fire on the space station's turbolaser batteries, but Darth Vader, aware of the danger of the rebel assault, took to the controls of his TIE Advanced x1 to attack the rebel starfighters. Escorted by two pilots he formed the dangerous Victor Squadron, and destroyed Naeco's fighter, killing the pilot.

Pyro Denton Explosive

This explosive was used by the Resistance in its commando operations.

Generally conditioned as a metal sphere of about 15 centimetres in diameter, this very thick powerful explosive was perfect for destroying strategic installations. Each sphere was equipped with an integrated timer and a magnetic device that allowed it to be placed in direct contact with part of the target to be destroyed. Despite being easy to use, the downside of this type of explosive was its weight. If the destruction of a target required a lot of spheres, transportation by commandos during the mission could be problematic.

Han Solo found an easy solution to this problem when he was charged with destroying the oscillator at Starkiller Base – Chewbacca. The Wookiee accompanied him on the mission, where his natural strength and stamina allowed him to carry the large amount of pyro denton explosives required.

PZ-4CO 'Peazy'

A communication droid assigned to the Resistance command centre on D'Qar, 'Peazy' shared the control of droid operations on the base with C-3PO, which allowed the golden droid to also focus on General Leia Organa's needs.

Its blue colour and specific design – based on the Tofallid physiology – meant that it could be easily and quickly identified by operators. 'Peazy' spoke with a feminine voice.

Quadjumper

The quadrijet transfer spacetug was manufactured by Subpro and was generally used in orbital transfer yards to quickly move merchandise from the huge transporters in orbit.

Its power and mobility optimised conveying time and therefore diminished the loss in turnover that was unavoidable for transport companies when moving shipping containers. Equipped with magnetic grappling hooks and powerful tractor beams, the quadjumper demanded good piloting skills. This type of craft was popular among prospectors and smugglers who appreciated its versatility in the atmosphere and space, along with its capacity to integrate numerous 'personal' modifications.

A quadjumper was parked on Dock 3 of the Niima outpost on Jakku, where it waited to be bought by the scrap dealer Unkar Plutt from a group of arms dealers. While trying to escape an assault by the First Order, Rey, Finn and BB-8 ran towards the craft, but it was destroyed by TIE fighters. With no other solution available, they set their sights on another old piece of junk, which turned out to be the *Millennium Falcon*.

Quarsh Panaka

A captain in the Royal Naboo Security Forces, Quarsh Panaka became Queen Padmé Amidala's bodyguard during the events that surrounded the invasion of Naboo.

Professional, demanding and stern, Panaka was a soldier who obeyed orders, but knew how to argue his point of view when it came to the protection of someone under his care, notably the Queen of Naboo. When Qui-Gon Jinn announced his desire to take the monarch to Coruscant, the captain was against the idea, but the young woman disregarded the judgement of the faithful soldier and accepted the proposition of the Jedi. Although Panaka resented the decision and took it as an insult to his ability, he showed no outward sign of this and accompanied her as she made her escape from their occupied homeworld.

He was soon tested again when their vessel was severely damaged by the blockade. Jinn's Padawan, Obi-Wan Kenobi, believed that the only solution was to go to Tatooine and make the necessary repairs. If going to Coruscant – capital of the Republic, a place of high culture, civilisation and home of official institutions – had seemed a bad idea to the pessimistic Panaka, this new destination, a desert planet in the grasp of Hutt gangsters, was sheer madness. To his horror, the queen accepted the Jedi's solution and on Tatooine, aware of his duty and faithful to it, he played along by staying in the vessel to protect the queen's double, leaving Amidala to accompany Jinn, Binks and R2-D2 on their uncertain quest for a hyperdrive.

Once on Coruscant, he opposed the queen's decision to return to Naboo. Despite his explanation that she would be captured and forced to sign the treaty imposed by the Trade Federation, Amidala ignored his objections once again. While his opinions as a bodyguard were not heeded, Panaka made up for it during the Battle of Naboo. From the streets of Theed to the Royal Palace, he fought bravely while protecting his monarch, until the eventual capture of Viceroy Nute Gunray and the liberation of his compatriots.

Qui-Gon Jinn

A Jedi Master, Qui-Gon Jinn discovered the Chosen One of Jedi Prophecy, and was also the first Jedi to achieve immortality within the Force.

Born on Coruscant, Jinn's sensitivity to the Force was detected at a young age and he was integrated into the Jedi Order to begin a long life of training and learning. When he reached the stage of Padawan, he was apprenticed to a Jedi Master who would eventually become the subject of much negative attention – Count Dooku. During the following years, Jinn became a Jedi Master himself and was assigned a Padawan called Obi-Wan Kenobi. Kenobi realised Jinn's head-strong integrity and strong values had played a big role in why his master had not joined the Jedi Council.

Before he took on the training of Kenobi, Jinn was a man ready to live a life devoted to the Force – to follow its most specialised and little-known ways – even if it sometimes conflicted with the strict path of his Order. Therefore he didn't hesitate to travel to a planet that was greatly imprinted by the Force, which could have been, according to legend, responsible for the creation of the midi-chlorians. On this world, five Priestesses of the Force detected his deep integrity and lavished an incredible knowledge on him: the secret of immortality within the Force after death. After he left the world of the five Priestesses, the Jedi continued to secretly learn, stage after stage, the different degrees of this discipline. However, he never had the time to master the entirety of all aspects of it.

During the blockade of Naboo, Jinn and Kenobi were sent to negotiate a peaceful outcome to the crisis, but suddenly found that they had to escape being killed by the Trade Federation. Once on Naboo, they saved Queen Amidala and found shelter on Tatooine where Jinn discovered a young slave boy named Anakin Skywalker. A host of indicators – an immaculate conception, elevated rate of midi-chlorians and superhuman capacities as a podracer pilot – persuaded Jinn that the boy was the Chosen One of Jedi Prophecy. In fact, he was so convinced in his belief that he decided to train Skywalker himself, despite the refusal of the Jedi Council to integrate him into its ranks. The Council was also sceptical about Jinn's other claim concerning a Sith warrior that he had briefly, but intensely fought on Tatooine.

His intuition about the Sith proved to be correct and he died in an epic conquest with Darth Maul on Naboo. With his last breath, the Jedi Master made Kenobi promise that he would take Anakin as his apprentice. His funeral ceremony was attended by all the Jedi and important politicians who hurried to pay their last respects to a man who had passed too quickly. Among the mourners was the person responsible for the Jedi's death, Darth Sidious, hidden behind the impenetrable face of Chancellor Palpatine.

In death, Jinn partially succeeded in using the principles of the five Priestesses. Although he was unsuccessful in projecting an image of his human form – except on a Force-amplifier planet – he was nevertheless able to communicate using his voice. Jinn continued to offer help, guiding both Yoda and Kenobi even further than he had gone on their way to eternal life. It was these lessons that enabled the two Jedi Masters to continue to appear to Luke Skywalker – even after their deaths – to help him become a Jedi Knight, and ultimately push his father to eliminate the Emperor, subsequently re-establishing the balance in the Force.

However, the historic importance of Qui-Gon Jinn was minimised. This would have been in part due to his early death and because he never made it to a position of authority on the High Council. After the Galactic Civil War, his relative anonymity could also be explained by the fact that for a long while it was considered that he had not only been mistaken in his identification of the Chosen One, but was also responsible for the release of a disaster of cosmic proportions upon the galaxy. The Jedi were massacred by his protégé, which in turn allowed the establishment of a dictatorial Imperial regime. The restoration of balance in the Force was a long and painful process, but one that Qui-Gon Jinn had foreseen.

Quinlan Vos

A human Jedi Master who hailed from Kiffu, Quinlan Vos' psychometric talents made him an expert hunter.

Over time, his independent character and sarcastic humour earned him the reputation of being a rebel. While on a secret mission during the Clone Wars with Obi-Wan Kenobi, he hunted down Ziro the Hutt – Jabba's uncle. Using his connections in the underworld, Vos managed to follow Ziro's escape to the Council of the Hutts. The hunt ended on the planet of Teth with the death of Ziro, who was thought to have been killed by the bounty hunter Cad Bane.

R

R2-BHD 'Tooby'

A droid based on Yavin 4, R2-BHD was seconded to Gold Squadron during the Battle of Scarif.

Nicknamed 'Tooby', it appeared that the R2-unit had just been delivered from the factory owing to its absence of colour and its lightly tarnished, silvery appearance. However, his appearance was misleading as this droid had actually served with the Rebellion for years. Caring, helpful and precise, R2-BHD considered the temperamental moments of some of its fellow droids to be illogical. Tooby frequently helped Jon Vander, Gold Leader, pilot his state-of-the-art Y-wing starfighter.

R2-D2 'Artoo'

A spirited astromech droid who was present at the key events of galactic history – often in the company of C-3PO.

Manufactured by Industrial Automaton, this type of utility robot was often assigned to maintenance, repair or starship piloting assistance. This three-wheeled unit with a blue and silver dome, was the property of the Royal Security Forces of Naboo. At the time of the dramatic events that disturbed this peaceful planet, he worked on Queen Amidala's royal starship. When the monarch fled in order to save her life, her chrome starship was hit as it forced its way through the blockade set up by the vessels of the Trade Federation. Under the intense fire that destroyed all of his astromech counterparts, R2-D2 patched the main propulsion unit. It was a pivotal and brave decision that immediately got him noticed by the Jedi and the queen.

During the long stop on Tatooine, R2-D2 encountered a very important future companion – C-3PO. This protocol droid was rebuilt by a young slave boy named Anakin Skywalker. The two droids watched as Skywalker won the Boonta Eve Classic podrace and was freed from slavery. Back on Naboo, the astromech droid acted as co-pilot to Skywalker aboard a N-1 starfighter. Together, they destroyed the Trade Federation flagship and secured an absolute victory over the Trade Federation, both in space and on the ground.

Before the beginning of the Clone Wars, the small droid was in the service of Amidala, who had faced two attempts on her life since becoming a senator. Under the protection of Skywalker, by this time a Jedi Padawan, the three of them travelled from Naboo to Tatooine, where they recovered C-3PO from the farm of the Lars family. Accompanied by the protocol droid, they continued on to Geonosis, where R2-D2 saved his mistress from trouble in the droid foundries. Following the battle that ignited the war with the Separatists, R2-D2, along with C-3PO, were the only witnesses to the secret marriage between Amidala and Skywalker.

Although he accomplished numerous missions during the Clone Wars, R2-D2 was particularly useful during the rescue of Chancellor Palpatine. He followed Skywalker in the assault of General Grievous' flagship, the *Invisible Hand,* where he successfully repulsed and destroyed several battle droids. He was also beside the young Jedi when he executed a difficult crash-landing of the *Invisible Hand* onto the surface of Coruscant.

After sharing many heroic moments with Anakin Skywalker, R2-D2 helplessly observed his master's massacre of the Jedi and the subsequent proclamation of the Empire. The astromech then set out one last time with Skywalker, who was now Darth Vader. R2-D2 landed on Mustafar and witnessed his master's fall to the dark side, which would lead Skywalker to choke his pregnant wife and duel with Kenobi. Along with C-3PO, R2-D2 took care of the unconscious Amidala and transported her back aboard her vessel, which Obi-Wan piloted to Polis Massa. After the birth of the twins and Amidala's death, R2-D2 and his golden friend entered the service of Bail Organa, a friend of Amidala's. In order to keep the existence of Luke and Leia secret from the Sith Order, Organa immediately took measures to erase the memory of the protocol droid, but the discreet astromech remained untouched.

Nineteen years later, Princess Leia Organa, senator and member of the Rebellion against the Empire, was travelling with the droid duo when her ship was invaded by Vader. Before being arrested, she inserted the secret plans of an Imperial superweapon and a holographic message for Kenobi into the databank of R2-D2. The astromech and C-3PO fled to Tatooine, but following a quarrel they separated in the immense desert. In spite of the argument, the two droids were pleased to see each other again after they had both been picked up by scavenging Jawas and loaded into their sandcrawler.

Sold to Owen Lars, who after many years didn't recognise either C-3PO or the unremarkable R2-D2, they made the acquaintance of Luke Skywalker. Knowing his priority was to deliver his message to the famous Jedi Master Obi-Wan Kenobi, R2-D2 ran away, and after an encounter with some Tusken Raiders, he finally accomplished his mission and delivered the message to the old Jedi.

The nature of Leia's call for help compelled Kenobi, Skywalker and the droids to head for Alderaan to deliver the Death Star plans to the rebels. To remain discreet, it was necessary for them to travel undercover on the *Millennium Falcon*, a ship that belonged to the smuggler, Han Solo. Upon meeting the ship's co-pilot, Chewbacca, the two became involved in a heated game of dejarik. The intellectual differences between the Wookiee and a droid capable of calculating thousands of flight plans soon became apparent, but knowing their tendencies for violent outbursts, R2-D2 was quickly convinced to let the Wookiee win. Then, along with his travelling companions, he discovered that Leia's adoptive father, along with the entire planet of Alderaan, had been destroyed by the Death Star – the plans for which R2-D2 was carrying.

After their vessel was captured by the space station, the occupants of the *Millennium Falcon* were forced to find a means of escape. As they made plans, they discovered that Princess Leia was aboard being held captive by the Imperials. R2-D2 helped his friends rescue the princess and made sure everyone avoided the dangers of the Death Star, particularly when he stopped a trash compactor from fatally crushing Skywalker, Leia, Solo and Chewbacca. Although Kenobi had been lost in a duel against Vader, the rest of the group escaped the Death Star and headed to the rebel base on Yavin 4.

At the base, the technical read-outs held by the droid were analysed. R2-D2's mission didn't stop there. He boarded Skywalker's X-wing starfighter and accompanied the young pilot during the rebel attack on the Death Star. R2-D2 didn't see the outcome of the Battle of Yavin as he was hit by a direct shot from Vader as he pursued Skywalker. Uplifted by the victory, rebel technicians worked on the R2-unit and the courageous droid looked like new as he attended the rebels' medal ceremony.

However, it wasn't all victories for the Rebellion. After a defeat on the ice planet of Hoth, the rebel fleet scattered and the astromech accompanied Skywalker to Dagobah aboard his X-wing starfighter. R2-D2 was unsure of where Skywalker was heading and the journey ended in a brutal crash-landing in a swamp. R2-D2 was then swallowed by a water-dwelling dragonsnake before being violently spat out onto dry land.

Next, the astromech found himself being beaten with the staff of an ancient, small green, being, who eventually revealed himself to be Jedi Master Yoda. From that moment on, R2-D2 stayed away from Yoda and guarded the X-wing as the Jedi Master taught Skywalker in the ways of the Force. After Skywalker experienced a vision of his friends in danger on Cloud City, he and R2-D2 left Dagobah, promising to return so Skywalker could finish his training.

Having landed on the floating city above Bespin, Skywalker and R2-D2 were quickly separated in the maze of passageways and elevators that constituted the city. The astromech was then reunited with the damaged C-3PO, Leia and Chewbacca, who had been freed by a repentant Lando Calrissian. The group escaped the Imperial forces who had laid a trap for Skywalker. They took the *Millennium Falcon* to save the Jedi, who had only just survived a confrontation with Vader, and R2-D2 saved the day by activating the vessel's hyperdrive, allowing them to flee the pursuing Imperial ships.

Skywalker sent R2 and C-3PO to Jabba's Palace as part of a plan to save Han Solo, who had been frozen in carbonite and captured for the crime lord. Unlike his gold-plated partner, R2-D2 was aware of the plan and convincingly played along in the charade while C-3PO panicked, sure that Skywalker had abandoned them. The little droid confronted the cruel EV-9D9, Jabba's torture droid, and earned, for his troubles, a role serving drinks on Jabba's sail barge, the *Khetanna*. This was a fortuitous turn of events, as the astromech ended up ideally placed to save the day when Skywalker, Solo and Chewbacca were sentenced to be executed at the Great Pit of Carkoon. Right on cue, he launched Skywalker's new lightsaber, which he had kept hidden in his dome, perfectly into Skywalker's hand. The Jedi freed himself and his friends, and eliminated the Hutt's henchmen. Meanwhile, R2-D2 cut the chains of Leia, who strangled Jabba. R2 then electrocuted the mischievous Salacious B. Crumb who had been attacking the defenceless C-3PO.

With the rescue mission a success and the barge destroyed, Skywalker and R2-D2 separated from their friends and set a course for the Dagobah system once again, where Skywalker fulfilled his promise to the dying Yoda. They then headed to the rendezvous point and joined up with the rebel fleet.

R2-D2's next adventure was on the forest moon of Endor, where the indispensable droid was part of the rebel mission charged with the destruction of the second Death Star's shield generator. With the help from an indigenous tribe of Ewoks, Solo, Leia and the rebels deactivated the battle station's shield. R2-D2's heroism saw him badly damaged while assisting the infiltration of the Imperial bunker. After the second Death Star was destroyed, R2-D2 was restored and joined the celebrations with the rebels and their new friends the Ewoks.

Many years later, after Skywalker disappeared into exile, R2-D2 voluntarily put himself into stand-by mode – a function that finally offered him the chance to sort out the astronomical amount of data he had collected over the years. Despite his inactivity, his service to the Republic and the Rebellion saw him carefully stored on D'Qar by the Resistance who were in conflict with a new enemy, the First Order.

He eventually emerged from his electronic trance having heard the conversation about the missing piece of a map that another courageous astromech droid, BB-8, had helped recover. The map, when complete, would show the location of the exiled Skywalker. In front of the Resistance leaders, R2-D2 and BB-8 pieced together the star charts and revealed Skywalker's final destination. It was only natural that R2 would then accompany Rey and Chewbacca on the *Millennium Falcon* to the planet of Ahch-To in search of Skywalker.

R3-S1 'Threece'

This feminine R-series droid was chief of staff to the team of astromechs at the rebel base on Yavin 4.

Nicknamed 'Threece', the unit had a silvery body surmounted by an orange-patterned, transparent dome through which she vainly displayed an Intellex V processor. She was perfectly organised and coordinated the technology maintenance of her team. However, because of her management skills and competitive character, she was not assigned to any particular starfighter.

R4-P17

Informally named 'R4', this astromech droid was assigned to the different starfighters used by the Jedi Knight Obi-Wan Kenobi.

The R4-unit had a feminine personality and handled hyperspace travel by calculating the faster-than-light jumps, as well as the maintenance of the ships to which she was assigned. She helped Kenobi aboard his Delta-7 interceptor during his pursuit of the bounty hunter Jango Fett to Geonosis, and also accompanied the Jedi Knight during dangerous missions on Teth, Rodia and Mandalore. She was assigned to Kenobi until the Battle of Coruscant, where she was destroyed by enemy buzz droids.

R5-D4

This astromech droid from the R5-series was produced in the factories of Industrial Automaton.

Sometime before the Battle of Yavin it became the property of a tribe of Jawas on Tatooine who tried to sell it to Owen Lars. After a brief interview with C-3PO, while Luke Skywalker conducted some basic technical verifications on R5-D4, the transaction concerning the two droids was quickly concluded despite the loud demonstrations of R2-D2. However, as it began to move forward, R5-D4 fell victim to a motivator breakdown, which stopped it clean in its tracks. C-3PO jumped on the opportunity to recommend that Lars take R2-D2 as a replacement.

RA-7 Protocol Droid

Exclusively produced for the Empire by Arakyd Industries, the RA-7 protocol droids were designed to accompany high-ranking military or official dignitaries.

The behavioural programming of this series gave them a strict and stern attitude. The RA-7 droids were nicknamed 'insect droids' because of the shape of their photoreceptors, but also came to be known as 'Death Star droids' because many of them were assigned to the protocol activities of the space station.

Rabé

One of Queen Amidala's handmaidens, Rabé accompanied the monarch with her colleagues Sabé and Eirtaé on Tatooine, then on Coruscant.

With her dark skin and jet-black hair, it was Rabé who introduced Anakin Skywalker to Amidala in her apartments on Coruscant when he visited her. She also actively participated in the battle inside Theed Royal Palace during the liberation of Naboo.

Raddus

An admiral in the fledging fleet of the Rebel Alliance, Raddus led the difficult orbital assault during the Battle of Scarif in his cruiser, the *Profundity*.

This Mon Calamari, born in the polar regions of his aquatic world, was one of the first officers to join the Rebellion. Previously mayor of the city of Nystullum, he took part in the mass exodus that followed the Empire's occupation. The Imperial troops believed that his vehicle was nothing more than a city-ship (a municipal building that consisted of just a simple tower that housed the administration of the city), but in actual fact it was a camouflaged starship that had the ability to extract itself from the ocean and rush towards the most remote places in space, where it could be converted into a war cruiser.

Although he was mainly stationed in the Telaris system, Raddus sometimes sat on the Rebel High Command on Yavin 4 when an important agenda required it. It was on one such occasion that Jyn Erso confirmed the existence of an operational combat station equipped with a weapon of mass destruction, which had already tested its power on Jedha City. Raddus agreed with the young woman that they should attack the location that housed the plans for the superweapon, but he was instead forced to comply with the more 'prudent' resolution of the Council.

Instead, he was assigned to escort Princess Leia Organa, who was aboard the *Tantive IV* docked with the *Profundity* for maintenance, to Tatooine, where she was to meet the former general of the Clone Wars, the Jedi, Obi-Wan Kenobi. However, following the announcement of the secret Rogue One operation on Scarif, the admiral changed plans and diverted his forces towards the tropical world, despite having received no authorisation to do so. In full preparation for the fight, he didn't even take the incoming communication from Mon Mothma. Upon his exit from hyperspace Raddus immediately issued his orders, which tasked Blue Squadron to pass through the shield gate to support the rebel forces on the ground, while the Red and Gold Squadrons would help to defend the fleet facing the Imperial forces.

Having received warning that access to the planet was about to be closed, he immediately ordered the shield ring to be fired upon and initiated a confrontation with the two Star Destroyers protecting it. As his capital ship was under the assault of numerous TIE fighters, the Mon Calamari initiated a plan to neutralise the *Persecutor*, one of the two menacing cruisers, in an operation that was achieved by the Y-wings of Gold Squadron and their ionic torpedoes.

Informed by Bodhi Rook of the absolute necessity to destroy the shield in order to be able to transmit the stolen plans, the commander of the rebel fleet devised a brilliant and difficult – but essential – idea, which required the sacrifice of lives in order to change the course of the battle and achieve its vital goal. He ordered the *Hammerhead*-class corvette *Lightmaker* to push the *Persecutor* until it smashed the superior bridges of the *Intimidator*, which was still travelling at full speed. The two huge space cruisers crashed down into the shield ring and destroyed it, and the *Profundity* was able to receive the precious files that had been transmitted.

Raddus' joy was cut short by the sight of the Death Star emerging from hyperspace. When its superlaser fired on the Citadel Tower, the admiral knew the deadly consequences for those who still fought on Scarif's surface. Despite maintaining his composure during the terrible event, the dark-skinned Mon Calamari was no less touched by it when he thought of those who were about to face their impending deaths. His declaration: 'May the Force be with you, Rogue One,' marked with sincere sadness, served to accompany them to their end. With no time to mourn, he immediately ordered all ships to jump to hyperspace – a manoeuvre that was cut short by the sudden appearance of Darth Vader's capital ship, the *Devastator*. Quickly disarmed, the *Profundity* was boarded by the Sith Lord, but his objective to retrieve the stolen Death Star plans evaded him, as they were already with Princess Leia Organa aboard the departing *Tantive IV*.

It was an ultimate source of pride for Raddus, who had waged the fight of his life: a short but intense battle in which his strategic talents were essential. He had played his part and paved the way for a young farm boy from Tatooine who would go on to destroy an infamous and deadly threat to both the Alliance and the galaxy.

Radiant VII, the

See **Republic Cruiser**

Ralo Surrel

A Rebel Alliance pilot during the Galactic Civil War, this major had once been a stuntman performing public shows in the Outer Rim, before he became a politician in the New Republic.

As part of the Alliance he became Garven Dreis' wingman with the call sign Red Eleven, and took part in the Battle of Scarif.

Rancor

Carnivorous reptilians native to the planet of Dathomir, these creatures were devoid of any intelligence, but had been naturally endowed with the necessary means to protect themselves.

They possessed a skin so thick that it almost qualified as a shell, had huge jaws filled with teeth and large, strong arms that finished in long, clawed fingers. In spite of an average 5-metre height, a 1.6-tonne weight and their inherent slowness, they were dangerous natural hunters. A lethal quality that hadn't escaped the notice of the slug-like crime lord Jabba the Hutt. He kept one of these great killing machines in a pit below the throne room in his palace and it represented a one-way ticket to death for all those the crime lord wanted to eliminate. The monster, lovingly named Pateesa, meaning 'friend' in Huttese, devoured both Oola the dancer and a Gamorrean guard who accidentally fell into the pit with Luke Skywalker. However, the creature met its fate at the hands of the Jedi, who killed it by dropping a heavy portcullis on its head that pierced its skull.

Rappertunie

A member of the Max Rebo Band, this green Shawda Ubb was the undisputed virtuoso of the Growdi Harmonique, an instrument that was played using the fingers, mouth and toes.

To play the instrument, which was a combination of a flute and a water organ, required highly synchronised skills, which the 30-centimetre-tall musician had perfectly mastered and regularly demonstrated.

Rasett Milio

The scientific administrator of the High Energy Concepts and Implementation Labs division of the Tarkin Initiative on Eadu, this researcher worked hard for twenty years to master the concept of generated chain reaction.

He succeeded in harnessing the energy released by the superlaser in one concentrated cone through the construction of containment channels and the use of force fields. This technical achievement had only one purpose: to bring death to cities and planets on the order of Orson Krennic – the director of this ominous project.

Rathtar

This strange amphibious creature was extremely dangerous and came from the same family of creatures as the sarlaccs, blixus and Umbara's vixus.

With their multiple tentacles and their radial mouths fraught with sharp teeth, these monstrous predators hunted their prey using light-sensitive orbs located on their backs. Responsible for the notorious Trillia Massacre, it was perhaps their aggressiveness and dangerousness that explained why only a few studies were ever made of them. A symbol of power, they nevertheless fuelled the fascination of collectors who, if they could afford to, were willing to spend astronomical sums in order to obtain a specimen.

It was for this reason that the vain King Prana – who loved rare and dangerous creatures and possessed his own zoo – employed Han Solo to deliver three rathtars to him in order to out-perform his rival, Solculvis. Solo loaded the three rathtars aboard the *Eravana* and, having already drastically reduced the number of men in the smuggler's crew, locked them up in airtight containers. During Solo's battle with both the Guavian Death Gang and Kanjiklub (two gangs he had borrowed a lot of money from to finance his expedition), Rey and Finn accidentally freed the rathtars, having become tangled within the *Eravana's* fuse cables. The ensuing chase spread death throughout the ship.

Ratts Tyerell

At just 79 centimetres tall, the Aleena Ratts Tyerell was the smallest of the podracer pilots to race in the Boonta Eve Classic Podrace.

Placed in pole position on the starting grid between Sebulba and Mawhonic, his advantage was somewhat wasted early on when he found himself lost in the middle of the pack. His situation quickly worsened when, while speeding through the Laguna Cave, his accelerator got stuck, which forced Tyerell to speed around the stalactites at an impossible pace – even for a professional pilot. The young racer died in the violent explosion that followed, making him one of the two official casualties of the race.

Raymus Antilles

A hero of the Rebel Alliance, Raymus Antilles was born on Alderaan and served the Royal Family Organa.

Antilles was the captain of the vessels *Sundered Heart* and later *Tantive IV*. Although he first joined the Rebellion because of his unswerving loyalty to the Organa clan, Antilles was nonetheless a key element of the underground diplomacy established by Bail Organa and continued by Princess Leia. The goal was to protect the Alliance through the use of the diplomatic immunity afforded to members of the Senate. Responsible solely for the transportation of the Organa family at the time of the Republic, he became a formidable rebel captain and broke through countless Imperial blockades after the fall of the Republic. Antilles died aboard the *Tantive IV*, where he was strangled by Darth Vader while trying to protect Princess Leia's identity.

Razoo Qin-Fee

This Kanjiklub member from the Nar Kanji human colonies was first lieutenant to Tasu Leech, leader of the Kanjiklub.

Equipped with his formidable wasp laser blaster, Razoo Qin-Fee was one of the most dangerous warriors of his gang. An arsonist and technology expert, he regularly developed strange weapons with extreme efficiency. He could be identified by his special haircut in the Zygerrian fashion, and often accompanied Tasu Leech during his piracy raids and debt-collection operations.

Rebaxan Columni Mouse Droid

A Rebaxan Columni-made communication and transmission droid that was used on the Star Destroyer *Finalizer*.

This type of small mobilised military droid was already in use on the Empire's interstellar cruisers before it was deployed in great numbers on all the bridges of the colossal First Order flagship to cover the large distances between the numerous stations of the *Finalizer*.

Rebel Alliance

Established to fight back against the Imperial regime, the Rebel Alliance was a military organisation that spent twenty-five years battling the Galactic Empire.

During the early years of the Empire's oppression, isolated rebel cells rose up to oppose Palpatine's rule. Over a fourteen-year period, these sparks of hope began to burn brighter and brighter, leading to a conflict between the rebels and the Empire that became a full-blown civil war. The Rebel Alliance grew to be a force to be reckoned with under the watch of its two formidable leaders, Leia Organa and Mon Mothma. Rather than focusing their forces in one place, their strategy saw them scattering their forces across the galaxy, making it more difficult for the Empire to crush them.

Having built up a fleet of modest but specialised war vessels, the Alliance had the opportunity to even the odds against the Empire by stealing the plans of a space station constructed in total secrecy and intended to cement Palpatine's rule of the galaxy. A flaw in the design of the Death Star led to its destruction by Luke Skywalker, a Jedi Apprentice whose sensitivity to the Force was only just awakening. However, the Alliance's bold move left it exposed. Flushed out of hiding, the organisation had no other option but to bolster a frontal assault against the Empire. It became a fugitive fleet pursued across the stars by the Empire.

After being tracked down to their new secret base, the rebels were defeated and forced to evacuate in the Battle of Hoth. While the Empire constructed its second Death Star the movement need to regroup and get reinforcements. The Alliance utilised the renowned network of Bothan spies to gather intelligence. They also integrated the Mon Calamari fleet, who were historically faithful towards the Republic.

Intelligence revealed that the Emperor would be present in person on the second Death Star to supervise the final stages of its construction. This crucial information filled the rebels with hope that they could finally take down the Empire by targeting its leader. This would be the Alliance's one opportunity to deal a death blow to the Imperial organisation. However, the move was risky as it required allies on Endor to destroy the generator that powered the protective shield surrounding the second Death Star. If destroyed, it would allow the rebel fleet to lead the assault against the massive superweapon.

On Endor, Han Solo and a small group of rebels were halted by the Imperial army and, in orbit around the forest moon, the rebel fleet was trapped between the second Death Star and the Imperial fleet. However, the Emperor failed to predict that the natives of Endor would ally themselves with the rebels. Equipped with a vital insider knowledge of their home, the Ewoks helped destroy the generator and allowed the rebel fleet to finally launch its assault against the space station.

The second Death Star was destroyed by a group of vessels led by Lando Calrissian, who piloted the *Millennium Falcon*. The Emperor failed to convert Luke Skywalker to the dark side of the Force, and died at the hands of Darth Vader, who passed away a few minutes later from the injuries his master had inflicted on him. Luke escaped the space station and joined his friends on Endor. The Empire lasted one more year until it was annihilated completely during the Battle of Jakku. The Alliance was dissolved and became the New Republic.

Rebel Fleet

Ships of all varieties came together under the banner of the Rebel Alliance to fight against the Galactic Empire.

After the Battle of Yavin, the fleet went from world to world, searching for the best place to hide. Its installation on Hoth provided a welcomed break for a short time, and although its time on the planet ended in a terrible defeat, the fleet was still able to save many of its craft. In spite of the losses, the weakened fleet tried a new tactic of sending small groups throughout the galaxy in a bid to scatter the Imperial starships, therefore depriving the Empire of the opportunity of winning another large confrontation. They knew that another substantial victory would only serve to strengthen the Empire's appearance of absolute power.

The absolute necessity of destroying the second Death Star saw the leaders of the Alliance regroup the fleet close to the planet Sullust before launching the attack on the dangerous weapon. During the battle, two Mon Calamari cruisers – the *Liberty* and the *Nautilian* – were destroyed by the space station's operational superlaser, while the Imperial fleet inflicted heavy damages to the rebel forces led by Admiral Gial Ackbar. Despite the loses, the ragtag band of fighters, cruisers and frigates fighting for the Rebellion were still capable of inflicting a biting defeat on the Imperial forces gathered in Endor, which resulted in the second Death Star's destruction. Following this battle and the restoration of the Republic, the rebel fleet became part of the New Republic Defence Fleet.

Rebel Radar Detector 9320/B

A portable short-range scanner that was manufactured by the Neuro-Saav Corporation.

With the ability to intercept all possible types of signals in a perimeter of 300 metres, this device could detect life forms, their movements, density, mass and volume as communication signals transported by energy waves. However, with no in-built database, the radar could offer little help in identifying life forms.

Rebel Soldiers

The rebel soldiers were the fighting infantry of the armed services of the Rebel Alliance.

These front-line soldiers were courageous defenders of the systems oppressed by the Imperial dictatorship during the Galactic Civil War. The troops were placed under the strategic responsibility of Mon Mothma, who was in charge of uniting the isolated cells of fighters to form an Alliance that was organised and coordinated. Under her supervision, the reluctant fighters and rebels became driven and disciplined soldiers and were capable of competing with the Imperial army, whose academy benefited from means far beyond those placed at the rebels' disposal.

The rebel soldiers participated in hugely important conflicts, such as the Battles of Hoth, Endor and Jakku, during which they showed the extent of their strategic and technological capacities.

Rebel Troop Carrier

This repulsorlift vehicle was used by the Rebel Alliance to transport small detachments on the battlefield.

These vehicles were designed to carry up to six people and were also used to transport staff around inside rebel bases.

Red Eight

See Zal Dinnes

Red Eleven

See Ralo Surrel

Red Five

See Pedrin Gaul *and* Luke Skywalker

Red Leader

See Garven 'Dave' Dreis *and* Wedge Antilles

Red Nine

See Nozzo Naytaan

Red Seven

See Harb Binli

Red Squadron

This famous Rebel Alliance squadron took part in both historic battles of the Galactic Civil War that led to the destruction of the two Death Stars.

Under the command of veteran pilot Garven Dreis, Red Squadron, comprised solely of X-wings, took part in the second and third assaults on the first space station. It was Luke Skywalker under the call sign Red Five who successfully hit the target that destroyed the first Death Star. Of Red Squadron, only Skywalker and Wedge Antilles (Red Two) survived the battle.

Red Three

See Sila Kott

Red Two

An unidentified Y-wing pilot.

This mysterious and unidentified rebel pilot was congratulated by Wedge Antilles during the Battle of Endor.

Ree-Yees

An insignificant henchman of Jabba the Hutt, this three-eyed Gran intended to make the most of the show when the Hutt threw Luke Skywalker – closely followed by a Gamorrean guard – into the den of the rancor.

As with most of those who gathered to enjoy the spectacle of them being eaten alive, he passed through three phases: a pitiless, sadistic joy to see the guard become a snack; then excitement at the prospect of the Jedi sharing the same fate; and finally disappointed incredulity when he tried to process the unthinkable – the death of the almighty predator. Frustrated, he joined the troop of courtiers who took their place on Jabba's sail barge to enjoy the execution of the rebels at the Great Pit of Carkoon. Little did he know that he was flying towards another disappointment.

Reek

A triple-horned, herbivorous creature from Ylesia and the Codian moon, the reek's popularity, which stemmed from its great strength and its capacity to endure injury, saw it exported all over the galaxy.

On Geonosis, they were used for the execution of condemned victims in the Petranaki Arena. At around 4 metres long and 3 metres high, their size and their habit of charging head-first enabled them to easily trample their victims or simply gore them with their horns. To ensure their domination over the massive beasts, the Geonosian masters fitted each reek with a ring in their nose. Anakin Skywalker used the Force to tame and mount a reek in the Petranaki Arena in order to fight the Separatist forces and save Padmé Amidala from a savage nexu.

Relby K-23 Blaster Pistol

A pistol produced by BlasTech Industries, the K-23 was used by the order-enforcement personnel of Cloud City at Bespin.

This blaster was known to inflict particularly painful injuries because of the very narrow beam. The production of this model was therefore subject to very strict supervision as it was notably banned from civilian trade, which meant that the quartermaster of Cloud City was obligated to obtain these weapons on the black market.

Rep Teers

Rep Teers was a female member of the Gungan High Council during the tragic events of the invasion of Naboo.

This Otolla Gungan was present when Qui-Gon Jinn recounted the events of the occupation taking place on the planet's surface and listened to his predictions of the harmful consequences it would have for the Gungan people. She agreed with Boss Nass when he scorned Jinn and let the two Jedi leave for Theed, guided by Jar Jar Binks.

Republic Cruiser

A starship used by the Galactic Republic to transport diplomats, ambassadors and Jedi during missions.

At the beginning of the Trade Federation blockade, Qui-Gon Jinn and Obi-Wan Kenobi used one of these *Consular*-class space cruisers, the *Radiant VII*, to reach the Trade Federation flagship. Although it was red, the colour of neutrality, the ship was brutally destroyed without warning on the order of Viceroy Nute Gunray, who obeyed Darth Sidious, killing its captain and its pilot.

Republic Senate

This assembly on Coruscant held legislative power in the institutional framework of the Galactic Republic.

Composed of hundreds of senators who each represented their homeworlds, it was controlled by a democratically elected Supreme Chancellor. The Senate voted on laws, possessed the authority to levy taxes, could make declarations of war, established the zones of free trade and took all measures necessary to retain the stability of the Republic. Although the chancellor had the authority to call for special sessions of the Senate, the chancellor also remained susceptible to a vote of mistrust that, if supported, could lead to impeachment.

The constitutional balance of power was broken by the long-term plot of a Sith Lord named Darth Sidious – who was in fact Sheev Palpatine, the senator of Naboo – when he became Supreme Chancellor in the wake of a conflict that he himself had secretly initiated. Through the same occult manipulations, he created a Separatist movement that plunged the Republic into the Clone Wars and started a vicious cycle of events. This resulted in the Senate's decision to grant the Supreme Chancellor increasing executive powers until he had almost complete autonomy.

Darth Sidious' hatred for the Senate – an element of the Republic he despised as strongly as the Jedi Order – matched the immense pleasure he took from destroying it from the inside. After he appointed himself Emperor and restructured the Republic into the Galactic Empire, Palpatine knew that the Senate, as it became 'Imperial', had also become nothing but an empty shell. Nineteen years later, he dissolved the last vestige of democracy, obsolete in a regime governed by the dark side of the Force. After the Battle of Jakku, the reinstatement of a new Senate on Chandrila was one of the first acts of the New Republic.

Republic's Anti-Slavery Laws

Padmé Amidala referenced this set of laws when she spoke with Shmi Skywalker, who, along with her son, was a slave owned by Watto.

This legislative text showed that the Galactic Republic had declared slavery illegal on the worlds it governed. However, even before the troubled period of the Clone Wars, the Queen of Naboo had gathered proof that the practice still persisted in the Outer Rim, at Mos Espa on Tatooine. The Empire, with its discriminatory policy towards non-human species, reinstated slavery. The new slaves were mainly vanquished enemies of the Empire, for example, the Wookiees were deported to the spice mines of Kessel when their homeworld, Kashyyyk, was conquered by Imperial troops.

Resistance

This independent paramilitary organisation operated under the command of General Leia Organa.

An iconic leader of the Rebel Alliance and hero of the Galactic Civil War, Leia had concerns about the remaining forces of the Empire that had vanished into the Unknown Regions after the Battle on Jakku, which she shared with the Senate of the New Republic.

Although a defender of peace, she warned the Senate against a blind demilitarisation policy that would weaken the New Republic's defences against any new potential threats. After being outvoted, then completely discredited by corrupt politicians, she headed to D'Qar to start a secret organisation to fight the rising power of the group known as the First Order. She gathered together all the faithful veterans, friends and politicians who still bore her goodwill to finance and support her movement.

With little financial support the young Resistance had to manage with the equipment it could salvage. With minimum staffing (mostly young, capable people, although not experienced), obsolete equipment and very limited resources, the Resistance's aim was to discover the First Order's objectives and thwart them. It also wanted to find Luke Skywalker – the last Jedi Master. To aid the search, the Resistance sent its best pilot, Poe Dameron, to Jakku to retrieve some new intel.

Luckily the Resistance could count on the experience of old veterans from the Rebel Alliance, like General Organa and Admiral Ackbar, to make the right decisions and build efficient battle plans. With the support of a network of spies that extended throughout the galaxy, it was able to rapidly deploy troops and intervene against the First Order's stormtroopers. On Takodana, the Resistance came to the aid of Han Solo, Rey, Finn and BB-8 – Dameron's precious astromech droid that concealed the crucial information gathered on Jakku.

Resistance Transport

This customised transport was designed by Slayn & Korpil and was used by the Resistance to transport troops.

The New Republic's aggressive demilitarisation politics had forced Resistance engineers to customise and develop utility vehicles to answer the needs of the conflict against the First Order. Transporters were used to deploy ground forces and were the result of assembling systems from various origins. The biggest element of the structure was made of parts that came from the B-wing Mark II, redesigned to integrate civilian transport compartments and engines from *Montura*-class shuttle modules that dated back to the Republic. Two miniaturised hyperdrives, inspired by designs stolen from the First Order, gave the transporter the capacity to travel at light speed. Its defence system, like its deflector shields, was from a Gyrhil R-9X laser cannon and the proton torpedo launchers were also from B-wing type crafts. This type of transporter, uncomfortable and difficult to manoeuvre, was able to transport about twenty passengers, but ideally needed a minimal escort made of fighters. They were frequently out of order and they required constant attention to keep them running.

Rey

This young woman, who lived on the planet of Jakku, was a wreck-raider, an adventurer and an unwilling custodian of the Jedi inheritance thanks to an unexpected sensitivity to the Force.

Rey had lived on Jakku since she was a child and over the years had learned how to adapt to the sand planet's extremely hostile environment. She demonstrated incredible mechanical skills and an understanding of how machines worked, which led to her becoming a wreck-raider who combed the Starship Graveyard in search of valuable parts. She carried her finds through the desert plains on her old speeder, although she always took care not to haul too much as she had learned that small cargoes were easier to defend from attack. She traded her merchandise to the Niima outpost scrap trader Unkar Plutt in return for emergency rations, which was the only food available in the region.

Rey endured all the hardships of her living conditions in the hope that she would one day be reunited with her family – who had left her on Jakku as a child – and she methodically kept track of the days that had passed, scratching each one onto the interior of the collapsed AT-AT she used as a shelter. Her austere lifestyle left no room for possessions, except for a few small items that had sentimental value, like the doll of an Alliance pilot she had made when she was ten years old and an old X-wing pilot's helmet that had belonged to Captain Dosmit Raeh of the Tierfon Yellow Aces. She also carried a quarterstaff at all times, with which she demonstrated extreme proficiency in combat.

Rey met BB-8, the droid that belonged to Resistance pilot Poe Dameron when he was captured in the net of a wreck-raider named Teedo. Having liberated BB-8, Rey agreed to guide the small droid to the Niima outpost to help him carry out his mission and here she met Finn, an ex-stormtrooper who claimed to be a member of the Resistance. Forced to flee from a TIE fighter attack with Finn and BB-8 aboard the *Millennium Falcon*, she found herself caught up in their mission to return BB-8 to the Resistance, in order to deliver the map that led the way to legendary Jedi Knight Luke Skywalker.

During her journey, Rey became more and more aware of the powers of the Force. An intense vision at Maz Kanata's Castle on Takodana and her subsequent encounter with the mysterious Kylo Ren progressively unveiled previously unknown abilities.

These new powers helped her survive dire situations and fight the First Order's troops, and Ren himself, on an equal footing.

Rey's powers were strengthened further when she finally located Skywalker on the solitary planet of Ahch-To and persuaded him to train her. Throughout her lessons, she was plagued by a Force connection with Ren and was drawn to him aboard Supreme Leader Snoke's ship, the *Supremacy*. After witnessing Ren kill Snoke, Rey rejected Ren's offer to join him and faithfully returned to the Resistance to use the Force for good, saving her fellow Resistance fighters from the advancing First Order threat on the planet of Crait.

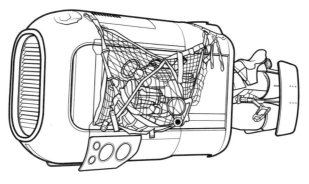

Rey's Speeder

Built by Rey, this hybrid-type customised repulsor-equipped vehicle was both a speeder and motojet.

She assembled and cobbled it together from spare parts found in dumps or bought from other wreck-raiders. This customised speeder offered stunning performance and, although it was able to transport heavy loads, it could, when empty, be as fast as a standard airspeeder. The heart of the machine was made of two turbo-reactor engines retrieved from a transporter and positioned one on top of the other, which were linked to powered amplifier intakes that came from an old Imperial combat ship. It also used racing swoop afterburners and a series of repulsorlifts foraged from crashed X-wings. Though the result was unbalanced, Rey's piloting skills compensated for the machine's flaws.

Her experience of living on Jakku and her knowledge of the local population convinced the young woman to install some security systems on her speeder – specifically a fingerprint-sensitive starter and an electrified chassis that could generate a powerful electrical discharge to shock anyone who was unwise enough to sit on the speeder uninvited. When nobody was looking and she wasn't carrying cargo, Rey enjoyed testing the power of its reactors by jumping in the air and doing complex tricks, which allowed her to show off her full range of piloting skills.

Ric Olié

A top pilot of the Naboo Royal Space Fighters Corps who served under Captain Panaka, this highly skilled pilot, whose sideburns were always impeccably trimmed, was also the personal pilot of Queen Amidala.

It was Ric Olié who was responsible for flying her to Coruscant when she fled Naboo following the Trade Federation's invasion, but it was a difficult challenge for the demilitarised ship to force through the blockade imposed by a heavily armed fleet of military freighters. However, with the help of astromech droid R2-D2 (who was able to quickly repair the essential shield generator), he was successful in the endeavour. After the stopover on Tatooine, the Jedi and the queen were joined aboard by Anakin Skywalker – a young boy who had just heroically won the Boonta Eve Classic Podrace. While on Coruscant, Olié taught the boy the basics of flying a starship – a brief training session that proved to be unexpectedly useful for the retaking of Naboo.

The plan was to draw the majority of the Trade Federation's droid army out of Theed in order to go in and capture their viceroy, Nute Gunray, while the Royal Space Fighters destroyed the Droid Control Ship, the *Saak'ak*. When the Theed hangar was liberated Olié and his pilots climbed aboard their N-1 starfighters and swooped on the *Saak'ak* in orbit around Naboo. Olié soon realised that the *Saak'ak's* deflector shield was far too powerful and the vulture droids pursuing them were decimating his fleet. Just when the battle seemed lost on all fronts Olié was surprised to see the Droid Control Ship explode and a N-1 starfighter fly quickly away from it. At the controls of that N-1 was the young Skywalker, the boy he had briefly taught how to fly the craft. Proud of the victory, Olié landed and joined the celebrations.

Ring of Kafrene

Located inside an asteroid belt in the Thand sector, this trading post was where Cassian Andor learned about the existence of the Death Star.

Originally a mining colony, this enormous construction was slung between two planetoids, and came equipped with its own docking bay, plus hundreds of imposing buildings and factories. It also boasted a labyrinth of narrow alleys, boutiques and habitats. The spirit of Kafrene was well summed up by a slogan painted in fluorescent letters above its docking bay: 'Where good dreams go bad'. In order to control the trade chaos that often erupted there, the Empire kept its presence on Kafrene known by sending a never-ending stream of stormtroopers to patrol the slums. It was during one of these patrols, in Sector 9, that Andor, an agent of the Rebellion, was forced to kill his informant, Tivik. Despite the alarm being raised, Andor successfully escaped by climbing up through the slums and getting lost in the teeming scrum of life on Kafrene.

Rishi Maze

This strategic zone was home to Kamino, the planet of the master geneticists and, by extension, homeworld of the Republic clone troopers.

As the principal source of armed troops for the Republic, Kamino was constantly watched over and protected. This job particularly fell to the Rishi station, a Republic outpost installed on a desolate moon of the Rishi system, which tried to intercept the communications of the Separatist army. This bastion was taken and then recaptured owing to the courage of the clone troopers and their officers, Captain Rex and Commander Cody.

Rodia

A swampy, jungle world in the Outer Rim Territories.

This planet at the edges of the galaxy was the homeworld of the Rodian species. The bounty hunter Greedo was one of the more notorious Rodians, known throughout the Outer Rim owing to his connection to the crime lord, Jabba the Hutt.

Rodian

A humanoid green-skinned species, the Rodians, who hailed from Rodia, possessed antennae on their head, bulging eyes and a thin snout.

They could be commonly seen throughout the galaxy in a variety of roles; some, such as Greedo, had become bounty hunters, others were musicians (Doda Bodonawieendo played for Jabba in his palace) and some were senators, such as Onaconda Farr, who represented Rodia during the last years of the Republic. The young Anakin Skywalker had a young Rodian named Wald among his friends on Tatooine.

Rodinon

This First Order officer was assigned to the Starkiller Base command room.

Faithful to the First Order's cause and highly disciplined, Lieutenant Rodinon was part of the huge contingent of technicians and officers required to make sure the supreme weapon of the First Order was kept in good working order and could be activated whenever required. He was present in the Starkiller control room during the Resistance's raid and remained convinced that his side would win until the central oscillator was destroyed by Poe Dameron's squadron. At that moment, following his survival instinct, he tried to flee as rapidly as possible. Although he was ordered to stay at his post by his direct superiors, he pointed out that even General Hux had left the doomed base.

Rodma Maddel

Rodma Maddel was a reconnaissance and intel agent for the rebel military.

Personally recruited by Cassian Andor, she served as a corporal in the urban combat unit. When she learned about the Rogue One operation to Scarif, the blonde-haired woman immediately volunteered to be part of the ground reinforcements disembarked on the beaches of the Citadel Tower. Her conviction and loyalty to the cause cost her her life during the desperate battle.

Rogue One

This codename was improvised by Bodhi Rook for the group that took part in the mission to recover the Death Star plans from Scarif.

The squad was diverse and had picked up recruits from all walks of life during its travels. Originally composed of Cassian Andor, his droid K-2SO and Jyn Erso for the mission on Jedha, through various circumstances they soon 'recruited' two former members of the Guardians of the Whills, Chirrut Îmwe and Baze Malbus, as well as a deserter from the Empire named Bodhi Rook. After the events on Eadu and Erso's failure to convince the Rebel Alliance to stage an immediate attack on Scarif's Imperial Military Research Centre, she was surprised to discover that soldiers were ready to follow her. In addition to the six original squad members, notable new recruits included Arro Basteren, Yosh Calfor, Eskro Casrich, Farsin Kappehl, Jav Mefran, Ruescott Melshi, Serchill Rostok, Taidu Sefla and Stordan Tonc. Although the squad successfully achieved its objective, there were no survivors. Everyone perished during the battle on the beaches, with the exception of Erso and Andor, who were engulfed by the wall of fire created by the Death Star's superlaser. These sacrifices allowed a young rebel pilot, Luke Skywalker, to destroy the devastating 'planet killer' station some days later.

Rogue Squadron

This Rebel Alliance group of fighters was famously involved in the Battle of Hoth, during which the fleet of snowspeeders led by Luke Skywalker were responsible for the defence of Echo Base as it was evacuated.

Despite the fact that several AT-ATs were destroyed during the battle, it was the Rebel Alliance's heaviest defeat. After a courageous fight from Rogue Squadron that allowed several rebel transports to pass through the Imperial blockade, the Imperial ground troops of General Veers succeeded in destroying the base's shield generator, and were able to enter the abandoned base.

Romba

This Ewok hunter found shelter in Bright Tree Village after returning from a hunt to discover that his tribe had been wiped out by the Imperial troops who had landed on Endor to construct a planetary shield generator.

He found protection at Chief Chirpa's side and later joined the ground operations against the Empire during the Battle of Endor. It was a victory that provided a small sense of justice for his now-extinct tribe.

Ronto

A herbivorous quadruped that could reach 4–5 metres tall, the ronto was very easily frightened despite its imposing height.

Tamed by the Jawas on their homeworld of Tatooine, the reptiles were a common sight in towns, such as Mos Eisley, or at the trading posts towards which they carried goods.

'Roofoo'

This pseudonym was used by Dr. Cornelius Evazan on Milvayne and Jedha.

Sentenced to death in a dozen systems, he fled with his accomplice Ponda Baba, renamed Sawkee, for new worlds. He furthered his criminal records on Milvayne through kidnap and slavery, but the rogue doctor never forgot to exercise his surgical 'talents' and often carried out procedures that resulted in mutilations. Once spotted by the authorities, the nefarious duo escaped to Jedha City to avoid investigation. Once there, the so-called Roofoo and Sawkee returned to their criminal ways and Evazan discovered that the chaotic city was the perfect place for him to continue his heinous practice.

The numerous altercations around the city provided him with plenty of wounded victims to employ his terrifying medical techniques on, which resulted in the creation of an unusual type of servant: the Decraniated. He used the same cybernetic technology to reconstruct a humanoid, Caysin Bog, who had been 'scattered' by an explosive attack by the insurgents. The sale of these poor creatures flourished but their existence attracted attention – notably from the bounty hunter Tam Posla. Despite being prone to violence, Roofoo restrained himself when jostled by Jyn Erso in an alley of the Holy City, preferring to make a quick escape with Sawkee, which proved to be a good idea as the city was annihilated soon after their departure.

Roos Tarpals

Roos Tarpals was the patrol leader at Otoh Gunga and a member of the Gungan Grand Army during the invasion of Naboo and the Clone Wars.

During the invasion of the Trade Federation's droid army, this Gungan was surprised to intercept someone that he knew well: the outlaw Jar Jar Binks, accompanied by two Jedi. Not malevolent but bound by duty, Tarpals immediately arrested the trio and presented them to the Gungan Council. Boss Rugor Nass showed leniency towards the prisoners and freed them – lifting the punishment of the clumsy Gungan. Tarpals encountered another surprise when, during Naboo's liberation, he became part of the Gungan Grand Army alongside Binks, who had been promoted to general, in recognition for his peace-making efforts between the Naboo and the Gungans, despite his lack of military expertise. The experienced Tarpals therefore made it his duty to keep an eye on Binks while on the battlefield, which resulted in him saving Binks from certain death by a tank. They were captured shortly after, but at the moment their fate seemed to be sealed the destruction of the droid capital ship deactivated all their enemies and left the Gungans victorious. The captain was later promoted to general.

Royal Blaster

See ELG-3A Blaster

Royal Palace Guard

Attached to the protection of the Naboo monarch and of the Royal Palace of Theed, this guard was a member of the Royal Security Forces.

They could also – as was the case with Padmé Amidala when she was senator – travel away from Naboo as representative bodyguards.

Royal Palace of Theed

A magnificent building located in the land capital on Naboo, the palace was the seat of royal power.

A massive complex of towers and rotundas with turquoise-tiled domes, the palace, located on a cliff, was the largest construction in the city. Its architecture was full of delicate details and reflected the sophistication of Naboo's peaceful people. The inside featured columns, arches and statues that had been chiselled by the best craftsmen and sculptors the planet had to offer.

It was also home to the government and, as the destination for visiting ambassadors and foreign diplomats, it was this emblematic building that was taken over by the Trade Federation during the occupation of Naboo. Just as symbolically it was here that Queen Padmé Amidala fought, weapon in hand, to reclaim her throne and free her people from the oppression of the droid army.

Ruescott Melshi

A soldier of the Rebel Alliance whose path crossed with Jyn Erso's, this sergeant was in charge of the Bravo Extraction Team that intercepted the turbo tank coming from the work camp on Wobani.

Having neutralised two stormtroopers, he identified the prisoner hidden under the identity of Liana Hallik as Jyn Erso – Galen Erso's daughter – who proved to still have some fight in her by stunning Melshi and her two other rescuers before being stopped by K-2SO. However, since he volunteered to follow her to Scarif, it's fair to assume that he held no grudge for her earlier actions.

His actions on Wobani saw Cassian Andor promote him to leader of the infiltration and combat mission around the Imperial Military Research Centre, accompanied by Pao, Chirrut Îmwe and Baze Malbus. In a remarkable display Melshi stealthily led his troops through the jungle zones, eliminating the sentries and planting explosive charges. Once Andor, Erso and K-2SO were inside the Citadel Tower, the captain requested that Melshi attract the majority of the garrison outside, and the order was immediately executed.

In addition to successfully deceiving the garrison into the belief that it was facing a huge assault on multiple fronts, the sergeant also had the necessary expertise to perfectly command his men during the most difficult second phase, as they fought an enemy that both outnumbered them and was equipped with more offensive weapons. Driven out from the tropical vegetation and cornered on the beaches by the AT-ACTs, his troops suffered losses, but Melshi managed to maintain control until the arrival of reinforcements brought by Blue Squadron.

Although the battle was fierce, the arrival of the elite Imperial death troopers only served to outnumber the rebels further and drastically increased their losses. Melshi himself sustained a shot to the shoulder, but managed to join the few survivors of his squad, which included Lieutenant Taidu Sefla and the two Guardians of the Whills. Cornered in the small cover of a bunker entrance, he received the last order of Bodhi Rook; in order to make the connection that would allow the stolen plans to be transmitted, a button – located in plain sight – needed to be pressed. Although Sefla attempted to achieve the objective, he was shot as soon as he exited the cover of the bunker. Melshi died shortly after – curled up on the sand – having never seen the success of Îmwe and Malbus' actions, nor what Erso and Andor accomplished, nor, finally, the destruction of the Death Star, a victory that gave meaning to this brave soldier's sacrifice.

Rugor Nass

Rugor Nass was chief of the Gungans during the invasion of Naboo. When the Trade Federation's droid army landed on Naboo, Nass met with the Jedi Qui-Gon Jinn and Obi-Wan Kenobi in the underwater city of Otoh Gunga.

Although the Jedi warned him of the consequences of his isolation, he stubbornly refused to become involved in the conflict and instead offered the Jedi a bongo submarine in which they could travel to Theed. Nass allowed Jar Jar Binks to accompany them and fulfil the life-debt he owed to Jinn, therefore freeing him from his previous sentence.

Having believed that he would never see them again, Nass was surprised when, some weeks later, the Jedi returned – accompanied by the Queen of Naboo. By this time the Gungans had evacuated Otoh Gunga and were instead hiding from the droid army in the swamps. Despite his mistrust of the Naboo, when Amidala requested his help with great humility he laid his previous feelings aside and sent the Great Gungan Army to join the Battle of the Great Plains. After the victory, he attended the funeral ceremony of Jinn and participated in the grand parade that culminated in Amidala's presentation of the Globe of Peace to Nass – a symbol of reconciliation between the Gungans and the Naboo following centuries of conflict. Many years later, despite not having held the official function of Boss since before the Clone Wars, Nass – as a sign of friendship – paid one last homage to Amidala by attending her funeral ceremony.

Rune Haako

This Neimoidian Trade Federation settlement officer, who also provided legal counsel to Viceroy Nute Gunray, was an important player in the Trade Federation's invasion of Naboo.

He was also one of the few that knew that the act of war had been instructed by Darth Sidious. Following each of the Sith's holographic appearances, Haako regretted their alliance and confided his concerns to Gunray, most notably when Sidious introduced them to Darth Maul. Following the Trade Federation's failure and defeat on Naboo, Haako was arrested. However, he remained faithful to the viceroy and the subversive plots of the Trade Federation, and attended the Separatist gathering held by the Confederacy of Independent Systems on Geonosis. He was even in a front-row seat at the Petranaki Arena when the Battle of Geonosis – the first conflict of the Clone Wars – broke out. Haako's political destiny was definitively sealed with Gunray's and, still influenced by Sidious, Haako found himself on Mustafar for one last gathering. It was there, on the lava planet, that he was betrayed by the Sith Lord and was assassinated along with the rest of the Separatist Council by Darth Vader.

Rystáll Sant

A Theelin-human hybrid, Rystáll Sant was one of three female backing singers in the Max Rebo Band.

A flame-haired artist whose white body was speckled with pink, she seemed to interest the famous bounty hunter Boba Fett, who was speaking to her when Princess Leia Organa arrived at Jabba's court.

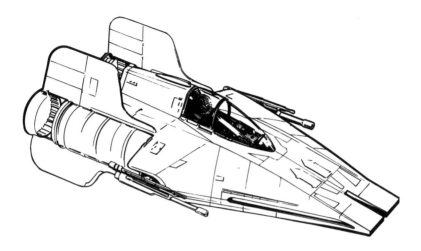

RZ-1 A-wing Starfighter

The galaxy's fastest one-seater starfighter the RZ-1 A-wing was heir to Jedi interceptors like the Delta-7 and the Eta-2.

The starfighters were manufactured by Kuat Engineering Systems, and came equipped with two laser cannons and twelve concussion missiles. However, what gave it a real edge was its pure, unrivalled speed, which even the dangerous TIE interceptors struggled to keep up with. The RZ-1 A-wing was made as light as possible when it was modified by the rebel technicians, who removed everything that could slow it down: armour, heavy weapons and shields. It was quite literally a cockpit with two big motors, which gave it extreme manoeuvrability without the help of an astromech droid.

It was entrusted to only the best pilots. Equipped with a hyperdrive and used by the Rebel Alliance since the very first confrontations against the Empire, RZ-1s fought during the Battle of Endor as part of Green Squadron. Two of them, flying inside the second Death Star, distracted TIE fighters in order to allow Lando Calrissian to speed towards the main reactor. And it was a RZ-1 A-wing starfighter that, after being hit, crashed into the bridge of the *Executor* Super Star Destroyer, leading to its destruction. These exceptional crafts were also used in the Battle of Jakku.

S

Saak'ak

See Droid Capital Ship

Sabacc

A popular card game played everywhere in the galaxy, where the principle of the game relied on a subtle mix of strategy and luck.

Perhaps the galaxy's oldest and most popular card game, Sabacc is played in a bewildering number of variations. All place a premium on betting and bluffing, and many include an element of chance that can turn a good hand into a bad one – or vice versa. The *Millennium Falcon* changed hands in a famous Sabacc game between Han Solo and Lando Calrissian.

Sabé

One of Queen Amidala's five handmaidens, Sabé had the special job of acting as the sovereign's decoy on several occasions during the dangerous times of the invasion of Naboo.

When the Royal Palace of Theed was taken over by the Trade Federation, it was Sabé – disguised as the queen – who stood in front of the viceroy and refused to sign the biased treaty, while Amidala remained hidden among the royal entourage, disguised as a servant. However, this strategy was limited – especially when Sabé had to make decisions only the real queen could agree to. Qui-Gon Jinn, their liberator, insisted that the queen be taken to Coruscant, in order to bring the problem to the Senate, but of course Sabé had to first obtain the discreet consent of the real monarch, before she could agree to the Jedi's proposition. It was a game that could often become strange, particularly when Sabé – still in character as the queen – ordered the real Amidala to clean R2-D2. Although it was a task that could be considered unworthy of a queen, Amidala saw it as a gesture of grateful appreciation to the little droid that had just saved them.

On Tatooine, a world full of danger, Sabé remained in the royal starship while the queen, protected by her anonymity, followed Jinn, who had guessed the real identity of the handmaiden. This exchange of identities continued for some time: it was Sabé that Supreme Chancellor Valorum and Senator Palpatine welcomed to Coruscant, but it was Amidala who privately spoke with Palpatine and addressed the Senate. Back on Naboo, it was Sabé who began the peace negotiations with the Gungans, but it was Amidala who concluded them, revealing her true identity to demonstrate her trust in Boss Nass. It was Sabé who led the assault on Theed Royal Palace as the queen, which led Viceroy Gunray to focus on her once Amidala had been captured, enabling her to take the Neimoidian hostage by surprise. After the successful liberation, Sabé reverted to her role as a handmaiden and sat quietly among the queen's entourage when Chancellor Palpatine and the Jedi Council arrived to celebrate the victory.

Sabine Wren

At just sixteen years old, this Mandalorian weapons and explosives expert was a vital member of the *Ghost's* crew in the rebels' fight against the Galactic Empire.

A graffiti artist with a colourful past, Wren joined the Spectres after abandoning her role as a cadet in the Imperial Academy. She used her creative flair not only to mount spectacularly explosive attacks on the Empire, but also to design the Spectres' starbird symbol. Unflinchingly brave, she helped rescue smuggler Lando Calrissian from Jablogian criminal Azmorigan's henchman, and utilised her data-slicing skills to unlock the Empire's five-year plan for the galaxy. After much persistence, she scored what was arguably her biggest win for the rebels by convincing Mandalorian warrior leader Fenn Rau to join the cause. She then helped to end the civil war on Mandalore and restored her homeworld's autonomy from the Empire. Following the Battle of Endor, Wren and Ahsoka Tano went on a mission to find Ezra Bridger, who had gone missing somewhere in the galaxy.

Saelt-Marae

Saelt-Marae was an informant of Jabba the Hutt's who could be found in the crime lord's palace.

A Yarkora with a characteristic camel-like head, Marae worked to discover potential plots against the master of the Tatooine underworld. It was in this capacity that he was present at the Hutt's court when the heroes of the Rebellion came to rescue their friend Han Solo. Marae could be seen on the staircase leading to the exit of Jabba's throne room, where, along with other such scoundrels, such as J'Quille, he blocked the exit to Princess Leia. His figure could also be identified on the Jabba's sail barge, the *Khetanna*, during the pleasure vehicle's trip towards its explosive destruction at the Great Pit of Carkoon.

Saesee Tiin

A Jedi Master and member of the Jedi High Council, this Iktotchi was one of the few Jedi that was favourable to the training of Anakin Skywalker.

A survivor of the Battle of Geonosis, Saesee Tiin tried to arrest Supreme Chancellor Palpatine along with a team of Jedi Masters, including Kit Fisto and Agen Kolar. They were led by Mace Windu, who demanded that the chancellor stop using his full powers. Alerted by Anakin

Skywalker to Palpatine's true nature as a Sith, he reassured Kit Fisto, who would have preferred that Yoda, Kenobi and Plo Koon had also been present for the encounter. Tiin confidently entered Palpatine's office in order to arrest him, but although the Jedi Masters were first to ignite their lightsabers, Palpatine struck with disconcerting speed and stabbed Kolar before he could make a defensive move. Tiin attacked the Sith Lord from behind, but Palpatine, unrelenting, turned round and brought him down by a blow to his side in a fight that lasted no more than a few seconds.

Salacious B. Crumb

This Kowakian monkey-lizard served as a jester in the court of Jabba the Hutt.

Salacious B. Crumb had a unique employment deal with the crime lord: if he succeeded in amusing Jabba at least once a day, he received food and drinks whenever he wanted them; but if he failed, he was executed. Always on a knife edge that most beings would find unbearable, Crumb seemed perfectly happy with the arrangement and plied his sadistic sense of humour and cheap tricks on the other members of the Hutt's court – making him despised by many.

His attitude towards visitors was just as intolerable and they were often met with cackling, insolence and wickedness. In the utter chaos that occurred aboard Jabba's sail barge, the *Khetanna*, he cruelly tortured C-3PO by pulling at the droid's photoreceptors. However, Crumb's fun was brought to an end when he was electrocuted by R2-D2 in an effort to save his friend. The odious little joker and his evil high-pitched laugh were silenced in the subsequent explosion of the *Khetanna*.

San Hill

Director of the InterGalactic Banking Clan, San Hill was a Muun from Scipio.

As director of one of the biggest banking conglomerates in the galaxy, he possessed a lot of influence and was very aware of the place his organisation had as a credible financing option for the Republic, and so naturally rallied to the Separatist movement. He was present at the secret meeting that preceded the Battle of Geonosis and guaranteed Count Dooku that his cartel would back him up financially. Betrayed by the Sith Lords, he was assassinated on Mustafar, along with all the other Separatist leaders, by Anakin Skywalker who had become Darth Vader.

Sanctuary Moon

See Endor

Sand People

See Tusken Raiders

Sand Skiff

See Bantha-II Cargo Skiff

Sand Sledge

Rey used this makeshift sledge to transport her finds during her expeditions inside the gigantic wrecks of the Starship Graveyard on Jakku.

Constructed from a metal plate from a Mon Calamari escape pod covered with the fabric of a recycled parachute, the sledge allowed Rey to hurtle down the long sandy slopes that formed near the huge wrecks of the Imperial ships. A hole in the plate, which was originally a fuel inlet, served as a fastener eyelet that helped to keep the salvaged parts in place and avoided the accidental loss of any valuable pieces during the trip down.

Sando Aqua Monster

A gigantic aquatic creature that lived in the watery core of the planet of Naboo.

At times growing up to 200 metres long, and powerfully muscular, it was presumed to be the largest marine predator on Naboo. A carnivorous creature, the sando aqua monster's teeth were sharp enough to pierce the thick shell of an opee sea killer, but it rarely ate the opee whole, preferring to consume its prey's soft meat and then discard the rest of the carcass for other smaller animals to feed on.

Sandtrooper

These special stormtrooper detachments were assigned to the Imperial outposts located in on desert planets, such as Tatooine.

The sandtroopers had the standard equipment of the Imperial soldiers, which had been improved and adapted to increase its suitability for the extreme climatic conditions. The armour featured a cooling system and a helmet equipped with filters that increased resistance to sandstorms, which frequently occurred on planets such as Tatooine. They were also equipped with a backpack that contained rations of supplies and water far superior to the standard ordnance officer, which allowed them to accomplish lengthier missions in the desert without the need to return to an Imperial outpost. To further help them on their long journeys, the sandtroopers on Tatooine also used dewbacks as mounts.

Sarco Plank

This Melitto ex-scrap seller frequented the Niima outpost on Jakku and led careers as both a bounty hunter and a tomb raider before moving into weapons.

A regular face among smuggler networks and other illegal activity circles, Plank made a lot of enemies in the region. Once he became a weapons dealer he sold different models of handmade blasters (often stolen) to travellers eager to brave the Starship Graveyard. Plank would enhance the weapons using Trandoshan doublers or triplers to boost their power and impress his customers. Thus he offered SoroSuub JSP-14 modified blasters, DH-17 from BlasTech and even a gun pompously called 'Night Special at Jakku'. Although he didn't have eyes, Sarco Plank could 'see' using his hypersensitive lashes.

Sarlacc, the

A 100-metre long carnivorous creature that could be found upright in the sands of Tatooine, waiting for its prey.

In its natural habitat it could eat the planet's fauna or the occasional lost desert traveller, who would fall into the gritty funnel that opened into the mouth of the beast, from which emerged tentacles and a beak. Then began the slow digestion of the still-alive victim, which some estimated could last for 1,000 years. When it came to food, the creature that inhabited the Great Pit of Carkoon was particularly spoilt: Jabba the Hutt brought it delicacies on a skiff in the form of those he wanted to get rid of. The Hutt considered it an alternative to being eaten alive by the rancor, with the added attraction of an accompanying open-air show.

However, on the day that a Jedi, a Wookiee and a debt-ridden smuggler were on the menu, things didn't go as planned and it was actually several of the crime lord's henchmen – including the infamous Boba Fett – who ended up in the Sarlacc's stomach.

Saw Gerrera

A controversial figure in the fight against the Empire, the Alliance considered him as both the 'first rebel' and an extremist – if not a terrorist.

Born on Onderon, a planet that was ridiculed for its initial neutrality in the Clone Wars but eventually fell under the occupation of the Separatist droid army, Saw Gerrera – with his sister, Steela – fought against forces that were superior in both number and weaponry. In need of assistance, Gerrera decided to call the Great Army of the Republic for support, but the Jedi Council – which commanded the army – chose not to intervene on a large scale. However, the Order did send military advisers to help Gerrera train his rebels and Generals Obi-Wan Kenobi and Anakin Skywalker, Commandant Ahsoka Tano and Captain Rex were dispatched to Onderon. With their expertise, the course of the war on the planet was reversed to favour the local guerrillas, even if, at one point, Gerrera was captured and tortured. However, during the final battle for liberation, the guerrilla leader paid a heavy toll for victory when Steela was killed. It was an act her brother would never forgive.

The transition of the Republic into the Empire under the guidance of Sheev Palpatine gave Gerrera the opportunity to drown his grief in action. It became a never-ending fight that he would always be part of: first on Onderon against a section of the Imperial army, then on several planets further afield.

Although he specialised in armed guerrilla warfare, networks of rebels gave him other opportunities. It was through one of these networks that he answered the call for help to extract a family – the Ersos – from Coruscant and to find them a hiding place in a remote part of the galaxy, far from the military-industrial complex of the Empire. He helped the family escape to Lah'mu, but unfortunately, four years later, he received a message from the father – Galen Erso – which warned him that they had been discovered and that Gerrera must return to the planet to look for the mother and the girl in a previously agreed hiding place, according to contingency plans that had already been put in place. On Lah'mu, Gerrera discovered that the scientist had been kidnapped and his wife, Lyra, was dead, but he found the eight-year-old Jyn hidden in the designated place.

As a man whose life revolved around the war, it was in the art of warfare that the child's education took place. He made her a child-soldier, but in spite of everything she brought to the cause Gerrera began to fear that one day she would become a bartering chip for her father, who was seen as an Imperial collaborator. Whether or not his worries were unfounded, Gerrera's growing unrest about the situation pushed him to abandon Jyn in a bunker with only a knife and a blaster for protection. In the eyes of the sixteen-year-old girl it was a psychologically brutal and unjustifiable act, but to Gerrera – an increasingly unbalanced, paranoid man with no children of his own – it was completely logical.

Over time, his methods drove him to alienate himself from others. Gerrera and his partisans formed one of the very first rebel cells, but his involvement in the first campaigns of the newly constituted Alliance revealed the gap between his tactics and those of Mon Mothma. Mothma, who seemed not to have seized the very nature of the Empire, still hoped for a political solution through the help of the Senate. The collateral civilian losses and damages and the use of torture were just two of the things that disqualified the Onderonian from the point of view of the Alliance. A Rebel Alliance outcast, Gerrera, who had sensed for twenty years that the Empire was plotting something huge, relocated to Jedha.

On Jedha, in the dark heart of the Catacombs of Cadera, Gerrera became an old warrior who fought his own demons as much as the Empire. A lifetime of fighting had left the partisan leader with terrible physical injuries and he was equipped with basic artificial feet, while a damaged pulmonary system forced him to permanently wear pressurised armour fitted with an oxygen respirator. His declining health forced him to ingest drugs and undergo treatment so dangerous that his medical droid, G2-1B7, had been tampered with in order to be able to administer it. Under constant pressure for decades and a victim of several attempts on his life, Gerrera's paranoia developed to the point where he believed that even the Alliance wanted to eliminate him. The arrival of an Imperial deserter, Bodhi Rook – who claimed to carry a message from Galen Erso – didn't reassure him, and he immediately subjected Rook to the mental torture of a telepath creature known as a bor gullet.

Gerrera's partisans also brought him Captain Cassian Andor and Jyn, who were trailing Rook, accompanied by Chirrut Îmwe and Baze Malbus, with whom Saw had recently tried to (unsuccessfully) cooperate with. Consumed by pathological distrust, Gerrera imagined that the girl he had once saved and educated had in fact been sent to kill him. However, once alone with her, he softened at her cold declaration that once her role of mediator was done, she would be finished with politics. Disarmed by her dismissal of the rebel cause, he proceeded to show her the content of her father's hologram message and from her reaction he understood that her anger and standing had been eroded by the distress created by her father's words. Conscious that she would take up the torch and too tired to flee, he told her to follow Andor and she made her escape. Gerrera chose to face the deadly wall created by the famous superweapon's destruction of Jedha City, and reassured to see Jyn's U-wing escape, in a last defiant gesture of freedom he removed his oxygen mask, and with outstretched arms he embraced the oncoming horror.

'Sawkee'

This false identity was taken by Ponda Baba during his flight through different planets alongside Dr. Cornelius Evazan.

It was under this name that the criminal escaped Milvayne and Jedha with his accomplice and went on to commit new misdemeanours elsewhere. Among the most serious, they were guilty of abductions and slavery, and under the pseudonym of 'Roofoo' his partner specialised in the surgical creation of Decraniateds that the pair sold at a good price. Wanted and tracked, notably by Tam Posla, to the streets of the Holy City, the two accomplices were in a decided hurry to leave the planet – so much so that they even passed by the opportunity to brawl with Jyn Erso. It was not the right time for provocation, but their natural attitude resurfaced some days later in a cantina on Tatooine, when they had resumed the use of their real names.

Scarif

A remote planet of the Abrion sector in the Outer Rim Territories, Scarif was the setting of the historic battle that triggered the Galactic Civil War.

A relatively small world, it was made up of jungle-covered volcanic islands that emerged from clear and shallow oceans. Under a beautiful blue sky dotted with white clouds, the islands also had attractive sandy beaches. Although Scarif may have looked like a paradise island, it hid dark and dangerous secrets. In fact, the planet possessed the dense metals that were essential to the construction of starships, but its remote position in the Outer Rim Territories made it too expensive to export these raw materials to the yards of the Core Worlds. However, the Empire turned this inconvenience to its advantage: it mined the world itself and produced all the projects that it didn't want the Senate to know about.

It was to this purpose that Palpatine's regime built the Imperial Centre of Military Research, topped with the Citadel Tower, on a main island in the northern hemisphere. The complex was connected by a system of wagons on repulsor rails that ran around a star-shaped network. There were landing zones and barracks located on inlets and gritty sandbars all around the base, and an excavation site in the southern hemisphere, known as Aurek-14, was scheduled to become a ship-building factory. An orbital station in the shape of a ring was also assembled to act as a gateway through the global shield.

Nine years before the Battle of Yavin, the Death Star – at the time still under construction – was moved from Geonosis to Scarif in order to continue its building. Its complete structural schematics were then integrated into the immense warehouse of data stored in the secure vault of the Citadel Tower. It was the discovery of this storage system that justified the launch of the clandestine Rogue One operation and therefore the support of the rebel fleet that led to the Battle of Scarif.

Scarif Shield

Also known as the shield gate, this protective force field surrounded the whole of Scarif, restricting direct access to the planet's surface.

A wheel-shaped installation, it was equipped with an entry portal that permitted authorised ships to enter Scarif's atmosphere. Once accreditation was verified, the portal gave access to Imperial ships by deactivating an opening in the centre of its structure. Besides the Imperial fleet buildings protecting it, defence of Scarif included turbolaser batteries, plus six hangars full of TIE fighters. During the Battle of Scarif, the shield's imperviousness to the firepower of the rebel fleet proved how perfect its design was. Admiral Raddus masterminded an incredibly bold manoeuvre to destroy that shield: he ordered the *Hammerhead*-class corvette, the *Lightmaker* to ram the Star Destroyer *Persecutor* into its sister ship, the *Intimidator*. As the two Imperial Star Destroyers plummeted into the entry portal, they destroyed it and successfully brought down Scarif's shield gate.

Scarif Vault

Data storage room located in the Citadel Tower of the Imperial Centre of Military Research.

This refrigerated warehouse was six floors high and contained three immense towers, all of which contained thousands of information files. These files contained intel of various types, including administrative reports, scientific communications and structural diagrams. The staff used a manipulator from behind a bay window to withdraw the electronic files. The vault was disconnected from all networks and had scanners in the entrance to restrict access. Because of its location, the probability of theft was considered practically non-existent. Nevertheless, it was central to the clandestine Rogue One mission, with Jyn Erso succeeding in stealing the plans to the Death Star from the Scarif vault.

Scimitar, the

See Sith Infiltrator

Scout Trooper

These elite soldiers of the stormtrooper corps underwent special training within the Imperial army.

They were evidently from the lineage of the Galactic Republic's clone soldiers and wore less protective armour than the basic troops, which gave them a superior mobility that was suited to their role. Scout troopers were trained to operate independently and specialised in reconnaissance and infiltration of hostile territory. The scout troopers used 74-Z speeder bikes and their special helmets, equipped with an optical visor, allowed them faster reaction times. They often piloted their speeder bikes at high speed in dangerous natural environments, such as the forests on the moon of Endor, where the trees created many deadly obstacles.

Scout Trooper's Blaster

Manufactured by BlasTech Industries, the EC-17 hold-out blaster had a short barrel, which made it excellent at close range, though it quickly lost its precision over longer distances.

Handy and small, it perfectly suited the scout troopers, especially when they were on scouting and infiltration missions in hostile territory and in close combat. These elite soldiers often carried the blaster attached to one of their boots, to ensure it was close at hand while they piloted their 74-Z speeder bikes.

SE-14R Light Repeating Blaster

Produced by BlasTech Industries, this model was mainly used by the Imperial army as an emergency weapon, which complemented the famous and dangerous E-11.

This repetition blaster, which looked very similar to the SE-14, which was commonly used during the Clone Wars by the Separatist droid army. Another variation, the SE-14C, was the weapon of choice for Dr. Evazan, but it didn't help him win his duel against Obi-Wan Kenobi during their dispute in Mos Eisley.

SE-2 Labour Droid

This basic utilitarian droid could often be found in charge of domestic tasks on farms.

It was easily identifiable by its gigantic eye, which was in fact a monocular photoreceptor with imagery in double shot. On Lah'mu, it was a model of this type, named Essie, which alerted Galen Erso to the arrival of Orson Krennic's shuttle.

Sebulba

Sebulba held the accolade of being the most vicious podracer pilot to race in the yearly Boonta Eve Classic Podrace on Tatooine.

A gifted professional pilot, he flew an enormous vehicle that had been customised with a few offensive elements (such as a flamethrower hidden in the left engine), in order to guarantee victory. Dreaded by the other pilots and venerated by the crowd, the Dug prepared himself for the famous race with a massage and manicure from two Twi'lek twins, which served as an arrogant gesture towards the other competitors.

Just before the start of the race, Sebulba sabotaged the vehicle of Anakin Skywalker, whom he maintained a bitter rivalry with. During the first lap of the race, his main competitor for first place was Mawhonic, who he quickly sent off the track. He was then challenged by Mars Guo, whose engine was destroyed by a piece of metal thrown by the Dug. On the third lap, Sebulba unleashed himself against Skywalker and cornered the young human on a part of the road that propelled him and his vehicle up in air. Following a tussle in which Sebulba's cockpit became entangled with Skywalker's vehicle, Skywalker managed to free himself and win the race, while Sebulba's podracer crashed in the desert sands.

Security Guard

Also known as a security officer, these police officers on the peaceful planet of Naboo often worked on a volunteer basis.

More comfortable with law keeping as opposed to the combat, the Naboo security guards nevertheless served as a courageous light infantry in Theed during the reclaiming of Naboo.

Security S-5 Blaster

Produced by the Theed Arms Manufacturing Company for the Naboo Royal Palace Guards, this handheld weapon could be customised to include a grapple launcher that was powerful enough to lift a man.

It was used by members of the Naboo Royal Security Forces, including Captain Panaka, and its versatility made it invaluable during the fierce battle inside the Royal Palace of Theed – particularly when the soldiers were forced to scale three floors to reach the throne room and arrest Nute Gunray.

Seek

A friend of Anakin Skywalker's on Tatooine, this red-haired boy was clearly not impressed by the talents of his pal to assemble a podracer.

He was so indifferent that he suggested they play a ball game instead and cruelly predicted that Skywalker would crash.

Senate Guard

This elite corps, recognisable by its blue cape, blue helmet with a crest, and a spear, ensured the security of the Senatorial District on Coruscant, where the Galactic Senate building was located.

The guards were stationed at key points throughout the building, such as the exits, halls and senatorial rooms, or could sometimes be seen escorting dignitaries. They also had a detachment permanently dedicated to the protection of the Supreme Chancellor. At the end of the Clone Wars, Chancellor Palpatine selected some members of the Senate guards to create his own private guards, which in turn formed the beginnings of the Emperor's Imperial guards. It was these Imperial guards that entirely replaced the Senate guards when they were dissolved after the formation of the Galactic Empire.

Sensorscope

Part of the standard equipment of R-series astromech droids, the sensorscope was an emitter–receiver device attached to a retractable antenna inside the dome of the droid.

It served to collect data through the use of a photo–receiver, and heat and motion detectors. This data was then protected and stored in the droid's internal memory system.

Separatists

The Separatists were a political and military movement that called for a definitive end to the Republic and its bureaucracy.

This movement, also known as the Confederacy of Independent Systems, was created by the Sith Lord Darth Sidious as part of his plan to become the supreme ruler of the galaxy. Sidious stoked the desire of certain conglomerates to cut loose from the rules of the Republic and persuaded the powerful Trade Federation to attack the small peaceful planet of Naboo. The blockade, followed by a ground invasion, was meant to expose the deficiencies of the Republic and its inability to manage such a crisis.

After the victory of the Naboo people over the Trade Federation's droid troops, the Separatist movement secretly regrouped under the command of Count Dooku, Darth Sidious' new apprentice. It brought together, among others: the Trade Federation (ruled over by Viceroy Nute Gunray); the Corporate Alliance (represented by Magistrate Passel Argente); the InterGalactic Banking Clan (directed by San Hill); the Techno Union (directed by Wat Tambor); the Commerce Guild (presided over by Shu Mai); the Quarren Isolation League (led by ex-Senator Tikkes), the Hyper-Communications Cartel (headed by Po Nudo) and some planetary leaders, such as Poggle the Lesser, archduke of Geonosis. The Confederacy of Independent Systems attempted to eliminate Senator Padmé Amidala several times before it was openly exposed during the Battle of Geonosis, the event that heralded the beginning of the Clone Wars.

The military power of the Separatist movement essentially came from the battle droid foundries on Geonosis and the Techno Union. As most of the leaders in the movement were traders the military operations were mainly conducted by Count Dooku and General Grievous. The latter, from his starship, the *Invisible Hand*, led many operations against the Republic troops.

After the Confederacy's defeat during the Battle of Coruscant and the death of Count Dooku, General Grievous gathered the Separatist leaders on Utapau, where he informed them of the situation and then sent them to Mustafar. It was on this molten world, controlled by the Techno Union, that they were assassinated by Anakin Skywalker (who had become Darth Vader) on the orders of Darth Sidious. Their deaths marked the end of both the Confederacy of Independent Systems and the Clone Wars. Their last project, the Death Star, became the jewel in the new Empire's regime.

Serchill Rostok

A reputed marksman of the Special Forces, this corporal was nicknamed 'The Rock' because of his ability to stand still, barely breathing, for fifteen minutes.

Rostok worked closely with his combat mate, Arro Basteren, who marked the targets, which 'The Rock' then shot with an A-300 blaster rifle configured to sniper mode.

The duo volunteered for the Rogue One mission and eliminated numerous stormtroopers on Scarif, before they lost the element of surprise and became outnumbered by the Imperial troops who carried superior weapons. The Rock perished in the dust and disappeared in the destructive wave triggered by the Death Star. His demise, and that of many other brave rebels, was avenged a few days later by the Force-assisted aim of a certain Luke Skywalker.

Seven-string Hallikset

This stringed instrument was owned by Sudswater Dillifay Glon, a member of the quartet who played at Maz's Castle on Takodana.

Although it had seven strings, no more than two fingers were needed to play a chord on the instrument – or at least that's what could be deduced from the fact that Glon had no more than three fingers and he used his thumb to help him hold the instrument. The hallikset was composed of a body, a fretboard with a saddle and gut strings, and sound was produced using the friction from a bow. The instrument was a manageable size and could be easily transported.

Shag Kava Band

This band worked in Maz's Castle on Takodana to entertain her varied clientele and Maz generously offered them bed and board in exchange.

When Han Solo, Finn and Rey arrived at the castle, the band was playing a soft tune made of short, distinct out-of-time notes. This travelling band had four members: the beautiful Taybin Ralorsa and Ubert 'Sticks' Quaril in the rhythm section, Infrablue Zedbeddy Coggins on the brass hypolliope and Sudswater Dillifay Glon on the seven-stringed hallikset. The band put up with the animated ambiance in the castle's main hall and provided subtle – but cheerful – music from one of the room's corners.

Shasa Tiel

This Ishi Tib was one of the accountants who managed the dubious fortune of Jabba the Hutt.

Her financial employment apparently allowed her to spend time at her employer's court and she therefore witnessed the arrival of both Princess Leia Organa, disguised as the bounty hunter Boushh, and Luke Skywalker.

Sheev Palpatine

An acolyte of the Sith Order, Sheev Palpatine brought about their return, initially in secret as the last Supreme Chancellor of the Republic, then as the much-feared Emperor of the Galactic Empire.

The embodiment of manipulation, Sheev Palpatine was an extremely powerful Sith Lord and achieved many victories for the dark side of the Force.

Born on the peaceful planet of Naboo, in his youth, Palpatine crossed paths with a Sith Lord – the sage known as Darth Plagueis – who chose him as an apprentice. Renamed Darth Sidious, according to the Sith rules inherited from the tradition of Darth Bane, he was trained in the ways of the dark side of the Force. At the same time, he began a political career using his public persona, which led him to Coruscant and the Senate. Having succeeded in making the leap from politician of a provincial world to the seat of galactic power, he judged his training to have finished. His master, Plagueis was said to have discovered the effects of midi-chlorian manipulation on prolonging life. Plagueis had not yet passed these secrets on to his apprentice when Darth Sidious killed him in his sleep. Now the master, Palpatine went to Dathomir and chose a young boy to take as his apprentice, who became Darth Maul.

From then on, Palpatine's life could be seen as a complex combination of secret strategies, to reach power – and to keep it. His first objective was to attain the most powerful position in the Republic, as opposed to just being one senator among thousands. Up until that point, he had presented a humble face; upright and innocuous about his ambitions. In fact, he presented himself as so insignificant that the then-chancellor, Finis Valorum, granted him access into his closed circle of friends and allies. Coming from a small unassuming world, Palpatine wasn't well known and did little to draw attention to himself. In short, the Republic ignored him. His plan, therefore, was to place himself at the centre of a crisis, in order to benefit from an enormous impetus of sympathy and to eventually replace his 'friend' Valorum as Supreme Chancellor.

As the secret adviser of the greedy Trade Federation, Darth Sidious pushed his 'allies' to arrange an invasion and blockade of his native planet, Naboo, as a formal protest against the Senate's taxation of a trade route that, among others, had previously been free. When Valorum unexpectedly intervened and dispatched two Jedi to Naboo to negotiate the peace between the two parties, Sidious attempted to eliminate them, but was unsuccessful. The Trade Federation's droid army reached the capital of Naboo and exiled Queen Padmé Amidala. Assisted by the two Jedi, Amidala escaped and broke through the blockade to land on Tatooine.

Sidious sent his apprentice, Darth Maul in pursuit, but the Sith Apprentice failed to stop them before they left for Coruscant.

The shrewd Sidious quickly disappeared behind the reassuring countenance of Senator Palpatine, and he planned to use Amidala to his advantage. From the outset, he conditioned her, arguing that the Senate was corrupt and would be disinclined to end the war on Naboo immediately. Amidala was left with only two options: the first was to depose the Supreme Chancellor by a vote of no confidence and hope that his replacement was more efficient, while the second option was to take the matter to court, which would take too much time. Amidala attempted to represent Naboo's plight in the Senate, but soon saw the infighting her speech caused and pursued the first option – a vote of no confidence.

Valorum was stunned when he was stabbed in the back by Naboo representatives to whom he had always been so favourable. Of course, it wasn't Palpatine who held the symbolic dagger, but his monarch. Although he didn't give the impression of any ambition for supreme power, the Senate, by its very nature, hated the emptiness left by the former chancellor's fast dismissal. Quickly the call went up for a new face to fill the position, someone upstanding, who inspired sympathy – like the senator that had come from the unjustly-invaded world of Naboo, and who was just beginning to emerge onto the political stage. Henceforth, Sheev Palpatine having no further need of her, allowed Amidala, who wished to return home to retake Naboo, to depart, so that he could take care of his election to power.

Nevertheless, he prepared a welcome party for the Queen and the Jedi on Naboo, and at the same time sent his Sith Apprentice, Darth Maul, to eliminate the Jedi and make sure that the Neimoidians killed the young monarch. However, Amidala escaped the Trade Federation and forged an alliance with the Gungans to engage the droid army in a big battle – a challenge that surprised Palpatine, because of his contempt towards the amphibious people and because of the enormous technological differences between the two armies. He therefore encouraged Viceroy Gunray to crush the primitive force. Unfortunately for Palpatine, although he was elected Supreme Chancellor, the droid army was defeated on Naboo and his apprentice was wounded and left for dead by Jedi Padawan Obi-Wan Kenobi. However, Darth Maul did kill Qui-Gon Jinn in the process. During Jinn's funeral ceremony, Palpatine savoured the joy of being undetected by the Jedi Council, which was worried by the Sith's resurgence. And during the Naboo victory celebrations, he approached the young Anakin Skywalker, promising to watch his career with interest. It was a strategy he would often repeat: always casually valorising and flattering the boy.

Despite being democratically elected to the highest position in the Republic, Darth Sidious could not directly attack the Jedi Order alone. He realised that it was necessary to position himself strategically and work with the different factions of the Republic and his enemy, the Jedi (at least in the short-term), so, Unbeknown to them all, he created an army. His plan was to militarise his adversaries and then, manipulate a war. Then, he would witness both sides weakening as they fought each other and, in the resulting chaos, he would restructure the galaxy into a regime of his making.

But first, he needed an apprentice who could be a public face and scapegoat if necessary. Sidious therefore turned to Count Dooku, a respected Jedi Master who had been disgusted by the corruption shown by the Republic. Step-by-step, he lured Dooku towards the dark side and eventually convinced him to leave the Order and take the name of Darth Tyranus. Together, they plotted to eliminate Sifo-Dyas – a Jedi who believed war in the Republic was imminent and was anxious to create a military force. They then took control of his project – which they kept in his name – and financed the production of an army of clones, which were produced on Kamino and were equipped with a microchip that made them subservient to Sidious. In order to avoid any outside interference, Dooku erased the data concerning Kamino from the Jedi Archives.

The creation of the outside enemy proved to be relatively easy. Building on the concerns of some planets that were unhappy with the Republic, and then multiple commercial, banking and financial organisations who wanted to maximise their profits and avoid taxation, Dooku founded the Confederacy of Independent Systems; a Separatist movement which, by nature, weakened the Republic regime while depriving it of thousands of solar systems. Under the secret direction of Sidious, Darth Tyranus officially took leadership of the Separatist faction.

Aware that the Jedi alone were not enough to maintain the fragile peace, the Senate proposed to vote for the creation of a Grand Army of the Republic. Amidala was opposed to this project and returned to Coruscant to participate in the vote, but barely escaped two assassination attempts. Hatched by the Separatists, these attempts were presented as revenge attacks by the Viceroy of the Trade Federation. While sheltered on Naboo with her protector, Anakin Skywalker, Amidala assigned her place at the Senate to Representative Jar Jar Binks. Following the revelation that the Separatists had amassed an army of combat droids, the Gungan was manipulated into petitioning a motion that gave full emergency powers to Palpatine. The Supreme Chancellor 'reluctantly' accepted and promised to restore the Senate its power at the end of the crisis.

With an imminent war on the horizon, the Republic and the Jedi had no other choice but to use the clone army that Kenobi had discovered on Kamino (an army which appeared to be the result of a lucky anticipation by a visionary Jedi Master). The Chancellor's first act was to permit the legal use of the clone army to counter the threat of the Separatists. The Battle of Geonosis, in which the Separatists' ground troops were defeated, was an immense victory for the Sith as the conflict, which had been secretly orchestrated by Darth Sidious, publicly ignited the start of the Clone Wars. In addition to the victory, Count Dooku returned to his master with the blueprints of a Geonosian superweapon in the shape of a gigantic space station – which would prove a pivotal part of the Sith's future militarised regime.

Darth Sidious continued to act in perfect secrecy – hidden behind his public appearance as the highest Republic authority. Nevertheless, the known resurgence of the Sith Order, Dooku's revelation to Obi-Wan Kenobi that a Sith controlled part of the Senate, and the slow but continuing increase in Palpatine's political powers, forced him to maintain his cover as he could never let it be known that he was the one that hoped to bring the Republic and the Jedi to their knees. In the carefully cultivated executioner-saviour-victim relationship that he had created between the Separatists, the Republic and himself, it was essential to him that he always appeared as the victim. Therefore, his plots also included several attempts against himself – one of the most spectacular of which was his abduction by the Separatist leader, General Grievous, during the Battle of Coruscant. As a victim, Palpatine made it almost impossible for even the most suspicious mind to contemplate events as anything other than how they appeared. Palpatine also continued to weave an even stronger tie with the young Jedi, Anakin Skywalker, which became apparent when he convinced Skywalker to kill Dooku. Sidious had therefore rid himself of Darth Tyranus, in anticipation of the arrival of a new apprentice, who was far more powerful than the Count.

Weaving his web around the young Jedi, he promoted Skywalker as his personal representative on the Jedi Council. Once again, it was a gesture designed to increase Skywalker's importance and although it was accepted by the Council, they only agreed to it to use the young Jedi as a spy against Palpatine, and did not bestow him the rank of Jedi Master. It was this insult from the Jedi Order that pushed the young man even closer to the Chancellor. During an opera performance, Palpatine told Skywalker the history of Darth Plagueis. In this disturbing story, he emphasised that there existed a means to save his loved ones from death, a fear that had consumed Skywalker after he discovered that his secret wife, Amidala, was pregnant. Palpatine cryptically explained that this life-saving power was an ability a Jedi didn't learn by himself. After this powerful meeting, which revealed the deepest anguish of the young Jedi, Palpatine finally knew how to proceed for his final act of manipulation. After the Battle of Utapau, he revealed himself as trained in the ways of the Force, including the dark side. Aware that Skywalker would instinctively remain loyal to the Jedi, Palpatine reminded him that exposing him as the Sith Lord would destroy any chance of saving Amidala from death.

The Chancellor was not surprised when four Jedi Masters stormed into his office to arrest him. But showing surprising skill and agility with a lightsaber, he killed Agen Kolar, Saesee Tiin and Kit Fisto in a matter of seconds. Mace Windu succeeded in disarming him after a savage duel, and used his lightsaber to deflect the Force lightning Palpatine struck at him. The rebound blast disfigured Palpatine. Thrown to the ground, pathetic and suffering, Palpatine sensed Skywalker's arrival and pretended to be gravely wounded. Driven to save his wife, the young Jedi came to Palpatine's rescue by cutting off Mace Windu's arm before he could strike the Chancellor. However, Skywalker's intervention had given Sidious the chance to restore himself and he used a surge of Force lightning to send Windu through the broken window to his death.

Sidious then gave Skywalker his new Sith name – Darth Vader – and ordered him to execute the Jedi in the Jedi Temple, and then the Separatist leaders on Mustafar. Sidious then activated the biological chip that was integrated into the brains of the clone troopers. This activation placed them in a trance – during which they blindly obeyed the Sith Lord. Forced to execute

'Order 66', they attacked and killed the Jedi generals who had commanded them, forgetting all bonds of friendship that had formed during the war.

Palpatine then reaped the rewards of the social change that he had sowed three years ago. For hundreds of years, the Jedi had benefited from a peaceful image as they acted as the guardians of peace and justice in the Republic. But in the conflict that he had orchestrated, the Sith Lord had forced the Jedi to transform their Order into one that was predominantly dedicated to war. Although their decision had been artificially induced, the militarisation of the Jedi Order was seen as a potential threat. Palpatine capitalised on this notion and, with his disfigured form, he made it appear that his attempted arrest had been part of a Jedi coup and his injuries had resulted from it. In a special session of the Senate, he announced the reorganisation of the Republic into a new Imperial regime, and declared himself Galactic Emperor.

He was later challenged by Yoda, who had survived Order 66. However, flushed by the success of his ten-year plan and euphoric at his near absolute victory, he defeated the most powerful Jedi and headed for Mustafar to find his severely wounded apprentice, who had been left for dead by Kenobi. Sidious saved Vader's life by enclosing him in armour. He then broke Vader's heart by lying to him that, mad with anger, Vader himself had killed Amidala. In the certainty that he would have a dedicated Sith cyborg by his side, the Emperor was free to admire the beginning of the works on his new, terrifying space station.

Nineteen years later, construction on the Death Star was almost finished when its plans were stolen by members of a dissident movement named the Rebel Alliance. Fearing for his strategic weapon, Emperor Palpatine sent Darth Vader in pursuit, who subsequently arrested Princess Leia Organa, after he failed to recover the documents on her vessel. Accusing her of being a rebel and arguing that her position as a senator was nothing more than a pretext, Palpatine dissolved the Imperial Senate – the last vestige of the former Republic. It was a move that he wouldn't have been able to make before, but with the Death Star almost complete, he no longer needed the bureaucratic mediator that was the Senate, and instead could impose order through fear. He gave the regional governors direct control over their territories, ensuring that there was no legislation to hinder his absolute power.

However, this early optimisation of the Imperial regime was short-lived, as the Rebellion destroyed the space station during the Battle of Yavin. It was a disaster for the Emperor's power base and an extensive loss in his command structure with key figures, such as Grand Moff Tarkin, among the casualties. Three years after this expensive setback, Darth Vader achieved an important victory on Hoth where he dispersed the major part of the Rebellion's fleet and begun a personal hunt for some of the hostile leaders. The Sith Lord then sensed a far more intense and personal danger.

After speaking to Vader, Palpatine was able to deduce that the young rebel responsible for the explosion of the Death Star was in fact the son of Anakin, Luke Skywalker. The Emperor was determined that this threat, who could potentially destroy them, should never become a Jedi, and so he accepted the proposition made by his apprentice that the young man should instead join the Sith. However, following his escape from Vader on Bespin, young Skywalker continued to haunt the plans of Darth Sidious and he unwittingly became part of the Emperor's plot to completely eradicate the Rebellion once and for all.

Through an elaborate ruse, Palpatine allowed the Alliance to obtain the plans and the location of the second Death Star, which was by that point almost complete, as well as implicitly confirming false rumours of delays and that he would be attending the weapon's construction in person. He created a window of opportunity for his enemies, who sprang into action without realising it was a trap. Not only was there an Imperial armada waiting for the rebel fleet and its leaders, they also found themselves in the line of fire of the Death Star's superlaser, which was in fact fully operational. As part of his scheme – a trap that was typical of the Sith Lord's plots – the Emperor also planned that Skywalker would succumb to the dark side.

When Darth Vader announced that he had felt his son's arrival on the forest moon of Endor, the Emperor ordered him to go there. He correctly predicted that the young Jedi, anxious to redeem his father, would surrender. And, as predicted, Vader escorted his son to the throne room on the second Death Star, and presented him to the Emperor.

Palpatine had skilfully prepared for this private meeting and dismissed his Imperial guards. He then revealed to Skywalker the trap he had set for his friends – that the Death Star was fully operational – and confronted him with the fact that he would unavoidably fall to the dark side. The Emperor succeeded in provoking the young Jedi to feel so much hatred that he eventually grabbed his lightsaber and prepared to strike the old man down, but in an instant, Vader's weapon came to the rescue of his master once again. To the sadistic joy of the Emperor, father and son fought against each other once again in a tragic duel. Although young Skywalker attempted to stop the fight several times to regain his self-control, his thoughts eventually betrayed the existence of his sister, Leia. When Vader proposed that they could perhaps corrupt her instead, the young Jedi was so horrified he unleashed himself completely and sliced off his father's mechanical hand and almost killed him. However, when he saw the injury he had inflicted, Skywalker realised that the dark side was trying to make him like his father and, horrified by his actions, he threw away his lightsaber and rejected the Emperor's offer to join him. Instead, he told the Sith Lord that he was a Jedi – as his father had been before him.

Infuriated by Luke Skywalker's refusal to turn to the dark side, Palpatine hurled his Force lightning at him, torturing him until he implored his father to intervene. Convinced of the loyalty of the apprentice he had shaped, commanded (and betrayed), just a few seconds before, the Emperor didn't anticipate for one moment that Vader would make a different choice and save his son. However, that was the choice Vader made – and it was accompanied by the return of Anakin Skywalker beneath the black armour. In a final act of defiance, the Jedi cyborg raised Palpatine and carried him to the mouth of the reactor, while the Emperor was still projecting Force lightning. Vader sacrificed his life-support system and threw the person responsible for his decay into the reactor. And with that, the man from Naboo, who became a Sith Lord, Galactic Emperor and architect of millions of deaths, was defeated.

Shmi Skywalker Lars

Shmi Skywalker was the mother of Anakin Skywalker, grandmother to Luke Skywalker and Leia Organa, and great-grandmother to Ben Solo.

A human slave on Tatooine, Shmi Skywalker gave birth to a boy she named Anakin. For nine years she never spoke of the mystery of his birth – until her son's path crossed with that of a Jedi Master named Qui-Gon Jinn, to whom she confided her secret. Anakin had no father and his conception was unexplained. Qui-Gon Jinn believed that Anakin was conceived by the midi-chlorians to achieve the prophecy of the Chosen One – who would restore the balance in the Force. The Jedi Master was able to liberate the boy from slavery, but not Shmi, who remained the property of Watto. Although the decision was not easy, she understood the opportunity that was on offer and allowed her son to leave with the Jedi. In spite of the boy's promise to return to free her, she didn't see him again for a long time.

Several years after those events, Shmi met a farmer named Cliegg Lars, who bought her from Watto, gave her her freedom and then married her. She finally lived a happy life on the Lars' moisture farm, but her happiness was brought to an abrupt end when she was kidnapped by Tusken Raiders during an attack. Although her husband initially searched for her, Lars lost his leg and some friends in a confrontation with the Tusken Raiders and, believing her to be dead, gave up his search. When her son, Anakin, by this time a Padawan, discerned her suffering through the Force, he returned to Tatooine to save her. However, the brutal treatment and torture she had suffered at the hands of the Tusken Raiders proved fatal, and she escaped only long enough to die in her son's arms. Outraged by the atrocity of her suffering and overcome by immense feelings of guilt and hatred, Anakin Skywalker killed all the Tusken Raiders present at the camp. Involuntarily, this kind, good-natured woman had caused her son to take his first step towards the dark side of the Force. Her death became such an important psychological issue for him that the manipulative Chancellor Palpatine encouraged the same terror when Anakin foresaw the death of the other woman in his life, Padmé Amidala.

Shock Trooper

A faction of combat specialist clone troopers who had been trained to operate in various hostile environments against Separatist forces, the shock troopers wore distinctive red and white armour and carried a DC-15 rifle.

During the Clone Wars they were particularly prevalent on Coruscant, where they kept watch on landing platforms and government institutions, such as the Senate. They also patrolled public plazas in order to keep the peace while keeping watch for dissidents; citizens of the capital world were required to present their identity cards on demand for checking. After the Jedi unsuccessfully attempted to arrest Chancellor Palpatine (following the discovery of his treachery), Palpatine employed shock troopers to accompany him to the Senate.

Shoretrooper

Also known as 'shoretroopers', these soldiers were specially trained and equipped for combat in tropical environments.

They were rare elite stormtroopers, and were notably assigned to Scarif. These troopers conducted surveillance patrols on the beaches and bunkers and defended the landing runways. Most shoretroopers were promoted to the rank of sergeant to enable them to order the squadrons of regular stormtroopers. Their helmets were equipped with fans in the frontal part and were streamlined with air conditioning, as well as being sand resistant, while their armour had a plastoid coating in order to fight salt corrosion. In addition to the standard issue E-11 blaster rifle, they also carried the E-22 upgrade.

Shu Mai

A Gossam from Castell, Shu Mai was the Presidente of the Commerce Guild and controlled the common financial assets of several organisations and many powerful societies all around the galaxy.

She was convinced that it would be a good thing to be free of the influence of the Republic and joined the Separatist movement created by Count Dooku. She took great care to keep her support for the cause secret. She was assassinated on Mustafar along with all the other Separatist leaders at the hand of Anakin Skywalker, who had become Darth Vader.

Sidon Ithano

This Delphinian pirate, who wore an impressive Kaleesh mask that hid his origins, was also known as 'The Crimson Corsair', 'The Blood Buccaneer' and 'The Red Raider'.

As with many other pirates, mercenaries and smugglers, Sidon Ithano spent time in Maz's Castle on Takodana. A man of few words, he preferred to leave his first mate, Quiggold, to do the talking. Equipped with an ivory-gripped laser rifle ripped from a member of Kanjiklub, he was a great source of anxiety for space travellers, who lived in terror of hearing the famous pirate's catchphrase: 'Lower your shields and surrender!' Captain Ithano still had enough credit with Maz that she recommended him to help her friends, and Finn managed to easily negotiate travelling aboard the *Meson Martinet*, Ithano's modified transporter.

Sifo-Dyas

A Jedi Master and ex-member of the Jedi Council, Sifo-Dyas hailed from the Cassandran Worlds and became a member of the Jedi Council shortly before the crisis of Naboo.

He supported the idea of a strong response in order to defend the interests of the Republic and he was in favour of the creation of a Republic army. These radical ideas led him to be excluded from the Council. Nevertheless, he pursued his fight and secretly ordered a clone army from the master geneticists of Kamino, pretending to act with the approval of the Galactic Senate and the Jedi Council. He reportedly died on Felucia after he had settled a quarrel between two tribes. His shuttle was blown up by the Pykes, whose syndicate he was supposed to have negotiated with. Sifo-Dyas was sent to Felucia by Chancellor Valorum, but his assassination was in fact ordered by Darth Tyranus, the alias employed by the fallen Jedi Count Dooku.

Sila Kott

This female Rebel Alliance pilot served within Red Squadron during the Battle of Endor under the Red Three call sign.

She died when her A-wing was shot down by a TIE interceptor, providing proof that, from that moment on, the new Imperial fighters were equal to the fastest combat crafts of the Rebel Alliance.

Silvanie Phest

Silvanie Phest was a member of a colony on the planet of Yablari that had recently converted to become part of the Disciples of the Whills.

The decision to follow the oldest religion built around the Force had unfortunately tragic consequences. As a demonstration of her new faith the Anomid had travelled to Jedha City and was collecting alms for the poor shortly before the Holy City was annihilated by the new Imperial superweapon. Donned in a red dress, Phest also wore a vocorder mask. Her species lacked vocal cords and a vocoder mask translated her subvocal harmonics into audible language. However, her metallic mask led to her often being stopped by stormtrooper patrols tasked with carrying out identity checks, as her anonymous attire could have been worn by anybody, especially those that were hiding from the Imperial authorities.

Sio Bibble

The governor of Naboo and a member of the Royal Advisory Council, during the blockade, this experienced politician was the first to understand that an invasion was in progress when communications were cut during the middle of a meeting.

Caught by the Trade Federation, he was freed, along with Queen Amidala, by the Jedi Qui-Gon Jinn and Obi-Wan Kenobi. A man faithful to his duty, Bibble remained in the palace in an attempt to lessen any acts of revenge Viceroy Nute Gunray may have sought for the monarch's escape. Darth Maul used Bibble's image to send a false message to the Queen in order to set a trap and discover her location on Tatooine. He was freed once more during the retaking of Naboo, and went on to attend the funeral ceremony of Jinn and the victory parade that celebrated the planet's liberation .

Sirro Argonne

This civil servant was in charge of managing the scientists who worked for the Tarkin Initiative on Eadu.

A former member of the Republic's Ministry of Science, Argonne took care of the researchers' well-being in their daily life and in the laboratory. However, the care he showed towards the Imperial project didn't save him from the execution ordered by Director Orson Krennic. He fell alongside his colleagues in front of Galen Erso, who had tried to save them by confessing his guilt.

Sisterhood of the Beatific Countenance

The Sisterhood was a Force-sensitive religious community that wore a dark red attire similar to the Guardians of the Whills, though their robes had a more complex design.

The sisters also adorned themselves in a number of other colours, and some wore an imposing hood, the Lorrdian hood of serenity, which could initially be mistaken for the vocoder mask worn by some members of the Whills. The Sisterhood's heavy attire completely covered them to hide any outer sign of individuality, and to help them follow their vow of silence (the famous 'Countenance'). Higher up in the Sisterhood's hierarchy, the gowns became blue and they took the name of 'Sullen Moon'. Despite the fact that anonymity was prized among the Sisterhood, the spiritual chief nevertheless distinguished himself as the 'Great Priest'. He and his supporters – including Toshdor Ni – were on a pilgrimage in the Holy City of Jedha when it was annihilated by the Empire.

Sith Apprentice

An individual who was chosen by a Sith Master to learn the dark side of the Force, and to become his or her successor.

Following the Jedi–Sith war, which devastated the Sith Order, Darth Bane, the only surviving Sith Lord, established the Rule of Two. It meant that only a Sith Lord and their disciple should exist at the same time. Some parallels could be drawn between Sith and Jedi training (lightsaber-fighting techniques, learning to use the Force), but Sith training differed on many points. The most important was the Sith's lack of consideration for life in all its forms. The other was in the ambiguous relationship between Sith Master and Sith Apprentice. The apprentice could be sent by his or her master on a mission alone, even if the outcome was likely to be death. The master could then use their apprentice as an expendable puppet. It was also not uncommon that, in return, a pupil killed their master after having learned everything they could. It was in that way that Darth Sidious killed Darth Plagueis in his sleep, despite the fact that Sidious was Plagueis' apprentice. By killing his master, Sidious replaced him as the Sith Master. The chaotic aspects of the Sith came from the value that they placed in the negative side of the Force: the will of power, the cruelty and the destructive lack of empathy.

Sith Infiltrator

This ship, named the *Scimitar*, was Darth Maul's personal infiltrator.

Used by the Sith when he was hunting for Queen Amidala on Tatooine, it held Maul's Sith speeder – the *Bloodfin* – and three DRK-1 probe droids. Based on a star courier produced by Republic Sienar Systems, this ship had been secretly modified to a high degree. With its two folding wings around a circular cockpit, it also featured six laser cannons and a surprising cloaking device that enabled it to disappear from the radar screens of its enemies.

Sith Order

This secret Order, whose followers were practitioners of the dark side, was born from a shadowy branch of the Jedi Order and had irreconcilable differences with the Jedi over their interpretation of the ways of the Force.

The Sith Order was created by a Jedi who sought further knowledge and power in the Force. He found that the light side of the Force, and the constraints necessary to its practice, only utilised a small amount of a Jedi's true power. He studied the dark side and discovered that its resources were potentially unlimited and that its use could be more personally rewarding. While the Jedi used their power for knowledge, or out of selfless concern for others or to defend without needing personal reward, the practice of the dark side, founded on conquest and power, offered much quicker benefits.

The conflicts that tore the two factions apart varied in intensity, but eventually resulted in the near-extinction of the Sith Order. However, having anchored their strength on the planet of Moraband, the Sith returned and planned to overthrow the Jedi once more. On this occasion they employed Jedi resources to the profit of the dark side and used kyber crystals to construct superweapons of a power never seen before.

Next came the time of the inner wars. The Sith Order, which didn't possess a code of conduct like the Jedi, was, by its very nature, vulnerable to infighting and disputes. The Sith practice, based on personal quests and individual gain, seemed to be incompatible with the idea of a collective organisation. The Jedi capitalised on this and after the Jedi-Sith War they destroyed the Sith Order. Unbeknown to the Jedi, one Sith survived, Darth Bane. Darth Bane established the Rule of Two, which decreed that only a Sith and his disciple could exist at the same time.

Unbeknown to the Jedi, for 1,000 years the Sith Order hid from view, and didn't reveal itself until the political ascension of the senator of Naboo – Sheev Palpatine – who was really a Sith Lord named Darth Sidious. He and his apprentice, Darth Maul, hatched a political plot to take control of the galaxy and to wipe out the Jedi. The Jedi Council felt the shadows of the Sith disrupt the Force and predicted the arrival of dark days for the Republic. That was the moment that Anakin

Skywalker appeared: a young boy extraordinarily sensitive to the Force, who represented a hope for the Jedi, but who was also a potential recruit for Sidious.

When Maul was defeated, Sidious took an ex-Jedi, Count Dooku, whose Sith name was Darth Tyranus, under his wing. The count was tasked with Palpatine's dirty work and created a Separatist movement within the Republic, with the view to leading the galaxy to war. During these events, Palpatine assumed a position that allowed him to control the conflict he had created. That war took place between a clone army commanded by the Jedi (who had been promoted to generals and commanders) and regiments of droid soldiers who fought on behalf of the Separatists.

Once he had achieved his plan, Sidious sacrificed Dooku and turned his attention to the recruitment of Skywalker to the dark side of the Force. To achieve this he told him the legend of Darth Plagueis the Wise, who had succeeded in finding the secret of immortality through a particular practice of the Force. It was this that interested Skywalker and which he eventually became obsessed with. He was quickly converted by Palpatine, who gave him the name of Darth Vader. With a Sith Apprentice as dangerous as Vader by his side, Palpatine then issued Order 66: a secret instruction implanted in every Republic clone trooper that turned them against the Jedi as soon as it was activated. The terrifying cull took place and after that Vader slaughtered every Jedi in the Jedi Temple on Coruscant. Palpatine then used the powers given to him during the Clone Wars to declare the Jedi as hostile against the Republic. The destroyed Republic, which had been torn apart by the fall of the Jedi, was restructured and took on the shape of an Imperial dictatorship.

Palpatine proclaimed the birth of the Galactic Empire to the applause of the Senate, which didn't know that the rise of its leader actually meant the Sith's return to power. Freed of the Republic and the Jedi, Sidious and Vader reigned over the galaxy for more than twenty years until they lost the Battle of Endor. Aboard the second Death Star, when Luke Skywalker, son of Vader, refused to embrace the dark side, Sidious modified his plans and attempted to kill the young Jedi using his terrifying Force lightning, which only the darkest adepts of the Sith Order could access. He underestimated Skywalker's capacity for resistance and also fatally misjudged Vader's reaction. Vader saved his son by sacrificing himself and re-established the balance of the Force, as the prophecy had foretold. Although he had killed the next to last Sith, the act was driven by a selfless love for another. As for the last Sith – Vader himself – he had disappeared when he acquired redemption by saving his son. He had become Anakin Skywalker once more, whose spirit then joined the Force.

A new era began where the Sith no longer existed and the Jedi were at the dawn of a rebirth. But no one had banked on the First Order – a new dark threat, led by the mysterious Supreme Leader Snoke, which emerged from the debris of the Empire in the Unknown Regions.

Sith Speeder

This FC-20 repulsor-fitted crescent-shaped speeder belonged to the Sith Apprentice Darth Maul, who named it *Bloodfin* and transported it aboard his interceptor, the *Scimitar*.

Built by Razalon, the speeder had no gun and was mainly used by the Sith warrior to swoop on his target once he had located it. He used it to reach Anakin Skywalker and Qui-Gon Jinn at full speed, then slowed down, twirled round and clashed with the Jedi Master – all of which took mere seconds. The *Bloodfin* possessed a very useful automatic stopping device, which enabled it to stand alone when the pilot was not riding it.

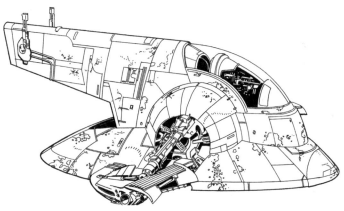

Slave I

A modified *Firespray-31*-class patrol and attack craft, developed by Kuat Systems Engineering, this model of pursuit ship was the property of the bounty hunter Jango Fett.

Its imposing engine, which supported the cockpit and the rest of the ship's structure, gave it a distinctive look, and its original design was reinforced by the fact that the ship, once in the air, flipped ninety degrees to allow the cockpit to face the front. *Slave I* was a heavily armed vehicle. Its arsenal contained two laser cannons, hidden missile launchers, a seismic bomb launcher, a tractor beam mounted on a turret, twin proton torpedoes, concussion missile launchers and a powerful ion cannon.

After Jango Fett's death during the Battle of Geonosis, his son, Boba, inherited *Slave I*. Following the many events during which the young Boba tried to avenge the death of his father, killed by the Jedi Mace Windu, *Slave I* was lost and passed from owner to owner. It once belonged to the Weequay pirate Hondo Ohnaka, who had the starship painted and added it to his collection before he was taken prisoner by the troops of General Grievous. Boba Fett eventually got his ship back, which he kept until his disappearance on Tatooine.

SLD-26 Planetary Shield Generator

A defensive energy field device capable of protecting an object from the size of a small moon to a large space station.

Manufactured by CoMar Fight Systems, this model of generator was used by the Empire to maintain the security of the second Death Star while it was under construction above the forest moon of Endor. Its other function was to generate a force field strong enough to counterbalance the gravity of the moon, in order to keep the space station in a stationary orbit. As a result of this, Endor experienced massive geological disruptions.

The generator could be easily identified by its pyramid tower topped by one big satellite dish, which contained several projection antennas surrounded by eight smaller dishes. Strategically the shield generator was of crucial importance for both the Rebel Alliance and the Empire. The Rebellion had to first destroy it in order to allow the fleet any hope of attacking the second Death Star, while the Empire used it as bait in a two-part trap. Imperial troops awaited the rebels sent to destroy it, and, as the rebel fleet came to the aid of its comrades, it would crash into the invisible shield wall, not realising quickly enough that it was still activated. However, during the Battle of Endor, the ships of the Alliance did detect this deadly danger in time and the ground units managed to escape their captors and destroyed the SLD-26.

Sleen Lizard

An endemic creature of the swamp planet of Dagobah.

The sleen lizard rarely ventured outside of its dark lair, except to hunt insects and other small prey that lived in and around the swamps.

Snoke

A mysterious character who bore the title 'Supreme Leader', Snoke hid in the shadows of the Empire's remains that took the form of the First Order.

The most important commanders of the organisation – General Hux and Kylo Ren – turned to him for guidance on the most important decisions. His origins were unknown and he appeared often through a holographic projector that showed an image of impressive proportions. He was also Kylo Ren's mentor in the ways of the dark side of the Force. As his flagship, the *Supremacy*, chased down the fleeing Resistance fleet, Snoke was killed by his own apprentice, Kylo Ren, as he tried to lure Rey towards the dark side of the Force.

Snowspeeder

This model of the T-47 series airspeeder, produced by Incom Corporation, was made famous during the Battle of Hoth when it was used by the Rebel Alliance.

Originally the T-47 was only available in a civilian version, designed to transport cargo with the help of magnetic harpoons. The cockpit, which could accommodate two people, was designed for a pilot and a logistical operator.

After the Battle of Yavin, it became impossible for the Rebel Alliance to access the products of military facilities, as they were completely monopolised for the purpose of the Empire. In addition, after the Senate was dissolved, rebel supporters could no longer issue clandestine orders under the cover of their diplomatic status. In light of this, the Alliance tried to militarise civilian devices and began with the T-47. The technicians added two powerful AP/11 laser cannons, reinforced the hull and transformed the cockpit so that it could accommodate a pilot and his or her gunner. They gave it the name 'snowspeeder' after the installation of the Echo Base on the ice planet of Hoth. The Alliance experienced numerous difficulties in adapting the technology to the cold weather, but the combat fleet was ready when it had to repel the assaults of the Imperial AT-ATs during the Battle of Hoth. To face the might of the Imperial vehicles, the pilots used the magnetic harpoons to tie cables round the legs of the machines, which rendered them immobile.

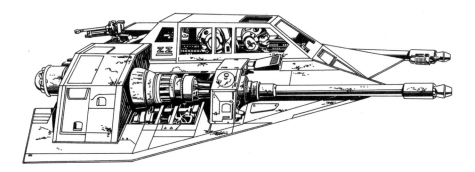

Snowtrooper

This elite class of stormtrooper was trained and equipped for operations situated in zones of extreme cold weather.

They wore a winterised uniform that was equipped with heating zones powered by a back-mounted energy generator. These devices allowed the soldiers to survive for several days in the most hostile conditions. During the invasion of the rebel base on Hoth, the Empire used the elite Blizzard Force detachment as ground combat troops.

Solar Sailer

An interstellar *Punworcca 116*-class interstellar sloop built by the Huppla Pasa Tisc Shipwrights Collective.

Count Dooku ordered the ship from the Geonosians before the beginning of the Clone Wars, which may have explained why its general design was close to that of the Geonosian starfighters. It was Dooku's primary vehicle for intergalactic travel, during which he would stir up conflicts under the guidance of his master Darth Sidious. The ship was equipped with a retractable sail that gathered interstellar energy that was then channelled towards the engine. The almost limitless fuel source gave the solar sailer a great deal of autonomy. Dooku used a FA-4 pilot droid to assist with take-offs and landings, and the ship was also fitted with a secured holonet transmitter that enabled Dooku to communicate with his master.

Sonn-Blas F-11D Blaster Rifle

Inspired by classic models used during the Clone Wars, this laser blaster developed by the Sonn-Blas Corporation formed part of the standard equipment of First Order stormtroopers.

A handy weapon providing reasonable range and firepower, the rifle offered a number of options to help its user adapt to his or her surroundings. Its compact design facilitated its use as a cover weapon, but its J-19 electroscope-aiming device also enabled more precise shots. Meanwhile, the removable main grip and the adjustable stabilisation grip in front of the barrel gave it added stability. Using energy ammunition, the Sonn-Blas F-11D blaster became the weapon of choice for First Order troops. An alternate model of this gun was also developed for Starkiller Base stormtroopers. Designed with the snowy environment in mind, it featured some modifications, including a demister filament on the sight and a cooler system for the barrel.

Sonn-Blas FMWB-10 Automatic Blaster

Developed by the Sonn-Blas Corporation, this heavy laser gun – also known as a stormtrooper's 'Megablaster' – was part of the assault arsenal in the First Order's infantry.

Designed for set firing positions, it was equipped with a fully articulated base that gave it great stability, and allowed for high-density continuous firing, or precision shots if using its integrated scope.

Sonn-Blas SE-44C Blaster Pistol

This blaster pistol was designed by Sonn-Blas Corporation as part of the First Order's stormtroopers' standard equipment.

Designed from ancient models used during the Clone Wars, the Sonn-Blas SE-44C was a handy and efficient weapon. Without a dedicated holster it could be attached directly to the reinforced betaplast waders of the stormtroopers using a magnetic device. This weapon was equipped with an integrated aiming support system and a vibrating pulsor in the grip that warned when ammunition was low.

Sotorus Ramda

The general in command of the garrison on Scarif, Sotorus Ramda let himself become too comfortable in his Imperial duty.

As a commander, Ramda had previously instigated the successful repression of an insurrection on Syni IV, which he hoped would take him closer to the central power. He had hoped for a promotion to Coruscant or one of the Core Worlds, and so was initially disappointed when he was posted to Scarif. However, the paradise setting combined with the feeling of invincibility that the extremely protected base provided meant that Ramda soon became overconfident and blasé.

It was this attitude that led him to doubt the demands of Director Orson Krennic concerning Galen Erso's communications. Ramda was shocked when the first rebel charges exploded in several positions on his supposedly impenetrable base. It was only after a handful of seconds passed, and under the impulse of a furious Krennic, that the grey-haired general emerged from his stupor and finally reacted to the hostile infiltration. Krennic judged his reaction to be too slow and promised to have him court-martialled and imprisoned for serious incompetence. However, that threat was shortly shattered when the Death Star's superlaser fired on the Citadel Tower.

Soulless One

The personal starfighter of General Grievous, *Soulless One* was custom-built by Feethan Ottraw Scalable Assemblies.

A Belbullab-22 starfighter, the ship was made for combat and was extremely manoeuvrable in the atmosphere. Its arsenal comprised of two quick-firing triple laser cannons and it also possessed a cutting-edge hyperdrive. The ship, which was present on Utapau during the duel between Obi-Wan Kenobi and Grievous, was later used by Kenobi as a means of escape following the issue of Order 66.

Space Slug

Gigantic creatures made of silicone, space slugs inhabited the natural excavations of asteroids and could grow up to a kilometre in size.

Also known as an exogorth, their diet consisted of mineral residues and other creatures constituted of silicone that crossed the asteroid belts they occupied.

Special Forces

Commando unit of the Rebel Alliance that specialised in the infiltration of hostile environments.

Recruits to this elite military branch of the Rebellion underwent four months of intensive physical and mental guerrilla warfare training, including ambush, sabotage and intelligence techniques. Under the command of General Crix Madine, these soldiers were commonly seen as the ultimate fighters and often sent on high-risk assignments. One of their most famous was the historic mission to the forest moon of Endor. The operation – placed under the command of General Han Solo – tasked members of the Special Forces, clothed in their light green and brown camouflage fatigues and equipped with blaster rifles, grenades and proton charges, to destroy the planetary shield generator of the second Death Star.

Special Forces TIE Fighter Pilot

The First Order's elite, these top pilots flew a modified version of the First Order's TIE fighter and answered to only the highest ranks of the Starkiller Base hierarchy.

They could be distinguished from the regular pilots by their reinforced equipment, shield and heavy turrets, but also by the left side of their cockpit, which was painted red. This symbol, the mark of ancient baron pilots from the Old Empire, could be seen on the pilots' helmets as two vertical red stripes. Special Forces pilots were known for their tenacity and stamina and never hesitated to take risks to shoot down their target. Armed with an SE-44C pistol, they were accomplished soldiers, totally devoted to the First Order's cause.

SPHA-T Walker

A heavy artillery cannon built by the Rothana Heavy Engineering, the Self-Propelled Heavy Artillery walker was one of the largest ground-based cannons in the Republic arsenal.

Requiring a crew of fifteen clone troopers, as well as additional gunners, the self-propelled turbolaser was attached to an imposing control platform. It rested on a chassis supported by twelve mechanical legs, which ensured the weapon's stability during firing. It also allowed the SPHA-T walker to change position and direction at will.

Sporty DDC Blaster

Manufactured in the Drearian Defence Conglomerate factories, this blaster was designed for civilian use.

It was favoured by diplomats and lovers of hunting sports, but was not intended for military combat. The model used by Princess Leia Organa, was the Satine's Lament, which was named after a high-ranking dignitary of the planet of Mandalore.

Squid-head

See Tessek

ST. 321

This *Lambda*-class T-4a shuttle was used by Darth Vader to travel to the second Death Star.

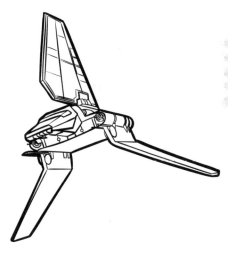

This elegant starship came with a captain assigned to the transportation of his prestigious passenger. However, sometimes Vader chose to pilot it himself, as he did when he went to the SLD-26 planetary shield generator based on the forest moon of Endor. It was in this very vehicle that he transported his son, Luke Skywalker, to the space station for a confrontation with Palpatine. Once the Emperor was dead, the young Jedi dragged his wounded father to the access ramp of the shuttle and it was there that they were able to exchange a few last words before the death of Anakin Skywalker. The young Skywalker piloted the ST. 321 away from the exploding second Death Star, accompanied by his father's body.

STAP (Single Trooper Aerial Platform)

This light repulsorcraft could be piloted by a single battle droid during reconnaissance and patrol missions and sometimes supported the heavy armoured vehicles of the Confederacy of Independent Systems and the Trade Federation.

Built by the Baktoid Armor Workshop, it was a slim, agile craft equipped with a pair of blaster cannons in order to strike back at the enemy. It was a STAP patrol that spotted and chased Obi-Wan Kenobi in the forest of Naboo, before Qui-Gon Jinn intervened.

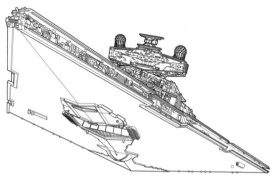

Star Destroyers

Huge warships produced in the Kuat Drive Yards factories for the Imperial fleet.

As symbols of terror and oppression, Star Destroyers were a hugely effective way for Emperor Palpatine to intimidate and bully disobedient systems. Their triangular shape and aggressive, seemingly sharp edges were proud symbols of the Empire's might, and the 1,600-metre starships were the sentinels of the regime, positioned in thousands of systems throughout the galaxy. Their characteristics and design evolved from the *Venator*-class destroyers used by the Republic during the Clone Wars, and were the basis for the *Resurgent*-class that were the jewel of the First Order's fleet.

Stardust

Stardust was Jyn Erso's nickname and the codename given to the Death Star's plans, in both cases chosen by Galen Erso.

During his daughter's first eight years, the only ones that he ever shared with her, the scientist lovingly called her by that nickname. The pet name, which possessed both a scientific and poetic meaning, stayed with the young child for a long time – even after the death of her mother and her father's capture on Lah'mu. Many years later on Scarif, Jyn – by this time a young woman – was faced with a gigantic bank of thousands of Imperial data files, among which she had to find just one file. Assisted by the advice from K-2SO she looked in the 'Structural

Engineering' section, although without any clue as to which was the correct file she had little hope of finding it as they all possessed cryptic names. Suddenly the name 'Stardust' appeared on the screen – as if her father had spoken to her – and she knew without a doubt that it was the file that contained the plans to the Death Star.

Starkiller Base

A one-of-a-kind combat platform installed on an ice planet. Starkiller Base was the result of an unprecedented mobilisation of the First Order forces.

Benefiting from technologically advanced studies around black energy transfer and hyperspace tunnels, it drained the energy from a star, and converted it into a powerful destructive ray. Created on the surface of an ice planet whose crystal deposits benefited from unique conducting properties, Starkiller Base boasted a colossal cannon, around which all the mechanical installations were built, including the control stations and barracks to defend the base. It was so huge it dwarfed even the famous Death Star.

Numerous stormtrooper units patrolled the planet's snowy landscapes, and were assisted by sentinel droids. To remain operational, Starkiller Base's supercannon needed a huge input of energy. This energy, directly drained from the nearest sun, gave the base the power to emit one shot that appeared to have a limitless range, and whose power could destroy a whole system. The Hosnian system, which was the seat of the New Republic, was destroyed in a matter of seconds by one of these devastating shots.

Hidden on D'Qar, and fully aware it was the First Order's next target, the Resistance used information collected through reconnaissance missions to uncover the one weakness in Starkiller Base's defence system. Destruction of one of the main oscillators would start a chain reaction that could cause the whole planet to explode. Assisted with a command team led by Han Solo and Finn, Resistance pilots located the flaw, and Poe Dameron succeeded in destroying the oscillator and Starkiller Base, temporarily stalling the First Order's activities.

Starship Graveyard

The dunes on the planet of Jakku were the final resting place for many wrecked starships after the Battle of Jakku.

As the last bastion of the Empire, Jakku was the location of the ultimate confrontation between the colossal interstellar Star Destroyers of the Empire and Alliance troops. The ships that were irreparably damaged during the battle plunged into the sand planet's atmosphere to crash among the dunes. An age of peace was ushered in with the signing of the Galactic Concordance, and Jakku became a paradise for wreck–raiders who would scavenge for valuable items amid the ship carcasses. Those items were mostly sold back to the First Order for a few meagre credits.

Statura

This Resistance officer was a member of High Command along with General Leia Organa.

Born on Garel, Statura took part in his planet's liberation during the war against the Empire when he was still a teenager. After the conflict had ended and the New Republic had risen, he decided to devote himself to applied sciences. He was recruited by General Organa to participate in a new movement created to protect the New Republic's citizens from a new threat. He became logistics manager and looked after the procurement of Resistance ships and supplies. His analytical skills allowed him to climb the ladder and he soon became a strong link in the command chain. Pragmatic and bright when having to evaluate the strategic situations that the Resistance soldiers faced, Admiral Statura was a precious asset against the First Order and an unwavering supporter of General Leia Organa.

Steelpeckers

These were scavenger birds that lived on the desert planet of Jakku.

Steelpeckers only ate metal and could often be seen plundering the Starship Graveyard, where they attacked the wrecks and metal parts that jutted out from the sand. Their iron-tipped talons allowed them to scratch and dent steel plaques before striking them with their beaks, to prepare it for ingestion. They stored vanadium, osmiridium and corundum in their gizzards to help the metal matter assimilate.

Stordan Tonc

A member of the Special Forces who fought on Scarif, this rebel corporal with a thin moustache and a light beard was nicknamed 'Stordie'.

A recent recruit of the rebels on Yavin, his hate for the Empire was rooted in the tragic revolt that occurred on Qemia 7. Luckily for Tonc, he was quickly incorporated into the unit he had dreamed of joining: the Special Forces. Jyn Erso's daring proposition to hit the heart of the Imperial army offered him the chance to satisfy his need for action and with his ranger companions he didn't hesitate to board the cargo shuttle. In sand and brown fatigues, his Czerka ACH-14 reinforced combat helmet tight and low on his forehead and his A-300 blaster in hand, he was ready to fight.

Once they arrived on Platform 9 of the Scarif complex, his mission – although secondary to that of his friends who had to infiltrate the base – was to secure the ship and help its pilot, Bodhi Rook, who he slightly mistrusted. The two of them devised a clever plan to make things difficult for the enemy by convincing it that there were multiple assaults on Landing Pads 2 and 5. Although this ploy delayed a confrontation, it soon became unavoidable and the Imperial forces, on maximum alert, deployed waves of stormtroopers who eventually reached the zone surrounding Platform 9. Although he warned his men and ordered them to hide, the time to act in plain sight came when Rook asked him to help establish communications with the rebel fleet in orbit. Quickly spotted, the young corporal fell during the violent battle around the shuttle.

Stormie

This toy was a favourite of the young Jyn Erso.

Even during the Galactic Civil War, children continued to play and Lyra and Galen's daughter wasn't any different. On Lah'mu she possessed many handmade toys, but her favourite was a doll that represented a stormtrooper, possibly a gift from when her father had worked for the Empire. When Director Orson Krennic came in search of the Erso family, his Imperial soldiers, known as death troopers, found Stormie abandoned in the muddy fields.

Stormtrooper

Extremely disciplined and conditioned to be completely loyal to the Emperor, stormtroopers were the iconic Imperial troops of the Empire.

Comprised of both human recruits and clones who had been serving in the Army of the Republic at the end of the Clone Wars, these front-line militia were often used to police worlds and enforce Imperial rule, unquestioningly carrying out orders.

Although they were trained at the Imperial academies, the stormtrooper corps was an independent faction of the Imperial army, which could be used in support of the main army or fleet whenever necessary. In order to effectively meet the challenges posed by the many different worlds and environments they were deployed to, specialist branches of stormtroopers were developed, including scout troopers, sandtroopers and flametroopers, to name just a few – each with their own variation on the regular stormtrooper armour.

The distinctive white armour of these fearsome troops was well-known throughout the galaxy. Comprised of white plastoid casing over a black body glove and finished with a full-head helmet that maintained complete anonymity, it was designed to offer protection from blaster bolts and other weapons, as well as difficult environmental conditions. They were also equipped with the best weaponry and frequently proved themselves to be highly adept warriors, even in the most difficult of situations.

Stratosphere

This secret project, conceived by the Galactic Empire, was stored as a cartridge in the secure vault of the Citadel Tower on Scarif.

It was unknown what stage this project was at as the two rebel agents who had infiltrated the vault were focused on their search for the Death Star plans. From its appearance there was no way to tell whether its codename had any bearing on its content.

Strono Tuggs

This Artiodac cook worked at Maz's Castle on Takodana.

Having lived at the castle for centuries, every day 'Cookie' (as he was nicknamed) would drag his deformed figure and club foot to the castle's kitchens where he prepared the tasty meals that Maz's guests savoured. His surly attitude and scarred face were the total opposite of the sweetness of his cooking, which included plates of fresh fruits, hammer-tenderised gornt meat, Chadian seasonings, subtle ubeses and local specialties, such as frals cushnips.

Subterrel

A planet of the Outer Rim, Subterrel was a mining world, essentially made of caverns and caves, which had been heavily prospected.

Its proximity to Kamino, the planet of the master geneticists, brought the societies mining its underground to regularly use Kaminoan technology. When Obi-Wan Kenobi asked his old friend Dexter Jettster about a toxic dart, Jettster was able to identify it as he had seen the saberdart in use when he was a miner on Subterrel, and went on to reveal to Kenobi where they were manufactured.

Sudswater Dillifay Glon

A regular at Maz's Castle on Takodana, Glon was part of the Shag Kava Band that entertained Maz's guests.

He generally offered his services in exchange for shelter and he played along with his fellow musicians, Taybin Ralorsa, Ubert 'Sticks' Quaril and Infrablue Zedbeddy Coggins, in subtle jams with light and bouncy melodies. Sudswater played the seven-string hallisket, a light instrument with a melodious tone.

SW-0608 Shuttle

This *Zeta*-class transport shuttle was the ship used by the Rogue One operation to infiltrate Scarif.

Initially located on Eadu, it was requisitioned and flown by the ex-Imperial pilot Bodhi Rook when the team had to make a swift exit from the planet, and eventually ended up on Yavin 4. When Jyn Erso was unable to convince the Rebel Alliance to take action, the stolen enemy ship came in handy once again when, loaded with determined rebel soldiers, it was able to pass through the Imperial control procedure because of its accreditation and the knowledge possessed by Rook. Once docked on Platform 9, the former Imperial pilot remained by the shuttle's side in order to transport the survivors at the end of the mission. Sadly this never came to pass, as both Rook and the SW-0608 were destroyed by the grenade of a shoretrooper.

Swoop Bike

This vehicle, a radical version of the speeder bike, functioned through the use of repulsorlift technology.

Many mercenaries and outlaws preferred them to speeder bikes and were attracted by their speed and power, and the dangerous aura that surrounded them. Secret swoop bike races were organised throughout the galaxy and the excitement of the events often helped bring communities together.

Sy Snootles

A Pa'lowick singer and member of the Max Rebo Band.

Sy Snootles was an amazing vocalist, with a pouting mouth and an enticing swing that was accentuated by her long legs. Unbeknown to her criminal audience, she also secretly worked as a spy for Jabba the Hutt.

T

T-14 Hyperdrive Generator

Produced by the Nubian Design Collective, this high-performance engine enabled ships to make the jump to hyperspace.

It was this fundamental piece of equipment that broke down on Queen Amidala's royal starship when she was escaping from the occupied planet of Naboo. This generator served as the stake of the bet between the scrap dealer Watto and the Jedi Master Qui-Gon Jinn – a bet that the Jedi Master won thanks to Anakin's podrace victory on Tatooine.

T-16 Skyhopper

A spacecraft categorised as an airspeeder, the T-16 was manufactured in the Incom Corporation factories.

The skyhopper was able to fly at more than 1,000 kph at a maximum altitude of a few hundred metres, and these features made it the favourite vehicle for young would-be pilots throughout the galaxy. It could be identified by its star-like shape made by three large wings, and its great manoeuvrability made it ideal for hunting. The skyhopper was also known to share the ergonomics of a part of its control system with the X-wing starfighter, which helped Luke Skywalker, the hero of the Battle of Yavin and former owner of a T-16, to become quickly acclimatised with the controls of the rebel fighter.

T-65B X-wing Starfighter

Produced by the Incom Corporation, those vehicles were the jewel of rebel fleet during the Galactic Civil War.

Equipped with four engines, each mounted on the back of a wing, this lean starfighter would spread its wings in attack mode, increasing the width of the laser cannons and forming the distinctive 'X' shape, visible from the front or the back of the ship. The pilot was aided by an astromech droid during flights, which could make small repairs in addition to its specific

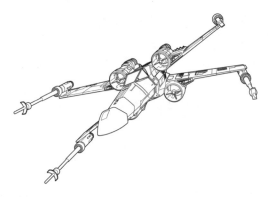

tasks of making space calculations. The technical specs of the X-wing were impressive: at 12 metres long it boasted four coordinated laser cannons, two proton torpedoes, a long-distance hyperdrive, energy shields and a sophisticated targeting system. Thanks to those advantages, the Alliance was able to stand up to the Empire, despite the fact that the Imperial forces were far superior in their might. The X-wings were greatly outnumbered by the TIE fighters of the Empire, but they compensated by using their superior aeronautic and military capabilities.

The X-wing was responsible for many inspirational feats throughout the history of the Rebel Alliance: there was the legendary Red Squadron of the Battle of Yavin, plus the escort that led the evacuation of the rebel base on Hoth, the second Red Squadron of the Battle of Endor, and the decisive victory during the Battle of Jakku, which ushered in an era of peace across the galaxy before the emergence of the First Order.

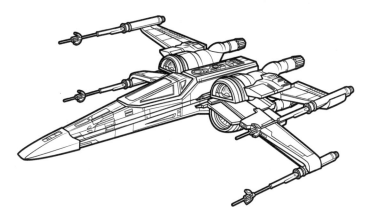

T-70 X-wing Starfighter

A single-seater combat starfighter designed by Incom FreiTek.

Constructed using a similar blueprint to its illustrious predecessor – the T-65 X-wing – this model benefited from several enhancements. Free from the panicked time restraints of the Civil War, its designers were able to work serenely to create a craft fast and powerful enough to take on the last Imperial cruisers that were still active. About 12 metres in length, the T-70 X-wing benefited from a new engine and incorporated some changes that allowed it to have a larger number of astromech droids, while it could carry a more diverse range of weaponry thanks to its secondary modular weapon pods.

Like the T-65, the wings of the T-70 could spread to facilitate the ionic engines, which cooled down the craft and allowed it to engage its four laser cannons. With its perfectly profiled retro-propulsors and electromagnetic gyroscopes, the T-70 X-wing had a crucial advantage during dogfights. It was able to pierce deflector shields with its eight MG7-A proton torpedoes, and the craft functioned as the spearhead of the Resistance forces under the command of General Leia Organa. Nevertheless, the number of units created remained low thanks to the aggressive demilitarisation politics led by the New Republic.

Taidu Sefla

A Rebel Alliance Special Forces soldier, Sefla was the highest-ranking officer to be a member of Rogue One.

The sprightly soldier immediately accepted the hierarchical reorganisation of the unit requested by Cassian Andor, which resulted in Sergeant Melshi leading it. At the end of the battle Melshi and Sefla, with Chirrut Îmwe and Baze Malbus, were the only survivors of their combat group, but they were cornered by death troopers in the entrance of a bunker. When Bodhi Rook requested that they press a button on a console that was located near to them but dangerously exposed, in order to make a connection with the rebel fleet, Sefla courageously attempted an exit, but was killed instantly by a shot from one of the elite black-armoured soldiers. His fall was followed by Melshi's, which forced Îmwe to try crossing the battlefield.

Takeel

A Snivvian mercenary, Takeel was a regular customer at Mos Eisley Cantina, where he developed a dangerous addiction to spice-based drugs.

Takeel offered his services to the highest bidder without thinking about the possible conflicts of interest that it could provoke. He was known by two nicknames: the first was 'Snaggletooth', which he shared with most of his fellow Snivvians (among which was his brother, Zutton) due to a unique and prominent tooth; the second nickname, 'The Hunchback', was specifically assigned to him.

Takodana

A Mid Rim planet and home to the famous Maz Kanata, Takodana was a lush world covered by lakes and forests.

Maz Kanata and her famous castle were located in a neutral zone that kept itself out of the great galactic conflicts. Welcoming adventurers from all sides, Takodana was the ideal location for any spy who wanted to gather strategic information. In search of the Resistance and aware that he would find support, Han Solo didn't hesitate to lead Rey, Finn and BB-8 to this planet.

Tam Posla

Tam Posla was an interstellar law enforcer of the Milvayne Authority who became a bounty hunter.

When Posla was assigned to investigate a series of abductions that were connected to slavery and surgery mutilation, he discovered that the horrors had been carried out by two strangers on the planets of the Inner Rim, who were hiding under false identities. Deeply affected by the atrocious crimes, Posla took it as a personal challenge to solve the case, even after – for unknown reasons – his superiors told him to stop his investigations. Revolted, he abandoned his official position and tracked the two psychopaths to another jurisdiction, Jedha, where similar crimes had been committed. Armed with his DH–17 blaster equipped with a customised magazine and still wearing his padded brown uniform and full helmet (which showed the Milvayne authority logo), he pursued his quarry through the streets of the Holy City. Posla was not to be confused with the partisan who took Cassian Andor and Jyn Erso to Gerrera, who wore the same attire except for the helmet and gloves. As Posla identified and 'locked on' his two targets, it was very likely that he escaped the tragic destiny of Jedha City. For their part, 'Roofoo' and 'Sawkee' were sighted with certainty a few days later in the Mos Eisley Cantina on Tatooine.

Tank Trooper

These Imperial combat drivers specialised in piloting the TX-225 GAVw / GAVr 'Occupier' assault tanks.

In most cases they patrolled the vehicle through the narrow streets of Jedha and escorted the cargoes of kyber crystals stolen by the Empire from the mines or the temples of the Holy City. The armour of the tank troopers was especially light as they counted on the armour of the tanks to protect them during an attack. Composed of a partial assembly of plastoid plates, their armour offered the necessary flexibility to move in the reduced space inside this type of vehicle.

Tantive IV, the

Manufactured by the Corellian Engineering Corporation, this consular vessel was a model in the CR90 line.

The *Tantive IV* played an important role during the Clone Wars and the beginning of the Galactic Civil War. This vessel was used by the family Organa of Alderaan, who acted as diplomatic cover for the emergent Rebel Alliance. Its last captain, Raymus Antilles, was killed by Darth Vader after the Sith Lord intercepted the vessel while searching for the plans of the Death Star that had been stolen by the rebels on Scarif. Princess Leia was captured immediately after she had concealed the plans in the memory of R2-D2, who later escaped the vessel in an escape pod in the direction of Tatooine. A short time later, Imperial forces destroyed the *Tantive IV* and claimed that it had been an accident that left no survivors.

Tanus Spijek

This Elom was at the court of Jabba the Hutt during the rebels' daring rescue of Han Solo.

A spy for hire, Tanus Spijek was also present on Jabba's sail barge, the *Khetanna*, when it made its last journey out towards the Great Pit of Carkoon.

Tarfful

A Wookiee general that hailed from Kashyyyk, Tarfful was large and powerful, like all Wookiees, and he took part in the Battle of Kashyyyk as the commander of the city of Kachirho.

Under the orders of Jedi Master Yoda he didn't hesitate to lead his troops to the front line. He was a long-time friend of Chewbacca, whom he rescued when he was taken prisoner by Trandoshan hunters. The two Wookiees helped Yoda safely leave Kashyyyk after Order 66 was given.

Targeting Computer

An electronic device that helped the user position his or her weapons according to a target previously locked on by sensors.

There were many systems and technologies used for these facilities but the general principle was the same, no matter the size of the vessel. The pilot had to align his device and calibrate his weapons through the projection of an electronic sighting that displayed the selected target/s. During the Battle of Yavin, Luke Skywalker succeeded in aiming the shot that destroyed the Death Star by using the Force instead of his targeting computer.

Tarkin Initiative

This initiative was an Imperial think-tank that could be found within the Advanced Weapons Research division.

Founded, as its name suggests, by Wilhuff Tarkin, it gave birth to the two Death Stars. Its logo was a hexagon in which straight lines crossed to symbolise a stylised kyber crystal.

Taslin Brance

Major Taslin Brance was a Resistance High Command officer who worked with General Leia Organa.

A specialist in communications, Brance was one of General Organa's most precious advisers. Convinced of the necessity to fight the threat the First Order represented, he joined the Resistance on D'Qar and became the transmission channel for all the important information about the First Order's moves, which gave General Organa and Admiral Ackbar and Statura the opportunity to make the right decisions at the right time.

Tasu Leech

The symbolic leader of the Kanjiklub, a Nar Kanjian warrior gang from the Outer Rim, Tasu Leech gained leadership through the gang's traditional way: he challenged his predecessor to a duel and defeated him.

Leech himself was challenged several times but was not vanquished. He used his charisma and his leader's legitimacy to maintain cohesion inside his troops and he led chaotic raids all over the Outer Rim, where they sometimes confronted their main adversaries, the Guavian Death Gang.

Leech was a fiery warrior and a leader of men, but he was no strategist. He relied on the gang's reputation and on the efficiency of his warriors to take advantage in skirmishes. Proud of his border origins, he refused to speak Basic (which he considered a 'soft language for soft people'), even though he perfectly understood it. His outfit was made of a reinforced plastoid body suit, some light armour pieces and a customised laser blaster called 'Huttsplitter', which had a gundark bone grip and a narglatch tusk vibro-spike bayonet. This random appearance was specific to the old Nar Kanji colonies, where ingenuity and the ability to make use of what was to hand were essential in order to break free from the oppression of the dreadful Hutts.

Although he specialised in extortion, piracy and ship theft, Tasu Leech sometimes invested in smuggling operations. After being deceived twice by Han Solo, he decided to pay a visit to the smuggler to get his money back.

Tatoo I and Tatoo II

Located in the Arkanis sector, Tatoo I and Tatoo II formed the Tatoo system in the region of the Outer Rim.

Its distinctive characteristic was its binary solar system around which revolved four planets, of which Tatooine was the most important.

Tatooine

This was the first planet of the binary solar system of Tatoo, situated in the Outer Rim Territories.

Tatooine owed a part of its renown to the fact that it was the cradle of two legendary destinies in the history of the galaxy: Anakin Skywalker, who was born on the planet, and his son, Luke, who at birth was placed under the care of his uncle, Owen Lars, a Tatooine moisture farmer.

Under the burning fire of the two suns, Tatoo I and Tatoo II, the desert planet, in its beginning, didn't offer an environment favourable to the development of indigenous life. Before Tatooine attracted the greed of the mining companies, its only sentient native species were the Jawas and the Tusken Raiders, but the surface of the planet and its high level of silica gave rise to

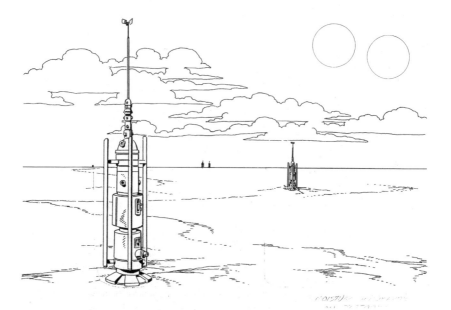

numerous speculations and the promise of fast and easy earnings that led to the explosion of the population. However, excavations indicated a concentration of metals with inappropriate properties that resulted in a raw material that was unfit for commercial exploitation.

The gigantic facilities that had been installed were then abandoned, which benefited the Jawas who recovered the abandoned material from the sands using their imposing sandcrawlers, which played a central role in their people's survival. Indeed, this material allowed them to take a place in the economic chain of the planet by providing the colonists, or the occasional visitor, with salvaged material. The Tusken Raiders didn't have this same chance and remained enclosed in the wild deserts of Tatooine. In addition, their temperament and their attachment to the desert repelled any ideas of cohabitation, or even interaction with any other population. Indeed, the Tusken Raiders thought that their people shared a bond with the desert and that its limited resources were theirs by right. The moisture farmers had the most contact with them, which often led to terrifying confrontations over whose right it was to harvest the water condensed by the humidity vaporators.

The planet's animal life entrenched itself in the depths of the deserts, which were sufficiently vast to prevent its extinction. Therefore, the famous and terrifying krayt dragons, as well as the restful banthas, could always be found on Tatooine and were objects of local mythology deeply anchored in Tusken Raider folklore. Other more or less wild species were also present in the dunes, mountains and canyons of Tatooine, among which were the dewbacks, rontos and womp rats. The dunes also sheltered the den of a terrifying sarlacc, an immense creature of which only the teeming muzzle of tentacles was visible from the outside. It lived in the depths of the Great Pit of Carkoon.

Tatooine was known to be one of the historic cradles of illegal activity in the Outer Rim. This was a direct consequence of the successive waves of colonisation that punctuated the history of the planet. A lot of mercenaries and smugglers tried their luck in trafficking the ores and some were even hired by companies. The introduction of the space trade routes took Tatooine out of isolation and the planet became one of the trading hubs for the surrounding systems. This cultural explosion caused the Hutt clan to take interest in the planet and they subsequently settled on Tatooine and built their far-reaching and powerful criminal organisation, which specialised in spice smuggling.

The two main cities of Tatooine were the spaceports of Mos Espa and Mos Eisley, which were home to the biggest concentration of trading activity on the planet, whether legal or not.

Taun We

The administrative aide to the Kamino prime minister, Lama Su, Taun We was also the coordinator of the clone army project destined for the Republic.

Gracious and slender, We welcomed Obi-Wan Kenobi when he arrived on Kamino and immediately arranged an appointment for him with the prime minister. We took part in the clones and facility review with the Jedi Knight and then presented him to Jango Fett, the genetic model of the clones, and his son, Boba.

Tauntaun

This bipedal creature native to the planet of Hoth was used as a mount by the Rebel Alliance during its installation of Echo Base.

The tauntaun belonged to a hybrid reptilian species, and had thick fur and powerful legs. They were hunted by carnivorous wampas but their speed allowed them to keep away from their natural predator. The discovery of the tauntauns and the fact that they were easy to tame was excellent news for the rebel command, whose technicians had immense difficulties in adapting their fleet of T-47 airspeeders to the extremely cold weather that swept across the surface of Hoth. These T-47s could only be used during daylight hours, so the tauntauns therefore allowed the rebels to carry out their surveillance patrols across a much wider timeframe.

Taybin Ralorsa

A regular at Maz's Castle on Takodana, Taybin Ralorsa – along with Ubert 'Sticks' Quaril – formed the rhythm section in the band that was charged with entertaining Maz Kanata's clientele.

She generally offered her services in exchange for shelter, along with her fellow musicians Quaril, Sudswater Dillifay Glon and Infrablue Zedbeddy Coggins. The band kept their music subtle and light, and when Ralorsa occasionally sang she would keep the beat with various instruments while swaying to the melodies that came from Coggins' hypolliope.

TC-14

This silver protocol droid from the TC-series served aboard the Trade Federation's Droid Control Ship, the *Saak'ak*.

She was charged with the task of welcoming the ambassadors of the Republic – Qui-Gon Jinn and Obi-Wan Kenobi – who she identified as Jedi for her Neimoidian masters Nute Gunray, Rune Haako and Daultay Dofine. While serving refreshments to the guests, a poisonous gas overwhelmed the room that left her so surprised that she let her tray fall. She was then required by her protocol programming to softly apologise to the Jedi. They spared her and let her leave, knowing that the real culprits were somewhere else.

Techno Union

This trade organisation specialised in high-tech technological industry and droid foundries.

Renowned for its battle droids, the Techno Union constantly developed new technologies and tried to establish itself wherever profit could be made, for example, on Mustafar, where the foundry buildings were protected by energy shields. Seduced by the possibility of avoiding the influence of the Republic, the Techno Union joined the Separatist movement through its director Wat Tambor.

Teebo

An excellent Ewok hunter with grey and black striped fur, Teebo was from Bright Tree Village on Endor.

Extremely brave, he ignored Han Solo's warnings and didn't hesitate to test him at the time of the rebels' capture. Once the decision had been made to free the rebels, he used his axe to cut the ties that bound a furious R2-D2, who then didn't hesitate to electrocute him twice. Later, at the Council of

Elders, he tried to make peace with the small droid, but a set of resonant beeps warned him not to and convinced him to fraternise with Chewbacca instead.

When Chief Chirpa decided to help the Rebellion, Teebo was responsible for sending the message to all surrounding Ewok tribes. He was then extremely involved in the Battle of Endor, where he was active on all fronts. He created diversions and ordered Paploo to steal an Imperial speeder bike, then he launched the ground assault from a branch by blowing a horn. At the end of the battle the wing of his hang-glider was hit, but Teebo survived and could be seen playing the drum during the victory celebrations.

Teedo

A small aggressive wreck-raider from Teedo, this term covered both the species and a single individual who roamed the south-west area of the Niima outpost on Jakku.

Perched on his luggabeast and equipped with an ionic spear that discharged paralysing surges, this small reptilian plundered the Starship Graveyard looking for valuable parts. He had optimised his mount for the long, lonely journeys with a retrieved monojet saddle, and he scanned the surrounding areas hoping to locate the specific energy signature that would indicate the position of an isolated droid that he could capture.

Teedo was used to living in the desert and had adapted his outfit as necessary: his sandals were made of droid rubber, which allowed him to walk on the sand without getting stuck; his mask was equipped with goggles that diminished the glare of the desert; and a dorsal device shaped as a metallic bottle recycled his bodily fluids. He also carried magnetic impulse grenades in case he was attacked. Just after he had captured BB-8, Poe Dameron's astromech droid, Teedo was confronted by Rey. Being familiar with the young woman and aware of what she was capable of, he released the droid and continued on his way.

Teemto Pagalies

This Veknoid podracer pilot from planet of Moonus Mandel took part in the Boonta Eve Classic Podrace.

On the starting grid, he could be found in the third row, stuck between Boles Roor and Clegg Holdfast, at the controls of his IPG-X1131. Although his performance in the first lap was commendable, having avoided all traps and obstacles on the course, during the second lap his right engine was hit by a projectile thrown by a Tusken Raider, which caused his podracer to violently crash. Although he survived, he was left feeling a certain hatred towards the Tusken Raiders.

Temmin 'Snap' Wexley

This Resistance reconnaissance pilot was born on the planet of Akiva, an old Imperial base liberated by the New Republic.

Wexley was the son of a Rebel Alliance veteran Y-wing pilot, and he was therefore naturally aware of the threat represented by the First Order. He soon joined the Resistance alongside General Leia Organa on D'Qar as an X-wing pilot. His flying skills and ability to quickly assess situations led him to the reconnaissance squadron. He never hesitated to take risks in order to scan areas far behind enemy lines if it helped his superiors develop the best strategies, and he was able to confirm the information supplied by Finn regarding the First Order's Starkiller Base. As the fleet only had a small staff he also participated in combat missions, during which he demonstrated his talents as a reconnaissance pilot. He took part in the Resistance's assault on Starkiller Base.

Temple of the Kyber

See Jedha City

Tessek

This Quarren worked as an accountant for Jabba the Hutt during the time of the Galactic Civil War.

It was a role the facial-tentacled amphibian fulfilled until the day the rebels killed his employer and destroyed his barge.

Thadlé Berenko

Naboo's emissary to the New Republic Senate.

Like her fellow senators, Thadlé Berenko followed the alternative movement of the Senate seat created after the Galactic Civil War, and therefore lived on Hosnian Prime. Berenko wore her hair styled in the ceremonial tradition of Naboo and wore a gown of Theedian origin adorned with recognisable patterns; she was the perfect representation of the small planet, just as Senator Padmé Amidala had once been. Berenko died during the destruction of Hosnian Prime by the First Order's Starkiller Base.

Thanisson

Thanisson was a First Order officer on the *Resurgent*-class Star Destroyer, *Finalizer*.

The product of the younger generation lulled by the tales of the Empire's great admirals, and encouraged to hate the New Republic as a source of chaos in the galaxy, Sergeant Thanisson was a disciplined young officer assigned to communications and traffic control in the landing zone of the *Finalizer*. He signalled the non-authorised take-off of the TIE fighter Finn and Poe Dameron were trying to escape with just before the cannons of the craft entirely destroyed the control room.

Thanlis Depallo

Commenor's emissary to the New Republic Senate. Like his fellow senators, Thanlis Depallo followed the alternative movement of the Senate seat created after the Galactic Civil War, and therefore lived on Hosnian Prime.

Depallo often rested his hands in a very specific way on his violet gown, and he treated his entourage with a haughty attitude that he obviously believed was befitting of his station. He died during the destruction of Hosnian Prime by the First Order's Starkiller Base.

Theed

The capital city of the planet of Naboo, Theed was once a farmers' village, built at the edge of a plateau on the banks of the Solleu River.

The river meandered everywhere in the city and was joined by many tributaries, which came from the core of the planet, before it ended its course in a waterfall on the side of the rocky plateau. These multiple waterways favoured trade between the Naboo and the Gungans, which particularly thrived after the Battle of Naboo, when the two people united to achieve a decisive victory against the droid troops of the Trade Federation. The architecture of the city, harmonious and elegant, reflected the profoundly peaceful culture of Naboo and its inhabitants.

Theed housed the Royal Palace, a huge building, which was home to both the royal power and administrative centre of the planet. The urban design was conceived and developed around this building, built on the edge of the cliff, whose facade dominated a huge esplanade where celebrations and official events usually took place. An architectural wonder, the care that had gone into its finishing touches showed great awareness of the Naboo people's devotion to art and handcraft. The Theed Royal Palace also housed the apartments of the elected ruler of Naboo, as well as the boardroom from which the planet was run. During the invasion of Naboo by the Trade Federation, the building was controlled by occupying forces, before it was reclaimed by Queen Padmé Amidala's bold strategy.

Theron Nett

Theron Nett was a Rebel Alliance pilot who took part in the Battle of Yavin under the call sign Red Ten.

Nett was part of the X-wing escort that accompanied Garven Dreis (Red Leader) during the final assault against the Death Star. He was also accompanied by Puck Naeco (Red Twelve) and was shot down by a TIE fighter as he protected Dreis' progression through the space station's narrow trench.

Tiaan Jerjerrod

Born on Tinnel IV, this officer of the Imperial army began his career in the design and development of special vessels for the Corellian Engineering Company.

The Empire noticed his work, and it was among its ranks that Tiaan Jerjerrod decided to pursue his career. This technocrat entered the group of high-ranking soldiers that advised the Emperor on military and martial matters, and he contributed to the construction of the first Death Star – the gigantic secret weapon that had the capability to destroy an entire planet. Although it was destroyed by a young rebel pilot with two simple proton torpedoes, Jerjerrod was promoted and reached the closed circle formed by the twenty recipients of the rank of Imperial Moff, who had been tasked with the perilous mission to supervise the faster construction of a new Death Star, bigger than the first one.

It was an epic task, at the same time taking all precautions not to raise any suspicions from the Rebel Alliance. He thus acted under the cover of the 'Director of Imperial Energy Systems' title. Although he succeeded in solving the major defect that had led to the downfall of the first space station, he had to confront the recurrent problems that faced every large-scale construction: the deficit of manpower, the interruption of raw material from the suppliers, lack of coordination between different building trades, and even budget cuts. As delays accumulated, Darth Vader warned him of the Emperor's imminent arrival and reminded him that he didn't tolerate failure. Jerjerrod then promised the impossible and maintained the work would be complete for Palpatine's arrival.

Luckily for the Moff, and to his huge relief, Palpatine didn't hold him responsible for the incomplete state of the station, but to his great disappointment, neither did the Empire's leader congratulate him for the gigantic progress that had been achieved in record time. In actual fact, the Sith Lord had no interest in those details because what he had considered to be essential had been done: the superlaser was operational to trap the Rebel Alliance. Always respectful to the highest authority of the Empire, the commander of the second Death Star obeyed the direct order to use the destructive device against the hostile fleet during the Battle of Endor. He therefore pulverised some of the cruisers, but couldn't prevent the change of events that favoured the Rebellion. The Emperor died, the station exploded, and among the thousands of names of those who died was Tiaan Jerjerrod, a gifted designer who became a cold technocrat for the Empire.

Tibanna Gas

Tibanna gas was mined in the upper atmospheric layers of the planet of Bespin.

It was a particularly rare and precious resource as it was used in the manufacture of numerous weapons and hyperpropulsors. After several commercial blockades, Bespin remained the only source providing the gas, a fact that garnered the planet a lot of attention. Cloud City became the only colony able to mine, refine and condition the gas for exportation.

TIE Advanced x1

A prototype starfighter of the TIE line that was produced for the Empire by the Sienar Fleet Systems.

Its size and aeronautical specifications were similar to those of the standard TIE fighter, but this advanced ship possessed heavier weapons and C-shaped wings, with three energy-gathering panels each instead of one. The ship represented an intermediary step between the v1 TIE fighter and the TIE bombers and starfighters that were produced soon after. Their aim was to compete with, and even to outclass, the X-wings of the Rebel Alliance. Notably Darth Vader used one during the Battle of Yavin.

TIE Bomber

Fighters of the TIE range, produced in the factories of the Sienar Fleet Systems, and used by the Imperial fleet during missions of aerial support.

These ships were fitted with concussion missiles, standard laser cannons, proton bombs, and gravitational and orbital bombs.

TIE Fighter

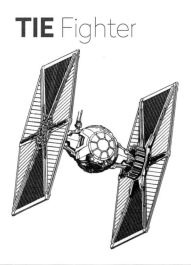

A single-seat space vehicle that became the emblem of the Empire, the TIE fighter was a product of Sienar Fleet Systems factories.

Small, very powerful and easy to manoeuvre, the ships were about 9 metres in height and could reach speeds of up to 1,200 kph, making them efficient hunters. Recognisable by their characteristic whirring sound, they were equipped with twin ionic engines that gave the craft its name ("Twin Ion Engine"). The principle of the double ion engine and the general design of the TIE were derived in part from the former Eta-2 *Actis*-class interceptors used during the Clone Wars. TIE fighters were not designed for long space journeys, but for short combat, exploration or reconnaissance missions, which could be launched from Imperial cruisers in orbit. Both the usual hyperdrive and deflector shield were sacrificed in order to maintain the TIE's light, agile weight; however, these two omissions left the craft vulnerable under attack. For this reason, TIE pilots were generally considered to be the bravest among the fleet's ranks, and they often took a superior attitude over their fellow pilots, believing that shields were tools for cowards.

TIE Fighter Pilot

This elite military class was formed to pilot TIE fighters, the emblem of the Imperial navy.

The recruitment and training programme for this group was extremely selective and strangely promoted pride and mutual loyalty by giving value to individual performances. TIE fighter cadets were trained to prioritise the objectives of the mission above any other element, which included helping other pilots. It was this principle that made this army corps one of the most competitive among the Imperial forces, which only kept the best, both in terms of expertise as well as involvement, courage and sacrifice. The chosen few naturally therefore exhibited a common behaviour based on arrogance and pride. They also took pleasure in the danger of piloting a TIE fighter. Deprived of both deflector shields and a hyperdrive, they believed that those amenities were only for cowardly pilots.

TIE Interceptor

A one-seat fighter recognisable by its four pointed solar panels, the Empire ordered this ship from its manufacturer, Sienar Fleet Systems, in an attempt to combat a serious fault that had been discovered with the classic model.

The classic TIE fighter struggled in space combat – particularly when up against the Rebel Alliance's A-wing starfighters whose speed was a problem for them. The TIE interceptor therefore possessed increased manoeuvrability and a speed designed to better compete with its adversaries – although it was still 50 kph slower than the A-wing. However, in order to optimise its superiority to many of the enemy craft, the interceptor was flown by only the most elite Imperial pilots. As with the previous model, it didn't possess a shield or a hyperdrive, but by fully charging its solar panels, the laser cannon was able to deliver quadruple the amount of firepower than it had before.

If the TIE Advanced fighter had been too costly to produce, the TIE interceptor would have served as a decent choice for the dangerous new fighter the Empire had been waiting for. By the time of the Battle of Endor the interceptor and other new TIE models made up twenty per cent of the Imperial fleet.

TIE Striker

An experimental one-seater craft, the atmospheric interceptor called TIE/sk model x1 was a new concept created by the Sienar Fleet Systems upon an order by the Empire.

It was tested by the military think-tank on Scarif, where it would be decided if the model would be deployed as a new-age fighter. This version of the TIE fighter was able to operate in high or low atmosphere, in particular during patrols of the top-level above-ground facilities. Distinguished by its elongated cockpit and its two pointed solar panels, this model was believed to operate at a speed even faster than a standard TIE fighter (1,500 kph). Despite its compact nature, the TIE striker was well armed with two heavy cannons that used anti-armour munitions, and a ventral bomb locker for ground support. The rapid-firing cannons integrated into the wings were planned for use in aerial combat, but this model never succeeded in entering into orbital flight. Its natural place was in clashes, such as the Battle of Scarif. This model remained in use in the Imperial armada until the Battle of Jakku.

Tivik

A member of Saw Gerrera's militia and an underground informant of Cassian Andor.

When they met on the Ring of Kafrene, Tivik was there to steal some munitions with other partisans from Jedha. Anxious to depart and sporting a wounded arm wrapped in a scarf, he confirmed the most incredible secret to the rebel agent: the existence of a 'planet killer' starship, which had been revealed by a deserter closely linked with an Imperial scientist named Galen Erso. At this point, Andor and Tivik were interrupted by a patrol of stormtroopers, which Andor was forced to get rid of. Handicapped by his injury and in panic, Tivik could not make it to the escape exit. With sincere regret but no hesitation, Andor shot his informant in the back. In war, it was important to learn the enemy's secret, but just as fundamental was that they never knew it had been discovered.

TK-421

This Imperial soldier was stationed on the first Death Star and was assigned to aid the team of scanners who had boarded the *Millennium Falcon* in order to discover if anyone was aboard the ship.

His role was to stand guard in front of the ship's access ramp in the company of another soldier. Some minutes after two specialists boarded the ship, he heard a noise followed by a voice asking for help. TK-421 boarded the vessel with his partner and fell into the trap that had been set by Han Solo and Luke Skywalker. The abandonment of their station was quickly noticed by Lieutenant Treidum, who noted the return of the two soldiers, but was unaware that it was the two fugitives hiding in the armour.

Tobix Chasser

Tobix Chasser was an Imperial army officer cadet who took part in the Battle of Scarif.

The secret weapon of the Empire – the Death Star – was a space combat station that needed to be staffed in order to keep it fully functional, and as such Chasser was in charge of overseeing the allocation of staff to the combat station. He ensured that only qualified hand-picked staff who knew how to keep a secret were assigned there.

Tobler Ceel

A general of the Grand Gungan Army.

The heroic Gungan Tobler Ceel fought during the Battle of the Great Grass Plains during the Trade Federation's invasion of Naboo.

Todes Halvax

An Imperial army technician on Scarif.

As system administrator of the command room located in the Citadel Tower, it was Halvax's job to resolve all possible technical problems so that the pivotal hub kept all of its strategic capabilities.

Toonbuck Toora

A Sy Myrthian senator during the period of the Galactic Republic.

With two little eyes and three beards, Toonbuck Toora represented the planet of Sy Myrth in the Galactic Senate.

Torture Chamber

Used to physically restrain and torment prisoners, the torture chamber was equipped with numerous devices that were used to torture a prisoner during questioning.

The chair was surrounded with multiple devices that generated intense shocks, which were delivered according to a protocol that prized gaining answers quickly.

Toryn Farr

Toryn Farr was a Rebel Alliance communications officer during the Civil War.

Three years after the Battle of Yavin, she was assigned to Hoth where she coordinated the defence and the evacuation of Echo Base. She succeeded in escaping aboard the very last transport, the *Bright Hope,* just seconds before the base was invaded by Imperial troops.

Tosche Station

A power and industrial resources distribution centre situated on Tatooine, this station supplied energy to many of the surrounding towns and was the main centre of technology-repair supplies in the Anchorhead area.

Luke Skywalker frequently went there in order to buy the necessary gear for his uncle's farm, but also to see friends and share their common dream of joining the Academy.

Toshdor Ni

A member of the Confraternity of the Beatific Countenance, this Lorrdian, like all those of his species, possessed a marked expression and a particular natural odour.

In order to conceal that and to physically respect his vow of silence, he wore the complete thick vermilion attire of the community and carried a censer that dispensed Qatameric incense. He was present alongside other pilgrims and the Great Priest in the Holy City of Jedha shortly before it was destroyed by the Empire's new superweapon.

Toydarian

A blue-green-skinned species from the planet of Toydaria, Toydarians had two wings, a long snout and webbed feet.

They also had the remarkable ability to be able to resist some uses of the Force, such as Jedi mind tricks, as Watto, the scrap trader of Mos Espa, demonstrated.

Tractor Beam

An invisible beam able to attract and take control of space objects, the tractor beam was civilian technology that, as was so often the case, the military put to its own use.

Tractor beams were originally used to move freight and merchandise, but were quickly installed on Imperial starships, where they were used to compensate for the lack of manoeuvrability between, for example, a giant space cruiser and a tiny starfighter, making the latter easier to lock on to. A powerful tractor beam, like the one installed on the Death Star, had the capability to attract middle-sized starships and completely incapacitate them. The *Millennium Falcon* ended up on the space station when it was caught in a tractor beam. In order to escape Obi-Wan Kenobi had to deactivate one of the seven energy generators that powered the beam.

Trade Federation

The Trade Federation was a powerful interstellar conglomerate that, driven by greed, wanted to buy or control every aspect of business, with a view to making as much profit as possible while avoiding Republic taxes.

The Trade Federation possessed a trade monopoly that had been conceded by the Senate, but after the commercial routes became subject to taxation, it became a military force and invaded Naboo, as advised by its secret Sith ally Darth Sidious, who was in fact Senator Palpatine. Although they suffered a rather humiliating defeat, it afforded Palpatine the opportunity to become Supreme Chancellor of the Galactic Republic. A decade later, the Trade Federation secretly became part of the Confederacy of Independent Systems, lending it its military might, while officially still supporting the Republic. Believing to the very end that they would profit from their double-dealing, the leaders of the Trade Federation thought they were finally set to reap the benefits of their long campaign when the Separatist leaders gathered on Mustafar. Instead, they found only death at the hands of Darth Vader – ensuring that the Trade Federation would never become part of the Galactic Empire.

Transport Gunship LAAT/i

The Low Altitude Assault Transport/infantry (LAAT/i) was developed and built by Rothana Heavy Engineering for the Republic.

Deployed for the first time during the Battle of Geonosis, the LAAT/i became one of the most common military vehicles of the Clone Wars. This basic transport, which could carry up to thirty clone troopers and reach speeds of 620 kph, was equipped with missiles and multiple laser cannons that enabled it to efficiently protect ground troops. Two bubble-protected turrets on the sides strengthened the weaponry of the ship. On Geonosis, the LAAT/i turned out to be an invaluable tool when it was used to create a security perimeter around the Jedi who had been cornered by the Separatist droids, and to carry troops to hunt down fleeing units.

Trash Compactor

A waste-processing apparatus that was used in space stations and large-scale starships.

Commonly composed of two mobile walls operated to compress the waste, the compactors generally had magnetically locking doors to ensure any potentially dangerous waste remained contained. It was in a trash compactor that Luke Skywalker, Princess Leia, Han Solo and Chewbacca almost lost their lives on the first Death Star. Luckily, Skywalker was able to reach C-3PO and R2-D2 on his comlink, at which time R2-D2 shut down the compactor before the heroes were crushed.

Troops Transporter

The Atmospheric Assault Transporter (AAT) was designed by Sienar-Jaemus Fleet Systems for the First Order's troops.

This craft could deliver up to two squads, or about twenty troops, from a planet's orbit or forward bases to the battlefield. Once empty, it rapidly departed the drop zone and returned after the battle to retrieve the survivors. Stormtrooper deployment took about thirty seconds. The craft's high cockpit allowed the pilot to have an overview of the situation at ground level. In case of breakdown, or if the main controls were off, the transport could be manoeuvred with its auxiliary controls.

Trugut

A currency used on Tatooine, in particular by the Hutts.

One trugut unit was worth sixteen gold wupiupi, and four truguts were worth one peggat, which represented roughly forty Republic credits.

TSMEU-6 Wheel Bike

The TSMEU-6 personal wheel bike was built by the Z-Gomot Ternbuell Guppat Corporation.

Composed of one giant 2.5-metre-diameter wheel – next to which the pilot could take its place – and four retractable legs, this all-terrain bike could reach 330 kph. Its speed, once the legs were deployed, was low (no more than 10 kph), but its legs enabled it to pass sizeable obstacles or travel from one type of terrain to another. Its arsenal was limited to a powerful twin laser cannon. On Utapau, General Grievous used this vehicle to escape from Obi-Wan Kenobi, but the Jedi eventually caught up with him, mounted on a varactyl.

Tuanul

This small village of settlers was located in the Kelvin Ravine, deep in the desert on the planet of Jakku.

Established by a small community of all kinds of people that were acolytes of the cult of the Force, the village of Tuanul was made from simple cob huts built around a vaporator tank. Its inhabitants shared a taste for deprivation and crafting. They made their own clothes from wool or fantabu skins dyed with tuanul berries and they fashioned their own belts and straps from gundark leather. Aware of the latent hostility of the desert that surrounded them, they created their own weapons using salvaged material. The ex-explorer and defender of the principles of the Force, Lor San Tekka made this village his retreat, and it was here that both the Resistance and the First Order came in search of information about the legendary Jedi Knight Luke Skywalker. Tuanul was devastated by a stormtrooper raid in which all of its inhabitants were killed on the orders of Kylo Ren.

Tusken Raiders

A primitive, indigenous people of Tatooine, who were also known as Sand People.

Although the exact time of their appearance on Tatooine was unknown, the Tusken Raider tribes quickly developed an extreme territorial attachment to the arid, inhospitable deserts. Convinced that they were the children of the desert and the only legitimate indigenous population of Tatooine, the Tusken Raiders did not accept the first colonists – who had come to exploit the unique atmospheric condensation of the planet – settling on what they considered to be their land. In an almost mystical belief, they considered that every drop of water their planet could produce belonged to them.

On average, Tusken Raider tribes were composed of about twenty individuals. Being nomadic, they didn't really have gathering places, although their camps could be found almost anywhere in the desert. Although the tribes chose to live independently of each other as opposed to in communities, it didn't prevent the development of a strong Tusken Raider culture composed of beliefs, customs and lifestyle. For instance, they revered their banthas with an almost cult status; as fellow creatures of the desert they shared an undeniable link that made them the only species deserving of the Tusken Raiders' respect.

Despite their forays into civilisation, Tusken Raiders personified the toughness of the desert and they remained brutal, ungovernable raiders with barbaric beliefs, who would often go to any lengths to achieve their goal. However, they were particularly apprehensive of krayt dragons, and they would often plan their journeys to avoid the areas known to be inhabited by the terrifying, gigantic lizards. Obi-Wan Kenobi once saved the young Luke Skywalker from a Tusken Raider ambush by imitating the scream of one of these dragons. Many years before that incident, Anakin Skywalker's mother was kidnapped by Tusken Raiders. He later found her dying in one of their camps, which, in revenge, he totally destroyed.

Twi'lek Twins

Ann and Tann Gella were the beautiful blue slaves who belonged to the Dug podrace champion Sebulba.

They would massage him and manicure his hands in the hangar before the Boonta Eve Classic Podrace on Tatooine.

Twin Pod Cloud Car

The twin pod cloud car, which had the capacity to fly in the upper layers of the atmosphere, was used by the law-enforcement forces of Cloud City at Bespin.

The device was made of two twin modules that sheltered a pilot and a gunner. These armed cloud cars were used for patrols and surveillance of the tibanna gas mining facilities.

Twin Suns of Tatooine

See Tatoo I *and* Tatoo II

Two Tubes

See Benthic *and* Edrio.

Tydirium Shuttle

This Imperial shuttle, stolen by Nien Nunb, allowed General Han Solo's rebel commandos to pass the Imperial blockades and land on the forest moon of Endor.

Although the mission began with a quip from the Corellian about the ship's unsuitability for Wookiees, the atmosphere soon became tense. To pass through the planetary shield the shuttle was required to emit, via its transponder, the correct code to the Imperial controllers aboard the Super Star Destroyer, the *Executor*. As the shuttle flew close to the Imperial cruiser, Luke Skywalker felt the presence of Darth Vader aboard, which only served to increase the concern of his friends. The Sith Lord also detected his son and asked Admiral Piett about the *Tydirium*. Although the code it used was a little old, it was still active and eventually Palpatine's right-hand man decided to let them pass in order to manage the situation himself. During that moment when time seemed to stand still, Solo instinctively suspected a problem and began planning an emergency escape, but despite all expectations the authorisation of passage was granted. The shield was deactivated and the *Tydirium* was free to land on the sanctuary moon, much to Skywalker's amazement.

Tynnra Pamlo

A member of the Imperial Senate, Tynnra Pamlo was also secretly the minister of education in the government of the Rebel Alliance.

While she represented her homeworld Taris during the reign of the Galactic Empire, her heart beat for the Rebellion. Pamlo worked with Alliance Intelligence and was very aware of the heinous attacks carried out by the Emperor's regime, among which were the Siege of Lasan, the sterilisation of Geonosis and the atrocities on Ghorman. She therefore had no difficulty believing in the existence of the Death Star when it was first revealed during a meeting of the Rebel Council on Yavin 4. Driven by fear of reprisals against her world and aware of the insufficient force of the rebel fleet to counter such a massive weapon, she was one of those that refused to take immediate action on Scarif. Nevertheless, a short time later back on Coruscant, the senator quit her role and courageously denounced the 'planet killer' in public.

Typho

A human who hailed from Naboo, Captain Typho was affiliated with the Royal House of Naboo and succeeded Captain Panaka as the head of security.

He held this post during the reign of Queen Amidala and remained unfailingly loyal to her. After she became a Galactic senator, it was this loyalty that drove him to follow her to Coruscant as her bodyguard. During the crisis that saw the development of the Separatist movement, it was his great caution that enabled Amidala to survive a bomb attack – but unfortunately the handmaiden who had taken her place as a decoy, while Amidala hid among the pilots, was killed.

Following the discovery of venomous kouhuns in Amidala's bedroom, Captain Typho supported the Jedi's idea to secretly send her back to Naboo under the protection of Anakin Skywalker. In order not to arouse suspicion, Typho remained on Coruscant to protect Dormé, another handmaiden of Amidala's, who took her place as a decoy.

Ubert 'Sticks' Quaril

A regular at Maz's Castle on Takodana, along with Taybin Ralorsa, Ubert 'Sticks' Quaril formed the rhythm section of the band that entertained Maz's clientele.

He generally offered his services in exchange for shelter, and played along with Taybin, Sudswater Dillifay Glon and Infrablue Zedbeddy Coggins in the light and bouncy jams that subtly filled the hall. Ubert played the xyloxan – a percussion instrument that was partially made of bodhar bones. The need to not disturb the clientele forced him to play with great softness.

Ugnaught

This humanoid species with a porcine appearance was native to the planet of Gentes.

The Ugnaughts endured many encounters with slavery throughout their history, which saw them scattered almost everywhere around the galaxy. A whole community was hired for the construction and the maintenance of Cloud City at Bespin – the installation that specialised in the extraction and refinery of the precious tibanna gas.

Umpass-stay

Although he played the drum in the Max Rebo Band, the Klatooinian Umpass-stay was also the band's bodyguard at Jabba's court.

While playing an enormous drum in a duet with the Weequay Ak-rev, he was brought to a stop by the drama that unfolded just a few metres from him, when the slave Twi'lek Oola was devoured alive by the rancor.

Unamo

This First Order officer was a radar operator on the main bridge of the *Resurgent*-class Star Destroyer, the *Finalizer*.

Chief petty officer Unamo was an experienced officer who worked under the direct command of General Hux. She tracked the *Finalizer's* primary objectives and reported on the target's status after each shot.

Unkar Plutt

Unkar Plutt was a scrap merchant from Crolute who traded ship parts salvaged from the wrecks spread all over the Starship Graveyard on the planet of Jakku.

Far from his natural aquatic habitat, Plutt's body suffered from the great dryness of the desert. His pinky skin had collapsed on his massive body and he stayed mainly in the darkness of his workshop, where he wore an imposing apron on his chest made of metal that was cut from a ship's hull. Installed at the Niima outpost, he managed a fruitful trade in spare parts. His booth was a converted old ground vehicle covered with surveillance systems to deter shoplifters, which stood on a blockhouse covered with awnings that the locals called 'The Concession'.

Unkar Plutt had an absolute monopoly on the combat rations he had salvaged from the stocks of the Imperial and rebel ships that had crashed on the surface of the planet, and he would exchange them for the spare parts that wreck-raiders, whether they were regulars or just passing through, brought him when they arrived in Niima. Among those wreck-raiders was Rey. With no competition, the Crolute was free to manipulate his rates in order to yield him the best interest and he would estimate the worth of parts from his own perspective, which assured him maximum profit when he sold them on the neighbouring worlds or to travellers passing through.

Plutt also maintained some cleaning posts that were fully equipped to wash and clean any parts to be sold in order to make them look their best. The fee for using these posts was deducted from the final price. Plutt was so focused on maintaining his monopoly, trading the best parts and getting the best deals that he would pay some villains to watch out for the forbidden exchange of imported foods or to acquire, by force if necessary, a particularly valuable part. However, the clumsy and obvious henchmen were not very efficient. Up until Rey stole the ship, Unkar Plutt had been the last owner of the *Millennium Falcon*, having stolen it from the Irving Boys, who had already stolen it from a certain Ducain, who had spirited it away from Han Solo.

UT-60D U-wing Starfighter

A transport and combat ship used by the Rebel Alliance.

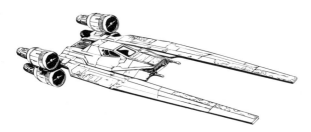

This craft was one of the last to leave the factories of the Incom Corporation before its mass production was prematurely halted by the meddling of the Imperial regime. Bail Organa succeeded in forging senatorial archives that caused a cargo of U-wings to 'disappear', allowing them to fall into the hands of the Rebellion. Their rarity made them all the more precious for the rebel cause. The U-wing's versatility made it a vehicle that filled several roles, including as a troops conveyor, fast mail deliverer, shuttle, evacuation ship and fighter. Its two wings were retractable, giving it both a flight and fight configuration. In its fight configuration, the U-wing was equipped with Taim & Baik KX7 double cannon lasers, which were stationary and required the pilot to move swiftly to hit their target. In order to remedy this limitation, the rebel technicians transformed one or two of the loading hatches into shooting stations by mounting a M-45 repetition ionic blaster to the craft. Although the cockpit held two seats and dual control, only one pilot was required to fly it.

A hyperdrive and four fusion engines completed this remarkable airborne weapon, which memorably aided the Rogue One mission on the beaches of Scarif. One Blue Squadron U-wing succeeded in passing through the planet's shield gate and not only brought down an AT-ACT, which helped the rebel soldiers who had been cornered on the beach, but after landing, the U-wing deployed troops that offered vital back-up to the already exhausted rebels on the ground. The U-wing provided aerial cover to the soldiers on the beach despite operating in a zone under heavy enemy fire, and although the U-wing was eventually shot down its versatility in action hugely contributed to the success of the Rogue One operation.

Utais

These inhabitants of the planet of Utapau coexisted peacefully with the Pau'ans in the cities built in the walls of the deep sinkholes found all over the planet.

The Utais were essentially in charge of subordinate tasks, notably as technicians on landing platforms. Small in size, their shape was adapted for life in the tunnels and their big black eyes enabled them to see in the dark.

Utapau

A planet of the Outer Rim situated in the Tarabba sector, Utapau was an arid and constantly wind-battered desert world.

Its surface was peppered by deep sinkholes, at the bottom of which water springs had enabled the development of an ecosystem. The many moons that gravitated around the planet – nine in all – strongly influenced the movements of those underground sources.

Utapau was also the native world of the Pau'ans, the Utais and the Amani. The Pau'ans and the Utais lived in cities built on the edge of the sinkholes, which extended into the walls in a series of cave and tunnel networks, while the Amani lived on the surface, in the deserts.

The capital of Utapau was the sinkhole settlement of Pau City and the main resource of Utapau was its mining. During the Clone Wars, the mining facilities – particularly for kyber crystals that were used in the construction of lightsabers – were a major stake for the different factions. The Separatist leaders took refuge on Utapau following their defeat at the Battle of Coruscant and the death of Count Dooku.

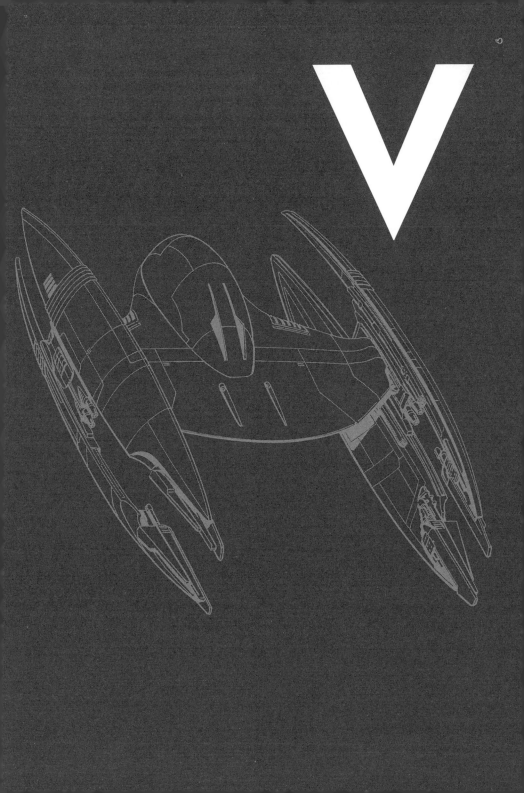

V-35 Courier

This landspeeder model, built by the SoroSuub Corporation, was more than 7 metres long and capable of reaching speeds of up to 120 kph.

This model was characterised by a far more angular design than the later ones. Produced two years before the Battle of Yavin, it was used by Owen and Beru Lars, who kept it, even though it was outdated, on their farm on Tatooine.

Valwid Ined

A brilliant forger based on Jedha, Valwid Ined worked primarily for Saw Gerrera.

The Vobati excelled in the counterfeiting of official documents and was able to create perfect forgeries of transit visas. Gerrera's partisans used these documents to pass effortlessly through the Imperial checkpoints at the entrance of the Holy City. Before the sacred city met its tragic destiny, Ined was in Tythoni Square during the insurgents' ambush of the tank. He wore a brown all-in-one, which was topped with a khaki headdress that entirely covered his face.

Vanden Willard

A native of the planet of Alderaan, Vanden Willard was a high-ranking tactical adviser for the Alliance, who was placed in charge of the defence of Yavin 4's Massassi Temple rebel base by General Dodonna.

Willard took part in two fundamental assignments during the Civil War: he assisted Dodonna in the strategic development of the attack against the Death Star and also developed the evacuation plan for the base.

Varactyl

A reptavian herbivore native to Utapau, these obedient animals, which measured around 15 metres in length, were particularly adapted to their rocky and plant-entangled surroundings, which made them very popular all-terrain mounts.

During the hunt for General Grievous and the Separatist leaders on Utapau, General Kenobi chose to ride a varactyl equipped with an adapted saddle rather than use a classic vehicle. The animal enabled him to efficiently pursue Grievous as he attempted to escape on a wheel bike.

Variable Geometry Self-Propelled Battle Droid, Mark I

See Vulture Droid

Vasp Vaspar

A member of the Imperial Senate and minister of industry in the secret government of the Rebel Alliance, Vasp Vaspar represented the Taldot sector.

He supervised the areas of the Rebellion's resources that were limited and secretly sustained them. More courageous than some of his counterparts, he was not against the idea of a declared confrontation against the Empire. Nevertheless, he found it difficult to believe that the rebel forces would ever be strong enough to attack the Death Star head on.

Veg-meat

This synthesised food could be found in the emergency rations that were retrieved by the scrap seller Unkar Plutt from the abandoned military kits in the wrecks of the Starship Graveyard on Jakku.

Freeze-dried and conditioned in small vacuum-packed portions, the veg-meat had the appearance of small silvery-green fragments. Once it had been cooked it turned green and had to be eaten in small bites. It contained the necessary nutrients to survive in hostile places and was generally conditioned with a share of synthesised bread for a full meal.

Verkle

This rodent with small tusks and thick brown and white fur lived on the forest moon of Endor and was successfully used by the Ewoks as a decoy in traps.

While on a commando mission the Wookiee Chewbacca was unable to resist the appetising odour produced by a freshly cut up specimen, which resulted in him – and all of his friends – being trapped in a huge net suspended a number of metres above the ground.

Vizam

This Kajain'sa'Nikto was at the disposal of the master of the underworld Jabba the Hutt.

Posted on the upper bridge of his employer's sail barge to witness the rebels' death, the orange Nikto witnessed them freeing themselves aboard their skiff. He used the cannon installed on the handrail to shoot at the vehicle where Chewbacca, Solo and Calrissian were precariously balanced. Having spotted the threat to his friends, Luke Skywalker killed Vizam with his lightsaber.

Vlex Onopin

This scientific programmer worked for the Tarkin Initiative.

A recipient of the prestigious diploma from the Magrody Institute of Programmable Intelligence, Onopin achieved titanic work during his years on Eadu, where he established the coded sequencers that calculated the crucial formulas required in the energy translations of kyber crystals. Every shot made by the Death Star was based on the variables calculated by Onopin's complex programmes. Just before ordering Onopin's execution alongside his scientific colleagues, Krennic reflected on how much he appreciated the scientist, but evidently it was not enough.

Vober Dand

Vober Dand was a Tarsunt controller in charge of ground logistics at the Resistance base on D'Qar.

He was motivated by the need to erase the threat of the First Order and he joined the Resistance, which was under the command of General Leia Organa. Dand was in charge of transporting equipment around the numerous runways of the base and was very picky when it came to protocol. Equipped with electrobinoculars and a communication earpiece, he would transmit his orders in a way that guaranteed both efficiency and fluidity, and his main concern was to avoid the creation of traffic jams. He remained on D'Qar during the raid on the First Order's Starkiller Base and regularly reported back to the Resistance command.

Volzang Li-Thrull

A member of Kanjiklub and Tasu Leech's sidekick, as was the case with most members of the gang, Volzang Li-Thrull came from the Nar Kanji human colonies.

A fierce warrior with a different look, he wore a helmet equipped with various lenses that he used to increase his precision with his tibanna gas rifle. He generally followed Leech – the charismatic leader of Kanjiklub – on his punitive expeditions and unwaveringly offered him assistance. Li-Thrull found himself face-to-face with an infuriated rathtar aboard the *Eravana*, Han Solo's freighter, having boarded the vessel to persuade the smuggler to repay his debts.

Vulture Droid

A combat craft of the Trade Federation, manufactured by the Xia Charrienses, the vulture droid was an automated vehicle that required neither a living pilot nor an independent droid.

It was able to execute extremely tight and fast manoeuvres, which would be impossible to execute without huge, potentially fatal, risks by even the most skilled human fighter pilots. On the other hand, this fighter lacked the ability to think on its feet like a true pilot. As the end of the Battle of Naboo demonstrated, the significant flaw in the vulture droid was that an entire fleet could be deactivated if the central vessel was destroyed. Despite this, the vulture droid had the strategic advantage of being able to operate both in the air and on the ground – it could alter its appearance and use its wings to walk on a battlefield. The vulture, marked in the blue and white colours of the Confederacy of Independent Systems, was most commonly found among the Separatist armada that attacked Coruscant when General Grievous attempted to abduct Chancellor Palpatine.

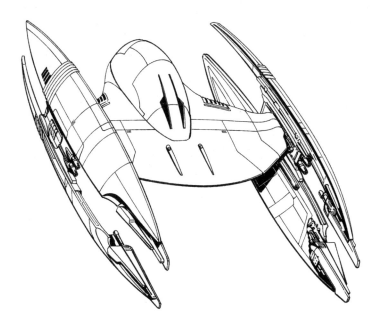

Wald

A close friend of Anakin Skywalker's on Tatooine, this short, young Rodian was also hooked on mechanics.

He was part of his friend's racing team and enthusiastically followed the podrace alongside Kitster Banai, C-3PO and R2-D2.

Walea Timker

A member of the Rebellion's Special Forces and a specialist in building fortifications during military operations, this female engineer ranked as a corporal and was transported to Scarif's beaches by Blue Squadron member Laren Joma's U-wing.

With the other reinforcement troops, she offered a second wind to the fighting rangers who had already suffered losses. Although the troops constituted a fairly modest reinforcement, they provided enough time for Jyn Erso to locate and steal the plans of the Empire's new superweapon: the Death Star. Although she died during the assault, Timker's sacrifice was not in vain.

Wampa

Carnivorous bipedal creatures that lived on the planet of Hoth, wampas, which grew up to 3 metres in height, were the masters of the food chain on their homeworld.

The advantage afforded by their height allowed them to rely on brutal and relatively simple hunting techniques. Nevertheless, they developed a sense of discretion and stealth, which were indispensable assets when they were hunting fast prey, such as tauntauns. In addition, the immaculate white colour of their fur provided them with a natural camouflage against the snowy landscape, which they used with dangerous efficiency. Wampas didn't just hunt when they were hungry. They were capable of storing prey by freezing it in the ice of their lair, in order to devour it at a later stage.

Luke Skywalker awoke to find himself hanging in the pantry of a wampa that had attacked him and killed his tauntaun. The predator had hung the Jedi by his feet until the time came to eat him, and was busy devouring the Jedi's mount.

Wan Sandage

A Devlikk podracer pilot in the Boonta Eve Classic Podrace on Tatooine.

As one of the podracers who was not very good, very little was known about him.

War Chariot

Big-wheeled transport vehicle used by the Gungan Grand Army.

Pulled by falumpasets, domesticated mammal quadrupeds, it transported ammunitions for the launchers (mainly catapults) to the Great Grass Plains. The carts were filled with energy balls that Jar Jar Binks accidentally released onto the battlefield after one of his clumsy misadventures.

'Wasp' Blaster Rifle

This customised blaster rifle was the property of Razoo Qin-Fee, Tasu Leech's lieutenant and fellow member of Kanjiklub.

This strange weapon was proof of Qin-Fee's passion for the latest technology and all kinds of weapon customisation. Equipped with a pump compressor near the grip and an external accelerator barrel cage, the 'Wasp' benefited from decent firepower. Its nickname came from the colour contrast between its yellow barrel cage – drilled to increase the cooling process – and the black barrel, reminiscent of the colouring of a wasp.

Wat Tambor

Wat Tambor was Emir of Skako and chief engineer of the Techno Union.

The air pressure of his homeworld was so specific that he could only survive on other worlds with the aid of the appropriate pressurised armour, which also forced him to express himself through an electronic speaker. Tambor was at the helm of the most efficient military power of the whole galaxy and during the Clone Wars he represented the interests of the Separatist Council, which he supported. He was briefly taken prisoner by the Republic, before his assassination on Mustafar with all the other Separatist leaders at the hand of Anakin Skywalker, who had become Darth Vader.

Watto

Watto was the owner of a scrapyard and a spare parts shop in Mos Espa on Tatooine.

Having been a soldier during his youth, the Toydarian settled in this territory of the Western Reaches to set up his business. As a fan of podraces and a confirmed gambler, he won two slaves, Shmi Skywalker and her son, Anakin, from Gardulla the Hutt. Watto found the young boy doubly interesting because he was an outstanding mechanic as well as a born pilot, and the winged scrap merchant decided to finance him so that he was able to participate in several competitions (although Watto was known to sometimes bet against his gifted but unskilled protégé). It was the demon of the gamble that had delivered Skywalker to Watto, and it was the same demon that took him away, after the scrap dealer bet with Qui-Gon Jinn during the yearly Boonta Eve Classic Podrace. The Jedi Master left with his young protégé and some years later, Watto, by then in financial difficulties, sold Shmi Skywalker to the farmer Cliegg Lars.

Always respectful of the powerful, when Skywalker returned to Tatooine in search of his mother, Watto provided him with all the necessary information to help him find her. Watto certainly didn't treat the free man, who was a member of the powerful Jedi Order with a lightsaber on his belt, in the same way that he treated the small slave boy he once possessed. Nevertheless, although the Toydarian was grumpy, lacking in affection, sparing with compliments, demanding and harsh, he was not the worst of the slaveholders in Mos Espa, who were so often cruel and violent.

Wedge Antilles

A pilot of the Rebel Alliance and the New Republic, Wedge Antilles, born on the planet Corellia, was a hero of the Battles of Yavin and Endor.

Like many of his fellow Corellians, Antilles quickly joined the Alliance, which was the only significant organisation that had decided to fight the decline of liberties and the oppression of the Imperial regime. Once joined up, he was assigned to missions as a navigator aboard cargo ships or as a laser cannon operator. It was during one of these cadet team-ups that he first met his pilot friends Biggs Darklighter and Jek Porkins.

During the strategy briefing before the Battle of Yavin, he put forward the young Luke Skywalker to take part in the mission and even saved him from certain death when he was pursued by a TIE fighter during the assault on the Death Star. Antilles, whose call sign was Red Two, witnessed the destruction of the squadron, and it was left to him and Darklighter to escort Skywalker and provide cover as the young pilot took aim to destroy the space station. But Darth Vader and his personal squadron were on their heels, which resulted in Darklighter's death and Antilles being forced to abandon the fight. However, Skywalker had time to conduct the victorious shot, owing to the help of Han Solo and the *Millennium Falcon*. Antilles and Skywalker were the only two survivors of Red Squadron.

Three years later, Antilles was part of the Rogue Squadron during the Battle of Hoth, which remained a historic defeat for the Alliance. The squadron, this time composed of T-47 airspeeders, was tasked with the protection of Echo Base's shield generator for as long as possible to permit the base's evacuation. During this mission, Antilles succeeded in destroying one of the Imperial AT-ATs. Having noted that the armour of these machines deflected basic laser shots, his gunner, Wes Janson, attached a towing cable to the armour of the AT-AT. Antilles then flew in a circle around the AT-AT until the tow rope hindered the walk of the vehicle, which finished on the ground. This manoeuvre exposed the AT-AT's weak point located at the junction of the neck, and it took Antilles just a few shots to make the Imperial vehicle explode.

Within a year of these events, Antilles attended the briefing of the mission that consisted of a coordinated ground assault on Endor with the aerial attack of the fleet on the second

Death Star. A group was deployed to the small forest moon to deactivate the energy generator powering the space station's protective shield. Once the operation had been achieved, the fleet would then have the chance to attempt a direct attack on the central reactor of the second Death Star.

The assault involved the Gold, Green and Red Squadrons accompanied by Lando Calrissian, who piloted the *Millennium Falcon*. But the destruction of the generator was delayed and the rebel pilots found themselves facing the Imperial fleet, which had used a pincer movement to trap them between its numerous ships and the second Death Star, which despite the intel that had been leaked, was operational. Once again, the rebel fleet paid a heavy price for this assault and, when access to the space station was finally possible, there were only a few fighters left to escort Antilles and Calrissian. Having passed through a labyrinth of ducts, each of them shot several torpedoes that destroyed the second Death Star just seconds later.

After that, Antilles pursued his career within the Alliance of the New Republic and left his name to a piloting manoeuvre that was taught to the cadets of the Resistance thirty years after the Battle of Endor.

Weeteef Cyu-Bee

The smallest, but also most destructive, of Saw Gerrera's partisans in the urban guerrilla warfare of Jedha City was Weeteef Cyu-Bee.

His facial expression, a permanent vicious grin, was a good indicator of Cyu-Bee's personality. At 80 centimetres tall, this bearded Tarpini was able to infiltrate any crowd without being spotted by stormtroopers. He specialised in explosives and collected very efficient sticky bombs that his comrades used against the tanks and the AT-ST. Equipped with his personalised hybrid blaster made from a DH-17 and an E-11 powered by tibanna gas, he was a sharpshooter who could also dangerously spray bullets during street confrontations. It was this particular skill that he demonstrated during the ambush on Tythoni Square. Hidden behind a low wall, he opened fire after the exploding charges had detonated. After the operation, he returned to the Catacombs of Cadera, where he saw Jyn Erso shortly before the evacuation of the base.

Wenton Chan

This pilot of the Rebel Alliance took part in the Battle of Yavin.

Chan was assigned to the assault led against the Death Star as part of the X-wing squadron, but his ship was destroyed during the raid that eventually became a Rebellion victory after the last attack wave led by Luke Skywalker.

Wes Janson

A lieutenant of the Rebel Alliance who took part in the Battle of Hoth, Janson was part of the crew of Rogue Three.

He was Wedge Antilles' gunner and as such took part in the aerial defence of Echo Base. He was the first to neutralise an Imperial AT-AT by tangling a cable round its legs. At the end of the battle and the evacuation of the base, he piloted an X-wing to escort one of the transports.

Wicket W. Warrick

This young Ewok warrior played a fundamental role in the Rebel Alliance's struggle against the Empire.

A small brown-furred warrior, Wicket W. Warrick was the liaison between the Ewoks and the rebels. When he discovered Princess Leia at the site of two crashed speeder bikes he was initially distrustful, but he soon accepted food from the princess, until he heard the arrival of an invisible enemy that started shooting at them. When he saw Leia arrested by a scout trooper, the little Ewok intervened and staged an attack – a diversion that allowed the princess to stun the soldier, commandeer his blaster and take down a second Imperial elite soldier on his speeder bike. Convinced that she was not an invader, he invited Leia to follow him to his village.

Later, when the Ewoks decided to help the rebels, Warrick hugged Han Solo and welcomed him like a brother in arms. Accompanied by Paploo, he quickly guided his new allies to the entry of the secret bunker that housed the planetary shield generator. Warrick remained behind with the droids, but as the rebel commandos approached the target he realised that his new friends were walking into a trap and went for reinforcements. He returned with a whole army of Ewoks who helped the rebels achieve their mission.

During the victory celebrations, he unwittingly disturbed Han Solo and Leia Organa when they wished to be alone, although they didn't hold it against him. Overcome by joy, he wriggled in time to the music alongside R2-D2 who, although not the best dance partner, was at least a new friend.

Widdle

Widdle was a young Ewok hunter and the brother of Wicket W. Warrick.

During the Battle of Endor, the greatest combat achievement of this indigenous little fighter was to help Chewbacca take control of the All Terrain Scout Transport vehicle piloted by Major Newland and Blanaid.

Wilhuff Tarkin

Born on Eriadu, sixty-four years before the Battle of Yavin, Wilhuff Tarkin was an officer serving in the headquarters of the Republic army before he became one of the main ideologists of the Imperial doctrine.

Tarkin's career really took off with the rise of the Empire. He was part of Palpatine's inner circle who knew how to brilliantly take advantage of the regime change. The first part of his career was marked by a very obvious preference for military tactics as opposed to political schemes, but it was his meeting with the then senator of Naboo, Sheev Palpatine, that made him re-evaluate his opinion. When he finally accepted his first post working for public affairs, his decisions still bore the stamp of his military education.

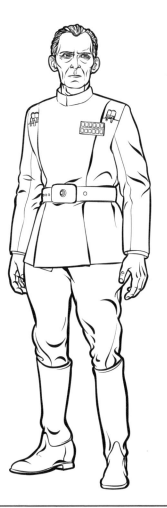

At the very beginning of the Imperial regime the Emperor assigned Tarkin to supervise the construction of the Death Star. It was a promotion he received for two reasons: first, to reward his loyalty, and, second, to distance him from the growing controversies that he had caused following missions led against enemy cells, in which he had displayed extreme brutality. Sometime later, he was promoted to the rank of Grand Moff.

At the time of the decision to spread the Empire to the Outer Rim, until then considered a lawless zone, Tarkin's methods made him the ideal candidate to install order and submissiveness in the region. One of the first planets he annexed as new Governor of the Outer Rim was Lothal. He confiscated the land of farmers in order to mine the planet's underground ores and established industrial complexes that would increase the production of military equipment. The displaced inhabitants were deported to Camp 43, nicknamed 'Tarkinville'.

Tarkin went to Lothal after hearing rumours of a rebel cell on the planet led by a Jedi. Although he was convinced that all the Jedi had died during the cull of Order 66, he was surprised to find that the Great Inquisitor had regularly failed to subdue this small group. Acting quickly, Tarkin organised an offensive that managed to capture Kanan Jarrus. After a fruitless torture attempt, he ordered that the prisoner be transferred to Mustafar, but the rebels succeeded in freeing their chief as he was taken aboard the *Sovereign*, Tarkin's flagship. They escaped aboard stolen TIE fighters with the Imperial fleet in close pursuit, when an unforeseen event confirmed both the rebels' biggest hope and the Empire's biggest fear: the existence of a structured and large-scale rebellion.

Three years later, the Rebel Alliance had the opportunity to deal a death blow to the Imperial organisation by stealing the technical plans of its space station. Tarkin transported the Death Star to Scarif, where the plans were located, and fired on the planet's transmission tower. However, he was too late and the group of rebels succeeded in transmitting the plans before the planet exploded.

After Imperial intelligence questioned the Organa family of Alderaan to learn if they had joined the Alliance, the Emperor tasked Vader with the mission to intercept and recover the stolen plans. The Sith Lord succeeded in capturing Princess Leia Organa, but the plans had already been sent to Tatooine in the memory unit of the droid R2-D2. Following these events, Tarkin organised a senior officers' meeting to evaluate the assessment of the rebel threat and the possible vulnerability of the Death Star.

Surprised by the resistance Princess Leia demonstrated during her torture by a mental probe, Tarkin revealed his cold, sadistic side by threatening to destroy Alderaan, Leia's homeworld. The objective of this cross-examination was not only to recover the plans that he knew to be in the hands of the rebels, but to discover the site of their base and destroy them before they could use the stolen information. Leia broke down and revealed that the base was located on Dantooine. Nevertheless, Tarkin ordered the destruction of Alderaan, to make an example of Leia's insubordination.

After Leia succeeded in escaping from the Death Star with the help of Han Solo, Luke Skywalker and Chewbacca, they took part in the rebel assault against the space station. At the peak of the combat the Imperial tacticians discovered that the rebels' assault had a very small chance of success and advised Tarkin to leave as a precaution. He refused and died in the explosion of the Death Star.

Wion Dillems

This rebel pilot used the Green Twelve call sign during the Battle of Scarif.

Although he came from a tree-loving tribe on Yelsain, this forester embraced the technological mastery of vehicles. He became a dangerous hunter of Imperial craft and kept his personal score on his helmet: each 'V' in a yellow or red circle meant twenty enemies shot down or destroyed. Dillems was usually posted to the ship of admiral Raddus – the *Profundity* – but on this occasion the long-haired, blond-moustached ace served as an emergency stand-in for another pilot who had broken their ankle. It was therefore as part of Green Squadron that he flew and fought in orbit above Scarif.

Wioslea

A female Vuvrian, terrestrial vehicles sales agent on Tatooine by profession, Wioslea shared with the rest of her species a very particular physical characteristic: an enormous head that was covered in multiple eyes of different shapes and sizes.

Even the two protruding tentacles on her face came from different areas of her head. When Luke Skywalker was in search of a buyer for his X-34 landspeeder, Wioslea took advantage of the recent XP-38's launch to negotiate a particularly low price. Skywalker, in a hurry to find the money to pay Han Solo for his and Obi-Wan Kenobi's passage to Alderaan, accepted the offer.

Wittin

This Jawa was present at the court of Jabba the Hutt on Tatooine.

Wittin was also a passenger on Jabba's sail barge, the *Khetanna*, during the battle that occurred at the Great Pit of Carkoon.

Woan Barso

Woan Barso was a refugee smuggler who helped transport refugees out of Jedha during the reign of the Empire.

In those uneasy times transportation to and from the Holy City was restricted to space pilots, such as Barso, who were the only people to have accreditations to reach the docks of the mesa. It was from those docks that the pilot helped anyone who wanted to escape the city leave – hidden in container tugs – and transported them to ships in orbit. Barso was concerned about how airtight his ship was, and so he permanently wore his orange spacesuit almost like a second skin. It was in this attire, but without his helmet, that he crossed Jyn Erso and Cassian Andor in the alleyways of the city, shortly before its brutal annihilation by the Imperial superweapon: the Death Star.

Wobani

This rocky planet was located in the Mid Rim. Its hostile nature, due to its heavy mineral make-up, was probably what inspired the Empire to install a prison colony on the grey rugged world.

Named the Imperial Detention Centre & Labour Camp LEG-817, the sinister place held common-law prisoners that were of no particular importance to the Empire, which was how Jyn Erso – incarcerated under a false identity for minor offences – came to be there. She was rescued from the colony by the Rebel Alliance's Bravo Extraction Team during a prisoner transfer.

Wollivan

A Blarina intergalactic scout and hyperspace explorer, Wollivan was a nosy character who kept a lot of astronavigational information and items.

A regular at Maz's Castle on Takodana, he benefited from the colourful clientele and often made deals with those around him, although his gambling addiction sometimes forced him to gamble his trinkets and maps away to luckier players. He used the Blarina's lack of distinctive features for his own benefit, it could be difficult to tell one Blarina from another, and never hesitated to pretend that he had numerous family relatives to plead mistaken identity if a customer or an angry gambler ever confronted him.

Womp Rat

These wild creatures, which were native to Tatooine, were considered by many a pest.

They could be particularly dangerous when they grouped together to form swarms and were feared by the inhabitants of Tatooine, who wouldn't hesitate to hunt them for sport. A particularly notable characteristic was that they were almost more dangerous in death than when alive, because the odour of their bodies was known to attract krayt dragons. During the rebel briefing that was held prior to the assault against the Death Star, Luke Skywalker compared the mission's odds of success with those of hunting womp rats through the canyons of Tatooine aboard a T-16 skyhopper.

Wookiee

The species native to the forest planet of Kashyyyk.

This tall, strong and hairy species supported the Republic during the Clone Wars before being enslaved by the Galactic Empire. One of the most famous Wookiees in galactic history was rebel hero and co-pilot of the *Millennium Falcon*, Chewbacca.

Wooof

Employed by the crime lord Jabba the Hutt, this Kadas'sa'Nikto was often confused with fellow rogue Klaatu.

Once a smuggler, Wooof managed the flotilla of sand skiffs and the orange-sailed barge, the *Khetanna*, that the Hutt kept at his palace. However, this work left him time to mingle with other members of the court and he witnessed the fateful arrival of Luke Skywalker. Wooof had another close encounter with the Jedi, which resulted in his death on the upper bridge of the *Khetanna*, after his blaster shot was deflected back at him.

Worrt

These carnivorous creatures were found in the deserts of Tatooine.

Chunky quadrupeds with globular yellow eyes and two cranial antenna they would squat without moving until an insect or small rodent passed close by. They would then suddenly extend their long tongue, which would roll itself round the prey and quickly whip back, so they could swallow their catch. These brown predators, which could grow up to 1.5 metres tall, found their best hunting ground in the desert. However, they could sometimes be found near isolated habitations, such as Jabba the Hutt's Palace.

Wupiupi

This metallic currency was used on Tatooine by the Hutts and at the Mos Espa Market, where gorgs were sold for seven wupiupi apiece.

A wupiupi was worth 0. 625 Republic credits, sixteen wupiupi were worth one truggut and sixty-four wupiupi were worth one peggat.

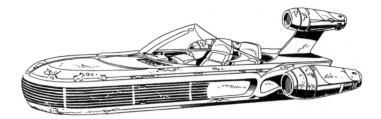

X-34 Landspeeder

These terrestrial vehicles were equipped with a repulsorlift engine that enabled them to hover up to a metre from the ground.

The repulsors created a power that allowed them to maintain a continuous lift – both when the vehicle was moving as well as when it was stationary. This power was augmented by turbines that generated propulsion and allowed the vehicle to reach a very high speed. Despite the repulsors, these vehicles were classified as ground vehicles rather than flying craft because, unlike airspeeders, they were only capable of flying at a low or mid-range altitude. The X-34 model quickly became obsolete after the release of the XP-38. Luke Skywalker possessed one of these vehicles on Tatooine, but he sold it to Wioslea in Mos Eisley. The money from the sale served as an advance to the cost of transportation for himself, Obi-Wan Kenobi, R2-D2 and C-3PO to Alderaan aboard the *Millennium Falcon*.

X-wing Starfighter

See T-65B X-wing Starfighter *and* T-70 X-wing Starfighter

XP-38 Landspeeder

This sportier successor to the X-34 was used as a ground vehicle for both civilian and military purposes.

The release of the XP-38, shortly before the Battle of Yavin, severely devalued its predecessor's second-hand price, even though the XP-38 didn't have any important improvements on the X-34. The main differences centred around the vehicle's appearance, which now had three engines, a sleeker and more aerodynamic design and a cockpit that was completely enclosed.

Xyloxan

This musical instrument bore many similarities to the traditional xylophone.

It was made of a metallic structure on which were tied various percussion elements and sound boxes, often made from organic matter like bodhar bones. It was the favourite instrument of Ubert 'Sticks' Quaril, a musician who regularly played at Maz's Castle on Takodana.

Y-wing Starfighter

Produced by the Koensayr Manufacturing Company, the Y-shaped crafts were among the longest-lasting commercial ships in existence.

The first models appeared during the time of the Republic, and were still in use under the New Republic. The Y-wing fighters also took part in the biggest military sagas of the Rebel Alliance. Originally these ships were made for two passengers (a pilot and a gunner), assisted by an astromech droid, while later models were produced for just one pilot. The Y-wing fighters of the Alliance were mostly already in use during the Clone Wars, which is proof of their durability and longevity. However, repairs were more frequent than on the later X-wings, which is why the Y-wings were stripped of their central hoods, which offered easier access to the machinery for maintenance. Their specific bomber abilities, and the fact that they were quick and versatile, made them the perfect companion to the X-wings. These long-lasting rebel starfighters participated in the assaults on both of the Imperial Death Stars during the Battle of Yavin and the Battle of Endor.

Yaddle

A Jedi Master and member of the Jedi High Council, Yaddle was from the same species as Yoda, but had auburn hair.

Although she sat at the Council during the events of the invasion of Naboo, this wise scholar left it soon after.

Yak Face

See Saelt-Marae

Yarael Poof

A Jedi Master and member of the Jedi High Council, he was present when the return of the Sith was revealed and when Qui-Gon Jinn presented the Chosen One, Anakin Skywalker.

This Quermian, characterised by his elongated neck, specialised in Jedi mind tricks. The Jedi Master Coleman Trebor replaced him on the Council shortly before the Battle of Geonosis.

Yarna d'al' Gargan

Jabba the Hutt's Askajian dancing slave, Yarna d'al' Gargan often performed artistic duets with the Twi'lek Oola in front of the throne of her Hutt owner.

When Oola performed dainty and graceful choreography, Gargan, with her generous six-breasted chest, improvised hers in a funnier way. She helplessly watched the dramatic end of her partner, then later saw the arrival of Luke Skywalker.

Yarua

A Wookiee who represented his planet, Kashyyyk, during the last years of the Republic.

Senator Yarua was present in the senatorial chamber when the vote of no confidence was upheld against Supreme Chancellor Valorum.

Yavin 4

The fourth moon of Yavin, Yavin 4 was covered by lush jungle that sheltered the Rebel Alliance base during the Civil War against the Galactic Empire.

Thousands of years before those events, a long-extinct race of warriors, the Massassi, settled on Yavin and built huge temples in the middle of the inhospitable vegetation. They were later enslaved by the Sith.

The Alliance headquarters, installed inside the largest temple, experienced its first victory against the Empire when the Death Star was destroyed during the conflict known as the Battle of Yavin. After this decisive moment of the Civil War, the rebels had to evacuate Yavin 4 and eventually installed a new base on Hoth.

Yoda

One of the most respected figures in galactic history, Yoda was known for his wisdom, his power and his actions as a Jedi Master within the Jedi Order in the last days of the Republic.

The most powerful Jedi to have survived Order 66, Yoda used his exile to study immortality in the Force. Although his face came to be one of the most known in the galaxy, there were also many mysteries that remained. Not much was known about his species, its name or homeworld, and there were few other representatives of his kind across the galaxy. Information about his first eight centuries was extremely scarce. He was estimated to have trained 20,000 apprentices, and his last official Padawan was Count Dooku.

Shortly after the invasion of Naboo, during which Yoda sat on the Jedi Council, Jedi Master Qui-Gon Jinn returned from Tatooine with two pieces of important news. Yoda listened as Jinn claimed that he had been attacked by a Sith warrior, and that he had discovered the Chosen One from Jedi Prophecy. Like the other members of the Council, Yoda remained sceptical of the re-emergence of their religious adversaries and questioned the admission of the young Anakin Skywalker into the Jedi Order, mainly because of the boy's emotional instability.

Thereafter, events tragically proved Jinn's theories – that the Sith had returned. Yoda remembered the rule of the Sith Order - that there must always be two, a master and an apprentice. It was impossible to determine which had attacked Jinn, and Yoda knew there may be another even more dangerous enemy out there. As for Skywalker, since Yoda could not oppose the last will of the dying Jinn, he reluctantly agreed for the young boy to become the Padawan of Obi-Wan Kenobi.

Ten years later, Yoda's former Padawan, Count Dooku, was now the figurehead of a Separatist movement that seriously threatened the Galactic Republic. Suspecting the Separatists of being responsible for the assassination attempts against Senator Amidala, the Jedi Council, along with Yoda and Kenobi, took the lead in an investigation. The clues led Kenobi to Kamino, whose coordinates were missing from the Jedi Archives, alarming Yoda, since only a Jedi could have erased the files. Yoda also discerned that Skywalker had experienced great suffering and he heard the desperate voice of Jinn. Yoda shared his vision with Windu, although at the time didn't understand its significance.

The plot thickened when Kenobi, on Kamino, identified the bounty hunter Jango Fett as being involved in the attempts against Amidala's life. He had also discovered an army of clones – genetically based on Fett – which had been ordered by the Jedi Sifo-Dyas for unknown military purposes. (Sifo-Dyas had died at the time of the invasion of Naboo.)

Kenobi followed Fett to the planet of Geonosis, where it was discovered that Count Dooku and his Confederacy of Independent Systems had gathered a massive droid army to confront the Republic. Jedi Master Mace Windu headed to Geonosis to attempt to rescue Kenobi with only 200 Jedi, while Yoda went to Kamino to take command of the clone army.

Yoda's subsequent arrival on Geonosis was extremely welcome, as the surviving Jedi were about to be decimated by the large droid army. The battle, which involved a massive number of forces and which had not been planned by either side, was intensely chaotic. However, the outcome quickly became clear: it was a Republic victory and a strategic Separatist retreat, which allowed Yoda to find Kenobi and Skywalker who had gone in pursuit of Count Dooku. When he found the Jedi Knight and his Padawan out of action, Yoda took their place and faced Dooku in a duel, using his talents with the lightsaber to subdue his former Padawan. Nevertheless, Dooku managed to escape through a ruse, leaving Yoda to face the bitter reality that the Clone Wars had begun.

The years of merciless conflict that followed saw Yoda operating on military and political fronts. Hoping to increase his influence over the Jedi Council, Supreme Chancellor Palpatine, the leader of the senate, appointed Anakin Skywalker as his personal representative. The Council were concerned about the Chancellor's ever-growing power, but begrudgingly accepted the interference. However, they refused to grant the young Jedi the rank of Jedi Master – a decision that infuriated Skywalker.

Yoda headed to Kashyyyk to oversee the defence against a Separatist invasion. Meanwhile, Skywalker told the Council that he had located the Separatist leader Grievous on Utapau, and wished to confront him. Yoda and Mace Windu were becoming increasingly worried about Skywalker's emotional state and sent Kenobi in his place to complete the mission. Skywalker saw this as a unbearable humiliation.

Yoda sensed Skywalker's passage to the dark side and narrowly escaped when his clone troopers' turned on him. Yoda survived Order 66 with the help of the Wookiees Tarfful and Chewbacca, who helped him leave Kashyyyk. Yoda joined Senator Bail Organa and Kenobi, and returned to Coruscant where all surviving Jedi had been told to return. Devastated by the betrayal and death of so many Jedi, Yoda knew they had to act quickly. He asked Kenobi to face his former Padawan, while he confronted Palpatine, now revealed to be the Sith Lord Darth Sidious: the architect of the dark side's rebirth.

A bad omen for what was to follow, the duel began badly for Yoda who was taken by surprise by the violent lightning strike of energy from his adversary. He immediately lost consciousness and, fully satisfied of his victory, Palpatine omitted to check his enemy, who awoke and fought back. With lightsabers drawn, a fierce physical and technical duel followed. Despite his great powers, Yoda had difficulty resisting the multiple assaults of the Sith Lord. Considerably weakened, the Jedi fled through the maintenance tunnels and was recovered by the faithful

Senator Bail Organa. In a crushing admission of failure, Yoda knew that he would be forced into exile and that the hostile Sith had won this battle.

Sheltered on the Polis Massa asteroid with Organa, Yoda witnessed the arrival of Kenobi, who had been victorious over Darth Vader. He returned with a wounded Amidala, who gave birth to twins, whom she named Luke and Leia, before dying. They were two 'hopes' that the Sith knew nothing of, so they were separated and hidden from the rising Imperial regime. Yoda left his two companions to take care of the necessary plans, and began his exile on the secluded swamp planet of Dagobah. It was in this austere life, excluded from the rest of the galaxy, that Yoda was able to fully explore the techniques that led to his immortality within the Force.

Twenty-two years later, Yoda was found by Luke Skywalker, who had followed Kenobi's instructions and asked to be trained as a Jedi. In order to test the young man, Yoda didn't immediately reveal his true identity, and instead played the role of an eccentric, inconsiderate being who had lived in solitude for several years. Luke was impatient and frustrated, leading Yoda to question Luke's resolve. However, Kenobi succeeded in convincing his old friend to train Skywalker in the ways of the Force.

In the challenging environment of Dagobah's swamps, the Jedi Master drilled his pupil in a set of exercises, from physical self-discipline to telekinesis. Young Skywalker was given a test to embark into the Cave of Evil. There, he faced a vision of Vader who he attacked and killed, only to discover his own face beneath the black mask. At the time, Skywalker failed to grasp the warning. Then when the impetuous Skywalker decided to leave, having had a vision in which he saw his friends in danger, Yoda was fearful it would be the last time he would see the young Padawan.

Upon his return to Dagobah, Skywalker discovered the old Jedi, nearly 900 years old, sick and dying. With his last breaths the ancient Jedi Master conveyed his final advice and confessions to the young Jedi. He told Skywalker that he must face Vader once again and warned him not to underestimate the Emperor's powers. He also confirmed that Vader was indeed his father and that another member of the Skywalker family also existed. With these final words his body simply disappeared – just as his old friend Kenobi's had. Although his body was gone, his consciousness remained intact, and he continued to communicate and appeared in a spiritual form.

Yoda's long life spanned almost a millennia of peace and justice in the Galactic Republic, which was ended by the return of the Sith. While his death on the eve of the Battle of Endor meant that he was not present at the Rebel Alliance's victory over the Empire, he nevertheless celebrated the victory by briefly appearing to Luke, with both Kenobi and Anakin Skywalker at his side.

Over thirty years later, Yoda, as a Force spirit, visited Luke Skywalker on the remote island of Ahch-To. A troubled Skywalker was trying to rid himself of his Jedi ties by burning the remaining Jedi texts, and was surprised that Yoda did not care. The wise Jedi Master helped Skywalker come to terms with his failed training of Ben Solo and rejoin the fight against evil.

Yort Cavwol

A duty officer based on Scarif, Yort Cavwol was responsible for providing reports on the routine operations at the base.

He reported to Lieutenant Adema and General Sotorus Ramda and it was a task he scrupulously carried out.

Yosh Calfor

Yosh Calfor was a bomb specialist in the Rebel Alliance and during the Rogue One operation on Scarif.

Deafened by the repeated use of thermal detonators, this first-class soldier wore an electro-ear implant. He thus heard Jyn Erso's call to take direct action against the Empire on Scarif and joined the crew known as Rogue One. His talent for handling the most dangerous explosives proved to be a considerable asset in the first phase of destabilising the defences of the Citadel Tower and he and his combat companions created the impression of a large rebel assault. Through his work, Calfor contributed to the success of Erso, Cassian Andor and K-2SO's mission, before he became one of the many victims of the terrifying Imperial counter-attack.

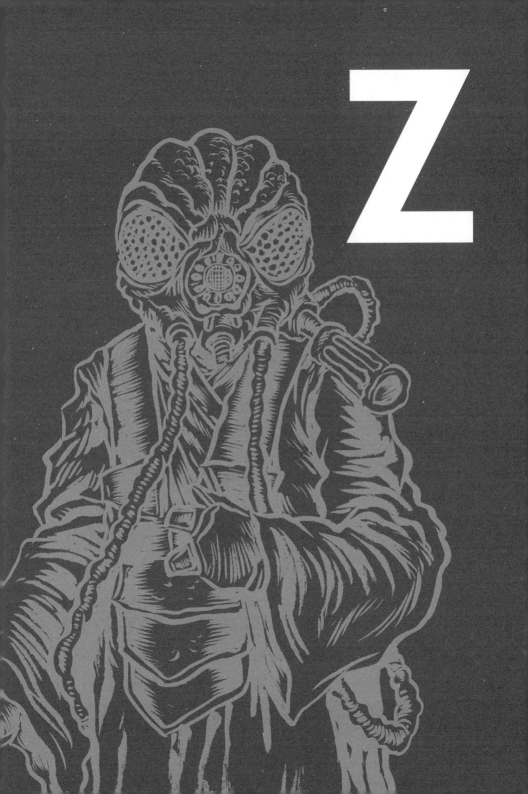

Z-6 Jetpack

Built by Mitrinomon Transports, this model of jetpack was favoured by the famous bounty hunter Jango Fett.

It contained enough fuel for around twenty controlled short bursts of lift, and offered a significant tactical advantage in the field, enabling its wearer to get close to a target, quickly change position or simply withdraw from a fight. Gyro-stabilisers ensured that the device had great manoeuvrability and its integrated rocket launcher could fire a grapple or a powerful remote-controlled, anti-armour missile. Boba Fett, the son of Jango, continued to use this type of equipment when he became a bounty hunter.

Z-6PO

See C-3PO

Z6 Baton

This type of weapon was developed to support stormtroopers who had to maintain order in territories that fell under the authority of the First Order.

Used for close combat, the Z6 was equipped with two retractable electroshock blades, and the magnatomic handle allowed fast rotations of the weapon for maximum effect. However, the particular advantage of this weapon was that its electroshock blade gave it the ability to block plasma fluxes. Therefore a stormtrooper who used this kind of club could confront, on equal terms, an adversary with a lightsaber.

Zal Dinnes

This rebel pilot, with numerous victories under her belt, engaged in the orbital fight during the Battle of Scarif.

As a member of the Yellow Aces squadron from the rebel base of Tierfon, she stayed with two other pilots and Jek Porkins on Yavin 4 after the dispersion of her unit under military pressure. Along with Porkins, Dinnes was integrated into Red Squadron and was given the Red Eight call sign. Despite this, her helmet still displayed the logo of the Yellow Aces, as well as a small 'V' for every twenty hostile vessels she shot down.

Zam Wesell

A Clawdite bounty hunter, Zam Wesell hailed from the planet of Zolan.

Her shape-shifting talents enabled her to take the appearance of anyone she wished in order to fool her targets or her pursuers. Nevertheless, she preferred to act from a distance and used her sniper rifle to do so, or occasionally used convoluted methods that involved venomous beasts, such as kouhuns. She sometimes worked with other bounty hunters, including Jango Fett. Fett offered her a contract on Coruscant, which was for the assassination of Senator Padmé Amidala. Making use of a probe droid, Wesell placed two kouhuns in the bedroom of the senator. However, due to the intervention of Anakin Skywalker and Obi-Wan Kenobi, her plan was thwarted. She was eventually captured by the Jedi Knights at the Outlander Club in the leisure district, but was executed from afar by Fett (who had used a saberdart) to prevent her from revealing the identity of her client.

Zama-shiwo

This form of martial art, native to the moon of Jedha, was practised by Chirrut Îmwe.

The disappearance of the Jedi created a void in terms of combined spirituality and combat techniques, and so some people were drawn to the ways of zama-shiwo because it was similar to Jedi physical exercises that helped teach body control. The central idea of this art was the perfection of physical awareness – both in terms of exterior placement and interior functions. It was believed that anyone who could master these techniques could also control things such as their heart rate, oxygen intake and other vital processes. The demanding and regular practice appeared to make some of the movements involved in this fighting style almost supernatural in appearance. It was also known as 'the inward eye of the outward hand'. This was how the blind Îmwe was able to defeat several stormtroopers using just his staff.

Zeta-class Transport Shuttle

The joint creation of the Telgorn Corporation and Sienar Fleet Systems, this versatile cargo ship was used by both civilians and the army – most notably the Empire.

The shuttle, which measured 35.5 metres in length, had two levels: a superior bridge where the cockpit was located and the lower freight locker that could be detached and dropped on site. It was equipped with four rotating wings that retracted up and inwards during landing, a bit like the mechanism of the *Lambda*-class T-4a shuttle. Hundreds of these ships were used during the Imperial occupation of Jedha to carry kyber crystals to Eadu where they were merged and refined for use aboard the Death Star.

Zev Zenesca

This Rebel Alliance pilot took part in the Battle of Hoth under the Rogue Two call sign.

Zenesca was part of the search and rescue team that was sent to look for Luke Skywalker and Han Solo, who had been declared missing in action the previous evening. He managed to locate them after they had survived the freezing night in an improvised shelter. Zenesca later participated in the fight against the AT-ATs alongside the rest of Rogue Squadron, whose mission was to protect Echo Base's defences that were essential to achieve a successful evacuation and to prevent an assault from space. His ship was destroyed by a shot from an AT-AT, which killed both him and his gunner.

Zuckuss

A bounty hunter from the planet of Gand.

His reputation was built on his efficiency and effectiveness as a hunter, and it earned him a place in the small group of bounty hunters gathered by Darth Vader to capture the crew of the rebel ship, the *Millennium Falcon*. In the end it was Boba Fett, who was working for Jabba the Hutt, who found the rebels. Fett received a double bounty from Vader and Jabba, which generated both admiration and envy from Zuckuss.

Zuvio

An inhabitant of the Niima outpost on Jakku, Officer Zuvio was the Kyuzo leader of a local militia that tried to keep order and enforce security in the small and diverse community.

He wore a traditional helmet and carried a vibro-axe made of salvaged metal, and he patrolled the different camps while remaining in contact with his two assistants via his sensor pack. Officer Zuvio was particularly committed to his job and his sense of justice gave him the reputation of being incorruptible.

Zygli Bruss

This emissary from the planet of Candovant was part of the New Republic Senate.

Like his fellow senators, Zygli Bruss followed the alternative movement of the Senate that was created after the Civil War. He therefore lived on Hosnian Prime, which housed the New Republic's institutions at that time. He usually wore the cosmopolitan fashion of the city-planet and his ultraviolet vision was one of the main characteristics of his species. He died during the destruction of Hosnian Prime by the First Order's Starkiller Base.